Mary,

I'm so … ,

you my latest book …

with a cozy armchair and a fuzzy blanket for a fun winter read!

A KING'S RANSOM

CORINNE AARSEN

978-1-9995353-2-2 (paperback)
978-1-9995353-3-9 (Kindle Unlimited)

Also by Corinne Aarsen

Historical fiction series: An Ordinary Immigrant

New Beginnings (2018)

Ties That Bind (2019)

Paranormal fiction series: The Travelers' Chronicles

The Reluctant Traveler (2018)

The Traveler's Stone (2018)

The Reluctant Thief (forthcoming)

The Travelers' Curse (forthcoming)

Romantic Suspense

A King's Ransom (2020)

Contents

Part I

Chapter 1 3
Chapter 2 12
Chapter 3 22
Chapter 4 28
Chapter 5 31
Chapter 6 37
Chapter 7 43
Chapter 8 50
Chapter 9 55
Chapter 10 62
Chapter 11 66
Chapter 12 73
Chapter 13 80
Chapter 14 83
Chapter 15 88
Chapter 16 92
Chapter 17 95
Chapter 18 100
Chapter 19 108
Chapter 20 114

Part II

Chapter 21 121
Chapter 22 127
Chapter 23 134
Chapter 24 141
Chapter 25 146
Chapter 26 156
Chapter 27 160
Chapter 28 167
Chapter 29 177

Chapter 30 182
Chapter 31 189
Chapter 32 196
Chapter 33 202
Chapter 34 212
Chapter 35 218
Chapter 36 225
Chapter 37 230
Chapter 38 234
Chapter 39 242
Chapter 40 246
Chapter 41 251

Part III

Chapter 42 265
Chapter 43 271
Chapter 44 279
Chapter 45 284
Chapter 46 290
Chapter 47 301
Chapter 48 310
Chapter 49 322
Chapter 50 331
Chapter 51 338
Chapter 52 341

Note from the Author 347
Acknowledgments 349

Having somewhere to go is home.
Having someone to love is family.
And having both is a blessing.

Unknown

Part I

Chapter 1

Janine Kirby sat on the living room floor, the shoebox with her deceased mother's keepsakes at her hip. She stared at the document in her hands, struggling to process what it revealed about her family, about the lies she'd been told all her life.

With rain slashing at her windows—making the last Saturday in May feel like March—Janine had assigned herself the task of sorting through the contents of her garage and storage room and setting aside items she found that belonged to Malcolm, her former fiancée. There were an astonishing number of his belongings still in her house, no surprise given their seven years together. They'd broken up three months before when he met the love of his life, who apparently wasn't Janine but rather Sandy Becker, two-time US Olympic medalist in free-style skiing. At the time, his abrupt change of heart had been devastating. Until, surprisingly, it wasn't. Within a few weeks of his leaving, Janine was astonished to find she didn't miss him, which led her to conclude that they'd been together out of habit rather than on account of a lifetime supply of love and passion.

Finding Malcolm's fishing rod and high school track and

field trophies was annoying; finding her mother's keepsakes box was a delight. She recalled stumbling upon it five years before when she'd been searching for legal documents relevant to her parents' estate. At the time—the day after the horrific three-car pileup on the Sea-to-Sky highway that took their lives—she'd been too emotionally fragile to do more than glance inside. Now, finding the box a second time, she took it up to the living room, poured herself a glass of her favourite Argentinian Malbec, set her playlist to the best-of-the-70's, and settled on the floor in front of the fire to examine the contents. She'd expected it to be an exercise in nostalgia, nothing more. She was utterly unprepared for what she found.

The childhood report cards attested to her mother's academic ability—Brenda van Birkhuis had always been smart—and reminded Janine of how proud her mother had been when Janine performed at the top of her class.

Finding the handful of letters her dad had written to her mother was insightful. They were from the summer of 1981, the year before her parents graduated from the University of Washington. Paul, living and working in his home town of North Vancouver, had been writing to Brenda in Seattle. Janine knew they'd married the following summer right after they graduated, Paul as a civil engineer and Brenda with her teaching degree. The letters were sweet, filled with loving sentiment so like her good-natured, warm father. Janine's eyes filled with tears as she read them. She'd often wondered why Paul, affectionate and devoted, had married the aloof, remote Brenda, but these letters, tender in tone and candidly expressive of his love, revealed he'd been privy to a sensitive side of her mother that Janine had rarely seen.

The identity of the children in the single black-and-white photograph was a mystery to Janine. The snapshot showed three tow-headed girls aged, she guessed, between two and six years. Attired in matching gingham dresses, they stood in front of a lilac bush. The two youngest were looking at the camera, their faces brightly beaming. The oldest girl was in profile, smiling indulgently down at the youngest child. Janine felt certain the girls were sisters given their matching clothes and hair. There was nothing written on the back of the photo to identify them, and since Brenda was an only child—who'd never talked about her family or upbringing except to say it had been unhappy—the identity of these girls, Janine knew, would always be a mystery.

Also in the box was a crayon drawing in a childish hand of three little girls standing in front of a house. Their pigtails were coloured a bright yellow. Were these the same three girls from the photo? If so, who were they? Equally as puzzling was the miniature pink bow with a rosebud centre. It looked little different from the decorative bows on one of Janine's night-gowns. Why had her mother kept such an insignificant item? The concert ticket stub for the rock band Queen—an event held at the Tower Theatre in Philadelphia on 2 February 1977—was even more perplexing. Janine had always been a huge fan of Freddie Mercury. Assuming Brenda had attended the concert, why had her mother never revealed that she'd seen an iconic performance of one of Janine's favourite artists?

When Janine unearthed a single sheet of heavy bond paper, folded in half twice, she didn't realize the axis of her world was about to shift. It was an official-looking document written in Dutch with the word *'Nederland'* in large font across the top followed by *Geboortecertificaat*. The page had typed row headings. The responses were hand-written in a neat, copper-plate script.

Janine had always known her mother's heritage was Dutch. Brenda had the blond hair and blue eyes to prove it. With her chestnut hair and brown eyes, Janine took after her father's side of the family. She was about to return the document to the box when a date, two days shy of her own birthday and a decade earlier, caught her attention: *27 Oktober 1977*. As she scanned the form, trying to figure out what made it important to her mother, she stopped breathing when she saw her mother's maiden name.

Janine grabbed for her phone, her fingers trembling as she opened a website that translated Dutch into English. Her heart was pounding, and she felt a strange sense of apprehension. Five minutes later, the document was fully translated. Her mother had given birth to a baby girl—Esme van Birkhuis—in a hospital in Aruba three months shy of her seventeenth birthday, father unknown.

Questions crowded into Janine's mind. Had the baby lived? If so, had she been adopted? Who was the baby's father? And why had Brenda given birth in Aruba, of all places, when she'd grown up—and likely conceived the baby—in Pennsylvania? Janine recalled her mother's claim that she couldn't tolerate heat and her refusal to ever vacation in hot countries. Could the birth of this baby in Aruba have put Brenda off the tropics? Janine typed *Aruba* into her phone's search engine, discovering that in 1977, the year of Esme's birth, the Caribbean island had still been ruled by The Netherlands. Since her mother's family was Dutch, perhaps she had relatives on the Dutch-held Caribbean Island. Was that why Brenda had given birth in Aruba?

Janine stared at the form, her mind whirling with questions. She was finding it understandably difficult to digest the fact that somewhere out there she might have a sister. For thirty years, she'd been under the impression she was her mother's only child.

When her eyes alighted on the baby's birth date, so close to her own, she suddenly understood something about her emotionally distant mother. Brenda had often become depressed in the days leading up to Janine's birthday. If her mother had given this baby up for adoption—or if Esme had died—it made sense that late October heralded a time of sadness for Brenda. Janine had never felt particularly close to her mother, but now her heart ached as she imagined what it might've been like to be pregnant at such a young age and so far from home and family.

Her mind drifted to her cousin Kevin, also an only child, who was like a brother to her. She'd grown up in Whistler—an international ski resort in British Columbia that rivalled some of Europe's best destinations—and Kevin, four years her senior, had been raised in Seattle, a four-to-five-hour drive south of Whistler. Every summer during their childhood, she and Kevin had vacationed at their grandparents' hobby farm on the Saanich Peninsula of Vancouver Island. After Kevin graduated from university—the same year Janine graduated high school—he moved to the UK where he completed his post-graduate studies in archeology, later landing a job at the University of Nottingham. Despite leading busy lives on two continents, the cousins remained close, with Janine making regular trips to Nottingham.

She glanced at her phone, calculating the time difference. It was 7:00 am in the UK. Would he be home? Or would he be camping out in his tiny caravan at a dig site somewhere, looking to unearth Anglo-Saxon artifacts and ruins? Janine tapped her cousin's landline number in her phone's contact list. Not for the first time, she wished he'd get a cellphone, but he was a technophobe who stubbornly refused to have his life dictated by technology. Not a surprise really, given he was more interested in history than in either the present or the future. He did make a few technological concessions—which she relentlessly teased him about—using a laptop for work, and utilizing the data from his grad students' ground-scanning technology to draw conclusions about concealed Anglo-Saxon settlements and burial sites.

Her gaze was drawn to the birth certificate as she listened to the double-rings of her cousin's phone. If he wasn't home, she'd leave a message on his archaic answering machine. It could be days—or even weeks—before he called back.

When Kevin answered, his voice thick with sleep, Janine was so surprised she remained silent for a moment.

"Hello?" he croaked again, clearly annoyed.

"Kevin," she said. "It's me."

"Jay-Jay!" he said, the delight in his tone undisguised. "How are you?"

"My mother had a baby," Janine blurted.

"Uh…say what?"

Janine could picture her cousin sitting up in bed and rubbing the sleep out of his eyes. "She had a baby in 1977 when she was sixteen years old."

"What?"

"You didn't know about it?"

"Know about…no…wow." Kevin's stammering made it clear he was trying his best to process Janine's surprising news. "Did she give it up for adoption? How did you find out?"

Janine told him about re-discovering the keepsakes box and finding the birth certificate. "Do you think your parents know?" she asked.

"If they do, they never told me. But why Aruba?" Kevin asked. "You think the baby's father was from there?"

"No, I think he was from Pennsylvania." Janine reached for the Queen concert ticket, staring at it as she shared the dates of both the concert and Esme's birth.

"Hell, I can't picture Aunty Brenda at a rock concert. A symphony, yeah. Maybe a musical. But *Queen?*"

"You know, I got an MP3 player for my birthday one year." Janine's tone was indignant. "I created a 70's playlist, which had some Queen songs on it. You know me, I love Freddie. I remember Mom and I had this strange kind of argument. She told me I should be listening to contemporary pop music in keeping with my age. I remember telling her how insane it was that I liked music from *her* era more than she did."

"And…*bah-dah-bump*….that was the perfect segue to tell

you she saw Freddie Mercury perform. Good lord, Jaynie, your mother was a dark horse, wasn't she? No offence, but I'm glad you take after Uncle Paul."

Janine smiled. This was not the first time they'd had that conversation. "I'm glad, too."

"What's the name on the birth certificate?"

"The baby's? Esme."

"Would the hospital have picked that name?"

"I don't know," Janine frowned. She tapped the speaker icon on her phone, then opened a browser while she continued chatting. "You know Mom. She was methodical. Everything she did was deliberate. I would assume she chose the baby's name. Oh my god, Kevin!"

Janine was staring at her phone screen. She'd typed in *meaning of girl name Esme* into the browser.

"What?"

"I just looked up the definition of Esme."

"What does it mean?"

For some inexplicable reason, Janine felt emotion welling up inside her. She had to swallow past the lump in her throat before she could speak. "It means *beloved.*"

"Jay-Jay," Kevin said, his voice soft with understanding. "I'm not sure you can read anything into that."

Janine's voice was wobbly as she continued, "Don't you think it's possible she loved that baby?"

"I think you're looking for evidence that your mother was a loving person, that she loved *you*. If she adored this baby, then you would find it easier to believe she also adored you. With all the reflection you did after your parents died, didn't you draw the conclusion that she *did* love you, but that she simply didn't know how to show it?"

Her cousin was right. Janine sighed. "I did. But now I feel, I don't know, *lied* to, I guess."

"That's understandable."

"I wonder," Janine said, speaking slowly as she formed

words around her thoughts. "Maybe that experience at sixteen is the reason, or part of the reason at least, why she was so remote. It must've been traumatizing. It scarred her."

Kevin made a sound of agreement, then asked, "Are you going to look for her?"

It took a moment for Janine to understand what Kevin was asking. She'd been so focused on trying to absorb the reality of the existence of a sister, she hadn't yet taken the next mental step. *Did she want to find Esme?* The answer was immediate. "Yes! Absolutely!"

"Well, I'd suggest throwing some money at a private investigator. You'll get results a lot faster than doing your own Google search. Aw, bloody shite!" Kevin had long ago adopted British slang.

"What?" Janine asked.

"I've got to go. My jackass grad student is at the door." Janine heard Kevin calling out to his visitor that he'd be a minute, then he was speaking to her once again, his tone enthusiastic. "We're taking his drone out to a potential dig site."

"Sounds like fun," Janine teased. She'd accompanied Kevin to his dig sites on multiple occasions. She would always bring a good book along to read while he worked or, depending on the location, would explore the countryside or shop in a nearby market town.

"Are you gonna be okay, Jay-Jay?" Kevin asked.

Janine smiled. She always felt better after talking to Kevin. "Yes, I'm fine. Go enjoy your day. I hope you find your Kevin-who."

He laughed at her play on words.

She knew her cousin lived for the day when he discovered the equivalent of the famous Sutton Hoo, a Viking burial site considered a literal treasure trove by experts and amateurs alike. Janine had been confused the first time Kevin told her about this exceptional find, thinking he was saying Sutton *who.*

Their ensuing conversation ended up much like the comedy routine, *Who's on First?* Since then, Janine often sprinkled a *Kevin-who* reference into their many conversations.

After the cousins said their goodbyes, Janine set aside her phone. She remained on the floor, staring down at the official looking document and feeling the thrill of her newfound knowledge plant a seed and begin to grow in her heart. *She had a sister!*

Chapter 2

Janine did a double take when she checked her phone for messages. She was standing in the cramped staff room of Café Art, which also served as their supply room, and had been about to leave for the day. She stared at the screen, her heart ricocheting in her chest like a pinball in an arcade game. Oblivious to the background noise of milk steamers, coffee grinders, and the hum of conversation coming from the coffee shop/art gallery she'd opened five years before, she scanned the private investigator's brief email then, with shaking fingers, tapped the icon to open the PDF attachment.

Three months before, she'd taken her cousin's advice and hired a private investigator. She'd been waiting with bated breath for her report ever since. As she scrolled through the lines of text, Janine grew increasingly impatient. This information wasn't new; it wasn't what she wanted to know. Finally, at the bottom of the second page, her breath caught. Here was something new. Yet, by the time she finished the four-page report, and despite the astonishing information the latter half of it contained, she was disappointed. The *one* thing she'd wanted to know above all else—information about Esme—still remained elusive. She'd had such high hopes and now felt crushed by disappointment.

It was too late in the day to call her cousin, so she instead texted her friend Nicolette. *Are you home? Care for company?*

She'd known Nicolette Dubois—the outgoing and successful manager of the nearby five-star spa—for years, but it wasn't until Janine settled permanently in Whistler five years before that they became good friends.

Janine's phone immediately chimed a response. *House to myself. Come on over.* Then it chimed again. *Need wine?* Another chime. *Is Malcolm being a dick again?*

Nicolette, ever loyal to Janine, always referred to Janine's former fiancée as *that dick Malcolm*. The town's grapevine—which was how Janine had found out that Malcolm and Sandy eloped—was now claiming that Sandy, who was sporting a baby bump, had a new job coaching the next generation of US Olympians at Mt. Hood. Janine was no longer bitter about Malcolm's change of heart, but she would be glad when the blissfully happy couple moved to Oregon.

Within only a few months of their breakup, Janine could find only two downsides to Malcolm's absence. She wanted kids. At thirty, and in a committed relationship, she'd assumed motherhood was on her near horizon. Biologically, she still had plenty of time; realistically, her options when it came to potential life partners were limited by her location. She ran a successful business in a small mountain town where there was an abundance of men—nature lovers and sports enthusiasts—but the majority were too young and too transient to be candidates for a long-term relationship.

The only other downside to being newly single was, simply put, the lack of sex. Malcolm might've been dragging his feet when it came to marriage and having kids—at least with her—but the sex had always been good. In the six months since his departure, Janine had enjoyed two flings, one with a construction worker a decade her junior who'd been in

Whistler for only two weeks, the other with an Australian tourist whose summer 2018 plans included cycling from Whistler to San Diego. In looks and build, the Australian reminded Janine of her cousin's gorgeous best friend, Dawson Delaney, a man she'd swooned over as a teen.

Janine tapped out a message to Nicolette. *Not Malcolm. I got the private investigator's report. Very disappointing. See you in fifteen? I'll bring wine.*

Janine gathered her things, then left the café, calling out a farewell to her remaining two staff who would work until 9:00 pm closing. As she walked towards her car, weaving between crowds of tourists, Janine barely noticed the threatening clouds building on the horizon, her mind occupied with the problem that stumped the private investigator.

JOGGING ALONG THE FORESTED PATH IN THE DIM LIGHT OF PRE-dawn the next morning, Janine's mind was still consumed by the contents of the private investigator's report. She shortened her stride as she neared a steep, downward sloping section of trail. In the shallow ravine, the muffled sound of her footfalls changed to loud thumps as she ran across the wire-meshed, wooden planks that traversed the bog. Once on the opposite embankment, she surged up the incline, gasping and straining to maintain her usual pace. Her legs felt heavy and her lungs restricted. Her entire body was unusually sluggish. This physical distress, she knew, was due to both lack of sleep and a hangover.

The evening before at Nicolette's, she'd had the lion's share of the Argentinian red and two generous helpings of her French friend's signature dessert, café liégeois. Janine could never resist the coffee-flavoured ice cream with its lightly sweetened coffee and Chantilly lace cream, although she usually indulged in only one small helping. But last night, she'd been upset. She had more wine, ate more dessert, and stayed up later than usual.

As the wooded path levelled out, Janine resumed her even stride, avoiding the protruding stones and exposed roots in the shadows of the tall western hemlock, Douglas fir, and Whistler pine trees that loomed like sentries on either side of the wide path. She absently noticed that the tamarack trees, interspersed amongst the evergreens, were showing the first hint of yellow. It had been a dry summer and the light showers of the previous evening had done nothing to quench the dry earth. She hoped the forecast, which promised more rain, would soon deliver the much-needed moisture.

Three months had passed since she'd discovered the birth certificate; yet, unearthing details about Esme seemed as impossible as grabbing hold of dried leaves in the wind. If she was still alive, Esme would be nearing forty. Where was she living? Was she married? Did she have children? What kind of work did she do? Was she happy? How did she take her coffee? What made her laugh? What made her sad? What was she like? Questions like these kept popping in and out of Janine's mind like moles in a whack-a-mole game. Usually while running she was lulled by the rhythmic sound of her feet on the trail. Running gave her the place and time to think, and she always left her phone and earbuds at home. But today she would've welcomed listening to some raunchy 70's rock tunes or clever Taylor Swift lyrics to distract her from the disappointing contents of the investigator's report.

The first half of the document provided information Janine already knew about her deceased mother. Brenda van Birkhuis had been born in York, Pennsylvania, the fourth-generation descendent of early Dutch immigrants. She'd met her future husband—Canadian engineering student Paul Kirby who was there on a rowing scholarship—at the University of Washington. After graduation, they married and relocated to his home town of North Vancouver.

Brenda upgraded her education degree at the University of British Columbia, then spent a few years teaching high school math and science. After Janine was born, she hadn't gone back to teaching; instead, the family relocated to Whistler when Paul took a job helping a development company transform the local ski resort into an international, all-season destination for outdoor enthusiasts. A few years later when Janine started elementary school, Brenda and Paul purchased a retail building and opened a video-rental store.

The information in the second half of the report provided Janine with previously unknown details. Janine's maternal grandfather had been Henry van Birkhuis, a minister in a Dutch Calvinist church in Pennsylvania. He died in the spring of 2012, six-and-a-half years ago. Janine's grandmother, Lena van Birkhuis, diagnosed with late-stage Alzheimer's, resided in a nursing home in Baltimore. Janine was astonished to learn that her mother had two younger sisters, Beatrice and Joyce, both of whom were married and also living in Baltimore. One had three sons, the other two daughters.

When Janine returned home from Nicolette's, she'd immediately retrieved the black-and-white photograph. The oldest child had to be her mother. Janine sat up in bed, examining every detail of the photo, trying to figure out why these three seemingly bonded sisters were no longer in each other's lives. Janine had always believed that her paternal grandparents—still sprightly despite their eighty-odd years—and her uncle, aunt, and cousin in Seattle, were her only family. Her mother never talked about her family, and Janine had assumed they were long dead. When Janine's parents were killed in 2013, she hadn't known to notify any family on her mother's side.

Why had Brenda withheld this information about her family, especially knowing how much Janine longed for more relatives? She was cognizant that a teenage pregnancy might well have been difficult for Brenda's parents to accept, especially given their ties with a conservative religion, but why hadn't Brenda's younger sisters kept in touch?

In the hours since learning about them, Janine was fluctuating between wanting to contact them and wanting to keep her distance. As an only child, she was mystified as to why the three sisters hadn't maintained contact over the years. She wished she knew who was to blame. Had her mother turned her back on those two adorable little girls? Or had they—Beatrice and Joyce—turned their backs on their older sister? Had the falling out occurred as a result of Brenda's teenage pregnancy?

Regardless, there was only one thing Janine desperately wanted to know: *Where was Esme?* Did her mother's sisters—Janine's aunts—know of Esme? And, since finding Esme was Janine's primary goal, if they didn't know where Esme was, did Janine even want to contact them? Janine couldn't decide.

Well after midnight, with more questions than answers crowding her brain, she finally clicked off her light, but it took some time before Janine finally fell asleep.

On the final kilometre of her run, Janine pushed hard, hoping to both dispel her lingering hangover and smother the churning questions. When she emerged from the forested path on the north side of Nordic Drive, the two-lane road winding from her neighbourhood down the mountain to the Sea-to-Sky highway, she ran across the pavement—there was minimal traffic this early in the day—and headed into her cul-de-sac on Tanglewood Crescent. Thirty seconds later, after a final burst of speed, she was in her driveway.

Hands on her hips, she paced in small circles behind her SUV until her breathing eased. Then, lifting her hands and tightening the ponytail that held her thick, pin-straight hair off her face, performed her usual series of stretches. As she did so, her mind continued to gnaw at the mystery of her mother's family. She needed a distraction, she decided. *Another Australian cyclist would do nicely!*

Retrieving the house key from the miniature pocket on her leggings, she let herself in the front door and headed straight to the kitchen at the back of the house. After her early morning run, coffee—high-quality coffee—was always her first priority.

While studying for her commerce degree, she'd been assigned a case study focused on the coffee business. She'd thoroughly enjoyed doing the research and, in subsequent months, furthered her studies about the industry simply for the pleasure it gave her, learning how and where coffee beans were grown, when they were picked, how they were roasted, and the variety of flavours that resulted. The summer between her third and fourth year of university, Janine enrolled in an intensive six-day course at the Coffee Quality Institute in California. She learned how to expertly analyze Arabica coffee, and later passed the standard 22 tests, successfully acquiring the status of "Q" coffee grader. After graduating from university, she snagged a dream job as a "green buyer", travelling to exotic destinations where coffee was grown, tasting a vast range of flavours and roasts, and purchasing the best of the best on behalf of her exacting employer.

Immediately following her parents' death, Janine took a month's bereavement leave from work. The assets she'd inherited included the house she'd grown up in and her parents' commercial building, which was leased to an insurance company. A few days later, lamenting the mediocre coffee she was drinking while sitting on a bench in Olympic Plaza—where the ski runs from both Whistler and Blackcomb Mountains converged—an idea occurred to her that there might be a niche in this multi-season tourist destination for an independently owned, non-franchised coffee shop. She spent the next two hours walking the pedestrian friendly streets of the village to assess her options, drawing the obvious conclusion that the ideal venue for her venture was her parents' commercial property. As the insurance company was expanding and had already given their notice to vacate, the timing seemed serendipitous.

When she ran her idea past Malcolm later that week, he'd been as keen as her to relocate from their condo in downtown Vancouver to the scenic mountain resort. As a self-employed mining engineer, he could work from anywhere. A week later, business plan in hand, Janine went to the bank and was approved for a loan. A month later, she and Malcolm were moving into her parents' house. After renovating the video store, devoting half the space to a coffee shop and half to a gallery featuring local artists, Café Art was launched, quickly gaining a reputation for its stellar coffee and one-of-a-kind artwork.

Janine's passion for good coffee dictated the purchase of top-of-the-line appliances in both her business and her home. Like she did every morning after her run, she set the plumbed, industrial Rancillio Silvia coffee machine in her kitchen to 205°F. She would make a single-shot espresso to drink at home. When she got to Café Art, she'd indulge in her usual tall macchiato, an espresso topped with cream and made from the highly caffeinated Robusta beans.

While she waited for the Rancillio to reach the desired temperature, she poured herself a tall glass of cold water, then leaned against the kitchen counter as she rehydrated and admired the view. On the highest mountain peaks, the dawn sun was dusting the snow a soft pink. She'd been looking at different versions of that view since childhood and still hadn't grown tired of it.

Setting her empty glass in the sink, she opened an airtight container of Brazilian Arabica beans, sighing with pleasure at the fragrance as she poured a measured scoop into the conical burr grinder. As a coffee connoisseur, Janine knew extracting the fullest flavour and allowing the oils to release evenly was best done with a kick-ass grinder. The Baratza was an expensive indulgence. It's two oscillating, serrated plates—burrs—

crushed the beans rather than cut them into grinds. And, when it came to coffee grinds, Janine knew size mattered.

When the Rancillio beeped, Janine forced hot water through the machine to heat all the elements. Adjusting the grind to the finest setting, she hit the power button, then circled the miniature basket under the funnel so the grinds distributed evenly. When it was full, she turned off the Baratza, tamped the grinds, then attached the portafilter to the machine. Thirty seconds later, she was pouring a perfect, Guinness-effect espresso shot into a vintage Italian espresso cup.

She took a satisfying sip of the perfectly brewed beverage, then headed up the stairs to her bedroom, taking another sip before setting the drink on the bureau beside her phone.

Janine frowned when she noticed the voicemail notification. This early in the morning it was likely from Kyla Storm, Café Art's assistant manager. If the capable Kyla was reporting a problem, then it was likely serious. Janine tapped to playback the voicemail on speaker, then slipped her shirt over her head. Seconds later, despite the automated voice dictating an international number she didn't recognize, Janine heard Kevin's deep-timbered voice. His tone was uncharacteristically intense.

Jaynie, it's Kevin. Look, I need you to do me a favour. I couriered a package to you—you should get it tomorrow. Can you keep it safe? Hide it as soon as you get it, okay? And keep it a secret. It's important, Jay—. There was a sound like a muffled curse, and then Kevin resumed speaking in a low, hurried tone. *I've gotta run, Jaynie. I'll call again as soon as I can.*

Janine replayed the voicemail three times, puzzled by both the content and the tone. What was in the package, and why was it a secret? More importantly, if it was something to do with his work—and most likely it was since he lived and breathed Anglo-Saxon history—why send it to her? He knew she had no appreciation for history.

As it was late afternoon in England, she tapped his name on her phone, sipping her espresso and waiting with forced patience as the overseas connection was made. A moment later, she was listening to the double rings of her cousin's phone. When he didn't answer, she left a message.

"Hey, Kevin," she stated after the beep. "I don't know if I should be worried or annoyed, your message is so cryptic. Of course, I'll keep the package safe, whatever it is." Her tone changed to light teasing. "Although I don't get why you have to be so secretive. Are you channeling Indiana Jones?" Her cousin hated being compared to the iconic movie character. "Call me when you get this."

Janine hung up, drained her espresso, then headed for the shower.

Chapter 3

The next day, well after four o'clock, Janine was finally able to gather her things and leave the café. She hadn't had such a hectic day in years. The evening before, Tanner Fieldstone, an employee scheduled to work the morning shift with Kyla, had phoned to say he'd fallen while mountain biking and was at the medical centre being treated for a broken wrist and sprained knee. Tanner's injuries meant Janine had to take his morning shift, starting at 5:30 am. She didn't mind the early morning, but she did mind ditching her morning run.

The line of morning coffee addicts became a challenge for her and Kyla to manage when the barista scheduled to begin her shift at 8:00 am arrived late. When the La Marzocco coffee machine broke down—something went haywire with the dual-boilers—she called the service tech in Vancouver who promised to arrive within two hours, but he later phoned to say he had a flat tire and would be delayed. They'd also run out of skim milk, the eighth deadly sin for their diet-conscious customers. Janine and Kyla handed out complimentary coffee cards to these customers. As if that wasn't enough, a disgruntled gallery client came in, wanting to return a painting she claimed her husband disliked. Janine knew it was more likely the husband was upset by the $2000 price tag, but she hadn't argued. The artist was popular and the painting would easily resell.

By the end of her frenzied day, Janine was reconsidering the feasibility of purchasing the neighbouring commercial space. She'd been toying with the idea of opening a roastery and boutique barista school that would offer half-day or evening training in home espresso and foam art. Given the day she'd had, she was re-thinking the wisdom of expanding.

Glad her eleven-hour shift was finally over, Janine headed into the cramped supply room where she and her staff stored their personal items. After retrieving her purse from her locker, she checked her phone and saw a dozen emails, the same number of text messages, half-a-dozen missed phone calls, and a voicemail. *This was why Kevin refused to get a cellphone,* she thought. She decided the messages could wait until after her run.

Ten minutes later, tossing her small purse and phone onto the side table by her front door, she ran up the stairs to her bedroom and changed into a pair of leggings, a maximum-support sports bra, a long-sleeved running shirt, and Nike trail runners. Downstairs, about to close the front door, she eyed the threatening clouds, then darted back inside. She tugged a cap onto her head, teasing her pony tail through the half-moon opening at the back, and slipped on her red, light-weight cycling jacket.

She decided to run the long loop that would end at the back of her house where a paved bicycle path wound from the town to a nearby lake. It was two kilometres longer than her morning route, but it was exactly what she needed to shed the day's stress. Ten minutes into her run, it started to rain. The wooded path protected her from the worst of it, but her jacket was water resistant, not waterproof, and she was soon soaked through. Forty-five minutes later, with rain lashing her face as she emerged from the shelter of the trees, she made her way along the paved path behind her house.

A few paces away from her fenced-in backyard she slowed to a walk, then jumped in startled surprise when a raincoat-clad Scottish terrier brushed against her ankles, barking a greeting. She turned and saw Piper's owner, the elderly Mrs. Winterburn, tucking the leash she'd just unclipped into the pocket of her oversize yellow raincoat, its hood concealing her thinning grey curls.

Mrs. Winterburn gestured for Janine to come closer.

"Hi, Mrs. Winterburn," Janine said as she approached her kindly neighbour.

"I'm so glad I saw you. FedEx tried to deliver a package," Mrs. Winterburn informed her. "I told them to leave it in your mailbox, but they said it required a signature, so I signed for you. I hope that's okay."

Kevin's package. Janine had completely forgotten about the strange voicemail her cousin had left the morning before.

"Yes, that's fine, thanks."

She held open the back gate of her neighbour's seven-foot fence. A few years before, Mrs. Winterburn had the over-height fence custom built to allay her fear that a cougar or bear might wonder out of the woods and mistake Piper for a grab-and-go snack while the dog was loose in the backyard.

Janine followed her neighbour into the landscaped, multi-terraced garden and up to the back door. Inside the basement entrance was a mudroom similar to the one in Janine's house. As they entered, Piper went directly to a mat and looked up at his owner.

"I'll wait here, too," Janine said, pre-empting whatever concerns Mrs. Winterburn might have that Janine would track mud into the pristine house.

Mrs. Winterburn nodded her thanks as she stepped out of her rubber boots and hung her raincoat, saying, "I'll be right back. The package is upstairs by the front door." Just then, her phone began to ring. "Oh! Just let me see who that is, dear," she said, hurrying up the stairs.

"Don't rush," Janine called, silently adding, *don't fall and break a hip!*

Janine could hear the muffled sounds of Mrs. Winterburn's one-sided conversation. Nothing about her tone indicated the older woman was trying to end the call quickly, so Janine set about removing Piper's doggie rainwear, wrinkling her nose at the unpleasant wet-dog smell. She retrieved the thin towel that hung on a hook in the mudroom, knowing Mrs. Winterburn used it to dry the dog. She towelled Piper, the little terrier obediently lifting each paw, clearly familiar with the procedure. When Janine stood to re-hang the towel, Piper yipped, then, tail wagging, trotted out of the room and scurried up the stairs.

Given Mrs. Winterburn's phone call showed no signs of ending, Janine went through her stretches. Finally, her call ended and with Piper at her heels, Mrs. Winterburn reappeared, apologizing for keeping Janine waiting and extending a flat courier envelope about the size of a mini iPad.

"Here it is, my dear. It must be important if it's been couriered, right? I couldn't help noticing it's from your cousin in England."

The widowed Mrs. Winterburn had never met Kevin, but that didn't stop her from being inquisitive. Janine gave her neighbour a neutral smile as she tucked the flat envelope into the back pocket of her rain-damp cycling jacket. It just fit. "Thanks for signing for me," she said. "It saves me a trip to FedEx tomorrow."

"I don't mind, dear. I know how busy you are."

Janine left her neighbour's house, then made her way along the path towards her own backyard. Unlike Mrs. Winterburn's, the entirety of Janine's sloping yard was devoted to grass. She jogged up the wet lawn and stepped onto the level rectangle of cement under the shelter of the overhead decking.

She reached for the zippered pocket on her leggings where she'd put her house key, but froze when she noticed the back door was slightly ajar. With each new gust of wind, it was soundlessly shifting; an inch forward, an inch back. She stared at the single cylinder deadbolt, her brain scrambling to remember the last time she'd used the basement entrance. The night before, she realized, when she'd taken out the compost. She must not have latched the door properly when she'd re-entered the house, and the rising wind had blown it open.

She hesitated, wondering if she might be wrong to assume the door was open because of her negligence. Had someone broken in? Whistler wasn't a mecca of crime. Bikes and sports equipment got stolen far too frequently, and recreational drugs were a problem, but it was generally a safe town. And anyway, she didn't have anything worth stealing, unless you considered surplus coffee cups a hot commodity. Her mother's wedding rings and jewelry, in their usual place in a decorative tray on her bedroom dresser, held little monetary value. Her emergency stash of cash and passport were in her safe, hidden under an empty box of coffee cups in her storage room. Thieves wouldn't know the safe was even there. Her other household items—television, stereo, and laptop—were years old, nowhere near the top-end of their product lines. The only items of any value were the Baratza Encore grinder and Rancillio Silvia coffee machine. But burglars intent on a quick sell weren't interested in unhooking and absconding with heavy, industrial appliances. She could certainly retrace her steps and use Mrs. Winterburn's phone to call the police, but she'd end up looking pretty silly if she made the call on account of a door she'd failed to properly latch.

Undecided, Janine leaned forward and put her ear to the crack of the open door, but with the heavy rain pounding loudly on her nearby tin-roofed garden shed, it was impossible to hear anything. Deciding to enter with an appropriate level of caution, she slipped inside, soundlessly closing the door behind her. She paused again, straining her ears to hear beyond the muffled sound of the wind and rain. The house was silent.

Despite her conviction that she must've left the door unlatched, Janine's heart was hammering as she stepped further inside and began cautiously and soundlessly investigating the downstairs rooms. It was late afternoon and the house was already semi-dark thanks to the overcast sky, but she could see well enough. In the storage room she confirmed the empty box hiding the safe hadn't been disturbed. With mild trepidation, she headed up the carpeted stairs, her footfalls soundless. At the top, she turned left, towards the living room, she noted that her cellphone and small purse were exactly where she'd tossed them on the side table by the front door. She'd scared herself for no reason, she realized. If there were thieves in her home, they would've swiped those items.

Despite her certainty that she wasn't being burgled, she crept towards the living room, sighing in relief when she saw the flat screen TV, the stereo, and the laptop on the coffee table, all untouched.

As she reached for the light switch, a large hand suddenly clamped around her wrist. She drew breath to scream, practically choking on the rancid taste of fear in her mouth, but his other hand was already pressed over her face, effectively muffling her shrieks.

Chapter 4

Janine's heart pounded a tempo of terror in her chest as she struggled to break free from the solid bulk behind her. At five-feet-nine, she was tall and fit, but she was a poor match for the overpowering height and strength of her captor. If only he'd remove his hand from her mouth, she'd tell him he could take whatever he wanted, including the $5000 in cash that was in the safe. Unable to move her upper body, barely able to breathe with his hand partially covering her nostrils, she thrashed against his hold, kicking out blindly.

She felt a measure of satisfaction when she heard his muffled grunt of pain, the sound resembling the first syllable of her name—*Jah!* She twisted her hips, catching a glimpse of her captor's expensive, hand-tooled cowboy boots as she lashed out again with all her strength. When the sole of her right foot smashed hard into his knee, she heard his surprised grunt of pain. *Take that, asshole!*

As she slipped out of his hold and sprang towards the front door, she heard him stumble backwards and fall against the wall behind him, heard the sound of the framed M. van Laar landscape getting knocked askew, heard as well a muffled thump from upstairs. *Holy shit! Were there two intruders in her house?*

In one smooth motion, Janine was swiping her phone off the side table with her left hand and flipping the deadbolt of the front door with her right. It took a full precious second to push down on the lever door handle and pull it open. As she shot out the open door like a human cannonball, she felt the man's hand slide down the back of her rain-slick jacket.

"Wait!" he called.

A ridiculous request, given his intentions.

Barely aware of the blinding rain, she sprinted at full speed across the wet, flat expanse of her front lawn. She knew she would have no problem out-distancing the asshole in his fancy cowboy boots even though the low cloud and downpour, combined with her panic, made it almost impossible to see.

In the next instant, the breath whooshed out of her lungs when she was grabbed by a second man. *Where the hell had he come from?* Shorter and stockier than the man inside her house, he lifted her off her feet and swung her around.

Janine screamed for help—*would her neighbours hear?*—but her shrieks of protest were abruptly cut off when the man who'd been in the house tore her from the second man's hold. They began to spar, their arms and legs striking with sharp, precise movements despite the blinding rain.

For a brief second, their odd behaviour trapped Janine in a freeze-frame of shock, but then she was once again sprinting towards the street. She'd barely taken half-a-dozen strides, though, when she was tackled from behind by the tall man wearing the cowboy boots. He effortlessly scooped her up and flung her over his left shoulder in a fireman's hold as he continued running towards the street. Janine tried to call for help, but she could barely breathe, her abdomen bouncing painfully against her captor's shoulder.

Behind them, she saw the second man struggling to his feet, his faded denim jacket soaked with rain. Two additional men streamed out her open front door, the first wearing a mustard yellow jacket and the second in black leather. The man in black yelled, *get the girl*, spurring his colleague to shift direction towards Janine. Then the man in the black leather coat swept his arm out towards the man wearing the denim jacket, a metallic object gleaming in his hand. In the next instant, he was deftly leaping away from the blood gushing from the gaping wound on his victim's throat. As the man in denim crumpled to the ground, the iron taste of blood filled Janine's mouth; she must've bitten her tongue.

Had she just witnessed a murder on her front lawn?

The next instant, Janine was flung inside an old van, her captor shoving her into the passenger seat. Despite her brain being scrambled by the horror unfolding on her lawn, she had the presence of mind to both shout for help now that she could once again breathe and scramble across the passenger seat to reach for the door handle. Her captor shoved at her hips, knocking her off balance and tumbling her onto the floor in front of the passenger seat. Her phone, which she'd been gripping like a lifeline in her left hand, went skittering out of her grasp, falling with a clunk against the exposed metal under the seat.

As the van shot into the street, she struggled to pull herself up from the floor, but then heard two sharp cracks in quick succession and the sound of shattering glass as the driver's side-view mirror suddenly exploded. *They were being shot at?*

"Stay the fuck on the floor or you'll end up dead!" her captor growled.

Janine instantly ceased struggling. She didn't want to be kidnapped, but she sure as hell didn't want to get shot either.

Chapter 5

Given the deluge of rain, Dawson wasn't hopeful the neighbours would see them and call the police, which was a crying shame. He could've used some backup right about now.

With Janine bouncing on his shoulder as he ran towards the van—which he'd left unlocked with its nose parked towards the exit, an old habit from his Secret Service days—he dug his keys from the front pocket of his jeans. He also noted two vehicles that hadn't been on the street when he'd parked twenty minutes earlier—a maroon sedan and a late model BMW M3.

He spared a glance over his right shoulder. Only a handful of seconds had passed since he'd scooped up Janine, but the big man in the mustard jacket was lumbering towards them, his hand, Dawson saw, reaching into his jacket. Thank Christ that stupid-ass hadn't had the sense to keep his jacket open when carrying a weapon, or he and Janine could very well be dead by now. Dawson didn't take more than half a second to take in the scene on the lawn, but clearly the man in black, who was now following Mustard Man, had knifed the man who'd grabbed Janine. *What the hell kind of cluster-fuck had Kev gotten them into?*

He tossed Janine inside the van, filing a mental reminder to apologize later for whatever bruises his rough handling inflicted. He had the vehicle started and in gear before he closed his door. Janine was screaming as she clambered for the passenger door handle. With his right hand, he gave her ass a hard shove, with his left, he flipped the all-lock button on his door console, at the same time accelerating into the street. As he maxed the speed of the windshield wipers, he saw Janine twisting and grabbing once again for the handle of the passenger door. *Jesus!* He was trying to save her life and she was doing her level best to get herself killed. His driver's side-view mirror suddenly exploded as two sharp pistol-cracks sounded in quick succession. Mustard Man must've finally freed his weapon.

"Stay the fuck on the floor, or you'll end up dead!" he bellowed at Janine. If he'd been armed, he would've waved his handgun at her; that might've made her more inclined to stay put. But he'd had no reason—*or so he thought*—to bother with the red tape of bringing a handgun over the border.

In his rear-view mirror, he glimpsed the blurry shapes of the two men diving into the maroon sedan. Thank fuck those shitheads hadn't had the sense to turn around before parking. That would give Dawson a two-second advantage. *But would it be enough?*

At the intersection of Nordic Drive, Dawson didn't slow; instead, scanning the approaching vehicles, he cranked the wheel hard to the left and shot into the street, the van fish-tailing on the rain-slick asphalt. He ignored the blaring horns as he sent the van careening down the winding mountain road, veering into the left lane to pass the vehicles ahead of him and forcing oncoming cars to swerve out of the way.

Flicking a glance at Janine, he could see the terror in her eyes. Years ago, she'd gazed at him with soulful adoration.

How could he ever forget? The image of her luscious curves was forever seared into his brain, not so much because she'd been utterly gorgeous, but because she'd been only fifteen-years old at the time.

At the bottom of the mountain, he took a sharp right far faster than was technically safe. He barely maintained control of the van as the road curved left, then right again. He floored the accelerator when the road straightened, merging north onto Highway 99, the same highway he'd driven at speed from Vancouver and the only major road in or out of the resort town.

WEDGED ON THE FLOOR IN FRONT OF THE PASSENGER SEAT, HER heart seemed to be keeping time with the high-speed wiper blades. When her captor swerved left off of her dead-end street and onto Nordic Drive. Janine clutched the seat with her left arm, her right arm bent to cushion her head from slamming into the glove box. She swallowed a scream at the sounds of blaring horns and screeching tires, expecting any moment to be squashed like a sardine between four walls of crunching metal. She thought of her parents then. Had they been in the same state of fear in the seconds before the semi-truck sheared the top off their SUV? The only good news for Janine was the van's age. It was a dinosaur without airbags. When they crashed, as surely they would, she at least wouldn't be decapitated when the non-existent airbag deployed.

She could hear her phone—and other objects in the back of the vehicle—clattering as the van hugged the twists and turns of the road. Keeping a wary eye on her abductor, she groped blindly with her left hand, intending to hit the emergency call button as soon as she reclaimed it. Since driving the van like a bat out of hell was requiring her captor's full attention, he wouldn't notice her calling for help...but first she had to get her hands on it.

As she curled her body forward and tucked her head low to give herself more reach, she felt the press of her cousin's envelope against her back. She'd forgotten about the package, the contents of which Kevin had begged her to keep safe. But now *she* wasn't safe. Her fingertips brushed against the phone —*yes!*—but she only managed to push it farther away. The man slammed on the brakes, and she heard it clatter and fall behind her into the cavity of the running board on the inside of the passenger door. *Shit!*

The man was muttering a stream of demented obscenities as he wove in an out of traffic, repeatedly flicking his gaze to the rear-view mirror and muttering about the assholes chasing them. From what she could see of his profile, he was handsome, his face angular and well-proportioned. The beginnings of a heavy stubble accentuated his strong jawline, and his dark hair, clearly in need of a cut, curled against his collar. The cuffs of his denim jacket were frayed, his jeans well worn, and he didn't have any visible tattoos. He didn't look like a criminal...not that she knew any criminals.

Even though she couldn't see the road in front of them, Janine was familiar with the small town and knew when he merged off Nordic Drive and onto the highway. With fewer twists and turns, he increased their speed. She knew they were travelling faster than the posted speed limit, and that they were heading towards the touristy section of Whistler, which meant there would be more traffic—more opportunities to crash. She needed to call for help, sooner rather than later.

"Goddamn idiot!" the man yelled as he laid on the horn. "Get out of the way!"

The car in front of them must've done exactly that as, in the next moment, he floored the accelerator but immediately braked again, causing the van to fishtail and inspiring yet another string of inventive curses. Shrieking in fear, Janine cushioned her head between her bent arms, fully expecting to crash. Miraculously, they didn't. The man twisted the wheel to the right, yelled another obscenity, and once again floored it as he turned right off the highway.

She couldn't figure out what road they were on as the van careened too fast around the next curve, but then he barked, "Where does Nancy Green Drive go?"

Janine gaped at him. "Up…up the mountain," she stammered.

"Goddamn it," he cursed, banging the heel of his hand against the steering wheel. "They're still behind us. Fitzsimmons Road! Where does that go?"

"Uh…" Janine stammered.

"Where?" he shouted as if she wasn't an arm's length distance away from him.

"Up to a dead-end," she answered in a rush. "Or…or left, back to the highway."

In the next moment, Janine's back was pinned uncomfortably against the van's uneven contours as they turned left.

"Fuck! It dead-ends."

"No!" Janine pictured the road in her mind's eye. "There's a sharp right that leads back to the highway."

Five seconds later, Janine braced herself. *Too fast! He's going too fast! The van is going to flip!* She held her body rigid, willing the vehicle to stay on the road. When she felt it finally straighten, she let out a ragged breath of relief. The man was handling the unwieldy vehicle on the slick roads with the skill of a race car driver.

She knew the road was straight for the next half kilometre and then it would curve left around Spruce Grove Park. *Enough time to find her phone!*

Janine kept her gaze on her captor as she groped behind her. The man must have sensed her scrutiny. When he flicked his eyes to hers, she felt momentarily pinned by his piercing gaze.

Her hand suddenly stopped its blind fumbling as she stared at him. He reminded her of someone…someone who had dark, magnetic eyes…someone like her cousin's old friend.

Then he lifted his gaze to the rear-view mirror and cursed.

On the straight stretch of road, Dawson glanced at Janine, their gazes locking for a heartbeat. Even in the fading light, he could tell she was desperately trying to place him. She'd always been transparent, her thoughts and emotions visible for the world to see on her expressive face. And now, he saw, she'd finally recognized him.

About time, he wanted to say, but when he flicked his gaze to the rear-view mirror, he saw the maroon car reappear and cursed instead.

Chapter 6

Dawson Delaney?

Having experienced multiple shocks in a short space of time, Janine seemed unable to process the truth of her kidnapper's identity. She gaped at him in open-mouthed incredulity. Dawson *freaking* Delaney? She felt her heart rate accelerate, and knew it had little to do with the racing van. She could easily picture his mesmerizing blue eyes—a shade darker and they'd be black—and his irresistible smile. Now, more filled out than he'd been at nineteen, but still with broad shoulders and long, lean jean-clad legs, the man was as gorgeous as she remembered. No, that wasn't true. The 2018 version of Dawson Delaney was off-the-charts hot. And his presence in Whistler, in this exact moment, could only mean one thing: He wasn't kidnapping her. He was *rescuing* her. She remembered how he'd torn her out of the grasp of that man on her front lawn, a man who must've intended her harm but who know, Janine felt certain, was dead.

But why was Dawson here? What the hell was going on?

And then he was addressing her, a devilish grin on his chiselled face despite the back wheels of the van slithering on wet pavement as he navigated the next curve. Janine cringed. In the next moment, the van straightened. Lordy, but this man could *drive!*

"You finally recognized me," he stated in a conversational tone as, barely slowing, he yanked the wheel hard to the right. "Took you long enough."

Janine tensed as she heard the blare of horns around them. Then they were accelerating again and she knew they were back on the highway, heading north towards Pemberton.

"Dawson Delaney?" Janine's voice came out as a high-pitched squeak.

"The one and only," he stated, flashing her the same irresistible grin he'd sported at the age of nine when she'd first lost her heart to him. They'd played together often when she'd visited Kevin in Seattle. As a teenager, her adoration for her cousin's best friend had morphed into a painful, embarrassing crush. The last time she'd seen him fifteen years before, she'd pathetically tried to gift him her virginity. He hadn't noticed; instead, treating her in his usual brotherly fashion. All these years later, it was disconcerting to find that she was still seeing him through her love-sick teenage eyes.

"We'll have to delay our happy reunion gab-session," he was saying. But then he slammed on the brakes and shouted, "Get out of the way, you idiot! Yes, you! Go-go-*go!*"

As he accelerated again, Janine glanced above her left shoulder and saw they were screaming past a semi-truck hauling a cargo of cars. "Good lord, how fast are we going?"

"About a hundred," Dawson stated, keeping his eyes on the road.

The highway's posted speed limit was 90 kilometres an hour, but Dawson was American, Janine realized. "We're going a hundred *miles* an hour?" She did the calculation in her head. *180 kilometres.* "Are you *crazy?* You'll get us killed!"

His tone was affronted, "Killed? I'm saving your life."

Janine struggled to get off the floor, desperate now to get

her seatbelt on. "*Saving* my life? You're *endangering* it!" she protested.

As if their conversation spurred his own need for safety, he clipped on his seatbelt. "Now that I know you won't jump out that door, you should buckle in."

Janine struggled to rise, but could barely move, pinned by the speed of the van as it hugged a long, arcing bend in the road. When the highway straightened, Janine finally unwedged herself from the floor and flopped into her seat. As they climbed a steep hill, the van's engine whining, she clicked her seatbelt into place, noting that dusk was descending early thanks to the low cloud. The rain had lessened and the rapidly swishing windshield wipers were squeaking in protest against the drying windshield. Dawson didn't seem to notice.

As they roared past a slow-moving eighteen-wheeler, its running lights gleaming, Janine asked, "Dawson, what the hell is going on? Who's chasing us?" At the same time, she leaned down to snag her phone from the floor, but the restricted range of her seatbelt held her in place and she couldn't reach it. "Why are you even here?" she asked as she pressed back and fiddled with the top of the seatbelt, trying to encourage it to release some slack.

They crested the hill, and Dawson allowed the van to coast even faster down the long, straight stretch ahead of them. Before he could answer her questions, she heard a popping sound, like a balloon bursting. In the same instant, the van veered into the oncoming lane, which was thankfully empty. Janine instinctively threw her arms up as Dawson fought to maintain control the van. A second later, they were in the ditch, bouncing over uneven ground, the sound of rocks and tree roots slamming into the van's sides and undercarriage as loud as thunder. They burst through a tall wire fence, barely missing the post. One second passed, then another, the van continuing to slow. Just when she was beginning to believe they might not crash after all, a sudden, grinding impact halted the van in its tracks, and she felt the pain of the seatbelt cut like a whip across her chest.

THE ASSHOLE BEHIND THEM HAD TAKEN THE OPPORTUNITY ON the straight, downward stretch of highway—and lack of oncoming traffic—to shoot out one of the van's back tires, likely with a .22 calibre rifle, Dawson guessed. At the speed they'd been travelling, and despite his expertise, it had been impossible to keep the van on the road.

The good news was that they went off the highway where there was a relatively shallow ditch rather than a ravine or a river. His foot was practically punching the brake pedal through the floor, but his efforts felt futile as momentum hurtled the van forward. Dawson concentrating on avoiding the massive trees all around them. In the same second the bouncing headlights illuminated a tall, wire fence, they punched through it, just missing the eight-foot post. The grade of the rough ground steepened, slowing the van considerably as they trampled over ferns, bushes, and brambles. When a majestic red cedar tree filled the windscreen, Dawson jerked the wheel right, skimming under its lowest branch. But in the next moment, within a handful of seconds after careening off the road and with a bone-chilling crunch of metal, the van's nose slammed into a fallen tree trunk, stopping them dead.

He immediately switched off the ignition. The sudden absence of headlights and noise seemed strangely ominous. He'd noticed the maroon sedan's brake lights glaring past them as he'd veered into the ditch. How long would it take them to backtrack and arrive at the crash site? Four minutes? Less? He had to get Janine the hell out of there. He was weaponless, and those bastards had a rifle, a pistol, and a knife—none of which were a match against his Swiss Army knife.

He looked towards Janine as he reached up and flicked on

the interior light. "You okay?" When he saw blood on her face, he panicked, the horror of re-living Cassie's accident momentarily keeping him frozen in place. "Jesus!" He moved then, reaching for her, but found he was stuck, at the same time realizing his seatbelt was still buckled. *Now is not a good time to lose your shit, Delaney!* He quickly released it, then reached for Janine, deliberately gentling his hands. "Janine, are you okay?"

She was blinking slowly, clearly dazed, her cap barely anchored on her head. He took her chin in his fingers and turned her face towards him, inspecting her wound—a shallow cut above her right eye. It could do with a stitch, he noted, but it wasn't life-threatening. *Thank Christ!* Aware of the ticking clock, he scuttled out the driver's door.

As he rushed around the back of the van, he brushed the rain off his face, then realized it was no longer raining. The moisture was blood. He must've slammed his forehead against the door frame when they crashed. He ignored it, realizing at the same time his cap was no longer in his back pocket.

A part of his brain registered the distant sound of a large truck on the highway below, and wondered if anyone besides their pursuers had witnessed the van careening off the road. As he came along the passenger side of the van, he also realized the interior light was acting like a beacon. Not that it really mattered given the swath they'd cut through the forest's undergrowth.

Regardless, he needed to get Janine the hell out of there, but the speed of their escape depended entirely on whether she was injured.

With a groaning creak of protest, he yanked open the passenger door. "Hold still," he said, one hand on her shoulder even though she'd made no move to exit. With the other, he removed her cap and tucked it into his back pocket. "Are you hurt?"

"Wh-at?" she asked in dazed confusion.

He unbuckled her seat belt, then helped her out. She stood, unsteady on her feet. He propped her against the van beside the open door. Keeping one hand on her shoulder to steady her, he explored her scalp, then quickly ran his hands down her torso and legs, breathing a sigh of relief when he realized she wasn't hurt. *Thank fuck!*

"What…what are you doing?"

Keeping his eyes and ears tuned to the forest around them, he said, "We gotta get out of here. Can you run?"

Chapter 7

Can you run? Janine lifted a hand to her forehead as she stared up at Dawson. One of his big, warm hands was on her shoulder, but his gaze was scanning their surroundings. Of course, she could run. She ran every day.

When he turned back to face her, she noticed the blood seeping from a cut on his left temple. "Oh my god, you're bleeding," she exclaimed, reaching a hand to his face.

Dawson avoided her inquiring touch as he leaned into the open passenger door and clicked off the interior light. "I'm fine. Can you run?" he repeated.

She didn't answer, instead asked, "What happened? Why did we go off the road?"

In the dim twilight, she saw Dawson's chin jerk towards the back of the crashed van. "They shot out a back tire."

She didn't have the wherewithal to resist when Dawson led her at a brisk clip into the woods. She felt certain the highway was in the opposite direction, *down* the mountainside, not up. She lifted a hand to her scalp, exploring the throbbing lump on her right temple as she said, "Shouldn't we go the other way?"

"Only if you want to get shot at," he stated in a low voice, at the same time checking over his shoulder.

She halted abruptly, digging in her heels and forcing him to stop. When she attempted to turn and retrace their steps, Dawson held her back. "I need my phone," she argued.

"No, you don't. I have mine." He patted his breast pocket. Frowning, he began patting all his pockets—jacket, shirt, and jeans—at the same time swearing under his breath. "Stay here," he added, turning and jogging back towards the van.

Despite his request, she followed him, albeit at a slower pace. She knew exactly where her phone was: In the cavity of the passenger door…which, she saw, was hanging open at an odd angle.

She tripped on the undergrowth, yelping and barely saving herself from falling, then abruptly dropped to the ground at the unmistakable sound of shattering glass and a weapon being fired. She envisioned another dead body, only this time it was Dawson crumpling to the ground. But he was suddenly at her side, very much alive, and dragging her with him into the forest. When she tripped again, he flung her fireman-style over his shoulder. She heard the unmistakable sound of a gunshot, then another.

"Put…me down!" she gasped, struggling against his hold.

He stopped, quickly setting her on her feet. *"Can you run?"* he snapped for the third time.

She heard one of their pursuers calling *this way*. She didn't hesitate. "Yes. Go!"

He leapt away, immediately tripped, barely saving himself from doing a face-plant. "Can't fucking see!" he snarled in an undertone.

Terrified of their gun-wielding pursuers, Janine followed Dawson up a steep incline, made even more difficult by the wet rocks, slippery ferns, and low-lying brambles. After barely three minutes, she felt herself beginning to lag.

Dawson turned and snagged her wrist, dragging her to their right under the low, sweeping branch of a massive coniferous tree, its lowest tips dusting the steeply sloping ground above them. She dropped to her knees, realizing as she did so that her chest was throbbing with a deep, aching pain from the impact of the seat belt. Resting her left hand against the trunk of the tree, she made a concerted effort to quiet her breath. A part of her brain registered that their sprint up the practically vertical slope hadn't caused Dawson any shortness of breath, yet she, who ran regularly and considered herself fit, was gasping as if she'd just qualified for the Boston marathon.

Her attention was caught by the sweeping arcs of two lights twenty metres below them. The fact that their pursuers had the wherewithal to bring flashlights showed a pre-meditated intent to pursue and capture, she thought, or perhaps even kill. She could hear two distinct voices, both male, calling to each other about which way to go.

She spoke in a low whisper, asking, "Who the hell are they?"

He turned to her but then cursed under his breath. "Your jacket, does it have reflectors?"

"Shit!" It was early evening, but with the low clouds threatening more rain, she knew her reflectors would shine like a beacon in one of those cones of light.

"Take it off."

Janine shook her head. "My shirt has reflectors, too."

"Fuck!"

At some point in the last fifteen years, she absently noted, her old friend had developed an unrestrained penchant for swearing.

He gestured, whispering, "Get behind the tree." But as soon as she moved, his hand snapped out and snagged her arm, staying her motion. "Jesus!" he whispered. "Your jacket is louder than a goddamn police siren."

He was right. The nylon fabric made swishing sounds every time she moved.

He shrugged out of his, holding it open for her. She took care to make no sound as she slipped her arms into his still warm, cavernous jacket. If there hadn't been men with guns after them, she would've buried her nose in his scent—wood smoke, the barest hint of coffee, and something nutty—peanut M&Ms?—mixed in with some indefinable scent unique to him. Any other time, it would've been heavenly.

She crouched behind his left shoulder, her heart pounding, as they watched the lights advancing towards them. In that moment of stillness, Janine was struck by the surreal nature of their circumstances. Had there really been a murder committed on her front lawn? Was she really in the woods fleeing from men with guns? With Dawson Delaney, no less?

As the sweeping beams of lights got closer and closer, she bit down on her lip, choking back an instinctive urge to flee. She must've made some small noise for she felt Dawson's big hand press lightly against her bent knee. She understood. *Make no sound.* She allowed Dawson's steady touch to anchor her as she willed herself to statue-like stillness. She heard one of the men trip, then curse to rival Dawson; heard the other ask, *how the fuck are we supposed to find her now?* When one of them suddenly shouted *here!* Janine realized they'd found something that made them swing their flashlights upwards, directly towards their hiding place. Then they resumed their pursuit with seeming ferocity.

She sensed more than saw Dawson pat his back pocket, heard him mutter under his breath. "Damn! They found your cap."

"But..." Janine lifted a hand to her head, only now realizing she was no longer wearing it.

"I took it off when I checked your head for injuries," he whispered as he dragged her out from under the low branch.

"It was in my back pocket, but it must've fallen out. Up!" he gestured. "As fast as you can."

"Wait," she said, shrugging out of his coat. "I can't run in this."

He slipped it back on, then led the way up the incline.

Janine followed as fast as she could, grabbing protruding roots and branches as handholds. It was a hard slog, made worse when the rain resumed. Without the visor of her cap, she was hampered by the downpour. At least their pursuers would be equally as hindered, she thought.

Within two minutes, the only thing propelling her forward was the sounds of pursuit. When a fallen tree blocked their path, she couldn't summon the strength to scramble over it. Dawson clamped hold of her wrist and hauled her over the obstacle as effortlessly as if she were a child.

Before resuming her climb, she paused and looked over her shoulder, then let out a ragged sob when she saw the lights of their pursuers too close for comfort. She forced herself to keep going up the mountain, following Dawson as fast as she could, knowing he'd slowed to keep pace with her. Her legs were quivering with fatigue, her lungs were heaving, emitting loud gasps. She wasn't sure how much longer she could keep going.

When she was about to call out that she had to stop, she saw Dawson above her, kneeling on a ridge. He reached down and clasped her forearm in his big hand. She put the last of her remaining strength into heaving herself up and over the bluff, but as she scrambled for a toe hold, a handful of rocks loosened, tumbling noisily downward. At the sound of a triumphant shout behind them, she cast a terrified glance over her shoulder. The arcs of light were bouncing up the incline barely ten metres below. Dawson had both his hands under her arms as he hauled her onto the ridge, steadying her on the relatively level ground before releasing her. As she rested her hands on her knees and sucked in great gulps of air, she noticed that Dawson, who was searching their immediate vicinity, didn't seem fazed by their efforts. He wasn't even breathing heavy. *What was he, a cyborg?*

It was easier to see on the ridge than in the shadow of the massive trees. Janine could make out a narrow trail hugging the edge of the bluff. *Not that way*, she silently pleaded. She wouldn't choose to traverse *that* in daylight.

Dawson must've drawn the same conclusion, as he once again was urging her to follow him up the next embankment. It felt less steep, but was still a challenge for Janine to climb. She reached blindly for handholds as the rain continued to slash her face. The brief respite helped but, within minutes, and despite the ever-present sounds of pursuit, she knew she had to rest again.

She saw Dawson reach the next bluff. With the last of her strength, and with his hands under her armpits, she heaved herself up and over the ridge. He quickly led her a few steps away from the edge, where she immediately dropped to her knees, realizing at the same time they were on a broad, flat expanse of granite. Ignoring the ache in her chest and head, she lifted her face to let the rain cool her heated skin as she struggled to catch her breath.

It was growing dark, but she could easily distinguish Dawson's contrasting shape against the trees. She sensed he was exploring the rock face, likely looking for a hiding place, clearly aware she couldn't run any farther. From where she crouched, she could no longer hear the sounds of their pursuers, but knew they were near.

Her heart-rate slowing and once again in control of her breathing, Janine got to her feet, realizing Dawson had disappeared from view. Keeping her elbows out from her sides so that her jacket made no noise, she moved forward, aware of the cliff's edge on her right.

Dawson suddenly materialized in front of her. He spoke in

a whisper as he claimed her right hand. "This way. Quiet as you can."

She followed him, half-blind, wondering how he could move so fast in the descending gloom. After a dozen strides, he stopped and placed her hand on a massive boulder that, by its silhouette, jutted up steeply from the cliff face. When he crouched and jumped off the edge of the cliff, she barely stopped herself from crying out in alarm. In the next moment, his hands were on her shins and she saw he was standing on some kind of ledge about a metre-and-a-half below the embankment, his head and shoulders level with her knees.

"Hurry!" he urged in a whisper. "I've got you. Quickly now."

Janine dropped to her knees and turned. She felt his hands on her waist as he guided her down and onto the ledge, which in the half-light looked to be about a metre wide.

Dawson whispered, "Keep your left hand on the rock." He gave her no time to argue as he led her forward, holding her right hand in his.

Hearing the sound of muffled voices behind them, she realized the men chasing them were cresting the ridge. When her teeth started chattering with fear, she ground her jaws together, shuffling as soundlessly as she could manage behind Dawson.

And then she could no longer feel the rain and realized he'd manoeuvred them under an overhang of rock. She sagged against him in relief.

Chapter 8

Janine could hear the muffled sound of their pursuers moving along the ridge above them. Dawson hadn't moved a muscle, yet she felt his body tense as if ready to leap on their attackers and tear them limb from limb if they dared approach. Despite an ache in her shoulder and a cramp in her foot, she forced herself to remain still and to breathe quietly.

The low rumble of voices came closer, although their words remained indistinct. Moments later, the sound of their voices began to fade, then disappeared altogether.

When she drew in her breath to speak, Dawson whispered for her to wait. She could tell by his posture that he remained utterly alert. With her own muscles silently screaming to be allowed to move, she shifted her focus from external to internal, willing herself to empty her mind, even for a few seconds, of the awareness of danger.

A minute passed. She realized the rain had stopped and she could also see a little better, either on account of the clouds having lifted a little or her eyesight having grown accustomed to the descending dusk. She could distinguish the dark silhouette of tree tops in front of her, their root base in the ravine far below them.

"I'll be right back," Dawson whispered, stepping away from her and edging around the far side of the jutting boulder. Then he was gone.

Disinclined to be left on her own, she felt her heart-rate accelerate at his sudden absence. She had to force down the urge to call out for him. Within half a minute, he was back, thank god, his big, reassuring hand once again clasping hers.

"Should we go down now?" she asked in a whisper.

She could see him shaking his head. When he spoke, he pitched his voice low. "Not yet. I'm going to follow them. I won't be gone long."

He was abandoning her? "What? No!"

He ignored her protest as he led her around the jutting rock. Seconds later, he dropped to one knee beside a dark shadow on the rock face about the height of her hip, tugging her down beside him. The shadow was a cave, she saw, at the same time realizing his intention.

"You can hide in there," he said.

Janine managed to speak in a low, controlled tone even though she wanted to protest loudly and vociferously. "No way. I'll come with you. I'll leave my jacket here," she added, lifting her hand to the zipper.

"We're wasting time," he argued in a whisper. "I need to track them, find out *something* about them, for god's sake. I have no idea who they are, or what they intend. If I can get close enough to eavesdrop, I can figure out what the hell is going on." He gestured to the cave. "It's empty, about the size of a pup tent. There's nothing furry in there, or cold-blooded. I checked. You'll be safe."

Janine shuddered. She hadn't even thought of disturbing a bear or a snake. "Why can't we head down the mountain?" she insisted in a matching whisper. "This is our chance to get back to the van."

"Could you find your way there, quietly and quickly, without being detected?" He didn't wait for her to respond. "Because I'm not sure I could. Think, Janine. They have a pistol, a rifle, and a deadly knife, all of which they seem willing to use. I've only got a Swiss Army knife. They could have backup, other assholes staking out the van as we speak. Do you really want to venture blindly down the mountain with night approaching without having a bead on their whereabouts or their intentions? Because I don't. I need to know where they are and what they intend to do next. Unless I know that, I don't have a chance of keeping you safe." He pressed a gentle hand on her shoulder, encouraging her to crawl into the cave. "Please. I won't be gone long. I promise. Will you trust me?"

"But…" She hated the idea of being left alone even while recognizing that Dawson was right. Those men were dangerous. "But what about you? What if they see you?"

She saw the flash of his teeth and guessed he wasn't smiling; snarling, more like.

"They won't."

Janine had no reason to doubt him given he'd clearly demonstrated he could climb a mountainside with silent stealth.

"Okay, but I'm not going in there. I'll wait here." She shifted to sit on the ledge, the rustling of her nylon jacket overly loud. Ignoring the unpleasantness of the wet stone under her butt, she leaned her back against the rock beside the cave entrance, wrapping her arms around her bent knees, aware of the cardboard courier envelope in the back pocket of her jacket. It seemed like days had passed since Mrs. Winterburn had given it to her, but it had barely been an hour. "As of now, I'm a statue." She wished she could see his face as he crouched beside her.

"Alright," he said. He rested a hand on her knees and

added, "I won't be gone long." Then he stood and, with barely more than a whisper of sound, was gone.

Being a statue was tricky, Janine realized, hyperalert to every sound as the minutes dragged by. She found herself imagining a cougar jumping onto the ledge looking to take shelter in the cave. *Not helping,* she scolded herself. Her thoughts moved to Dawson. What if a cougar or a bear pounced on *him* while he was sneaking through the woods? Or, and this seemed more likely, what if he tripped in the dark and fell into a ravine and broke his leg and couldn't come back? *Still not helping*!

A pebble was digging painfully into her butt cheek. She managed to wiggle away from it without making more than a whisper of sound. Settling back, she felt the outline of the now soggy cardboard envelope against her back. Her thoughts turned to Kevin, struck by the coincidence that, on the same day she received a package from him, she was kidnapped—albeit by a friend—then chased out of town and shot at. The insanity of their circumstances had to somehow be connected to the package. Was Kevin in some kind of trouble? The notion seemed preposterous. She couldn't think of a scenario that would link her history-obsessed cousin to gun-wielding criminals. But what if he was, in this very moment, in as much danger as she and Dawson? *Also not helping.*

Janine forced herself to deepen her breathing, telling herself to empty her mind of thought for a single breath, then one more. After a minute or two, she began to feel steadier. But then her heart started ricocheting in her chest again when she heard a faint scuffling along the ledge to her right. When a bulky shadow appeared from around the jutting shadow of rock to her right, she uttered a faint *eek*, at the same time realizing it was Dawson.

"Coast is clear," he said, his tone making it obvious that he wasn't concerned about being overheard. "They're halfway down the mountain."

"Thank god!" She scrambled to her feet, barely stopping herself from launching into Dawson's arms and clinging to him like a life buoy. When she opened her mouth she found herself blurting, "I need to pee."

His voice held amusement. "Well then, I've got a tree I'd like you to meet."

Chapter 9

Dawson was beyond relieved they were safe, at least for the moment. But could he continue to keep her safe? That was the question of the century. It was getting too dark to see, but he felt certain as she rose from her crouch at the cave mouth that she was regarding him with utter trust, the same way she'd looked at him all those years ago.

That summer when he'd been nineteen, he'd readily agreed when Kevin said his young cousin would be tagging along with them on their Independence Day weekend at the lake. Apparently, Kevin's maternal grandmother in Portland had broken her hip, and his parents were driving down to spend a few days sorting things out for the elderly lady, leaving Janine in the care of her older cousin. Dawson had met his best friend's solemn, whip-smart cousin frequently throughout their childhood, and had always enjoyed her company. Four years younger than he and Kev, she'd hero-worshipped her cousin and, by virtue of being Kev's best friend, allotted him the same elevated status. Dawson hadn't thought twice about agreeing she join them that weekend; only, he'd expected to greet a pig-tailed, metal-mouthed kid. The moment he saw Janine in her cut-off jeans and midriff-baring tank top, he'd choked on his tongue. When she gave him her usual exuberant hug, he'd practically flung her away. He was a healthy, hetero man whose dick came to an appropriate level of attention when a woman's breasts were pressed against his chest. Only Janine wasn't a woman. She was a freaking fifteen-year-old *girl*, for Christ's sake! His brain had known that, but his dick hadn't. *You are a lecherous, loathsome dog,* he'd berated himself.

He'd vowed to keep his distance from her, but then Toby Shaw showed up *sans* girlfriend. Their other friends were all coupled off, but broken-hearted Toby was intent on drowning his sorrows in the arms of the nearest available woman, who happened to be Janine. Who was *not* a woman, despite curves that argued otherwise. Dawson had no choice but to protect his friend's young cousin from Toby. He went for a lot of dips in the lake that weekend, dips that had nothing to do with the glorious weather.

And now he was back in her life and he'd done nothing so far but scare the be-jezus out of her. Although, to be fair, when she'd entered her house through the jimmied back door, she'd scared the be-jezus out of him.

Late that morning, he'd discovered a voicemail message Kev had left on his office phone the previous day. Why the hell Kev hadn't called his cell, Dawson didn't know, but Kev's message conveyed his fear that Janine might be in danger on account of a package he'd sent her. He'd practically begged Dawson to go to Whistler in person if he couldn't get in touch with Janine by phone. Kev then apologized for not having time to explain, recited her contact info, and ended the call with an *I owe you big time. Mega big.* Even though he hadn't seen Janine since that fateful weekend, Dawson hadn't thought twice about acting on Kev's request.

Janine hadn't answered any of the half-dozen calls he'd made. The first time, he left a voicemail, re-introducing himself, explaining why he was calling, and asking her to call him back as soon as possible. She hadn't. Luckily for her, his beater van had already been packed for a late summer camping excursion. Instead of heading east to the Cascades, Dawson went north. If Kev's fears proved to be unfounded and Janine was fine, there were innumerable places Dawson could fish and camp in Garibaldi Park near Whistler. But if Kev's cousin *was* in some kind of danger, then Dawson would be on hand to help. He owed Kev that much.

As he drove north, he phoned Janine repeatedly. She didn't answer and he didn't leave additional voicemails. He cursed Kev for failing to provide Janine's husband's info—he was certain Kev had told him she'd recently gotten married—and also repeatedly phoned Kev's UK number. As his friend hadn't answered, Dawson left three highly explicit messages demanding more info and telling Kev to call him back—on his blooming cell this time.

He'd also devised a basic plan—his only choice given the appalling lack of info. Upon arrival in Whistler, he would immediately head to Janine's home. If neither she nor her husband were there, he'd charm one of her neighbours into telling him where one of them worked. He seemed to recall Kev saying she ran an art gallery. Or maybe it was a coffee shop? He'd visit all the coffee shops and galleries in town if that's what it took. Once he found her, he'd be able to reassure himself—and Kev if the Luddite would ever answer his dinosaur-age phone—of her well-being.

The US/Canada border queue had been short. Barely more than four hours after departing Seattle, Dawson was parking his van on Janine's street. He turned off the ignition and took a moment to take in his surroundings. The street, a dead-end, was forested on the east side. The opposite side of the long road was lined with a couple dozen modest, older homes. There were less than a handful of cars on the street. A white Audi Q5 was parked in Janine's driveway.

The rain drumming on the roof of his van wasn't letting

up, so he slipped his denim jacket over his long-sleeved shirt, the flannel lining a welcome layer as he stepped out of the vehicle. His senses on full alert, Dawson pulled the bill of his cap low as he walked with long, lazy strides to Janine's front door. Stepping under the roof's overhang, he rang the doorbell, then turned to scan the street. Not a soul or a curtain flick in sight.

When no one answered, he retrieved his phone from the breast pocket of his shirt and tapped Janine's number. Almost immediately, he heard a rotary phone ringtone coming from near the front door inside the house. He ended the call, then tapped her phone number a second time. The same ringtone sounded from inside the house. Janine's phone was clearly home, but she wasn't. Ending the call, he considered whether she could be inside the house, perhaps hurt or unconscious or —god forbid—dead. He entertained that gruesome thought for only a second before dismissing it. Kev's voicemail had been cryptic and urgent, possibly even alarming, but there was no cause, as yet, to jump to worst-case scenarios. Regardless, the situation needed further investigation.

Dawson tucked both hands into his jean jacket pockets as he strode around the side of Janine's house. Once there, he saw there was no gate to her fenced backyard. He guessed that, from the front, the yard could only be accessed through the attached garage. He would have to go the long way around, either walking north past the dozen or so houses back to Nordic Drive—the same route he'd driven—or south past three houses to the end of the cul-de-sac.

He chose the shorter route and, as expected, found a narrow trail hugging the perimeter fence of the last house. The thick forest temporarily sheltered him from the rain, but when he stepped out of the trees and onto the paved path, empty of both pedestrian and bicycle traffic, he was once again being lashed by wind and rain.

Habit had him scanning left and right as he headed

towards Janine's backyard. The houses, he saw, had walk-out basements perched above steeply sloping yards, most of which were enclosed by wooden fencing of varying heights. Entering Janine's yard through a back gate, he walked up the sloping lawn. Under the shelter of the upper floor deck, he rapped on the back door. While he waited for a response, he peered into the basement windows, but the shades were drawn and the windows appeared securely locked. To complete his investigation, he crossed the yard to a garden shed situated near the neighbour's tall fence. The pounding rain was even more deafening here thanks to its tin roof. He checked the padlock on the door, which faced the house and the top of the lawn. It was secure. When he stepped to his right and peered into the single, small window, he saw the usual assortment of lawn and garden supplies, as well as a bright yellow kayak and a couple of life jackets hanging from pegs on the bare timbre walls.

He heard the muffled yip of a small dog, and realized Janine's next-door neighbours had entered their back yard and entered the house. As the seven-foot fence prevented him from catching their attention, he decided to pay them a visit and ask where they thought Janine or her husband might be.

As he stepped around the corner of the shed, he saw two men darting through Janine's back gate, their heads ducked against the rain. One wore a black leather bomber jacket zipped up to his chin, the other a canvas jacket in dark yellow, the closed buttons straining against his protruding middle.

Dawson quickly slipped back behind the shed. One glance had been enough for him to know that the larger man, the one in the mustard-coloured jacket, was wearing a shoulder holster, obvious in the way he held his beefy arm ever so slightly out from his left side. Dawson assumed he was carrying either the compact Glock 19 or a 9mm Smith & Wesson, both handguns popular with serious-minded criminals. But this was Canada, for Christ's sake! Why were armed men scurrying into Janine's backyard?

Concealed from their view thanks to his location between the tall fence and shed, Dawson pulled off his cap and stashed it in the back pocket of his jeans so he wouldn't be noticed peeking around the corner of the structure. He saw Mustard Man furtively scanning the yard while the man in black, his back to Dawson, quickly and expertly jimmied the lock. He doubted these guys were the brains of whatever operation was going down; their bulk, dress, and skill at B&E indicated brawn. So, who was pulling their strings?

Dawson drew back, remaining behind the shed, oblivious to the rain that slicked his dark hair as he replayed Kev's voicemail in his mind. The archeologist had admitted sending a package to his cousin and expressed regret for having done so, implying it might put Janine in danger. Dawson could only guess, given Kevin's obsession with the past, that the package contained something of historical value. Dawson also knew private collectors would go to criminal lengths to get their hands on priceless artifacts. Had these dickwads come to steal whatever it was Kevin had sent to Janine? He wondered how Kevin had gotten mixed up with a criminal element of Anglo-Saxon history—if there even was such a thing. Or, was it Janine and her husband who were rubbing shoulders with lawbreakers? *Not Janine,* Dawson immediately thought, remembering the solemn, earnest child she'd been when he'd first met her at age nine. He'd seen her often enough over the next decade to feel certain she didn't have a criminal bone in her body. He couldn't say the same for her husband, though.

His thoughts coming full circle, he concluded there was only one important question. *Where the hell was Janine?* His first priority, now that those assholes had broken into her house, was to keep Kev's cousin well clear of them.

Intending to sneak out the backyard before jogging back to his van, Dawson peered around the edge of the shed, then was astonished to catch the briefest glimpse of a woman—it had to be Janine—disappearing into the house through the back door. *What the hell?* Had she just entered her house despite evidence of a tampered lock?

Rattled by her unexpected appearance and intent on getting her the hell out of there before the criminals noticed she'd returned, he made to step out from behind the shed, but paused when he saw Mustard Man peering out an upstairs window. Dawson waited for a heartbeat, then another, feeling his blood pressure rising. If this asshole didn't move away from the window in the next half second, Dawson would have no choice but to break his cover. He cursed silently as he stared up at the man. *Turn away from the goddamn window!* As if responding to Dawson's silent command, the man stepped back and disappeared from view.

Dawson immediately sprinted to the back door, cursing silently as he slipped into the house. *Had Janine not goddamn noticed that the goddamn lock had been goddamn tampered with? Why the fuck hadn't she called the police?* That last question was easy to answer. She hadn't called for help because *she didn't have her goddamn phone!*

Chapter 10

It was while she was relieving her bladder, with Dawson a good ten metres away, that a thought popped into Janine's mind. Might Dawson somehow be associated with criminals? Was *he* a criminal? Perhaps a rival of their pursuers? Was she making a mistake in thinking that, because he was Kevin's childhood friend, he could be trusted?

Janine immediately dismissed her suspicions. Giving in to paranoia was a waste of time. Besides, this was *Dawson freaking Delaney*. She'd known him since childhood. She'd met his parents and his four older sisters. And he worked for the US Secret Service. Although, now that she thought of it, she remembered Kevin telling her he'd left his job. Regardless, she trusted her cousin implicitly, and Kevin would never associate with criminals.

When Janine rejoined Dawson, the silhouette of his image a barely discernible contrast against the overcast sky, he addressed her before she had a chance to speak, his tone accusatory. "Didn't you notice your lock was broken when you came in through your back door?"

Immediately defensive, she protested, "Of course I did!" But then she deflated, emitting a humourless chuckle. "Okay, that's not true. I did notice that the door was open. I *didn't* notice the lock was broken. Oh my god," she muttered, dropping her face onto her hands. "I'm such an idiot." She jerked her head up then. "Wait, how did you know I came through my back door?"

Dawson told her what he'd witnessed, stating that seeing her slip into the house and knowing the intruders were inside shaved ten years off his life. He also shared his theory that there were two rival groups after Janine, which would explain the altercation they'd witnessed on her front lawn.

"But why? I mean, is all this…" Searching for the right word, she swept her arm out to indicate their surroundings, her nylon jacket swishing loudly.

"This clusterfuck?"

"That seems an apt description. This all has something to do with Kevin, doesn't it? Do you think…?" Her voice shook and she couldn't finish her sentence. *Do you think he's dead?*

"Janine, don't do that. Giving in to your fear that he might be hurt—or worse, dead—won't help us or him. We can assume he's in trouble, yes. But can we agree to operate on the assumption he's okay?" Dawson asked. "Anything less will handicap us—especially you—from thinking clearly."

Janine nodded. "I can do that." And she could. She would picture her cousin safe.

"You thirsty?" he asked.

Janine was startled by his sudden change of topic. Now that he mentioned it, she realized she was parched. "Yes. Very."

"Come on."

There was sufficient contrast in the dark shadows along the relatively flat bluff for Janine to follow him. Within half a minute, she could hear the sound of trickling water. Thirty seconds later she was crouched beside a narrow, rock-lined brook.

"Good lord, that's cold!" she said when she started scrubbing her filthy hands. When she was certain they were clean, she cupped the water and sipped until her thirst was quenched. "Very good, though," she added.

"You should rinse the cut on your head," he suggested.

She dabbed carefully at the broken skin, the cold water cooling on her throbbing temple. When she asked if he'd washed his wound, he dismissed her concern.

Finished, she stood and faced him. He stood silhouetted against the darkly overcast sky, his arms crossed over his chest, his stance typical alpha male. From his profile, she could tell he was gazing out into the distance. She wished she could see his face. She asked a different version of her earlier question. "What do you think is going on? And shouldn't we be going down to the van now? My phone's there. I can call my friend Nicolette to come pick us up."

She could see Dawson shaking his head. "That's where *they'll* be."

"You can't know that."

"I can if I heard them say they would stake out the van."

"Shit!" she exclaimed, then added, "But my phone is there."

"Is it worth dying for?"

Thunder rumbled overhead, low and menacing, as if giving appropriate weight to Dawson's question.

"No, of course not, but…"

A light shower of rain began to fall.

"Jesus," Dawson muttered. "Don't you just love the west coast?"

As they moved under the boughs of the nearest evergreen tree, she asked, "Did you hear anything else?"

"They don't relish telling someone named Bart that they didn't get what they came for."

"Which is?" she asked.

"Didn't you hear them at your house?" He imitated the man in black, *"Get the girl."*

"I forgot about that." She sucked in her breath. "And, just after we left the van, one of them said something about finding *her*. They mean me, don't they?"

"What he said was, *how the fuck are we supposed to find her now?*"

"Setting aside the question of why they want me, it's clear we can't go back to the van. But we still need to get to the highway and catch a ride back to town."

"Can you find the highway in the dark?" Dawson asked.

Janine looked around them. The obvious direction to go was down, but they could easily end up in a blind valley. "No," she admitted with reluctance, then added. "Good lord, you're not suggesting we spend the night here?"

"What I'm suggesting," he grumbled, "is we have this discussion in the shelter of that cave."

Chapter 11

The sheer darkness inside the damp cave would've been terrifying had Janine been alone. They didn't have a flashlight, but Dawson did something to his wristwatch to make it glow, illuminating the small interior. The ceiling to the right of the entrance was low, sloping down into a flattened crevice about twenty centimetres high. The largest part of the hollow was immediately in front and to the left of the oblong entrance, about a metre deep, the same in height, and double that in length.

Twigs and stones—and likely animal bones, Janine thought without humour—dug into her palms and kneecaps as she followed Dawson inside. She shifted around to face the entrance and settled on his left, their backs against the wall, their knees drawn up. Above her head there was a good ten centimetres of space, but the crown of Dawson's head was just below the low ceiling. Rain was pattering loudly on the stone ledge in front of their feet, but thankfully there was no wind blowing the wet into their refuge.

For the first time, Janine felt the cold and was grateful for Dawson's warmth beside her. She was also feeling the presence of a whole host of bruises. Despite these inconveniences, she realized their situation could've been much worse. They could've been captured or shot, possibly killed. They'd also avoided slamming into a tree at high speed multiple times during their mad escape thanks to Dawson's expert handling of the van.

Dawson clicked off the glow feature on his watch. "Might as well let our eyes adjust."

A sudden flash of lighting momentarily illuminated the cave. In the second after it was gone, Janine was completely blind.

"Do you think he's dead?"

"Kev?" Dawson asked.

"God! No! I thought we weren't going there?"

"We're not. Jesus! Sorry. You mean the guy on your lawn?" Dawson sighed. "I only caught a glimpse but, yeah, I think he's dead."

A flash of lightning once again illuminated the cave, followed two seconds later by a loud crack of thunder. The rain came down even harder.

"Why were you at my house at *exactly* the right time?" Janine asked, lifting her voice a little to be heard above the sound of the rain.

"Nothing but luck," he said. "Kev left a…I don't want to frighten you, but he left a pretty cryptic message on my phone. He said he sent you something and was worried about your safety because of it. He basically begged me to make sure you were okay. I phoned you half a dozen times, left a message, texted you…"

Janine recalled all the missed messages she'd ignored. "Sorry. It was a crazy day, and I didn't have a spare second to look at my phone…" She shrugged, drawing her knees closer to her chest and hugging them, trying to ward off the cold. "I was intending to deal with the messages after my run, but then this happened." She turned her face towards Dawson even though she couldn't see him. She knew he had a degree in criminology and had joined the US Secret Service after graduation, but she didn't know much else. "You work for the Secret Service, don't you?"

"Not anymore."

Dawson's tone was cold and clipped, making it abundantly clear he didn't want to elaborate. Once again, she wished she could see his expression.

He continued in a neutral tone. "My brother-in-law and I have a company in Seattle that specializes in home security consultations and installations."

"Well…looks like *I'm* in need of a security system," Janine stated, her tone wry.

Dawson's surprised chuckle dispelled the tension. "That you are," he agreed.

"What did Kevin say to make you drive all the way to Whistler?" Janine asked, her teeth chattering slightly.

"You're shivering." Dawson shifted, and the next moment she was snuggled into a cocoon of warmth, his open jacket at her back, his left arm holding her snug against his big frame.

She didn't hesitate to settle against him, feeling like a heat-seeking missile who'd found its home. What was it about men and their internal furnaces? She was tempted to undo one of the buttons on his shirt and snake a hand inside, certain that doing so could warm her cold hands in seconds flat. Thinking of her hand on his bare chest brought to mind the memory of how he'd looked all those years ago at the lake, the dark hair on his sculpted chest tapering to a thin line dissecting his hard abs, disappearing invitingly into the low waistband of his swimming trunks.

"What exactly did Kevin say?" she repeated. Below her cheek, she could feel the appealing vibration of Dawson's voice as he responded.

"He said he'd made an important find, that he sent it to you, but was now feeling this object put you in danger. He asked me to make sure you were safe, then rattled off your phone number and address. I tried calling him a few times, but…"

She felt him shrug.

"Wait. Where is *your* cellphone?" she asked, lifting her head from his shoulder.

In the dark, her forehead brushed against his jawline. The roughness of his stubble on her bare skin felt intimate. What would he do if she lifted her hand and trailed her finger along his raspy chin? She dropped her head, resting her cheek once again on his shoulder. *Dawson Delaney, you are entirely too distracting!*

Dawson sighed. "Last time I had it, I was on your front step. I put it in my jacket pocket, but these damn pockets," he made a gesture she couldn't see. "They're too shallow. It probably fell out, along with my cap, when I had that little dust-up on your lawn. Or maybe when we crashed. I don't know." He sighed, clearly frustrated. "Kev might have called me back by now."

"In the voicemail he left for me," Janine shared, "he said I was to keep the *package* safe. He didn't express a concern about *my* safety."

"When did he leave the voicemail?"

"Monday morning about 6:00 am." It was now late Tuesday evening.

"That's about the same time he left one for me, only he left it on my office line. I'd been on a job site, and didn't check that voicemail until late this morning. But he was definitely worried about *your* safety. And Kev, of all people, knows I take that word *very* seriously."

Janine wasn't surprised given his former career. "But it's a long way to travel based on a cryptic voicemail. Seattle to Whistler is a good four or five hours."

"Well, I owe Kev for…it doesn't matter. What I do know is that if I'd listened to it yesterday, we wouldn't have been chased out of town today."

"How did Kevin sound? Did he seem worried?"

"He was..."

"What?" Janine asked when Dawson hesitated. This time when she lifted her head, she deliberately pulled her chin in to avoid touching him. Another flash of lightening illuminated the cave. In that split second, she saw his thoughtful frown, his eyebrows dark accents above his brooding gaze.

"Concerned? Pissed? Scared? Apprehensive?" he said. "All of the above?"

Janine reached behind her and unzipped the back pocket of her jacket, tugging out the envelope. "Can you turn your watch light on? I need to know what he sent me."

"You have it *with* you?" Dawson asked, clearly startled.

Janine told him she'd been given the package minutes before entering her house through her back door.

They examined the envelope in the glow of Dawson's watch. The edges were intact despite the soggy cardboard. Whatever was inside was still there, although the small bulge gave no indication of the contents. Janine ripped the cardboard tab. When she tilted the envelope towards the light and peered inside, she glimpsed a pink-hued, plastic bubble sleeve the size of her palm. She retrieved it, then set the soggy cardboard aside. The plastic was secured with an inch-long piece of clear tape—*cellophane*, her cousin would say, having adopted British lingo.

She and Dawson exchanged a look before she tugged it open. Peeking inside, she saw a small, gold disc. "I think it's a coin," she said, letting the object slide onto her open palm.

Dawson shifted his wrist to better illuminate the object as she displayed it between her thumb and forefinger. In the centre was a six-petalled rosette, the edges embossed with square-edged capital letters: R E X A L F R E D. She turned it over. The back was etched with the profile of a man's head—sharp jaw, a jutting, Roman-looking nose, a pointy beard—

encircled by the Roman numerals D C C C X C. That was a date, she knew.

"A Roman numeral X is ten," Dawson said. "D and C could be one hundred, five hundred, or a thousand. Do you recall?"

"D is five hundred, C is one hundred," Janine said.

"So…890. How do you remember that?"

"My grandfather collects Victorian coins."

"May I?" asked Dawson.

Janine handed the coin to Dawson. She watched him examining it, asking, "Do you really think that coin is sufficient reason for those men to break into my house? And then chase and shoot at us? And knife someone on my front lawn?"

Dawson handed it back to her. "It doesn't seem possible, does it?"

Sighing, Janine tucked the coin back into the plastic bubble envelope, then slipped it into the zippered pocket of her leggings with her house key. Dawson clicked off the glow feature on his watch, then suggested she sit on the empty cardboard envelope, which she did, before resettling against his warmth.

"Kevin has a lot to explain," she stated into the darkness. "I still can't believe you drove all that way on account of a cryptic message, but I'm glad you did. I don't know where I'd be right now if those men had found me instead of you." In quiet sincerity, she added, "Thank you, Dawson."

"You're welcome."

"But…at the risk of negating my appreciation for your timely intervention…why the blazes did you kidnap me instead of simply telling me who you were?"

"I didn't kidnap you. I *rescued* you."

Janine chuckled. "Is that what you call it? But seriously, why couldn't you have said, *Hey, Janine, remember me? Dawson Delaney? I'm here to rescue you from the bad-asses burgling your home.*"

He snorted. "You don't seem to realize, I was trying to get us the hell out of there *unnoticed.*"

"Fair enough. But in the van, you had time enough to utter strings of expletives. Is Cursing 101 a pre-req for the Secret Service?"

She felt him tense again at mention of his former employer. What was *that* about?

"Yeah, sorry," he said, his tone clipped. "I've been told I tend to swear a lot when I'm under pressure. It's a bad habit."

"I don't care about the swearing. But honestly, Dawson, you should've told me who you were. I was beyond terrified."

"You're right. And I'm sorry. I handled the situation badly. I'm out of practice, I guess."

Lightning flashed, followed by an instant crack of loud thunder.

"Damn. It's getting worse," Dawson said as the rain pounded down.

"At least there's no wind," Janine offered. After a moment, she added, "I still can't believe you drove all this way just because of Kevin's voicemail."

"It's not that much of a stretch. You probably didn't notice, but my van is full of camping gear. I was just about to head out on a solitary fishing trip. I simply drove north instead of east to the Cascades."

Janine remembered hearing items sliding back and forth in the back of the van—his camping gear. "The Cascades might be having better weather," Janine observed as she listened to the drumming rain. She lifted her wrist and checked the time. "Wow," she announced. "Are you thinking what I'm thinking? That it feels more like the middle of the night instead of only 10:00 pm?"

Chapter 12

Are you thinking what I'm thinking? Dawson barely prevented himself from snorting in derision.

What he'd been thinking was how good she felt nestled against his side. Having Janine against his chest was playing havoc with his libido. Her scent was messing with him big time, too. Even soggy and sweaty, she smelled damn good, the rain dampness mixed with the faint scent of coffee and some fragrance he couldn't identify, something citrusy, probably from her shampoo or body lotion. Tantalizing images of lifting her onto his lap and kissing the shit out of her right then and there had been plaguing him ever since he'd pulled her against his side.

Are you thinking what I'm thinking? Yeah. Not likely.

He heaved a resigned sigh, reining in his wayward thoughts. "When's the last time you talked to Kev?" he asked.

"Um…four, maybe five weeks ago. I think he's been camping in his caravan a lot. They're having a really dry summer and for some reason that makes archeology all the more interesting. You know him, he gets excited about pottery shards and shoe buckles and midden heaps—that's medieval speak for landfill, by the way."

Janine's stomach suddenly growled loudly.

Dawson chuckled. "When's the last time you ate?" Dawson asked.

"I had a turkey on rye…" She lifted her wrist and checked the time. "Ten hours ago. Aren't you hungry?"

She felt him lift a shoulder in a shrug. "Not so much. I had a burger and fries at a drive-through in Squamish a half-hour before I got to your house."

When Janine shifted, her hand, which had been laying on his chest, settled on his abdomen, close to his belt buckle. In spite of the discomfort of the cave, his dick responded immediately, no thanks to his mind projecting the image of Janine in frayed denim shorts and a girls-gone-wild tank top. He'd felt like a total pervert fifteen years ago, unable to stop himself from imagining what it would be like to peel off that tank top and fill his hands with her luscious breasts. He was definitely a breast man; always had been. But lusting after an innocent fifteen-year-old girl? That was loathsome! Janine, an adult now, was off-the-charts sexy. He had to remind himself that she was also another man's wife and that he was here to protect her, not have sex with her.

He suddenly remembered her saying she'd call her friend Nicolette to pick them up. Why hadn't she suggested calling her husband? *Good lord, was Janine gay?*

"Aren't you married?" he asked.

"What?" Janine seemed momentarily thrown by his unexpected question. "Oh! Kevin told you I was engaged? Yeah, I was. We broke it off six months ago. He fell in love with someone else."

Dawson felt blood surge in his veins. *Janine was single, hetero, and no longer fifteen…* Then he realized what she'd said and became immediately indignant. "Jesus! He *cheated* on you?" He couldn't imagine why anyone would go looking elsewhere if they had Janine in their bed, in their heart. *Now, that's a strange thought,* the voice in his head said.

Dawson felt the negating shake of Janine's head against his shoulder.

"I don't think so. He had the decency to break up with me before that happened."

"So *he* said," Dawson muttered, realizing the rumbling thunder was growing distant.

"I believe him. Anyway, they're married now." In a too bright voice, she added, "*And* they're having a baby."

Dawson had four sisters. He knew how to interpret a woman's insincerely cheerful tone. *She'd* wanted to have this slimeball's baby. He pictured Janine pregnant—naked, and pregnant. Round and lush and fertile—gorgeous!

Jesus! What was *wrong* with him? Why the hell was he finding it so hot to picture her *pregnant*? Naked, *yes*. Pregnant, *no!*

Over the years, Dawson had been in a number of long-term relationships, but he'd never been tempted to pop the question or start a family. His sisters had long ago given him the nickname "George" on account that George Clooney took serial monogamous relationships to a whole new level. The fact that George had fallen in love for real and gotten married four years before and was now a devoted family man hadn't changed Dawson's nickname. His sisters still called him George.

"How long were you together?" he asked.

"Seven years. Engaged for the last two."

She might think her tone disguised her hurt, but he could hear it. It made him want to punch something.

"He kept dragging his feet when it came to setting a wedding date." She sighed, then added. "In hindsight, I should've connected the dots."

"So, you're still…"

"No! I'm not still in love with him. The question is, was I ever? I ask myself that a lot. I mean, shouldn't I be missing him?"

"You're not?"

"Not since about week three."

Wasn't *that* interesting.

"And you?" she asked into the silence. "Are you in a relationship?"

"Nope," he said, although the immediate response in his mind was, *not since Cassie died.*

The months following the accident had been hell. At the time, he'd been dating a pediatrician, a woman named Sarah Anders. They hadn't officially been living together, but she kept some of her belongings at his place. He'd come home one day and realized Sarah's things were gone, then had to wonder how long they'd been gone.

It had taken months to lift himself out of the downward spiralling vortex of self-loathing after Cassie's death. Kev's friendship during that dark time had helped immeasurably.

"Do you see marriage in your future?" she asked.

He debated whether to be honest, then realized this wasn't some awkward first date with the usual twenty questions. This was Janine, his childhood friend. "Honestly? I want what my parents have. I don't see the point in marriage unless I can picture my wife and I in our nineties, holding up the cashier's line in the grocery store with our side-by-side walkers and shouting *can you repeat that, dearie* to the clerk when she's counting out our change."

He could feel Janine's smile against his shoulder. It made a light flick on inside his heart.

"How long have they been married?"

"Coming up to fifty-five years."

They fell into silence then, lulled by the sound of the rain, lost in their own thoughts. Against his chest, he could feel Janine moving her chin slightly, and surmised she was chewing on her lower lip. He wanted to duck his head and have a taste.

Stop it, he scolded himself.

Dawson lifted his wrist and looked at his watch. The

glowing numbers indicated it was close to midnight. "Look, why don't we try sleep for a few hours?" For a fleeting moment, he considered suggesting sex to pass the time, but didn't relish the idea of getting slapped. "When it's light enough to be certain of our direction, we can start making our way to the highway. And anyway, I'm starting to feel like a pretzel in here. If we shift around so that we're lengthwise, facing the cave opening, we can stretch out our legs."

They repositioned themselves, moving to lay on their right sides, their upper bodies in the hollowed-out portion of the cave and their feet tucked into the lower cavity. He cushioned her head with his right arm, draping his open jacket over her and spooning her against his front, pulling her close. The ground was hard and uneven, but Dawson had the bonus—in addition to being sheltered from the rain—of having Janine in his arms. He'd take that any day over a soft bed.

Into the somewhat awkward silence that fell, Janine said. "My Café is going to be seriously under-staffed tomorrow morning."

They chatted for a while, updating each other on the events of their lives over the past fifteen years. When Janine touched on the unhappy circumstances of her parents' car accident, an event he'd known about from his relationship with Kevin, he said, "I thought about sending you flowers when I heard, or a card. I wish I had. God, what a tragedy." He pulled her closer, offering the only comfort he could.

"It's okay," Janine said, then added. "My parents dying wasn't the worst part of that accident, you know. There was one other fatality, a four-year-old girl. I found out her name was Annabelle Labonte. She was travelling with her grandparents because her mother just had a new baby. Every time I think of those young parents having to bury their four-year-old daughter, and those grandparents who survived when Annabelle didn't, my loss seems so minor in comparison."

Dawson wanted to place his lips on her temple, not in a

sexual way, but to indicate his understanding. "You're asking yourself," he said, *"what right do I have to grieve, when the pain the other family is going through is so much worse?"*

"Exactly," she breathed. "How did you know?"

He wished he could see her face. "We all have shit to deal with, Janine," he said, then instantly regretted his words. He didn't want her asking probing questions, so he added, "But their loss isn't *bigger* than yours. It doesn't work like that. You have the right to mourn your parents." He felt her nod.

After a moment, she said, "I think about that family often. I'm sure the grandparents blame themselves. They probably waste countless hours second-guessing the actions that led up to that crash. I'm certain they're plagued by thoughts of what they could've done differently."

Now it was Dawson's turn to ask, *how did you know?* But he didn't allow himself to voice the question. That was an emotional minefield he didn't think he'd ever be ready to navigate. In a voice thick with emotion, he said, "I'm just so goddamn sorry you had to go through that, Janine. Were you close with your parents?" He had only a vague recollection of them.

"I was really close with my father. He was a sweet, gentle man. My mom…she was aloof. Remote. Like she had only a limited reserve of love and it had already been used up before I came along."

She told Dawson what she'd recently discovered about her mother.

"Why Aruba?" he mused.

"I don't know, but it has to be the Dutch association. Maybe even a family connection. I have so many questions, but mostly I just want to know whether Esme is alive and, if so, where she is."

"Are you going to contact your mother's sisters?"

She yawned expansively, then said, "I haven't decided yet. I didn't even know they existed until two days ago. I'm just…"

When she didn't finish her sentence, he said, "It's not a decision you have to make right now. You'll know when you're ready to make it."

"Yeah, I know," she said, her voice heavy with sleep.

He was about to offer to apply his skills as an investigator to look for Esme when he realized Janine had fallen asleep.

Without disturbing her, he adjusted his position, trying to get more comfortable. The cold stone floor was godawful, but having Janine in his arms, even in a platonic way, was freaking awesome. He pulled her closer, telling himself it was for the sole purpose of sharing body heat and had nothing at all to do with how good she felt in his arms.

Chapter 13

When Janine awoke, her first impressions were of the juxtaposition of the cold and unforgiving stone directly beneath her—the square of soggy cardboard beneath her hip was ineffectual—and the welcome heat emanating from Dawson behind her. She opened her eyes, disappointed to see it was still dark. At least the rain seemed to have lightened to a barely perceptible drizzle. Careful not to let her jacket rustle—she didn't want to wake Dawson—she checked the time: 5:09 am.

Janine willed herself to fall back asleep, but her mind was too busy picturing Kyla heading to the coffee shop and expecting Janine to be there. Her thoughts shifted to the previous day's events. *Was Kevin dead?* Her mind skittered away from that terrifying thought. As Dawson said, it was better to only entertain the possibility of him being alive. She prayed fervently that, wherever he was, her cousin was safe.

She'd been gazing sightlessly out the cave entrance, lost in thought, unaware of time passing, when she realized she could see the treetops silhouetted against the pre-dawn sky. It would soon be light enough to make their way down the mountain.

Janine turned her head, intending to wake Dawson, but

paused as she gazed at him. He lay on his side facing her, his right arm pillowing both his head and hers, the other draped, along with his open jacket, possessively around her waist. In the barely there light, she couldn't make out his distinct features, but could detect the dark sweep of his eyelashes fanned against tanned cheeks. He'd always had killer lashes, even as a boy.

As she gazed at him over her shoulder, Janine felt the same powerful pull of attraction she'd experienced as a teenager. That weekend at the lake, he'd spent a lot of time with her, keeping up a constant flow of friendly banter, his goofy sense of humour repeatedly sending her into fits of giggles. She'd wanted so badly for him to kiss her, but the only time he'd touched her was when he helped her in or out of the speedboat. He'd behaved in a brotherly fashion, treating her the same, she suspected, as he did his sisters. She'd both loved those moments with him and resented them. She hadn't wanted to be treated like a sister. But she also hadn't known how to flirt or how to make him see her as a woman. *Well, Janine, you're not fifteen anymore.*

She was aware of the contours of Dawson's welcome warmth curving around her. He was built just the way she liked, long and lean. She felt a kick of heat deep in her abdomen at the tantalizing mental image of Dawson looming over her as he thrust inside her. She dropped her gaze to his lips and imagined skimming their fullness, first with her fingertip, then with her lips, tasting him on her tongue.

Her eyes widened when the very lips she was staring at suddenly curved into a smile. She glanced up in alarm. His eyes, framed by thick, sooty lashes, were like midnight pools of ink. There was no mistaking the hot embers of desire heating their depths.

"I…I didn't know you were awake." she stammered, turning to look out the entrance of the cave. "It's getting light. We should go."

Dawson took his time propping himself up onto an elbow. "I've never liked that word," he said around an unhurried yawn.

Janine turned to regard him, a question on her lips, but was distracted by the rooster tail on his head. She had to suppress the urge to reach up and tangle her fingers into his thick hair. If she let herself do that, she knew she'd pull his head down and kiss him.

She had to make a concerted effort to remember his comment. "You never liked what word?"

"Should."

She shook her head, uncomprehending.

"You know, shoulda-woulda-coulda?" He was looking down at her, his eyes dark, his early morning voice grumbly and rough, his mussed hair and dark stubble elevating his leading-man good looks from gorgeous to irresistible. "It's a waste of time thinking about what I shoulda-woulda-coulda done. Either do it," he paused, dropping his gaze to her mouth. "Or don't." As if to demonstrate his theory, he dipped his head and kissed her.

In her mind, Janine was hearing the excited shrieks of her fifteen-year-old self. *Dawson freaking Delaney was freaking kissing her!* Her adult mind, as excited, was also evaluating the sweetness of his kiss. She would've pegged him as a full throttle kind of man, kissing a woman the same way he drove, demanding the highest performance and giving the same in return. She hadn't expected this gentle exploration, the light sandpaper roughness of his stubble barely discernible on her cheeks.

As she lifted her hands to finally do what they'd been born to do—tangle in his hair—she only fleetingly considered her need for a toothbrush. As a wave of pure lust swept through her, she opened her lips in an unmistakable invitation for more. All thoughts, including those of her cousin and where they were and why, evaporated as the kiss turned from sweet delight to a molten eruption of liquid, pulsing desire.

Chapter 14

When Janine abruptly looked away from him—*in embarrassment?*—Dawson leaned up on an elbow and shifted his hips away from her. When he'd opened his eyes to see her staring at his mouth, he assumed she was contemplating kissing him. His optimistic dick immediately came to attention and seconded this motion.

He yawned, attempting nonchalance as he dropped his gaze to her face. A part of his brain was aware of dawn approaching, aware too that the morning was calm, with no obvious wind and only the lightest patter of rain. When she said they *should* go, he knew she was right. It was time to start making their way down the mountain. But he'd learned a valuable lesson about the word *should.* It implied obligation and guilt; of doing something even though your heart wasn't in it. He had *should-ed* himself to death after Cassie died, and he much preferred the satisfaction of doing something, anything, as long as it felt honest and authentic. Applying *should* to future actions or *should-haves* to past regrets sucked. Maybe they *should* leave, but if that was the case, why did he feel so utterly compelled to stay in this stone cocoon and kiss her?

He did exactly that, his mouth curving up slightly at the sound of her surprised, in-drawn breath. He paused for a millisecond, feeling her warm exhalation on his face, giving her time to stop him. But she didn't, so he dipped his head further and brushed his lips lightly against her *thank-you-Jesus-for-inventing-kissing* mouth. She tasted even more delicious than he'd imagined.

Her earlier embarrassment had him expecting a tentative response, but he was delighted to discover he'd grossly under-estimated her. Within seconds, she'd ratcheted up that sweet, ten-out-of-ten first kiss into a streaking comet of heat. She seemed to both melt and explode beneath him, and his semi-uncomfortable boner morphed into a pulsing raging hard-on that was impossible to ignore.

Janine was on fire. Her tongue in his mouth was hot lava, igniting and matching his long overdue desire for her. Wanting to taste more than just her mouth, he shifted to half lay on her, knowing his arousal would be fully evident as he draped his leg over her length. The cold stone beneath them wasn't remotely comfortable, and he silently cursed the lack of a soft, king-sized bed. But the discomfort didn't stop him from trailing kisses along the smooth line of her utterly delectable jaw. She lifted her chin in invitation, her sigh of pleasure his new favourite sound.

She arched her hips, pressing her body in unmistakable invitation against the length of him. *Jee-ZUS!* He lingered for a moment as he tasted the hollow in her throat, forcing himself to cool his jets, all the while revelling in the feel of her fingers in his hair and the rapid beating of her pulse against his lips. He couldn't remember ever going from zero to full throttle, except that time with Marla Banks. In his defence, he'd only been fourteen at the time and she a highly experi-enced—and magnificently well-endowed—seventeen.

He lifted his head, reclaiming Janine's lips as his hand drifted down the length of her long, exquisite body, then up to cup the curve of her breast, cursing the layers of fabric—jacket, shirt, bra—that denied him access to her skin. His need intensified as she arched herself into his exploring hand.

He hadn't noticed that she'd pulled the tail of his shirt out of his jeans, but he was instantly aware when her cold fingers sparked sizzling lines of electricity along the bare skin of his back. He fumbled for the zip of her jacket, wanting, desperately needing, to fill his hand with her lush curves. He intended to make her moan, make her arch her back as he kissed and licked her breasts, buried his face in them. But first he had to get his hands on them.

Her jacket open, he finally slid his hand under her shirt and touched her gorgeous velvet skin. His exploration made note of her hefty running bra. It would take some doing to get it off, but for the moment he was happy simply touching her, feeling her pebble hard nipples responding through the thick fabric.

Except it *wasn't* enough.

Without breaking their kiss, he shifted onto his back in the small confines of the cave, pulling her with him. He was vaguely aware of the unpleasant granite beneath him, but he was more attuned to how it felt to fill both his hands with her lush curves. Her nipples hardened into candy corn under his caress, and he felt his cock swell with equal fervour. When she drew up her knees on either side of his hips and pressed her hot mound against him, he just about launched his rocket. He hadn't climaxed from dry humping since he was a teenager, but he was close to losing it now, as if he were still that pervert who'd been so goddamn hot for fifteen-year-old Janine. But she wasn't underage anymore. *And* she wasn't married. *And* she clearly wanted him as much as he wanted her, that was certain. *Jesus, she felt good!*

When she broke their kiss and sat up slightly, keeping her head low to prevent bumping against the ceiling, his first instinct was to protest. But when she let him slip off her jacket and then began fumbling with his belt buckle, he realized there was not a single thing in this world to complain about. He debated slipping off her shirt. Was it too cold? Probably. He satisfied himself with lifting the hem to expose, yup, the sexiest, no-nonsense sports bra he'd ever laid eyes on, which in no way detracted from how hot she was, despite the visible absence of a handy release clasp.

He must've made a sound of approval, because she laughed suddenly, low and sexy. His hands were happily occupied, so he didn't bother helping her with his belt. He needed those nipples in his mouth. He needed to bury his face in the swelling warmth of her curves, and then he needed to lose himself in the liquid heat at her core.

He moved a hand to the front of her leggings, reaching inside. "Jesus, you're wet," he said in a voice he didn't recognize as his own. He groaned with pleasure as he slipped a finger into her slick heat, then two, knowing when he buried his cock where his fingers were, he truly would explode.

That tantalizing thought made him finally tune into the one-word message his brain had been sending in a kind of Morse code since the moment Janine had ratcheted up the heat of their kiss.

Condom. Condom-condom-condom. Condom.

His hands stilled. Like every single, virile male, he never traveled without condoms. *Of course* he had condoms. They were where he always kept them. In his shaving kit.

In the *goddamn van!*

Why the hell had he stopped the high-school habit of carrying a condom in his wallet? *Why?*

Janine had his belt and the top button of his jeans open. Her hand was on his zipper, her eyes at half-mast, clearly delighting in the occupation of his hands. But when he froze, so did she.

So close! So goddamn close to the exquisite touch of her long fingers enveloping the firm length of his cock.

He couldn't see her face clearly but knew she'd finally received the same message.

Condom.

Condom-condom-condom.

Condom.

Chapter 15

Dawson's voice was hoarse with desire. "Please tell me you never go for a run without a condom. *Please.*"

Janine felt his fingers thrust inside her as he uttered the second *please*. She half closed her eyes and bit her lip, wanting, desperately wanting, to continue what they'd started. Good lord, if this is what kissing Dawson Delaney did to her at age thirty, it's a good thing she hadn't kissed him at fifteen.

His right hand was cradling her heat, his left caressing her breast, lightly brushing the pad of his thumb against her pebbled nipple. His touch was sending shivers of pleasure down her spine, igniting every nerve ending. She'd been so close to freeing the rigid length of his cock, so close to igniting the climax she so desperately wanted, a climax fifteen years overdue. *Damn! Bloody, double damn!*

Janine hadn't given a thought to needing protection. Had he not stopped them, would she have remembered? She didn't know.

Moving her hands away from his half-open jeans, she slumped forward, resting her palms and forehead on his chest. Of course they had to stop. She had no idea what his recent sexual activity was, and she wouldn't dream of having unprotected sex. She'd had two sexual partners since Malcolm, but neither of them had her abandoning all rational thought. Granted, neither of them was Dawson *freaking* Delaney!

She lifted her hips, inviting him to remove his hand. Only, he didn't take her up on her unspoken request; instead, he sank his fingers deeper into her slick, velvet heat, his movement so surprising—*so good*—it forced out a hoarse *aahhh* from her open mouth.

He repeated the movement, then again, her body instinctively grinding onto his hand, her hips welcoming each thrust. *Oh god,* the thought, knowing she was on the crest of an orgasm and knowing, too, that she *should* stop him. What had he said? *Shoulda-woulda-coulda.*

And then she was convulsing and shuddering as an intense climax rippled through her.

A full minute later, she was still collapsed on Dawson's broad chest, still working to slow her breath. His fingers remained buried within her, and she could feel the length of his hard cock against her abdomen. She didn't dare lift her head, too embarrassed to look at him. She'd just had a freaking orgasm—*with Dawson* freaking *Delaney, no less*—in a cold, damp cave. What was *wrong* with her?

This time when she lifted her hips, he did remove his hand. She was aware of his arousal, and wanted more than anything to take him into her mouth. If only she *had* tucked a condom instead of her house key into the pocket of her leggings.

Her mind went to the coin nestled beside the key. She sighed. They had to get off this mountain and figure out what the hell was going on with Kevin. But first, she'd have to lift her head and look Dawson in the eye. She could do that, couldn't she?

He had one arm around her, cradling her to him, the other stroking her hair and what she knew had to be a very disheveled ponytail. Neither of them had yet spoken.

She became aware of a pebble pressing painfully into her right kneecap, and of the mild but persistent ache of the wound at her temple. She rolled off Dawson without looking at him, turning to retrieve her jacket. Her entire body felt achy and bruised. Funny, she thought. She hadn't noticed any of that while she'd been devouring Dawson. She sat up and slipped her arms into her jacket, the sound of the nylon fabric explosive in the awkward silence. Finally, knowing she could avoid it no longer, she lifted her eyes to meet his gaze.

He was leaning on an elbow, his smile wry, patiently waiting for her to look at him. Desire still darkened the midnight pools of his eyes, but she also saw a glint of humour.

She suddenly swivelled her head to look outside, realizing that if she could see his expression so clearly, it was easily light enough to leave. Sure enough, dawn had arrived.

"Our first priority," he stated, waiting for her to look at him before continuing, "Is to get the hell off this mountain. The second…"

She smiled suddenly, certain she knew what he was going to say next. They chimed the answer in unison. *"Get Condoms."*

"I'm sorry you didn't…you know," she added, waving her hand in the general direction of his crotch. Then, despite willing herself not to, she glanced down, her gaze taking in the all-too evident bulge. She met his gaze, allowing her eyes to shine with the promise of what would come at the first opportunity they had to get naked.

Dawson mirrored her smouldering look, but his words surprised her. "Don't even think that wasn't good for me, because it was. *Freaking awesome good."* He sat up and kissed her on the lips, hard and brief. He lifted his hips and adjusted his jeans and buckled his belt, then stated, his face only inches from hers and his voice a hoarse whisper. "But next time? My tongue will be where my hands were, and then my cock."

Janine felt her eyelids half close at the image of Dawson's head buried between her legs. *Good lord!* Was her desire for him so intense and unrelenting because of an unfulfilled fifteen-year-old crush? Or would she have found him utterly sexy and irresistible if yesterday had been the first time she'd clapped eyes on him? She didn't know.

The sexual tension evaporated abruptly when Janine's stomach growled loudly.

They both chuckled. Dawson shifted his gaze to the dawning light outside the cave. "There's some luck, at least. Looks like the rain stopped."

Chapter 16

Once they emerged from the cave, they paused to stretch their stiff muscles, sore from the hours spent lying on the cold, unforgiving stone, and likely also from the residual effects of the crash. Janine's clothes were still damp, but she knew whatever cold she felt would dissipate once they started moving. Looking around, she got her first clear view of where they'd spent the night.

The slab of rock in front of the cave, less than a metre in width, served as a kind of natural ledge hugging the jutting granite that formed the cliff. Towering evergreen trees clung to the steep banks of the ravine below them, the uppermost branches of the tallest well above them.

Dawson was already gesturing for her to follow him back the way they'd come. After he helped her scramble up and over the bluff, she turned to give him a hand, but he effortlessly lifted himself from the rock ledge in one smooth motion.

Good lord! The man made her positively drool. He was so incredibly sexy. She mentally assigned herself the future task of mapping every inch of him with her hands, and tongue, and lips.

Dawson suddenly advanced on her and pulled her roughly

against him. He paused, his eyes sizzling with heat as he stared at her open mouth before claiming it. She melted against his long frame, burying her fingers in his hair and luxuriating in the feel of his hands sliding down her back. When he dropped his hands to her ass and pulled her against him, there was no way she could miss his arousal. Her bones turned to liquid and an ache of desperate need bubbled up from her core. She wished there was nothing between them but skin. *Well, that and a thin layer of latex.* She heard a moan and realized it came from deep within her own throat.

When he tore his mouth from hers, she felt his teeth and lips and tongue on her neck, his moist touch and rough stubble sending tingles of delicious sensations along her skin, playing havoc with her pulse. "I want…" she whimpered.

But he abruptly pushed her away, taking a step back.

"I know what you want, Janine," he said in a voice husky with desire. "I want it, too. But the next time you look at me like that, with that come-fuck-me look in your eyes, make damn sure you've got a condom."

She had been looking at him like he was a delectable lollipop she wanted to lick and suck and taste. "Shit. Yeah. Sorry," she said, admitting to the role she'd played in their brief display of fireworks.

"I need a drink," he grumbled, turning and heading towards the stream they'd visited the previous evening.

Janine followed, smiling, guessing he would've preferred the kind of drink that came in a hip flask.

After quenching their thirst, they moved to stand near the edge of the bluff under an old arbutus tree. Its crooked branches with their distinctive reddish-brown, peeling bark reached precariously over the edge of the cliff as if wanting a view of the pristine waterfall that trickled down into the ravine.

Dawson aimed his arm northwest. "I'm guessing the highway is that way. What do you think? Recognize any of these peaks?" he asked, gesturing at the mountains around them.

Janine was thankful the clouds were showing patches of blue sky. She pointed to a peak in the west, half-hidden by clouds. "That pointy one there with the smaller pointy bit on the left that you can barely see? That's Mt. Cayley." She shifted her arm in much the same direction he'd indicated, only more to the north. "The highway is somewhere there."

She dropped her arm and looked around them, taking in the massive juts of stone that rose from the cliff's edge, some towering a good three metres above her head, others leaning haphazardly towards the tree-covered ravine. The stone would soon be covered in pale green lichen as the autumn rains continued. From where they were standing on the small, rock-strewn meadow, there was no way of knowing the cave existed.

"How did you manage to find the cave last night, in the dark?" she asked.

Dawson indicated the jutting granite boulders with his chin. "It's not uncommon for these giant slabs of rock to have nooks and crannies. I'd hoped to find an overhang, that's all. A good spot to hide. Discovering the actual cave was a welcome surprise."

Mention of the cave had her remembering where his hands had been a few short minutes ago. She wasn't convinced she could ever look at him without reflecting her desire, so she kept her gaze averted, mindful of his earlier warning.

"So, we go that way," Dawson said, pointing. "Avoid the van, but find the highway. Agreed?"

"Agreed," Janine said, turning to lead the way.

Getting off this mountain was their first priority, then coffee, food, a shower, a phone call to her cousin, and then… sex with Dawson. In a bed, this time, and with a condom.

A condom? *More like a dozen!*

Chapter 17

It was approaching 8:00 am when Janine heard the muffled roar of a distant transport truck. Five minutes later when they stepped out from the cover of trees, she saw what they'd been searching for. And more.

"Well, I'll be goddamned," Dawson said, clearly pleased. "This is a stroke of luck."

The northeast-bound cars and trucks on the two-lane highway, fifty metres below them, were travelling towards Pemberton, Janine knew, while the vehicles heading in a southwesterly direction were making their way towards Whistler, Squamish, and eventually Vancouver. But the highway wasn't what surprised them. It was the truck stop on the north side, with the requisite convenience store, gas station, and diner, plus an extensive parking lot that could accommodate multiple eighteen-wheelers. A large billboard above the utilitarian, one-story building read, *Ivy's Pies.*

"God bless Ivy," Janine said with heartfelt sincerity, already salivating. She needed coffee, and for once didn't care that it would very likely be atrocious.

"Shit!" At her exclamation of concern, Dawson became suddenly alert, twisting around to look behind them. She realized her expletive had him expecting to see the men who'd chased them.

"What?" he asked, clearly confused.

"Do you have any money?"

Dawson gave an exaggerated snort. "What good are you, woman? You don't carry condoms. You don't carry money." He patted the back pocket of his jeans. "I may not have condoms, but I do have a credit card."

Janine's eyes fell to the perfect ass he'd just patted, wondering if Ivy's Pies sold condoms.

"Jesus," Dawson muttered, sucking in a deep breath as he stared at her. "What did I tell you about looking at me like that?"

"I wasn't!" she denied, pressing her lips together and repressing the urge to giggle. Except she had been. *Geez Louise, Janine! What is* wrong *with you?*

"At the first opportunity," Dawson said through clenched teeth. "You and I are going to fuck like there's no tomorrow."

From anyone else, Janine would've been offended at his crude remark. But it was Dawson, and her only response was a surge of heat.

"You are so goddamn beautiful," Dawson said, his tone low. He looked away, running a hand through his disheveled hair. "The sooner we get there, the sooner we can—"

"Indulge in some seriously bad coffee," Janine interrupted with a smile.

"That first, definitely. Come on," he stated, leading the way down the steep embankment.

It took twenty minutes of scrambling over thick undergrowth, fallen logs, and craggy knolls before they finally made it to the road. They waited on the south side until a gap in the traffic allowed them to jog across. As they walked along the potholed, half-gravel, half-asphalt frontage of the truck stop, Janine began to slow, eying the people coming and going from the gas pumps, convenience store, and diner. She put a hand on Dawson's arm and stopped.

"What if they're in there?" she asked.

Dawson shook his head. "Highly unlikely. They're either staked out at the van, or at your Café, if they know you own it. They won't be drinking bad coffee and eating greasy sausages here on the one-in-a-thousand chance we show up in this exact spot. And even if they are, they're not going to pull out their weapons and attempt anything. Not with all these people here. It's too public. This isn't a scene from *Pulp Fiction*."

Janine nodded, accepting his logic. They resumed walking. "If my life were a movie, it sure as hell wouldn't be *Pulp Fiction*," she muttered.

"*Romancing the Stone*?" he teased. "I always liked that ending."

Janine laughed. "*You* like rom-coms?" Good lord, the man got sexier with each passing minute.

"I *like* alligator-skin boots," he corrected.

At the entrance, situated between the convenience store on their left and the diner on their right, Dawson held the door open for her, following her into a generous foyer.

The fragrant smell of coffee and greasy sausages assaulted her senses. "Bad coffee has never smelled *so* good," she stated.

Directly ahead of them were restrooms. At either end was an open doorway, one leading to the convenience store, the other to Ivy's Pies. On their immediate left was a rack filled with local papers and tourist pamphlets advertising fishing and mountaineering excursions. To their right was a payphone. *People still used pay phones?* The floor, Janine saw, needed a mop. She wouldn't dream of letting Café Art's floor get this grimy.

"The coffee won't be up to your exacting standards," Dawson teased.

She saw humour dancing in his eyes. *God, the man had pretty eyes*. She grinned in answering amusement. "Whatever standards I might've once had? They're long gone." She nodded to the women's restroom. "I'm going to take a few minutes to wash up," she said, moving out of the way of two burly men exiting the restaurant, both wearing grease-stained John Deere caps.

"I'll do the same," Dawson replied. "And then I'll detour to make a purchase," he added, jerking his chin towards the convenience store. "I'll meet you in the diner."

Janine laughed at him over her shoulder before pushing open the door of the restroom. No doubt he'd buy the biggest box of condoms on the shelf. The thought made her thrum with anticipation.

The first thing she did was wash her hands thoroughly at one of the two sinks, then drink from the cold water tap. After her thirst was quenched, she paused, staring at her reflection in the mirror. Dawson's words echoed in her head: *You are so goddamn beautiful.* Her face was streaked with dirt, the cut on her forehead crusted with a line of dried blood, and her ponytail was an unrecognizable tangled lump. She couldn't believe he found her desirable, looking the way she did. Malcolm had always been fastidious about sex, often insisting they both shower first. But Dawson, despite her dishevelment and her morning breath, hadn't been able keep his hands off her. She grinned as she ticked items off her mental checklist. *Coffee, food, get a ride home, phone Kevin, shower, then…sex with Dawson in her king-sized bed.*

At the thought of her house, she sobered, seeing the man with his throat slit. She felt a wave of self-disgust wash over her. Her home was likely a crime scene. How could she let her lust for Dawson Delaney eclipse her concern for whatever mess her cousin might be in? A frown creased her forehead as she stepped into a cubicle. She needed to talk to her cousin, the sooner the better.

A few minutes later, as an older woman joined her at the sinks, an idea occurred to Janine. Would this stranger let her borrow her phone? "Hi. I'm wondering if you would be willing to help me," Janine said. "I lost my phone."

The woman was frowning her disapproval, her critical gaze sweeping Janine from head to foot.

"I know I look a fright," Janine said, giving the woman her friendliest smile. "But would you consider letting me borrow your cellphone? I have a calling card number, so it wouldn't cost you anything."

The woman was shaking her head. "I don't think so," she said, hurriedly jerking out a couple paper towels. Without a backward glance, she scurried out of the restroom.

Janine sighed, dried her hands, and followed the woman into the foyer.

Chapter 18

The first thing she saw when she exited the restroom was the pay phone. The sight of this close-to-obsolete means of communication stopped Janine in her tracks. She didn't need to borrow a stranger's cellphone.

Janine absently noticed Dawson taking a seat at a table in the diner. A middle-aged waitress in an old-fashioned, puke green uniform was approaching him, a pot of coffee in one hand and a large, plastic-coated menu in the other. Hopefully he had the sense to order everything on the menu, she thought as she went to the phone. Because of the short cord that forced her to stand directly in front of the phone box, the only part of the restaurant she could see was the cash register counter just inside the door.

Janine dialed. At the prompts, she keyed in the Café's calling card number. A minute later, she was listening to the two short rings, followed by two more in quick succession, all the while silently chanting, *pick up, pick up, pick up*. Then—*thank god*—the phone was answered.

"Kevin!" she stated before he could speak. "It's me, Janine. Are—"

She was interrupted by the voice of a strange man with a

lilting accent. "Cousin Janine?" he asked in a pleasant, conversational tone.

"What…? Where's Kevin? Is he okay?" Janine's initial thought was that her cousin wasn't well and a friend was with him, answering the phone while Kevin rested. But when the man with the Irish accent continued, his deceptively mild tone belying his threatening words, dread flooded through her.

"You haven't been answering your mobile, lass. It's good news for Kevin here that you finally decided to ring, because your right arse of a cousin doesn't seem inclined to answer the simplest of questions despite…how shall I put it?…Gerald's *persuasive* fists. Perhaps you can influence him to improve his manners, yeah?"

Persuasive fists? A hot rush of anger momentarily outstripped Janine's fear as she pictured her cousin being pulverized. At six feet, Kevin was a big guy, but he was a scholar, not a fighter.

Janine gripped the receiver in a white-knuckled fist and spoke in a low, threatening tone. "I want to talk to Kevin," she demanded. "Where is he, goddamn you? Tell me he's okay!" *Oh god, please don't be dead, Kevin. Please don't be dead.*

The man chuckled, the sound cold enough to crack ice. "Janine, lass, stay calm. Can you do that?"

"I *am* calm! Tell me where Kevin is."

"I make the demands here, not you," the man snarled, his words sending a lick of fear shivering down her spine. "And I'll tell *you* nothing until you tell *me* something."

Janine had to swallow before she could speak. "What… what do you want to know?"

"Your tosser of a cousin sent you a package, yeah?"

Janine placed her free hand against the waistband of her leggings, feeling the small bulge of the plastic-wrapped coin. Was this tiny object a reason to hurt Kevin? To chase her and Dawson up a mountain? Knife that man on her lawn? *Who are you messed up with, Kevin? What have you gotten yourself into?*

The man's tone turned harsh. "Janine? Are you there?"

"Yes. I'm…I'm here," she stammered.

The man sighed audibly. "D'ya have the package?"

"Yes. Yes, I have it." Janine didn't even consider lying. Clearly the coin was valuable, but not more valuable than her cousin.

"Good. Bring it to me."

"Bring it to you? *To England?"*

"Yes, *to England,"* he mocked, mimicking her accent. "To Kevin's house."

Janine had to stop herself from echoing his words. "But… can't I just courier it?"

"Are you not listening, lass? I said, *bring it!"*

She realized she should be extracting some kind of proof of life before being coerced into action. "Not before I talk to Kevin," she challenged. "I'll only come if he tells me to."

The man's chuckle was filled with mirth. He responded in a light, almost teasing tone. "You've got some gumption, lass. I very much look forward to meeting you, I surely do." Then he was snarling, "But you'll do as *I* say, you manky bitch, or you won't be seeing your cousin alive again. You understand me?"

Terror clawed at her stomach. Her mouth felt parched of moisture. She could barely speak her next question. "Yes, but please, is he…is he alive? Is he hurt?"

The man resumed his mild tone. "He's breathing fine *now*, don't you worry. But he's not what you call a cooperative man, is he? A mite stubborn, that one. And a slow learner. You'll be wanting to make sure that trait doesn't run in the family. You get my meaning, Janine?"

Dread threatened to overwhelm her. Kevin was an archeologist for god's sake, and not the Indiana Jones type. What the hell had he gotten himself into?

"Yes. But, please." Janine hated the wobble in her voice that made her come across as cowed. But she was no actress. Her terror and concern were real. Whatever anger she'd felt earlier had been superseded by the threats of this faceless, formidable man. "Please, can I talk to him?"

"Of course, lass. He's right here."

After a pause, the familiar sound of her cousin's voice filled her ear.

"Jaynie?"

"Kevin!" Janine slumped against the phone, vaguely aware of people in the foyer. She glanced behind her long enough to confirm the two young women and an older man had no interest in her. "Are you all right? What's going on?"

"Don't belief any-fing dis vanker says."

Kevin had been beaten so severely, she realized, he couldn't enunciate his words properly. Janine didn't notice the silent tears slipping down her cheeks. "Oh my god, Kevin, you're hurt!"

"I'm fine. Nuh-fing for you to vorry 'bout, Jaynie."

"But Kevin, you're…I…" *Where to even start?* "Kevin, we were shot at, and—"

"Oh by god, Jaynie, I'm so sorry," Kevin said, anguish in his tone. Then he spoke fast and clipped, adding, "Don't do vat dey ask. Don't trust anyvone, except—"

His words were cut off. Janine could hear muffled sounds of a struggle. She went rigid, her hand clenching the receiver, her free hand fisted in impotent fear and rage. *What were they doing to him?* "Kevin," she whimpered. "Oh my god, what's happening?"

Janine noticed a customer looking over his shoulder at her in concern while at the counter paying his bill. Given his paunch and the greasy hair under his Kenworth cap, he was likely a trucker. She saw the question in his eyes and turned her back on him, lowering her voice and repeating, "Kevin? Are you there?"

The stranger's Irish-accented voice responded. "What was I saying about your cousin being uncooperative?" The man sounded amused.

Bastard! Janine cursed silently, feeling utterly powerless and wholly afraid.

"It's not a family trait, now, is it, lass?"

"No." Janine barely got the word out, too choked up with anger and terror to speak. "Please don't you hurt him," she insisted, but her voice was completely devoid of authority.

"Me? *I* haven't laid a finger on him," the stranger assured.

Janine wiped absently at her wet cheeks. "Please, I'll do whatever you say. Just don't hurt him."

The man let out an audible sigh of pleasure. "Ah. I love to hear a lass beg, I surely do."

Janine squeezed her eyes tightly shut. She hated this man, hated his melodious voice. But she would do whatever he asked. "Please, just don't hurt Kevin. Where do I send the package?"

"You weren't listening, lass. You'll deliver it in person, to your cousin's home, yeah?"

"But..."

The man threatened, "You'll come alone, Janine. And you'll tell no one your destination, you understand?"

"Yes, I understand," she said, nodding. "I'll come alone."

"And Janine?" He waited for her to respond.

"Yes?"

"That American friend of Kevin's? Name of Dawson? The one who owns the security company? You don't contact him, you hear? Or your cousin dies. *You tell no one.*" After a second or two of silence, he added, "Now, lass, I need you to convey your understanding."

"I understand," she said in a frightened whisper. She didn't know how Kevin had gotten into this predicament, but she understood what she had to do to get him out of it.

"Tell me what you intend to do," the man demanded.

"I'll come alone, and bring the package, and..." *Dawson!* If she wanted to see Kevin alive, she couldn't let Dawson know what she was about to do. "And I won't tell anyone where I'm going."

"Good. I'll ring your cousin's house in twenty-four hours. You better be there to answer."

Twenty-four hours? "What? No! I need more time. You don't understand. I'm stranded. I have to get home and the airport is hours away, and—"

"Twenty-four hours," the man repeated. "Deliver the package, *alone*, and maybe you'll see your cousin alive. Thwart me, and you'll both die."

Before she could say anything further, the stranger with the musical accent and deadly threats hung up. The dull hum of the dial tone droned in her ear.

Dazed, Janine slowly hung up the receiver, staring at it, her hand resting on the oblong of black plastic. The sounds from within the restaurant and store slowly filtered into her stunned mind, bringing her back to the present.

Twenty-four hours? Good lord! She had to act fast. She had to get Dawson. They had to leave. Now!

She was about to turn and do just that when she froze. She couldn't tell Dawson, not with Kevin's life on the line. She knew, without a doubt, if she relayed the conversation she'd just had with—*God, she hadn't thought to get the man's name*—with the freakishly scary Irishman in Kevin's house, then Dawson would insist on travelling with her, or possibly even going instead of her. She'd spent less than a day with him, but knew with certainty he wouldn't tolerate her meekly following that terrifying man's bidding. But if she wanted to protect Kevin from further harm, what choice did she have but to go to England alone?

If she was headed to the UK, she would need her passport. And that was a problem. It was in her safe in the basement storage room of her house. The question was, would her home be swarming with police?

But she couldn't think about that right now. First things

first; second things second; third things third. That philosophy had worked when she'd opened her business, and it would work now. And right now, the first task she needed to accomplish was to get a ride to Whistler.

Janine whirled towards the exit, promptly colliding with a young man with a pimply face.

"Sorry," she said absently, momentarily distracted by the slogan on his hoodie. *Me drop everything. Work on your problem.* She resisted the urge to break out into hysterical peals of laughter. If only someone *would* drop everything and work on her problem.

"Sorry," he echoed, stepping back and gesturing for her to precede him outside.

At his polite response, Janine heard the echo of her mother's oft-repeated sentiment: *Good manners, good mother.*

"You okay?" the young man asked when she didn't move.

She realized she was staring at him, which was very bad manners. She gave herself a mental shake, and quickly darted out the door in front of him, immediately turning right so Dawson wouldn't see her through the diner's windows.

"I'm fine, thanks," She stopped abruptly and faced him. "Are you for hire?" she asked, gesturing at his chest. He was twirling a set of keys in his hand. Perhaps he could drive her to Whistler.

The young man looked confused for a moment, glancing down to remind himself what he was wearing at the same time his pocket began emitting the sound of an electric guitar riff. He dug for his phone, giving her an amused grin, clearly assuming she was making a joke as he turned and walked away, his phone to his ear.

Damn! So much for getting a ride with the polite young man.

She eyed a car parked at a gas pump, a young man filling the tank, a young woman in the passenger seat. Janine could see the tops of two small heads in the backseat. A vehicle with children was *not* an option. She took a few steps towards the outside entrance of the convenience store, glancing over her shoulder at the young man who, she saw, was absently eyeing her from where he stood leaning against his car. Should she approach him? His manners had her believing she could trust him. But his car was directly in front of the restaurant's windows, and he seemed deeply engaged in his phone conversation.

Feeling panic rise and threaten to overwhelm her, she paused and leaned against the cinder block wall of the low-slung building, clutching her arms against her stomach, hunching forward slightly, and forcing herself to breathe through a wave of nausea.

Chapter 19

"Thank you!" Janine called over her shoulder as she stepped down from the extreme height of the semi-truck's cab.

The trucker with the Kenworth cap she'd seen paying his bill while she was on the phone had exited the convenience store at the same time she'd been having a panic attack. As he approached, he'd paused and asked if she was alright. Janine nodded, then asked if he was heading to Whistler. He'd immediately offered her a ride. She'd accepted, but refused to walk with him to his vehicle.

He'd glanced towards the diner, mistakenly assuming she was running from an abusive man inside. Nodding decisively, he told her to wait for him just beyond the gas pumps. Two minutes later, she was climbing inside his eighteen-wheeler, all the while suppressing thoughts of Dawson and how he would feel once he realized she'd left without him. Her priority was Kevin, and since Dawson's presence would jeopardize Kevin's safety, she could not allow Dawson to learn of her intentions.

On the drive to Whistler, the trucker—*Reginald Winston Becker, but you can call me Reggie*—shared his family size bags of Doritos and cherry-flavoured Twizzlers. Best of all, he was also willing to share his Thermos of truck-stop coffee. She was grateful for all of it, despite it being the worst coffee she'd ever tasted, brewed she felt certain, from a low-quality Robusta that was long past its shelf life. She could tell that the carbon dioxide that gave coffee its distinctive taste had 'de-gassed' for far too long, and the flavour had escaped. She also knew the water hadn't been set to the recommended 205°F, but was likely closer to the boiling point, perhaps even as high at 210°F. Over-heated water destroyed the volatile oils and the subtler flavours of coffee. Not that she was kicking a gift horse in the mouth. She was thankful for both the caffeine and the high-calorie junk food.

Reggie was a talkative man, and Janine only half-listened to stories about his ex-wife and grown sons, grateful he wasn't nosy about her situation. Her own mind was busy trying to figure out how she was going to retrieve her passport from the safe in her basement given the likelihood that her house was a crime scene. Even if she did manage to retrieve it, before heading to the airport she would need to phone Air Canada and purchase a flight. Except she didn't have a phone. To complete all the tasks that needed doing, including a shower, a change of clothes, and a ride to the airport, she would have to enlist Nicolette's help.

While she'd waited on the far side of the gas station for Reggie to pull up, she'd set her Fitbit stopwatch for twenty-four hours, calculating in her head the time it would take to get from Ivy's Pies to Kevin's house. She gave herself four to six hours to get to the airport, another one to four before the flight departed, then a nine-hour flight, with another hour or two at Heathrow to disembark. That left her as many as nine or as little as three hours to take the train from Heathrow to Nottingham, with a short taxi ride to her cousin's house.

The timeline was only barely doable, and there were so many variables out of her control. Assuming she got there in time, what would happen when she delivered the coin to the brute at her cousin's? That surely couldn't be the end of it, but she had no capacity to imagine what would happen next.

Twenty minutes after leaving the truck stop, Reggie pulled to a stop at a red light at the intersection of Highway 99 and Lake Placid Road in Whistler. Before he allowed her to leave his cab, Janine had to reassure him she had good friends who would help her get away from her imagined abusive partner. When he insisted she take a soggy bag of sausage rolls with her, she didn't argue, instead tucking them into the back pocket of her jacket and thanking him profusely for his kindness as she exited the tall cab.

Janine broke into a fast jog as soon as her feet hit the pavement. After passing the ski club, she veered off the main road and wove through the backstreets towards her house, knowing she had to avoid being recognized. Her stomach was roiling with anxiety—or maybe bad coffee and Twizzlers. If police were at her house and they detained her, she'd have to tell them about the threat on Kevin's life. But would they let her go? Meanwhile, the clock would be ticking.

She felt exposed as she ran, and repeatedly glanced over her shoulder. It was a relief to enter the forest. She stopped abruptly as a jogger approached, crouching down with her face averted as she re-tied her shoelace, not rising until the jogger moved past and disappeared around a bend. A few minutes after she resumed running, she veered off the path, stepping carefully on the uneven ground until she could get a clear view of the front of her house.

Peering out from behind a tall red cedar, Janine saw yellow crime-scene tape encircling her front yard, including the driveway and garage. Two police cruisers were parked on the street, and a sedan with a tall antenna was in her driveway behind her SUV. Yellow numbered markers dotted her lawn. She felt a surge of panic, and tamped it down with deep, even breaths. She'd anticipated this, but it was still a shock.

She counted four uniformed police officers and a handful

of people in street clothes wearing booties over their shoes, two taking photos, the other three talking, periodically turning and gesturing at different areas of the crime scene. A half-dozen onlookers were standing on the street, watching from behind the police barricade, some snapping photos on their phones. Janine's attention was caught when a curtain moved in the upstairs window of her neighbour's house. She saw Mrs. Winterburn at what she knew was the woman's guest bedroom window peering down at the scene. Janine turned to leave.

Once back on the wooded trail, she resumed running for a couple hundred metres, then veered right onto a downward sloping path before ending up on the bicycle path behind her house, which was thankfully deserted. A moment later she was behind Mrs. Winterburn's tall wooden fence, which concealed her as she approached her own backyard.

From where she stood, her yard appeared empty. She scanned the kitchen and dining room windows on the middle floor and the master bedroom window on the upper level. From her vantage point, her house looked deserted, but she knew it wasn't, knew as well that if someone inside were to look out one of the windows while she was dashing up her yard, she'd have no chance of getting to Nottingham within the allotted time.

Quelling her trepidation, she ran in a crouch behind her own shorter fence, stopping to peer over the top of her gate. Seeing no one in the yard or at the windows, she opened the gate and ducked under the crime-scene tape. Her heart hammering in her chest, she sprinted up the yard, angling towards the garden shed. Taking temporary cover between it and the seven-foot fence, she paused, deliberately slowing her breathing, then almost jumped out of her skin when Piper's frantic barking from the other side of the fence startled her.

"Holy Christ!" Janine whispered, lifting a hand to her heart. "Piper, *be quiet!*" she hissed from her side of the fence, hoping

the dog would recognize her voice and cease and desist his misplaced guard dog antics.

When Piper didn't stop, Janine suddenly remembered the sausage rolls Reggie had given her. She quickly retrieved the bag, tore it open, and tossed the contents over the tall fence. And just in time, too, she thought, hearing Mrs. Winterburn's back door open.

"Piper! What are you barking at?"

Janine rolled her eyes at the question. The dog barked if a breeze ruffled his coat, for god's sake.

"Piper!" Mrs. Winterburn's voice rose in alarm. "What are you eating? Stop that! Piper, *come here!*"

Piper ignored his owner, loudly snuffling up every crumb of the treats that had fallen like manna from doggie heaven.

Janine froze when Mrs. Winterburn's back door banged closed. She heard her neighbour approaching the dog, stopping little more than an arm's length away from where Janine stood. She was frighteningly aware of how noisy her jacket would be if she so much as breathed.

"Piper!" Mrs. Winterburn's voice scolded. "Come on, no more of that. Up you get."

Janine waited until she heard Mrs. Winterburn re-enter her house, then rested the back of her head against the garden shed and breathed a sigh of relief. Crisis averted. But there was no time to waste. She turned, heard the swishing sound as the underside of her arm brushed against her torso, and realized she'd have to shed her coat before entering her house. She quickly shrugged out of it, then stuffed it under the base of the shed.

Seeing no one behind the windows at the back of either house, she darted out and ran the additional steps to the cement patio under her deck. At her back door, she experienced a strange sense of déjà vu. This was where it had all started late the previous afternoon. Ever so slowly, she pressed down on the door handle. She took a deep breath, knowing if she opened the door and encountered a police officer directly inside, any chance of getting to Nottingham within twenty-four hours would evaporate. She didn't know what would happen to Kevin if that happened.

Don't think about it!

She pushed the door open, thankful its hinges were silent. Seeing the mudroom unoccupied, and with her heart hammering in her chest, she silently stepped inside, closing the door behind her. She paused momentarily, aware of the sound of muted conversation filtering down from the floor above. A cellphone rang. Someone answered it.

Her footfalls silent, Janine stepped out of the mudroom and turned right, slipping through the open door into her supply room. A quick glance told her it was empty. She went straight to the box that covered the safe, lifting it off carefully. With a brief glance over her shoulder towards the open door, she keyed in the numbers, thankful she'd changed the default settings to silent. The muted click as the tumblers unlocked sounded, at least to her ears, as loud as a thunderclap. She froze, listening, releasing her tension after a moment when the muffled sounds from above remained unchanged.

She let out a silent breath, then turned the handle and soundlessly opened the small door. She stuffed the cash down the front of her pants, tucked her passport into her bra, then shut the safe. Pressing the re-lock button, she re-positioned the empty box above the safe.

Now all she needed to do was exit her house without being seen.

Chapter 20

As she ran along the paved cycling path, Janine reflected on how easy it had been to sneak into, and out of, the crime scene that was her home. She could only assume the police had searched the lower level of her house, and then confined the rest of their activities to the front yard and upper levels.

She'd forgotten to retrieve her jacket before fleeing her backyard, but that was of no concern. She'd successfully gotten a ride to Whistler, and liberated her passport. Step three was arriving at Nicolette's undetected so she could shower and change and purchase a flight. Then a ride to the airport. Her biggest concern now was whether her name would be flagged when she went through airport security. Regardless, she had no choice but to book the flight and attempt to board the plane.

As she ran towards Cheakamus Way, Janine encountered only a handful of people. She kept her chin down, conveying an unfeigned inward focus as she pelted past them. At Nicolette's house, Janine retrieved the key from its hiding place under the cast-iron cat in the small rock garden, checking the countdown on her Fitbit as she did so. *22:36.* Still on track.

With Nicolette at work, and her partner Julia in Vancouver —she only came up on the weekends—she knew her friend's townhouse would be empty. Despite her certainty, as soon as she let herself into the townhouse, Janine called out, "Nicolette? Are you home?" The house was quiet.

Janine headed to the kitchen where, with quick and efficient movements, she set a cup of Keurig coffee to brew. Her next task was to book a flight to London, but without a computer or a cellphone, she needed the phone number for Air Canada. Using Nicolette's landline phone, Janine scrolled through the pre-programmed numbers. Nothing for Air Canada, but their local travel agency, Aspire Travel, would do nicely.

She pressed the call button, then picked up the TV remote and flicked on the small television in Nicolette's kitchen. The travel agency answered on the second ring, but Janine was immediately put on hold. With the phone tucked at her ear, she began scrounging for a pen and paper, but stopped abruptly when the news anchor spoke her name. Startled, she gave her full attention to the television, which was broadcasting a previously taped video of the front of Janine's house. The scene was lit by floodlights, the footage clearly taken sometime during the night.

Janine Kirby has been missing for an undetermined period of time after her home was burglarized. It is still unknown if anything was stolen. Police are asking for anonymous tips if they know anything about Ms. Kirby's whereabouts.

"Well, hi Nicolette," a cheerful woman stated in Janine's ear.

Janine paused. She hadn't considered the travel agent would have call display.

"Nicolette?" the voice repeated. "Can I help you?"

Shit! Janine recognized Deb Bailey's voice and hung up the phone. Why hadn't she realized she couldn't identify herself to any of the locals who worked at the travel agency? Could she even use her credit card? What if the police were tracking her credit card activity?

Janine stared at the TV, but the news anchor had moved on to a story about a house fire in Squamish. She picked up the remote and turned it off, deciding that the surest way to purchase a flight without anyone discovering her intention was to ask Nicolette to buy it for her. Since her absence was on the news, her friend would also be worried sick.

Finding the programmed number for the spa on the phone, she hit the call button, scrambling to prepare a story about why Nicolette's home phone number would appear on the spa phone's call display if one of Nicolette's staff answered, but this time she got lucky.

"Julia?" Nicolette asked in a wary, surprised tone.

Janine spoke fast. "Nicolette, don't give away that it's me. Say, *hi Angie*."

Janine heard her friend gasp. A moment passed before Nicolette responded in an overly bright voice. "Oh...*Hi, Angie.*"

"Thank you." Janine closed her eyes briefly in relief. "I'm safe. I'm in your house. Obviously. Can you talk freely?"

Janine heard the sound of a door closing, then, "*Holy freak out, Janine!* I've been worried *sick.* I didn't watch the news this morning, so when I got to the spa, the girls were all asking what happened to you, and I didn't know what they were talking about, and then—"

"Nicolette!" Janine interrupted. "I'm okay. But I need your help, and it's urgent. I don't have time to explain. Please, will you help me?"

"Yes, *of course*. Sorry, only...Are you really okay? What the hell is going on? Is it true a man was found *murdered* on your *front lawn?*"

"He's dead? Shit! I don't know who he is. Kevin's in trouble, and I need—"

"Kevin?" Nicolette. "Who's Kevin?"

"My *cousin!* Look, I need—"

Nicolette interrupted again. "Your cousin? The one in England?"

"Yes. And I have to get to the airport, and—"

"The airport?" Nicolette snorted. "You mean, the police station, don't you?"

"I can't involve them. Nicolette, please, just trust me. I need—"

"I'm coming right over," Nicolette interrupted.

"No! That's not—"

Janine heard a click. "…necessary," she said to the dial tone. She sighed, unsurprised by Nicolette's vivacious, take charge approach. Her friend had never been mistaken for someone with patience.

Tossing the phone aside, she retrieved a carton of cream from the fridge, splashed a dollop into the mug of coffee, then scrounged through her friend's cupboards until she found an energy bar. Tearing it open, she took a big bite as she hurried up the stairs, careful not to spill her drink. She would take a quick shower, then scrounge through Nicolette's clothes to find something suitable to wear, 'suitable' being the operative word.

She and Nicolette were same size for the most part, with Nicolette smaller in the bust. But Nicolette's taste for colourful, trendy clothes that she complemented with high heels and bold jewelry—all of which suited her mocha skin, snazzy hairdos, and regal bearing—would make it challenging for Janine to find something comfortable, despite the many options in her friend's abundant closet.

Part II

Chapter 21

"Will you be okay?" Nicolette asked.

They were standing on the wide sidewalk beside Nicolette's car at the curb-side drop-off for international flights at the Vancouver airport. Janine held a borrowed overnight bag in one hand and wore Nicolette's small, cross-body travel purse—with passport, cash, and Kevin's coin tucked into the inside pocket—across her torso.

"I will be once I see Kevin," Janine said as she checked the countdown on her Fitbit. *19:12.* As long as her flight wasn't delayed, she could meet the imposed deadline.

She'd put her filthy clothes through the shortest wash cycle at Nicolette's, but as there hadn't been sufficient time to dry them, she'd dressed in a pair of her friend's dark wash skinny jeans and a snug black T-shirt with a colourful mandala pattern on the front. The jeans fit perfectly, but she'd draped a long scarf in muted shades of aqua around her neck to disguise how the too-small shirt hugged her bustline. Even though she'd taken out the removable padding from the borrowed underwire bra, her breasts were barely contained in the lace cups. Janine assumed she'd have better luck with the borrowed panties when Nicolette handed her an unopened pack-of-three underwear—until she'd opened the package to reveal skimpy thongs. At least they were cotton, she'd grumbled to herself. On her feet Janine wore half-size-too-large riding boots—the flattest heels in Nicolette's extensive collection.

Her trail runners—still damp from scrubbing them clean at the kitchen sink—were in a zip-lock bag in the borrowed overnight case, along with her damp running clothes. She didn't know when she'd be able to dry them, but she'd been loath to leave them behind. She'd also packed two of Nicolette's plainest and largest cotton tops, some toiletries, four pairs of socks, the two additional thong panties, and Nicolette's lightweight down jacket. The colour, blinding white, was not a choice Janine would've made but, like the candy floss underwear, it had been the best of the poor choices available to her.

Nicolette had purchased a seat for Janine on the first available flight to Heathrow. Janine intended to refund her friend the cost of the very expensive, last-minute flight as soon as she had the chance.

Her friend was more concerned with exacting a promise from Janine to buy a pay-as-you-go phone at Heathrow and to send frequent updates. She'd also written down all her contact info and tucked this into the borrowed purse so that Janine could program-in the details as soon as she bought the disposable phone.

During the commute to the airport—with a quick detour at the Tim Horton's drive-through in Squamish for coffee and a sandwich—Janine relayed the previous day's events to her friend, even showing her the coin. She'd also explained how she knew Dawson, obviously avoiding any mention of their pre-dawn fireworks. Now was not the time for *that* conversation.

Ever since leaving the truck stop, Janine had been waffling between feeling certain she'd done the right thing in fleeing without Dawson and believing she'd made a terrible mistake. Now that she was about to head into the unknown—and feeling completely unequal to the task—she felt his absence acutely. But having Dawson with her would put Kevin in unnecessary danger, and she simply couldn't risk that.

"Thanks again for helping with the Café," Janine said. She knew she could rely on Nicolette to sort out the staffing issues. "And for purchasing the flight."

Nicolette waved off Janine's thanks. "Stop thanking me. Just stay safe and come home soon."

Janine glanced warily at the revolving doors leading into the terminal. "If I get through security, then all I have to do once I'm there is hand over the coin. As soon as Kevin is safe, I'll be back." Janine knew this claim was false. It couldn't be that simple, she knew; yet, she also couldn't envision what would happen after she arrived at Kevin's house.

Nicolette frowned. "What about this Dawson guy? If he really is Kevin's friend, you should ask him for help, regardless of that Irish creep's threats. I would feel better about you leaving if I knew there was someone to watch out for you."

"We've been over this. Kevin's safety is the priority. You know I have to go alone."

Nicolette grimaced. "I know what that creep said, Janine, but it doesn't feel right."

When a horn honked, they looked over and saw a car waiting to take their spot at the curb. Nicolette gave a friendly gesture to signal her intent to leave, then turned and hugged Janine. "You promise to buy a phone as soon as you get there?" she asked, walking backwards.

"I will." Janine raised a hand in a wave. "Thanks for everything!"

"Anytime, my friend," Nicolette called back, adding, "Be safe!"

Janine watched as her friend got into her car, then waved a

last time as she pulled away, the driver in the waiting car immediately pulling into the vacant spot.

Once inside the airport, Janine went directly to the security queue.

What if they wouldn't let her through? What if she got through security and onto the plane, but it had mechanical failure and couldn't depart? What if the plane departed on time, but bad weather prevented them from landing at Heathrow? Or, what if she got to Heathrow and was stopped at customs and prevented from entering the country? What if she got to Kevin's place, but he wasn't there?

She sighed her exasperation, forcing herself to desist with the litany of unhelpful what-ifs. It wasn't like her to focus on worst-case scenarios. She usually approached life as a problem-solver, applying creative and innovative thinking in her quest for solutions. But she'd never before been in a situation that had such high personal stakes, which made pivoting to solution-oriented thinking all the more difficult.

Shuffling forward in the queue, Janine tried to school her expression to appear relaxed and bored, knowing cameras were aimed at every traveller. Twenty minutes later, feeling sick to her stomach, she stepped out of her boots and set her belongings into bins on the conveyor belt. When her passport was scanned, no one batted an eye. When she walked through the scanner, nothing beeped.

Another obstacle successfully navigated.

She felt her shoulders relaxing as she retrieved her belongings and pulled on her borrowed boots. As she made her way into the belly of the airport, she looked for a store that sold underwear—the proper, full-bottomed kind—and bras larger than a C-cup.

Two long hours later she was in the queue to board the plane. She hadn't found any options when it came to bras, but at least she had a couple pairs of cotton boy-short panties in her bag. She'd also exchanged half her cash for British pounds sterling. At the gate, the attendant scanned her passport and waved her through. Janine breathed another sigh of relief as she strode down the ramp towards the plane.

Once inside, she found her economy seat. The passenger in the window seat, a fiftyish man in a navy suit, was reading a newspaper and ignored her. For the moment, no one occupied the middle seat. She kept her fingers crossed no one would.

After stowing her bag in the overhead compartment, she sat in her aisle seat, tucked her borrowed purse under the seat in front of her—keeping her toe on it to keep it in place—and buckled her seatbelt.

She glanced at the time. Would the plane depart on schedule? Nothing, as yet, hinted it wouldn't, but still she sighed, impatient to be in the air, impatient to land, impatient to be on the train to Nottingham, impatient to see Kevin and assure herself he was fine.

A passenger stopped beside her, clearly intent on occupying the empty seat on her right. She reached to unbuckle her seatbelt, keeping her face averted to hide her disappointment, then gasped in surprise when her eyes fell on familiar hand-tooled cowboy boots.

Her head snapped up. She stared at Dawson in disbelief. His eyes glittered like midnight sapphires as he stared down at her in silent accusation. Janine understood the anger, saw as well the underlying hurt. And, beneath that, recognized the ever-present tug of attraction.

"Dawson?" she finally managed to squeak. How could he *be* here?

"In the flesh," he snapped. He busied himself stowing his bag in the overhead bin, then shrugged out of his jacket and stuffed that in as well.

Janine noticed he'd showered and shaved, and changed into a pale green plaid shirt and a pair of faded jeans that accentuated his long, lean legs. She absently wondered if his wardrobe had any shirts that weren't button-front plaid.

She was forced to stand so that he could move into her row. Resuming her seat, she eyed him with growing consternation as he folded every gorgeous inch of himself into the cramped middle seat—one clearly not made to fit a man of his height. As she re-buckled her seatbelt, she heard the echo of the stranger's words, his musical, lilting accent amplifying rather than diminishing his threat. *That American friend of Kevin's? Name of Dawson? The one who owns the security company? You don't contact him, you hear? Or your cousin dies.*

When she spoke, leaning away when his shoulder brushed against hers, her tone was rife with accusation. "Dawson, you can't be here!"

Chapter 22

It wasn't difficult for Dawson to read the conflicting emotions in Janine's wide gaze. Her eyes were like bronzed mirrors reflecting her every emotion. As he buckled his seat-belt, he deliberately brushed against her shoulder, intent on invading her personal space. When she drew back from his touch, glowering at him in dismay, it only fuelled his need to be contrary. He knew he was being childish, but her abandonment had stung and he wanted to punish her, push her buttons, stubbornly convinced that doing so would make him feel better. His sisters would take him to task for his childish behaviour, but they weren't here.

The look in her eyes, a marbled maelstrom of clashing emotions—dismay, fear, trepidation, and concern mixed with the ever-present attraction and even pleasure—weakened his resolve to punish her. He was tempted to gather her close and comfort her, say whatever needed to be said to annihilate her worry and fear. A part of him wanted to be gentle and ask, *Why'd you run, Janine? Don't you know how crazy worried I was when you disappeared? And why would you want to face whatever challenges are ahead on your own when I'm right here, ready, willing, and able to face them with you?* But, right now, he was still too hurt and angry to be gentle.

"You can't be here," Janine protested.

Dawson scoffed his annoyance, focusing his attention on rolling up the cuffs of his sleeves. "You think I'm that easy to ditch?" He looked over at her and raised his eyebrows, daring her to respond as he shifted his legs. *He hated flying economy!*

She was still too stunned, it appeared, to do more than stare at him. He almost—*but not quite*—took pity on her as she huddled away from him, her left shoulder bumping against passengers filing down the aisle. Her indignation at his unwelcome presence was pissing him off. She'd been hot and yielding in his arms a few hours ago; now she was acting as if he was covered in cow shit. That hurt. Knowing it would annoy her—he childishly *wanted* to annoy her—he claimed her hand. It was a block of ice, and his stubborn resolve to punish her almost faltered.

At the truck-stop, he'd assumed she was taking longer in the bathroom because she'd been dirty and grimy from their night in the woods. But it wasn't until he'd practically inhaled half his stack of flapjacks that he'd finally gone looking for her.

He'd knocked on the door of the ladies' room, calling her name. When no one responded, he took the liberty of entering, worried she'd fallen and hurt herself. But the stalls in the women's restroom were empty. He'd barrelled out of there, almost knocking over a scowling, middle-aged woman about to enter, consumed by the terrifying thought that his instincts had been way off, that the men who'd been pursuing them the night before had taken her. A total fluke they'd found her, but one he should've anticipated. He blamed himself. He'd been so distracted by lecherous thoughts of getting Janine naked, he'd lost his edge—although, truth be told, he'd lost that edge the day Cassie died. Regardless, he'd been reckless with Janine's safety. Totally fucking inept.

He'd burst into the parking lot, frantically searching for her, but the only person nearby was a pimply kid leaning against his car while talking on his phone. There were numerous vehicles—semi-trucks, cars, pickup trucks—entering, exiting, as well as parked in the large lot. Janine could be in any one of them.

"Janine!" he shouted, jogging through the parking lot, fighting the panic that threatened to overwhelm him. *Damn it!* This is why he'd left his job. He couldn't stand this feeling of helplessness, not when it led to someone he cared about getting hurt. *Dying!*

He knew the high-octane panic that bubbled just beneath the surface of his skin was fuelled by his growing feelings for Janine. In the short time they'd been together, she'd pulled on his heart strings. He'd embarked on this trip to Whistler as a favour to his old friend, but before falling asleep in the cave he'd already decided that, when this shitstorm was over, he wanted to see more of Janine. *But now she was gone, and it was his fucking fault.*

He jogged up and down the length of the long parking lot, stopping everyone he encountered, demanding to know if they'd seen a tall, pony-tailed brunette woman wearing a red cycling jacket. He'd done a full loop and was back where he'd started, with no sign of Janine and no clue as to where she'd gone.

"Hey, man. You looking for the chick in the red coat?"

Dawson whirled, eyes blazing. His fierce gaze landed on the young man who was no longer on his phone. Dawson was in his face in two long strides. "Where is she? What do you know?" he snarled.

The young man bowed his back against his car, his hand blindly scrambling for the door handle in an attempt to get away from the hulking, angry man towering over him. "Nothin', man! I don't know nothin'."

Shit! Dawson forced himself to back up a step, at the same time holding up both hands in a gesture of reassurance. Adopting a non-threatening tone, he said, "I'm sorry. *Please,* just wait. *Wait!* Did you see the woman, brunette pony tail, red cycling jacket? Did you see her leave?"

The boy had the driver's door open, suspicion radiating from him in thick waves.

Dawson made a concerted effort to further dial down his intensity. This frightened young man was his only chance of finding Janine. He couldn't blow it.

"Look, I'm her *friend.* I swear to you. Damn it, kid, if you believe one thing, then, please god, believe that." Dawson did everything in his power to make his sincerity vibrate off him, but there was nothing fake about the tears that choked his throat and glistened in his eyes when he said, "I'm her *friend.* Honest to god, kid. But there's some nasty fuckers after her. I'm not one of them. I promise you, I'm not. Only I can't find her, see? And now I'm scared as all fuck they've grabbed her. I swear I'm telling you the truth, kid. *I fucking swear it.* Please, believe me. *Please* tell me what you saw."

The young man still seemed uncertain as to whether he would be putting the unknown woman in danger if he shared what he'd observed with this forbidding man, but at least he responded, albeit with suspicion. "Dude, nobody *grabbed* her."

At the kid's welcome words, Dawson felt suddenly dizzy. He stumbled back half a step and then had to lean forward and keep his hands on his knees as a wave of relief almost knocked him flat. *Thank fuck!*

He sucked in a deep breath, then stood up. He knew his eyes glimmered with unshed tears as he addressed the kid. "Nobody grabbed her? You're certain?"

The kid seemed eager to help now, as if witnessing a big, alpha male like Dawson reduced to tears was sufficient evidence of sincerity. "Nobody grabbed her. But whoever she was talking to on the phone? She was scared, man. *Totally* freaked."

On the phone? Dawson wanted to snatch the kid's cell and check his call history, but he made himself stay put. "She borrowed your phone?"

"No." The kid jerked his chin towards the entrance to the diner. "She was on the payphone."

Dawson looked in the same direction. He'd noticed the payphone in the small lobby, but it hadn't dawned on him she'd used it. *She'd called Kevin!* That's why she'd been gone so long while he was in the restaurant drinking shit coffee and making short work of his breakfast. But if she'd talked to Kevin, why the hell hadn't she told him?

"I don't think *she's* in trouble," the kid volunteered. "But she seemed pretty twisted up about someone named Kevin."

Dawson pinned the kid with laser like focus. "Tell me everything you heard."

The young man lifted his hands, in defence or apology, Dawson couldn't tell. "I barely heard anything, man. Only snatches. She was talking low. And she sounded scared. Really scared. She said shit like…um…*don't hurt him*. And, uh…" The kid looked off in the distance, crinkling his face in concentration. "Something about a package?" The kid shrugged. Then, looking slightly hopeful, suggested, "Drugs, maybe?"

Dawson almost snarled. "Did she look like a drug dealer to you?"

The kid shrugged. "I saw this movie once, where this rich housewife—"

Dawson motioned impatiently as he interrupted. "What else do you remember?"

"Well, just before she hung up, she said…*I'll come alone*. That kinda creeped me out. So, I asked if she was okay, cuz, you know." He shrugged. "She seemed upset, man. Like, *I'll come alone?* That's freaky creepy, isn't it?"

It *was* freaky creepy, but Dawson was so pleased with the kid, he could've kissed him. Everything made sense now. Janine had called Kevin's house, only Kevin hadn't answered.

Whoever had, a) inferred that Kevin was hurt, b) told Janine to return the package Kevin couriered, and c) ordered her to deliver said package in person and alone. It didn't take a genius to know she'd also been given a deadline to perform all of the above. *That's* why she'd disappeared. That son-of-a-bitch on the phone had scared her, and she was now doing what she'd been ordered on threat of Kevin getting hurt. He was disappointed she hadn't trusted him, hadn't turned to him for help despite what the cocksucker on the other end of the line said. That hurt. But he could live with that knowing she wasn't in any immediate danger. Except she would be, if she went to England alone.

Dawson turned and looked in the direction of Whistler. He needed to go with her. His eyes gleaming with intensity, he turned back to the kid and addressed him in a low, confiding tone. "Hey, you want to earn a hundred bucks?"

The young man jerked his chin into his neck and regarded Dawson in utter horror. "Fuck, no! Get away from me, you perv."

"Jesus Christ!" Dawson protested in equivalent horror when he realized the kid thought he'd just been sexually propositioned. "No! Kid, that's not.... *No!"*

The young man looked relieved, although his eyes still held a modicum of cautious suspicion. "Oh. What do I have to do for it?"

Dawson gestured in the direction of Whistler. "Drive me to my van, which has its nose planted in a tree a few miles down the highway."

The kid brightened. "Hey, she wanted to hire me, too."

"To drive her to Whistler? And you *turned her down?"* Dawson snapped.

"No! Chill," the kid protested, proudly thumbing at the words on the front of his hoodie. *Me drop everything. Work on your problem.* "I thought she was joking. Kinda funny you both wanting to hire me, don't you think?" he asked, giving

Dawson an engaging grin. When Dawson merely stared at him, he shrugged and added. "Whatever, dude. I'll do it. Easy hundred bucks."

It was risky taking a detour to the van, but without Janine, Dawson knew he could sneak within ten feet of the assholes staking it out. His passport was in the back pocket of his jeans, with his wallet, so it wasn't essential to retrieve his duffle bag, but he wanted to see if he could find their phones. If he couldn't get near the van, so be it, he'd leave. Then he'd start the real work of tracking her down, which wouldn't be overly difficult given his contacts. In fact...he knew exactly how he'd do it.

He was practically humming with anticipation. "Kid, I'll give you *three* hundred if you drive me to my van, wait for me while I retrieve some of my things, and then drive me to Whistler."

The young man's eyes nearly popped out of his head. "Dude," he said with a grin, holding out a closed fist in an invitation to bump. "That's what I call a *stealy-deal-of-a-dealy-oh.*"

Chapter 23

The plane had taken off while Dawson relayed his account, and they were now at cruising altitude. He kept his voice low so the passengers in the row ahead wouldn't overhear, which also gave him an excuse to lean in close to Janine. Everything about her smelled clean and fresh—not that she hadn't smelled good before.

Although she remained uptight and pensive, her eyes clouded with anxiety, her hand, at least, was a little warmer than when he'd first claimed it. His anger had also dimmed significantly now that he'd found her.

The airplane was going through some turbulence, and the captain announced she was leaving the seatbelt sign on until they were clear of it. Janine pulled her hand from his as if she needed both of her hands to check her seatbelt clasp.

"And? Did you find your van?" she asked.

Dawson glanced longingly at her hands, which were now clamped between her denim-clad knees. "It was easy to spot given one of your Mounties had his police cruiser parked, lights flashing, on the side of the road where we hit the ditch. Why are they still called that? It's not like they're mounted."

He could see he'd disconcerted her with his sudden

change of topic. She had trouble switching focus quickly, he realized. He liked that about her, that she gave her full attention to whatever was engaging her beautiful mind. In this case, she needed a nudge. "Royal Canadian *Mounted* Police? You don't *mount* a police cruiser. So, why are they still called *Mounties?*"

Feeling chagrined that he'd initially elevated her jangled nerves, he was trying to make up for it by being silly, hoping to diminish her tension. He was pleased to see her expression of fond exasperation, her shoulders and body language less tense than when he'd first joined her. By the time they landed in Heathrow, he intended for Janine to not only renew her trust in him but also promise to stick to him like glue, despite what the cocksucker on the other end of the phone said.

"You're an idiot," she accused, but she was smiling and shaking her head in mock disapproval.

He shrugged good-naturedly. "So my sisters never cease to remind me."

"There's still the Musical Ride, you know."

It was his turn to shake his head. "Formation riding that's strictly PR? That hardly counts."

"Did you talk to the Mountie?" she asked.

"Hell, no," Dawson stated. "He was leaving when I showed up with the kid. Given our bat-out-of-Whistler yesterday, I'm pretty certain my van has been reported for erratic and reckless driving. But his presence on the scene at least did a good job of scaring the bad guys away—if they were even still there. I was in and out in under five minutes."

She sighed, and he knew she was wishing she'd been with him so she could've looked for her phone. He'd found it after searching for less than thirty seconds—under the van on the passenger side and relatively dry—but he was still a little pissed that she'd so easily abandoned him. He wasn't ready to give it to her.

When Janine turned to face him, a vertical furrowed line

between her eyebrows, he was tempted to try and erase it with the tip of his finger.

She kept her voice low as she asked, "But how could you know I would be on this flight?" She pointed to her lap and added, "*In this seat.*"

Dawson shifted, trying to get comfortable in his *too goddamn cramped* seat that had *no goddamn* legroom. *Fucking economy.*

"It wasn't hard to put two-and-two together," he grumbled. In response to her wide-eyed confusion, he addressed her in a clipped, hissing tone that revealed just how much anger he still harboured. "Jesus, Janine. The real question isn't how the hell I figured all that out. It's why the fuck didn't you trust me? Why didn't you come straight to me after that phone call? After everything we've been through, everything we talked about, everything we *did*." He was glad to see her flicker of embarrassment as she recalled exactly what they'd done that morning. In his world, you didn't get intimate like that unless there was some trust involved. "How the hell can you *not* trust me? But you *ditched* me. And that *hurt*, Janine. It goddamn stung." He continued with less ferocity. "It still does, if you must know. You scared the crap out of me. I thought those assholes snatched you. Did you think of that when you were making your fleet-footed getaway?"

Janine closed her eyes and dropped her forehead into her hand. "Shit!" he heard her mutter under her breath.

"I get that Sylvester wasn't inclined to trust me at first, but you…" Dropping this unusual name made her look at him, which was the response he'd intended.

"*That's* his name? *Sylvester?*"

When they shared an amused grin, he saw the fear in her eyes diminish another notch. *That's more like it.*

"Get this," he said in a conspiring tone, dropping his shoulder and tilting his head close to hers. He wished he could slouch in his seat, but the lack of leg room had him sitting ramrod straight. "He was on his way to visit his girlfriend in Deep Cove. Want to know *her* name?"

"Please tell me it's not *Tweedy*," Janine said, laughter dancing in her eyes.

"Her name is *Twyla*. But since she and Sylvester started dating, you can guess what nickname she's earned."

"But," Janine insisted, growing serious once again. "You still haven't explained how you came to be on *this* flight in *that* seat."

"You mean this stupid, I'm-in-economy-jail seat?" Dawson practically snarled, gesturing in annoyance at his cramped space. "I'll tell you, but only if you hold my hand."

Janine looked startled. "What? Why?"

"Because I like holding your hand. And I'm pretty certain you like holding mine."

Janine mock glared at him. "If I do, will you stop being mad at me?" she asked.

"You figured out I was mad, huh? Geez, what gave it away?"

She shook her head at him, but at least she lifted her hand in invitation.

He clasped it in his, intertwining their fingers. "I knew you'd be heading to the airport," he stated. "After stopping at the van for my duffle bag, I got Sylvester to drop me off at the float plane terminal at Green Lake."

Janine made a sound of envy. "I didn't even *think* of the floatplane."

"How did you get here?"

"Nicolette drove me."

Dawson nodded. "Ah. And what did you tell her?"

"Everything," Janine said.

Dawson cocked an eyebrow at her, deliberately dropping his gaze to her breasts, which were unfortunately completely hidden from view thanks to a billowy scarf that hid her curves. He lifted his eyes to meet her gaze, delighted to see an answering heat in her gorgeous eyes. It was always there, simmering just below the surface.

Janine shook her head at him. "Okay, not *every*thing. But you still haven't answered my question."

He smiled. "It was easy to narrow your flight options. Really, there were only two. This one on Air Canada. Or a departure on British Airways a few hours later."

"So you chose the earlier departure. And, if I wasn't on that flight, you'd wait for me to arrive on the Heathrow side?" Her brow furrowed as she thought this through. "But that doesn't explain seat *18-J,"* she insisted.

"Yeah, well, for that I had to call in a favour from a former colleague."

Janine frowned. "You used to work for the airline?" Her face cleared. "Oh. The government. Doing security?"

"Well…it's classified," he stated, giving her a sheepish grin.

He shifted, trying to ease his cramped posture, but it was an exercise in futility; yet, he wouldn't want to be anywhere else in this moment except sitting next to Janine, who fascinated him on every level. But her presence was the *only* reason he was putting up with this *stupid goddamn seat.*

"You're American. You shouldn't have access to *private* information at a *Canadian* airport about a *Canadian* airline."

"I once did some contract work for Canadian Immigration. Well, more like, a *division* within Immigration."

Janine gaped at him. "Even if you did, that doesn't give you access to airline passenger manifests," she insisted.

Dawson feigned insult as he met Janine's gaze. "Clearly you have no faith in my powers of persuasion, or my charm. I can be hard to resist, you know." He bent his head towards her and added in a stage whisper. "I know you *know."*

Janine glared at him. "You're too arrogant for your own good, do you know that? For the record, I find it very disturbing that someone in Canadian Immigration—and I'm guessing that someone is a hetero woman who melts into a puddle if you so much as deign to look at her—would share an entire passenger manifest. That's *very* disturbing."

"One person in three hundred is not an entire manifest."

"Well, in my books, 0.33% is still an unacceptable margin."

"Technically, she didn't divulge anything confidential."

Janine pulled her hand out of his and lowered her table tray. The flight attendants had the refreshments cart out, although they were still a few rows away. "Do I need to recall your attention to exhibit A?" she stated in a huffy tone, crossing her arms. "The body in seat 18-J?"

Janine was looking at him as if he was one of the bad guys. Dawson had to remind himself he was supposed to be earning her trust, not pissing her off. He couldn't afford the stress of having her leave him again.

"Look, it's not as bad as you think," he stated, his tone conciliatory. "During our former collaboration, it was necessary to be more candid than the rules allowed in order to achieve what was, at the time, a mutually desirable outcome. So, me and my Canadian colleague developed a very basic code. *I can neither confirm nor deny* meant *confirmed*, while *no comment* simply meant *no*." Dawson shrugged. "When I landed here, I phoned her. She simply responded with either, *I can neither confirm nor deny*, or *no comment*."

Janine scowled at him. "And the seat number? You got *no comment* eighteen times, and then another ten times when you started reciting the alphabet?"

Dawson shook his head, grinning. He loved Janine's clever brain. "Nah. I simply asked her to recommend a seat on a Boeing 787. She suggested 18-J."

Janine pointed at his cramped knees pushing against the seat in front of him. "And you're pleased with her recommendation?" she asked sweetly.

In that moment, the passenger in 17-J tilted his seat back, reducing what little space Dawson had. He scowled.

Janine laughed. "You're just lucky it wasn't already taken."

"Yeah, I'm a lucky son-of-a-bitch, aren't I?" he grumbled. He chose not to share the fact that the seat had, indeed, been taken. Like Nicolette, she didn't need to know *every*thing.

Chapter 24

Ever since he'd shown up—once her brain had started functioning again—Janine had been frantically trying to figure out how to lose Dawson a second time. She quickly realized that wouldn't accomplish anything given he knew her final destination. But Kevin's well-being was contingent on her showing up alone. If she didn't, and they hurt Kevin further, she'd never forgive herself, or Dawson. There was nothing for it but to convince him not to accompany her to Nottingham. And to succeed in doing that, she had to keep him at an emotional distance.

That last part of the equation was proving near impossible. He was clearly intent on diffusing her tension, which was sweet. She liked that about him. She also liked his goofy sense of humour. It was just so…idiotic. And endearing. It didn't help that he was off-the-charts sexy, or that she loved the feel of his big hand holding hers, loved his warmth beside her as his shoulder brushed hers. She was practically humming with pleasure—and not just sexually—simply from being near him. She'd forced herself to release his hand—twice now—because touching him was a distraction she couldn't afford. How was she going to succeed in convincing him not to come with her when all she wanted was for him to do exactly that?

She realized he was eyeing her mouth as she gnawed on her lower lip. It was clear he wanted to kiss her. As much as she wanted that too, she couldn't let it happen, not if she wanted to de-complicate her present circumstances.

"It's not that big of a deal, Janine," he insisted, raising his eyes to hers. "It might have been unconventional, getting *this* seat on *this* flight, but it's not like we breached Canada-US security protocols."

"What? Oh." Janine shook her head. "No, I wasn't thinking about that. It's just…" Her words trailed off as she absently began fiddling with the trailing fringe of her scarf.

She was watching Dawson shift in frustration, moving an inch here, an inch there, then ending up right back where he started. She took pity on him. "Oh, for god's sake," she stated, pushing up her table tray and snapping open her seat belt. She stood up and moved into the aisle, turning to address him. "We're trading seats. Hurry up," she added, gesturing at the approaching attendants. "Before I change my mind."

She saw Dawson hesitate, as if he was considering arguing, but the thought of having the extra leg room an aisle seat offered was clearly too appealing to turn down.

"Your turn," Dawson said when they were resettled into their seats, each with a coffee and a package of cookies on their open table trays. She winced in distaste after taking a sip of her drink.

Janine realized there was no point in withholding anything about the conversation she'd had with the Irishman. Sitting slightly sideways and speaking in a low tone, she shared the threatening exchange, making no attempt to hide either her concern for Kevin or her underlying accusation about Dawson's uninvited presence. She found she was relieved to talk out the problem with him. He had expertise when it came to people like that Irishman. When she described how Kevin hadn't been able to enunciate his words properly, she saw Dawson's gaze darken. Strangely, he wasn't surprised when she shared how the man had mentioned Dawson by name and warned her not to enlist his help.

"He insisted I couldn't involve you," she said, hating how her voice, even pitched low, sounded shrill with worry. "How does he know your name, or that you're a security expert?"

Dawson shrugged. "I might've left a few messages on Kev's machine during my drive to Whistler."

She looked at him in confusion. "What did you say?"

Dawson's tone was disgruntled. "Just to *please* not call my security company for help if he wasn't willing to provide the details I needed to do my job."

Janine gave a low hoot of laughter. "Uh-huh?" she challenged, crossing her arms. "You said *please*? No F-bombs or WTFs or any of your other less-than-eloquent adjectives?"

"I might've sprinkled in a few. But they were all highly appropriate for the occasion."

His amused grin and the sparkle in his eyes loosened a butterfly—more like ten—in her stomach, forcing her to look away. She found the man utterly irresistible. But she had no business thinking about him like that, not with Kevin's safety at stake.

Janine shifted to regard him, her tone grave. "Dawson, the fact that you're here is a problem. A big one. You can't come with me to Nottingham. You just can't. If I don't arrive alone, they'll hurt Kevin, and that would be my fault. I'd never be able to forgive myself." Her voice faltered on the last few words, her eyes filling with unshed tears.

"Hey, no, stop that," he soothed in a gentle tone, reaching for her hand.

She deftly avoided him, stuffing her used napkin and cookie wrapper into her empty coffee cup. She would not allow him to distract her from what was most important—Kevin's safety. She glanced at the passenger in the window seat, saw he'd tilted his seat back and had a mask over his eyes. Whether he was asleep, she couldn't tell. She turned to face Dawson and spoke in a low tone. "I'm serious. You can't come with me."

Dawson sighed, drained his coffee, then snapped up his table tray with an impatient gesture. He stacked his empty cup with hers, then turned slightly to face her. When he spoke, his face close to hers, his tone was low and deadly serious. "Janine, I'm going with you to Nottingham. We're going to—"

"No! *We* are not, Dawson. If you show up with me—"

"We," he hissed, "are going to make a plan that won't compromise Kevin's safety. But *I am* going with you, Janine. Get that through your pretty head. Nothing you say or do is going to change that. When we disembark in Heathrow? You are *not* going to ditch me again. And *together*, we will make sure Kevin doesn't come to further harm. Okay?"

Everything Dawson said sounded good. Better than good. She wasn't equipped to do any of this—whatever *this* turned out to be—by herself. She certainly didn't want to encounter that scary Irish guy on her own. Nor did she believe that simply handing over the coin would be the end of things. But she had no capacity to predict what might come next. Having Dawson with her would make all the difference. But his presence put Kevin's well-being, perhaps even his life, at risk.

"But if you show up with me—"

Again, Dawson interrupted her. "No *buts*, Janine. I *am* going to Nottingham. As Dick Irish-Asshole said, I know a thing or two about security. But he thinks I'm an expert in home security, which I am. What he doesn't know is that I've had shitloads of experience dealing with assholes like him. And that means you're going to let me apply my skills and expertise to extricate Kevin from whatever shitstorm he's stirred up. In return, you stick to me like glue. I intend to keep you safe, Janine, but I can't do that if I don't know where you are."

Janine saw something change in his eyes when he uttered that last statement. Was it fear? Was he making a promise he didn't feel he could keep? Regardless, she knew she didn't have a hope of preventing him from travelling to Nottingham, with or without her. "Can we make a plan that at least makes them think I'm alone?"

Dawson made a non-committal sound. "We'll make a plan where those cocksuckers don't get a chance to hurt you."

"But it's Kevin we need to be concerned about, not me."

Dawson eyed her, his gaze serious. "My first priority? It's protecting you, Janine. I won't budge on that. Yes, I intend to disentangle Kev from whatever mess he's in, but only while keeping you safe. But you have to promise not to ditch me again. Not knowing your whereabouts will split my focus, and that would compromise us all."

Dawson accompanying her to Nottingham was going against what the Irishman—what had Dawson called him? Dick Irish-Asshole—had mandated. But clearly, she'd lost the argument. And losing had never felt so good. She felt tears welling up in her eyes.

This time, she was the one reaching for his hand. "Okay, then," she said, taking comfort in the feel of his calloused hand possessively clasping hers.

The relief in Dawson's eyes made them gleam a deep Mediterranean blue. "Okay, then," he echoed.

Chapter 25

"Dawson, why did you leave the Secret Service?"

Janine saw him stiffen in response to her question, but in the next moment shrugged and his expression cleared.

"My brother-in-law spent ten years in the police force before realizing it wasn't for him. He suggested we start a company specializing in home security. I thought it was a great idea. We mostly install systems on large estates, but we can do any kind of security. Do you know," he said, warming to his topic, "there's tons of DIY home security systems out there, but homeowners make all kinds of shit-stupid mistakes. It's *always* better to hire a professional, even if only for basic advice. Can you believe people still hide their house keys under their front mats or garden gnomes? I mean," Dawson paused, shaking his head in disgust. "Why *lock* your door? Why even *close* your door?"

Janine smiled to herself, deciding it was best not to divulge how she'd accessed Nicolette's home.

Dawson eyed her, his gaze enigmatic.

"What?" she asked, suddenly self-conscious.

"I have something for you."

Janine eyed him as he got to his feet and began

rummaging in the overhead bin. On her right, the passenger at the window indicated he needed to use the bathroom. Janine picked up the trash from her table tray—the flight attendants hadn't yet returned to collect it—then closed it and shuffled into the aisle. Once there, the stranger extended his hand for her trash—*good manners, good mother,* thought Janine approvingly. She smiled, handing the items to him.

Once her and Dawson resumed their seats, she recognized what he was holding out to her. "Hey!" she stated, sitting up and swiping it from his hand. "That's my phone." She looked at him accusingly. "How long have you had this?"

Dawson put a hand to his heart and feigned hurt. "Well not since last night, if that's what you're suggesting. I can't believe you'd think that."

Janine realized she had, and felt mildly chagrined. "You found it in the van this morning?"

"*Under* the van. It must've fallen out the passenger door when I helped you out."

Janine touched the home button, but the screen remained black. "It's dead," she said, disappointed.

"It's not dead. I turned the power off." When Janine looked at him, he shrugged. "I didn't have your password and couldn't put it on airplane mode." He jerked his chin up, indicating the overhead bins. "I bought you a power cord, and a UK adaptor."

Janine kept her finger pressed on the home button until the apple icon appeared. "I don't know whether to thank you or hit you. Why the hell didn't you give this to me as soon as you sat down? *I* could've put it on airplane mode."

Dawson sighed, then stated in a monotone as if reciting an oft-repeated sentiment. "Because sometimes I behave like the four-year-old I still am."

Janine shook her head in mild disgust, guessing his sisters had accused him of such behaviour on more than one occasion. "You were pissed at me for ditching you. Withholding my phone was punishment?"

Dawson lifted a shoulder. "Go ahead, say it. I'm an idiot. My sisters tell me all the time."

Janine studied him. She wasn't annoyed, exactly. She understood that his worry about her being snatched by their pursuers had freaked him out. She had briefly considered his feelings when she left Ivy's Pies, but she hadn't allowed it to shift her focus. "I get why you were mad, and I'm sorry for abandoning you. I honestly thought I was doing the right thing, the *only* thing I could do to keep Kevin safe."

He gave her an inscrutable look. Something in his eyes… surprise…tenderness? She wasn't sure.

"For what it's worth, I'm sorry I didn't give it to you right away." He nodded at the phone. "But I did plug it in. It's fully charged. And now I need you to purchase Wifi, then let me borrow it."

Sobering immediately, Janine nodded. Once the phone powered on, she switched to airplane mode, then tapped her Air Canada app and purchased the flight's Wifi. She quickly tapped out a text to Nicolette, briefly telling her Dawson was on the flight with her and he'd found her phone. Then she handed the device to Dawson, at the same time realizing the police could track her now that she'd activated her cell. Not that it mattered. Her only concern had been ensuring nothing prevented her from departing Vancouver. Regardless, she asked Dawson if he thought the police would attempt to track her credit card or phone activity.

"You're reported missing, so yes, they might try, but it's not like in the movies. For one thing, it can take days to get the authority to do so, at least in the US. Then the problem is, do they have appropriate access? The simplest is obviously tracking location using GPS, either SUPL-based or CP-based. The first protocol requires an internet connection because it uses the TCP/IP network—"

"Um," Janine interrupted, holding up a hand. She was faintly amused that Dawson had the ability to bore her. "What you're saying is, go ahead and use my phone?"

He feigned hurt. "Well, shoot. And here I was about to wax poetic on triangulation theory." He gestured with the phone. "Does this have WhatsApp installed?"

Janine took the phone back and swiped until she found the app, then returned it to Dawson.

He tapped in a number and held it to his ear.

"Who are you calling?"

Dawson gave her an apologetic look as he started speaking. "Joanie. Yeah, hi…Look, I need you to do something for me…Yes, I know what time it is," he said, glancing at his wristwatch. "Fine. I'll pay you." Dawson gave Janine an amused look, then said to the person on the other end of the call, "Never mind whose phone this is…Oh? She called?"

Janine detected a note of dismay in Dawson's tone, and felt certain it had something to do with the 'she' he'd just referenced. Janine wished she could hear both sides of the conversation.

"Tell her whatever you want, I don't care…No, I *really* don't care…Joanie, that's not in your job description….You don't have one? Well, write one then….Look, could you shut the hell up for half a minute? I'm on a plane to Heathrow… Never mind why, but I lost my cellphone….*Jesus Christ, Joanie, never mind!*" Dawson gave Janine an exasperated look.

This Joanie person was obviously his secretary, Janine surmised. They certainly had a casual way of communicating. She supposed it was too much to hope that Joanie was a grey-haired woman with a frizzy bun—it was an old-fashioned name, after all.

Dawson continued his phone conversation as they both rose and shuffled back into the aisle to allow the passenger assigned to the window seat to re-enter their row.

"Look, Kevin Kirkby left a voicemail for me at work. Can

you retrieve it from my email inbox?…Yes, that's still my password…It is *not* stupid.…No, the P is caps, but not the L.…No, that's *not* it. The underscore is between the S and the L…No! Lower case L."

As they resettled in their seats, Dawson closed his eyes and recited his password in a toneless monotone, indicating lower and upper case, spelling out *Princess_leia10!* "Yes, that's it," he confirmed in a resigned tone.

Janine sputtered with mirth as she heard Dawson recite his password. *What was it with men and Princess Leia?*

"Send Kev's message to this number…Never mind, who.…Yeah, and one more thing. Rent a car for me at Heathrow airport. I should be there in about seven hours.…You're a peach, Joanie.…Yeah, yeah. I love you, too."

Janine had been listening intently to Dawson's side of the conversation, amused by and a little jealous of the affectionate banter between him and his secretary. Even while telling her off, his voice was laced with fondness. But her eyes bugged out at his closing sentiment. She turned away and blindly grabbed the airline magazine from the seat pocket in front of her. He's likely seduced every secretary he's ever had, she thought in irritation. In fact, he probably can't be around any woman—including her—for longer than five minutes without getting into their pants. *God, Janine, you fell for his so-called charms as if you were still that pathetic, swooning fifteen-year-old.*

When Dawson tapped her arm with her phone, she took it without looking at him.

"Let me know when that email arrives, okay? I want to listen to Kev's voicemail again and re-evaluate his exact wording and tone in case I missed something."

The flight attendants appeared at their row with the dinner cart, reciting the meal options—beef, chicken, or vegetarian. The window-seat passenger asked for chicken. When the young man at the head of the cart looked at Janine, she shook her head and politely said, "I'm not hungry."

"She'll have the chicken," Dawson stated. "And a red wine each."

Disregarding Janine's frown, Dawson released her table tray, then set down the foil-covered meal.

"And for you, sir?" the flight attendant asked, a purr of approval in his voice. "I'm guessing the beef?"

Janine wanted to roll her eyes. The flight attendant was obviously gay, and clearly had no qualms about flirting with Dawson. Well, he was welcome to him!

"I'm that easy to read?" Dawson asked in mock disgust.

The flight attendant smiled his delight. "I'm good at predicting peoples' tastes."

Janine tried to tune out their banter as Dawson paid for the wine. After the flight attendants moved on, she glared daggers at him. "I said I wasn't hungry."

"What's made you so pissy all of a sudden?" Dawson asked as he lifted the foil from his tray, releasing steam. "Janine honey, you can shoot darts at me with those pretty eyes all you like, but they bounce off. Four sisters gives a guy thick skin." He frowned at her when she didn't respond to his teasing. "Seriously. You have to eat. You'll be no good to Kev if you show up faint with hunger."

She *was* hungry. And the food smelled good, despite it being airplane fare. Janine removed the foil covering her meal, revealing the chicken breast, mashed potatoes, a mixed medley of colourful vegetables, a dinner roll, and a cup of fruit cocktail.

She glanced over at Dawson's tray. "You have a pudding cup for dessert," she observed, hating the petulant tone in her voice.

Dawson glanced at her tray. "And you have fruit cocktail."

"I don't like fruit cocktail." Janine knew she was being contrary. She didn't care.

Dawson exchanged her fruit cocktail for his pudding. "Isn't it lucky for you I'm such a generous guy?"

"Generous to a fault," she muttered, imagining him generously bestowing his powers of seduction on every women who crossed his path.

"What's that supposed to mean?"

She turned on him, unable to hold her annoyance in check. "I can't believe you'd tell your secretary you *love* her. And in front of me, after what we—"

Janine blushed and turned away, but not before she saw the grin light up his face.

"You're jealous," he accused, clearly delighted.

Janine glanced at the man in the window seat, saw that he was looking at her with interest. He'd clearly heard Dawson's accusation. "I am *not*," she hissed under her breath, stabbing a baby carrot with her plastic fork, wishing it was his heart.

"I'll have you know, I *do* love my secretary. And I intend to tell her that, frequently. It means she does what I ask. Well, with only minor grumbling."

Janine refused to look at him.

"But unlike you," he continued in a congenial tone. "She wouldn't be jealous if she heard me telling another woman I love her."

This time she did glare at him, but he only quirked an eyebrow, and said, "*She* knows how to share."

Janine fumed, wishing she'd managed not to reveal her jealousy, more mad at herself than him.

"Ever since she almost died when we were kids," he continued, "I've had no qualms telling her I love her. We all do. My parents, my *other* sisters—"

Janine turned to Dawson, realization dawning. "Are you telling me your secretary is your *sister?*" She recalled once being at Dawson's house with her cousin—riding there on the back of Kevin's bike, if she remembered correctly—a house that seemed overrun with a pack of older girls. One of those girls must've been Joanie.

Dawson bit into his dinner roll, devouring half of it in a

single bite. A teasing glint glimmered in his eyes. "Uh huh," he said, pausing to swallow a mouthful of food. "Joanie is closest to me in age. Actually, we're Irish twins."

"You're a *twin?*" Janine hadn't known that.

"No, *Irish* twins. Siblings born less than twelve months apart. Joanie's birthday is the end of January. Mine's mid-December. We're the same age for six weeks."

"Oh, *that's* what Irish twins means," Janine said, feeling like an idiot as the last of her misplaced anger evaporated. She cut into her chicken. "So, is she the sister who almost drowned?"

Dawson nodded, then proceeded to tell her how it had been his fault they'd even been on the river that day. They'd often canoed on the small lake behind their house, but that summer when Joanie was ten, the family had been holidaying at a riverside campsite. He'd convinced Joanie to come canoeing with him without asking their parents' permission, but the rushing water hadn't been anything like the calm surface of the lake. The boat had capsized, and Joanie had hit her head on a rock. He'd barely been able to get them both to shore. He'd been grounded for the rest of the summer, and hadn't protested his punishment, convinced he deserved to be grounded for life. Seeing Joanie barely conscious, the blood gushing from a cut on her head as she struggled to keep her mouth above water, had scared the adventure right out of him.

Janine wondered if that experience, at such an impressionable age, had contributed to his chosen career with the Secret Service and, later, to his decision to run a security company.

After finishing their meal, they continued chatting about what it was like for Dawson to grow up with four siblings and, by the sounds of it, too many cousins to count. His descriptions of his loud, boisterous family were hard for Janine to fathom.

When the flight attendants came by a little later to clear their dinner trays and offer refreshments, Janine ordered decaf coffee, knowing it would taste terrible, but needing even a low quality hit before attempting to sleep. At the same time, Dawson purchased a set of earbuds.

Coffee in hand, she checked her phone. Nicolette had responded. *Thank god Dawson showed. Stick to him like glue, girl!* There was also a message from an unrecognizable number. She clicked on it.

Tell George he owes me.

When she showed Dawson the message, he laughed. "That's Joanie for you."

"But who's George?" Janine asked.

Dawson appeared chagrined as he shared why he'd earned the nickname. Then he plugged in the earbuds, gave Janine one and put the other in his ear. When she was ready, he tapped the download icon.

Dawson! I need your help. I was hoping to talk to you. Look, I think I did something stupid. Really stupid. I found something that's valuable, priceless really, and I sent it to Jaynie for safekeeping. Now I'm thinking that was a mistake. Could you phone her? Here he rattled off Janine's number. *And if she doesn't answer, or you talk to her and you think there's a reason to be concerned, could you go up to Whistler and check up on her? Make sure she's safe? I know it's asking a lot, but I'm worried. Her address is 2010 Tanglewood Crescent. Look, maybe I'm freaking out for no reason, but if I'm not…Shit, man, I'm sorry, but I'm in a bind here and I'm not sure how to get out of it. As long as Jaynie is safe, that's all that matters. I'll try calling again as soon as I can, okay? Thanks man. I owe you big time. Mega big.*

Janine had been frowning at the underlying note of alarm in her cousin's voice. She shared a look of concern with Dawson after the message finished. "Could you play it again?"

After their third listen, Janine removed the earpiece. "Considering the limited information he provided, all I can say is thank you for making that long drive. I mean that, Dawson. I don't know where I'd be if you hadn't been there."

He shrugged, folding his table tray into place and

stretching one of his long legs into the aisle. "You're welcome. Did you keep the message Kev left on *your* phone?"

She shook her head.

He leaned forward to look past Janine at the passenger on her right. The man was wearing an eye mask and seemed to have fallen asleep. "Can I see the coin again?" Dawson asked in a low tone.

Janine retrieved her purse, digging out the coin and handing it to him. While he examined it, she dealt with the messages on her phone, smiling a little when she listened to Dawson politely introducing himself and letting her know he was on his way to Whistler. His tone gave no indication of urgency or concern. She wondered how she would've reacted had she listened to his message before she went for her run. Regardless, she didn't delete it. She also did a brief internet search, showing Dawson the results, which claimed that while some old coins sold for as low as fifty pounds, others sold at auction in the tens of thousands of pounds. They agreed, with their limited knowledge, it was impossible to guess the value of Kev's coin.

When the lights in the cabin dimmed, she put her phone and the coin in her purse and tucked it under the seat in front of her. Accepting a blanket from the flight attendant, she reclined her seat and rested her head on Dawson's shoulder even though she knew she wouldn't be able to sleep, not with all the unanswered questions whirling in her brain.

Several hours later she awoke, stiff necked, when the flight attendant's voice on the public address system announced that breakfast service was about to start.

Chapter 26

Janine stood beside Dawson at the car rental counter in Heathrow Airport sipping a triple-shot americano, hoping it would give her a much-needed jolt of energy. It was 9:00 am local time, and she'd just texted Nicolette to let her know they'd arrived.

According to her Fitbit, there was just under six hours left in their countdown. Had she been alone, she would've been worried that relying on trains, with a transfer in London, would prevent her from arriving at her cousin's by the deadline. But with Dawson—and, more importantly, his credit card—they were able to rent a car, something she wouldn't have been able to do with cash. As long as there were no issues with traffic, they would arrive at Kevin's several hours in advance of the deadline.

She'd woken from her too-short sleep worrying about her cousin. How badly hurt was he? What would they find when they got to his house? Would he even be there? Would the creepy Irishman? And what would happen once she handed over the coin? Surely the Irishman and Gerald's 'persuasive' fists wouldn't simply exit stage right, would they?

While they ate their breakfast, she posed her questions to

Dawson and he somewhat reluctantly shared the conclusions he'd drawn. The coin, Dawson conjectured, was from a much larger cache, which was the true prize Dick Irish-Asshole was after. Kevin clearly wasn't divulging where he'd found it. That meant Dick Irish-Asshole's intention wasn't to gain possession of Janine's coin, but to gain possession of Janine, and then use her as leverage to get Kevin to divulge the location of this larger cache of coins.

Janine could've kicked herself when Dawson shared his theory. It made perfect sense. She'd been so focused on getting to Nottingham, so overwhelmed with worry for Kevin, that she hadn't been able to think clearly, hadn't connected what now seemed like obvious dots. But Dawson had. Janine felt certain his theory had merit.

Standing next to Dawson at the car rental counter, her mind preoccupied with worry, she absently admired both the scrawl of Dawson's signature and his good manners as he thanked the clerk. As they resumed walking towards the exit, Dawson slung both their overnight bags over his shoulder.

Noting Janine's furrowed brow, he said, "Stop imagining worst case scenarios, Janine. We won't know what we're dealing with until we get there. It's a foolish waste of time to worry it to death."

Stung by his words, which landed on her ears like a sharp reprimand, she found herself blinking back tears.

Dawson matched his stride to Janine's slower steps, adding, "Wasn't it Erma Bombeck who said, *worry is like a rocking chair: it gives you something to do but never gets you anywhere?*" He smiled over at Janine, then abruptly stopped walking when he saw the silent tears coursing down her cheeks.

"Shit!" He immediately dropped their bags and pulled her

against him. "Hey, hey, hey," he soothed in a low tone as Janine began to cry in earnest.

He took her close-to-empty coffee cup from her hand and tossed it with effortless precision into a nearby trash bin. His sisters were right. He was an insensitive idiot. His words had been thoughtless and inconsiderate, and hadn't taken into account Janine's fragile emotional state or her significant sleep deprivation. "I wasn't thinking," he said, pressing his lips to her uninjured temple before adding, "I'm sorry if that came across harsh. It wasn't meant that way. Hey, now, sweetheart, don't cry."

"I'm *not* crying." Janine began digging through her pockets, finally finding a crumpled tissue. "Okay, I *am* crying, but I don't know *why* I'm crying," she said, wiping her nose. "I'm not a crier. I'm really not."

He gave her a tender smile as he cupped her face, forcing her to meet his gaze. "Give yourself a break. You're exhausted. The past thirty-six hours have been an emotional roller coaster. You're crying because you're worried about your stupid-ass cousin, and I said something idiotic. Janine honey, I'm sorry."

Dawson saw the apprehension and worry staining the luminous depths of Janine's shimmering eyes, the mahogany lashes wet with tears. It was impossible not to kiss her. He intended it to be tender, but her immediate and eager response had him instantly revved. The unpleasant and sudden blare of the PA system, the male voice heavily accented in what he knew was a northern Geordie accent, startled them apart.

When he lifted his head, he saw that her gaze was as liquid with desire as he was hard. He dropped his forehead to hers and breathed in the scent of her, making a concerted effort to dampen his ardour. But hell, she ignited him as easily as a match to dry tinder. "We're going to have to rescue your cousin soon, because I can't wait much longer to get you naked."

She gave him a wobbly smile and said, "Okay."

He planted a brief, hard kiss on her lips, then picked up their bags. He slung his own over his shoulder, but strategically carried Janine's in front of him. *God almighty, Delaney, you haven't had to conceal a boner in public in years. What the hell is wrong with you?*

As they resumed walking, he glanced at her. She gave him an amused smile, briefly dropping her gaze to the location of her bag.

Noticing a bank of restrooms, Janine said, "I better make a detour before we head out."

Dawson watched her disappear into the restroom, reminded of how she'd ditched him at Ivy's Pies. In case she was attempting the same feat, he kept his eyes trained on the entrance, at the same time focusing on what it would feel like to sink into the freezing depths of a glacier-fed lake. By the time Janine exited the ladies room, he had her bag over his free shoulder.

Janine looked energized when she rejoined him, as if her brief sojourn in the ladies room had been a rejuvenating experience. "I have a present for you," she announced, then amended her statement, her smile wide, "Well, for us."

He gave her a quizzical grin. "Oh?"

On her palm, she displayed a handful of neon-coloured, foil packets. "Did you know?" she informed him, tucking the items into her purse. "Condom dispensers have a slogan that says, *Fly safe, carry a condom*. I feel safe, now. Do you?"

"*Jesus,*" he said, shifting Janine's carry-on bag in front of him. "You'll be the death of me, woman."

Chapter 27

Janine had always found the English landscape thoroughly appealing no matter the county, but as they drove through the East Midlands, the scenery was devoid of its usual charm. Upon entering Nottingham's city limits, she barely gave the medieval castle that dominated the skyline, jutting up from the promontory known as Castle Rock, a cursory glance. Over the years, she'd learned interesting tidbits about her cousin's adopted city, like how in pre-Saxon times it had been known as 'Snottingham' and, more recently, its classification as a UNESCO city of literature, but these details held no appeal in light of her concern for Kevin.

It was early afternoon, twenty-two hours since Janine had been ordered by the man on the phone to deliver the coin. They'd made good time on the drive from Heathrow. She'd even slept for twenty minutes, and they'd stopped at a rest area. But the closer they got to Kevin's house, the more butterflies of worry flaked loose in her stomach.

Dawson navigated the black VW Golf onto Kevin's street, rolling slowly between the parked cars jammed into every conceivable space on both sides of the road. Kevin's house was the fifth in a row of eighteen two-bedroom terraced houses on the north side of the street. Most of the two-up-two-down units on either side of the road looked as neglected as Kevin's. When her cousin was first offered the job at Nottingham University, the fixer-upper had been the only option in his limited price range. He'd intended to modernize it but hadn't yet made any improvements.

Janine's gaze locked on her cousin's house as they slowly drove by, the cobblestones loud under their tires. Dawson had earlier warned her they wouldn't immediately park. He intended to observe from a distance and gather intel, whatever that meant. The drapes were open at both the front reception room and in Kevin's bedroom, but there was no detectable activity inside. She saw that the sentry-box-like structure that was his front porch seemed to be listing even more to the left than it had at Christmas. Directly below his front room window were nine large flagstones. Although she couldn't see from the street, she knew all were badly cracked and in need of replacement.

Dawson drove to the bottom of the street, turned the corner and went around the block, pulling over just before Kevin's street. From this vantage point, they could see the postage-stamp-sized walled gardens—a misnomer, in Janine's opinion, since none of these tiny paved areas boasted anything green or plant-like—behind the row of terraced houses. All were empty of activity, except for one near the bottom of the gently sloping incline where a toddler was pushing himself round and round on a wheeled plastic wagon.

Dawson re-started the Golf and once again turned into Kevin's street. A handful of houses beyond Kevin's, the driver of a parked car pulled out. Dawson nipped into the spot, parking with the driver's side half-on, half-off the sidewalk on Kevin's side of the street.

Janine immediately unclipped her seatbelt and reached for the door handle, but Dawson put out a hand to stop her from exiting, at the same time unclipping his own seatbelt and lowering their windows.

"Let's keep an eye on things for a bit," he stated, turning off the ignition and adjusting the angle of his side-view mirror. When she began to argue, he shook his head. "We can't go in blind. We don't know how many assholes might be there, or if they've got weapons. We made good time, so there's no reason to rush in half-cocked." He frowned, looking at the reflection in the rear-view, then the side-view, mirrors. "*If* anyone is even in there."

Janine trusted Dawson, but that didn't make the waiting any easier. She was picturing Kevin, hurt and bleeding, perhaps passed out on his sofa or in his bed, in dire need of medical attention. The longer they remained in the car, the longer her cousin went without care. Sighing, she adjusted her side-view mirror to an angle that allowed her to see the street directly in front of Kevin's house. There were a few trees and overgrown hedges on the street, but none blocked her view.

She frowned suddenly. "Wait. What do you mean, *if* anyone is even there."

He lifted a shoulder and said, "I'm pretty certain it's empty."

Janine looked over her right shoulder at the front of Kevin's house. "You can't know that."

Dawson also turned to look over his shoulder. His face, mere inches from hers, stirred an erotic memory of their intimacy in the cave. He'd shaved on the plane before they landed, but already she could see the hint of dark stubble on his jaw, heard the rasp of it as he idly scratched the underside of his chin with his thumbnail.

They both morphed into high alert when a car turned into the street, then relaxed as the vehicle drove past them. It stopped at the bottom of the road to let in a teenage girl. A moment later, the car turned left and disappeared from view.

"What makes you think Kevin's house is empty?" Janine asked.

"Let's just say it's a feeling I have."

Janine frowned as she stared at his profile. Nothing he did struck her as fanciful. Goofy yes, when he was relaxed, but she wouldn't have pegged him as someone who made non-empirical claims. "You have a *feeling* it's empty? And you're taking that seriously?"

Dawson glanced at her, unbothered by her incredulous tone. "Yup."

Well, *that* was interesting, Janine thought. She chewed on her lower lip, her gaze drifting back to the reflection in her side-view mirror as she thought about his claim. He'd probably had to trust his gut—or instinct, or whatever a person wanted to call it—a lot in his line of work. Even in her business, she'd learned to do the same. But *her* gut was guided by facts and figures and the expertise that came with experience. What Dawson was claiming was a stretch.

"So…you're basically saying you have a super power? Some kind of laser vision that allows you to penetrate brick walls?" She meant for her tone to be teasing, but it sounded disparaging.

Dawson chuckled, clearly unbothered, keeping his focus on the mirrors. "No. But I'd put money on Kev's house being empty."

She looked over her shoulder again. "So, you're saying Dick Irish isn't there, but neither is Kevin?"

Instead of answering, Dawson said, "Why not call Kevin's landline?"

Janine retrieved her phone, put it on speaker, and taped his number. They listened in silence to the characteristic double-rings until the answering machine clicked on.

"Do I leave a voicemail?"

"No."

She disconnected the line. "Can we go in now?"

Dawson made a sound of negation, keeping his eyes on the mirrors. "Let's wait a bit."

She sighed. *More waiting?*

His eyes still glued to the reflection in the rear-view mirror, Dawson asked, "Dick Irish-Asshole told you to answer the phone at Kev's at the twenty-four hour mark, right?"

"Yes, in two hours and…" Janine glanced at her Fitbit. "Make that one hour and fifty-six minutes."

"So…what's he planning? That's the question." Dawson was staring at the reflection in his side-view mirror, his right thumb distractedly tapping the steering wheel.

Five minutes passed in silence. She respected Dawson's willingness to trust his gut, she truly did, but Janine desperately needed to see for herself if her cousin's house was as empty as Dawson claimed. Impatient, she suggested, "Why don't I go knock?"

"We've already discussed this, Janine. There's no *I*. There's only *we*. Or, better yet, *me*."

Janine sighed. They hadn't *discussed* this topic, they'd *argued* about it. She'd wanted to approach Kevin's front door alone, as instructed, with Dawson in the car in case anything went sideways. He'd refused to entertain her suggestion.

When another minute passed, she asked, "So, if Kevin isn't in there, and Dick Irish isn't in there, where are they?" She touched a finger to her temple, absently aware of a mild headache. "What if Kevin is seriously hurt? Do you think they would bring him to a hospital? Oh, god," she uttered, her tone sharp, dropping her hands into her lap. "That's *ridiculous.* If they're the ones who beat him up, they sure as hell aren't going to bring him to the emergency room."

"Don't go worst case," Dawson reminded her in a gentle but firm tone, unpinning his gaze from the mirrors to regard her. He claimed her hand and gave it a reassuring squeeze. "Janine honey, stay focused on the facts."

"Yeah, well, that isn't bloody well working for me," she

grumbled, blinking back tears. "We don't *know* the facts, Dawson." She shook her head, dropping her free hand to the door handle. "I think we should go in. I really, really do. That's *my* gut talking."

"Whoa, heads up," Dawson said, looking over his shoulder.

Janine turned to do the same, her face close to Dawson's, deliberately anchoring herself in his unique scent as she watched a miniature black and grey car, a cross between a Smart car and a dune buggy, pull onto the flagstones in front of Kevin's house, stopping nose-to-nose with his porch. Had Kevin replaced his beat-up panel van with an electric car? In the same instant, Janine realized the driver was a woman.

"Hello, sweetheart," Dawson stated with undisguised interest. "Who might *you* be?"

Janine could only see her upper body as the woman stepped out of the car, but it was enough to conclude she was gorgeous. Her cascade of copper hair, glinting in the sunlight, fell in thick waves to mid-way down her back, framing a pale, pretty face. As she strode around the back of her car with the confidence of a super model, Janine's eyes widened at the sight of her flawless legs showcased to perfection by the high-heeled wedge sandals and a short, flared skirt.

At Kevin's front door, the woman tossed her gorgeous hair over one shoulder and dug into her cavernous bag. A moment later, she withdrew a key, opened the door, and disappeared inside.

Janine turned to regard Dawson. Although the woman could no longer be seen, he seemed transfixed, his gaze glued to Kevin's front door. Janine got the impression he'd been dazzled by that hair and those legs. *Don't be juvenile,* she scolded herself, remembering how silly she'd felt after she'd learned Joanie was his sister. But Dawson's gaze remained riveted on Kevin's house as if his vision really could penetrate brick.

"Who do you think she is?" Janine asked, hoping to break whatever spell had been cast on him.

At her words, Dawson abruptly turned and resettled in his seat. He gazed unseeingly out the windscreen as he tapped a thumb against the steering wheel. He didn't answer, and seemed to have forgotten her presence.

"Dawson?" Her voice was sharper than intended. Although he turned to face her, she could see his attention remained on the leggy woman inside Kevin's house.

"I want to meet her," he stated abruptly, practically vibrating with anticipation. "Don't you?"

Janine was about to add a disparaging remark that would've conveyed her admittedly juvenile jealousy, but Dawson was already rolling up the windows, almost leaping out of the car in his haste to meet the new arrival. She followed, dragging her feet. Her gut's message was loud and clear. This woman was nothing but trouble.

Chapter 28

The sun was warm against her back as Janine knocked on Kevin's front door. They'd left their jackets and overnight bags in the car, but she was still wearing the scarf and her cross-body purse. Dawson was standing an arm's length away from her, partially concealed by the jutting structure of the porch. Janine wondered if he didn't want the beautiful woman inside to think they were a couple.

You're not a couple, Janine hissed to herself. *Now, stop behaving like an insecure teenager.*

When the door opened, Janine was struck speechless for a brief moment as she gazed at the exquisitely beautiful woman. The woman's face had the sculpted bone structure of a Grecian goddess, with a flawless, alabaster complexion. The light dusting of freckles on her perfectly tilted nose and near her hairline enhanced her beauty rather than detracted from it. Her generous lips gleamed with a hint of gloss—the only obvious cosmetic Janine could detect. Her green eyes, framed by thick lashes a shade lighter than her vibrant hair, swept over Janine, one perfectly arched eyebrow lifting as if in triumph.

Before either woman could speak, Dawson moved to stand

beside Janine. The woman at the door seemed briefly taken aback, but in the next instant, her gaze transformed into warm pleasure.

Dawson, Janine saw, was grinning at the flawless creature like a besotted puppy. *Seriously? Your head is that easily turned?*

The woman, her attention back on Janine, said, "You must be Janine, Kevie's Canadian cousin, yeah?"

Now, wasn't *that* interesting? Her accent was as Irish as Dick Irish-Asshole's. Janine glanced at Dawson to see if he was thinking the same thing, but he didn't seem willing, or able, to tear his smitten gaze away from the vision at the door.

"Yes, I'm Kevin's cousin." Janine replied. Despite Dawson's previously stated belief that the house was empty, she added, "Is he here?"

The woman's eyes filled with moisture, making their green depths shimmer attractively. She addressed Dawson as if he'd asked the question. "I don't *know* where Kevie is," she stated in a soft, trembling voice. "He's not answering his mobile. I'm not sure if I should be worried."

"About Kev? You know him, always off digging in the dirt somewhere."

Dawson seemed eager to save the day and be proclaimed her hero, Janine thought, watching in silent misery as he fell under the woman's spell. What a fool she'd been to think she could hold the attention of a man like him, whose sexy James Bond vibe perfectly suited this exquisite Irish beauty. Sure, Janine had managed to capture his undivided attention when the two of them had been stranded in the woods, but that was likely attributable to adrenaline, which apparently did crazy things to a person's libido.

The woman turned to Janine and held out her hand to shake. "Pardon me! I've forgotten my manners. I'm Tiffany O'Sullivan, Kevie's girlfriend."

Janine forced herself to keep a neutral expression on her face as she shook the extended hand. Women flocked to her tall, ruggedly handsome cousin like moths to a flame, but he was generally oblivious. He'd had two long-term relationships since moving to the UK, both with scholars who shared his passion for archeology and fieldwork, and who dressed as he did, in cargo shorts, T-shirts, and hiking boots. Janine couldn't imagine someone like Tiffany catching Kevin's attention for longer than a millisecond.

Dawson introduced himself, making no effort to hide his pleasure at being the recipient of her attention.

Please, come in," she said, gesturing for them to follow her inside.

Janine met Dawson's gaze. He blinked slowly at her, then again. Shaking her head—the redhead's brazen sex appeal had clearly cast a spell of idiocy on him—she stepped into Kevin's cluttered reception room, taking perverse delight in blocking Dawson's view of the short skirt that swayed against the woman's disgustingly perfect thighs. Janine found herself feeling put out by the woman's sense of ownership of Kevin's house. Granted, she had a key, but still, it was annoying.

Inside the front room, Janine looked around as if half-expecting to see her cousin. The room, furnished with mismatched, salvaged cast-offs, was overflowing with Kevin's usual paraphernalia—textbooks, research papers, academic journals, and historical objects, some recognizable, others a mystery. Nothing looked different from her previous visit. The wall-to-wall carpet was still threadbare and stained, the lopsided, dented electric heater still stood in the unused hearth, the baseboards were still missing along one wall, and the striped wallpaper—trailing green vines on a faded two-tone merlot background—was still peeling at multiple join-lines.

"Excuse me a moment while I use the loo," she heard Dawson say.

At least the Irish beauty's presence hadn't completely addled his brain, Janine thought, knowing he would check the two small bedrooms and bathroom on the second floor—which the Brits called the first floor—to see if it was as empty as he'd predicted.

Familiar with the layout of her cousin's home, Janine moved through the reception room and poked her head into the kitchen at the back. It was also empty. Returning to the front room, Janine saw the message indicator light on Kevin's answering machine wasn't lit; yet, she knew Dawson had left more than one message for Kevin. Dick Irish must've deleted them.

Janine heard the toilet flush upstairs as she paused beside a Victorian-style armchair upholstered in faded green velvet, absently noting the frayed arms as she checked the time on her Fitbit. Ninety-one minutes until the scheduled phone call with Dick Irish. She regarded the woman, who was standing by the low, futon sofa rooting through her giant purse. When she pulled out a phone, tossing her purse onto the rickety side table where the old phone and answering machine sat, Janine's brain finally kicked in as she processed what the Irishwoman had said.

"Did you say Kevin's not answering his *mobile?*" Janine shook her head. "He doesn't have a cellphone."

The woman's smile was disdainful. "Perhaps I'm a good influence on him," she stated, the ice in her eyes melting as Dawson re-entered the room.

Dawson gave Janine a minute shake of his head, indicating that no one was upstairs, then tucked his hands into the back pockets of his jeans and rocked on his heels, beaming a smile at Tiffany.

"Why don't I fetch us some lagers," the woman volunteered. She didn't wait for their reply, instead turning and sashaying out of the room.

As soon as Tiffany and her legs disappeared, Janine whirled on Dawson. *"She's lying!* Kevin doesn't have a mobile. And *she's* not his girlfriend."

"I know," Dawson whispered back, keeping his eyes on the doorway into the kitchen.

Janine gaped at him, but he was addressing Tiffany as she re-entered the room, her phone in one hand and four tall beer cans yoked together with plastic packaging rings in the other.

"Please tell me you found that beer in the fridge," Dawson stated in an affable tone.

"You Americans," she teased, giving him an indulgent smile as she distributed the beers. "Shall we sit?" Tiffany asked, gesturing for Dawson to join her on the sofa.

Turning, Janine rolled her eyes as she removed a handful of academic journals—something with *Pontifical* in the title—from the Victorian armchair, then took a seat.

On the sofa, Dawson cracked open his beer and took a sip, then pulled a face. "Welcome to the land of warm beer." Despite his complaint, he took a second generous sip. Giving Tiffany an engaging smile, he asked, "How long have you been working to cure Kev of his Luddite ways?"

Tiffany took a delicate sip of her beer, then said, "I don't want to *cure* Kevie of anything. He's perfect just as he is."

Janine assumed it was deliberate on Tiffany's part that some of the froth clung to her upper lip. Because Dawson seemed fascinated by it, Janine's tone was edged with annoyance when she blurted, "Kevin doesn't have a girlfriend."

Granted, her cousin was appallingly bad at keeping in touch, so it was possible that he might have a new girlfriend. But not Tiffany. Janine couldn't picture her rumpled cousin dating a woman with such practiced polish and poise. Janine noted the darts in the Irishwoman's eyes, and wouldn't have been surprised if the redhead suddenly hissed and unsheathed a set of claws from under her perfectly manicured fingernails.

"Kevie and I are still in that new, special place," she informed Janine before turning to Dawson. "You know what that's like," she added, bestowing another high-wattage smile on him.

“So, when’s the last time you saw him?” Dawson asked.

“Yesterday morning. We were supposed to have dinner last night, and…” She lifted her hand and made a graceful gesture, at the same time shaking her head, her hair sweeping against her bare arms. “He didn’t show, but he sent me a text, so I know he’s okay. It’s just, he’s being so cryptic, and that’s not like Kevie, is it?”

Dawson shifted so he sat half-turned towards Tiffany on the low couch, his right arm slung across the back. “What do you mean by *cryptic?*”

“Here, I’ll let you read it.” Tiffany’s long hair fell forward as she tapped her phone, at the same time shifting to mirror Dawson’s pose, bumping knees with him.

“When did Kevin get a cellphone?” Janine demanded, her tone icy.

Tiffany flashed a humourless smile at her. “I may not have influenced him—*yet*—to reno, or,” she added with a smile at Dawson as she handed him her phone, “store the lager in the fridge. But do credit me with having some influence on that mulish cousin of yours.”

When Dawson cleared his throat loudly, Janine forced herself to withdraw her own dagger-throwing gaze from Tiffany and regard him. He gave her another of his intensely unfathomable looks before looking down at Tiffany’s phone. “He sent this last evening. *Tiff, darling, I’ve been delayed, and can’t meet at the restaurant as planned. Can we meet later? I’ll text you as soon as I can. Thanks, darling.*” Dawson lifted his head and met Janine’s gaze, adding, “He signed off with an I-heart-Tiff.”

“Yeah, he does that,” Tiffany stated, looking pleased with herself.

Janine coughed in response to the sound of retching in her head.

“Then there’s some from Tiffany,” Dawson stated for Janine’s benefit as he scrolled through the messages. “She’s wanting to know where he is, and asking him to call. Then another from Kev. This one just a couple hours ago. *Tiff darling, something's come up at work. I'll be busy until around ten tonight. Can you do me a favour? My cousin Janine, the one from Canada, will likely be arriving at my house soon. Can you meet her there? And ask her to meet me at the left lion tonight at ten. Tell her to bring the package. Janine will know what that means.*" Dawson looked up at Janine, adding, "He added another I-heart-Tiff."

Janine knew Kevin hadn't written those texts. For one thing, she couldn't picture him using the word 'darling' as an endearment, no matter how gorgeous the girl or how in love he was. It just didn't fit her cousin's profile. And, more importantly, he never called her 'Janine'. Ever. He either called her Jaynie or Jay-Jay.

Janine realized that, while she'd been distracted by her thoughts, Dawson had asked Tiffany why the texts between her and Kevin only went back a day. Tiffany was explaining she'd lost her mobile and replaced it only the day before.

When Tiffany held her hand out for her phone, Dawson returned it. "Wouldn't your previous text strings be in your cloud profile?"

She looked down at her phone, tapped a few times. "I haven't had time to check why they're not showing up," she stated, her tone frustrated. Tiffany shifted on the couch, her skirt revealing a few more inches of her endless legs.

When Dawson didn't pass up the invitation to look, Janine angrily plopped her unopened beer on a stack of books beside her chair. Women had built-in radar that recognized self-aggrandizing, manipulative predators like Tiffany, but men just got stupid. Janine knew for damn sure this woman was *not* Kevin's girlfriend. She didn't know why Tiffany was claiming to be her cousin's girlfriend, or why she was so intent on flirting with Dawson, but it had everything to do with Dick Irish, of that Janine was certain. Which, she also realized, made Tiffany dangerous. Perhaps Janine would be wise to tread carefully.

"Kevie and I share a fascination for Anglo-Saxon artifacts," Tiffany was telling Dawson. "That's how we met, at the Winfarthing Pendant exhibit at the University Museum. We've been inseparable ever since." She turned to Janine. "When I got that last text, I came rushing over here to meet you. Does his message make sense to you? Do you know what package he's talking about?"

In the next moment, the mobile in Tiffany's hand began emitting a whistling ringtone. Janine couldn't place the familiar tune at first, then realized it was the nurse whistle from the movie *Kill Bill*. Isn't *that* freaky, she thought.

"It's Kevin," Tiffany exclaimed. In her excitement, she fumbled the phone and dropped it; in her haste to retrieve it, she accidentally kicked it under the sofa.

Janine observed Tiffany's flustered attempts to retrieve her phone. Dawson had immediately dropped to his knees in front of the sofa and was trying to reach for the whistling phone, but Tiffany's frantic efforts somehow kept blocking him. By the time Tiffany retrieved it, the phone was silent.

"Shite!" Tiffany cursed, as they resumed their seats on the sofa. Tiffany stared at the screen, mumbling in an undertone, "Kevie, darling, leave a message."

When the phoned pinged indicating a voicemail, Tiffany made a pleased sound and tapped the screen, then rested the phone on the palm of her hand. They all leaned forward to listen.

The rumble of Kevin's deep voice was unmistakable. Janine looked over at Dawson, but he was frowning down at the phone and seemed unaware of Janine's intense stare.

"Tiff, tell Janine I'll explain everything when I see her, okay? Remind her to bring the package and meet me at the left lion at ten. That's the soonest I can get away. Thanks, darling. I'll be in touch again soon."

"Well, that's him alright," said Dawson, sounding pleased. He retrieved his can of beer and took a swig, then leaned back against the sofa, casually propping a boot against the cluttered coffee table. He lifted his brows as he looked at Janine and asked, "He sounds just fine. Right, *Jaynie?*"

Janine didn't know why Dawson would feel reassured by that message, or why he'd emphasized her name, but she, for one, was not soothed. "Why didn't he call *my* cell?" Janine challenged, retrieving it from her purse, the strap of which was still across her torso. She checked her phone for new messages. There were none. "Why call *her* if the message is for me?"

"He likely hasn't programmed your number into his mobile yet. Why don't you and I exchange numbers, yeah? That way I can reach you if Kevie texts me later."

It made sense, even if she didn't trust Tiffany. Regardless, she would delete the woman's info at the first opportunity.

After programming their phones with each other's numbers, Tiffany gave Dawson an expectant look. He shrugged. "I'm in the same boat as you. I lost my phone yesterday and haven't had time to replace it. You can reach me on Janine's phone."

Her brow creased in a delicate furrow, Tiffany asked, "Do you know what Kevie meant when he said, *bring the package?*"

"He can't mean the coffee you brought him, can he, *Jaynie?*"

"Uh…" she said.

Dawson suddenly yawned expansively. "Wow, that jet lag is catching up with me. I need a nap."

Tiffany glanced at her wristwatch, the robin's egg blue watch face an attractive pop of colour on her pale arm. "I should go. I don't want to be late for work."

Dawson, slouched wearily against the sofa, rolled his head to regard Tiffany. "Where do you work?"

"I waitress in a pub." She rested a hand on his forearm, and asked, "Do you know where the left lion is?"

When Dawson came to his feet, Tiffany's hand fell away.

"Sure. It's in the town square," he answered, his words muffled as he tried to swallow another expansive yawn.

Tiffany picked up her bag and tossed her phone into its cavernous depths, then unfolded her mile-long legs to stand beside Dawson. She took the few steps towards the small porch, gesturing gracefully towards the door. "I left Kevie's key in the door. You might as well keep it."

Janine had always thought it strange that, in the UK, most people locked themselves in, leaving their house key dangling from the inside key hole.

"Sure, thanks," Dawson said as he trailed after her, stopping when she turned to face him.

"Thank you, Dawson," she gushed. "I was so terribly concerned, but I'm not anymore. Not now you're here."

Janine succumbed to a fit of coughing.

Both Dawson and Tiffany turned to eye her. Dawson said, "You okay, *Jaynie?*"

"Yup, fine. Don't mind me," Janine croaked, reaching for her can of beer and cracking it open.

"Well, good-bye then, Janine," Tiffany said, waggling her fingers. "It was nice to meet you."

Janine stood up and lifted her beer can in salute. "You, too. Good-bye." *Good riddance, more like.*

Tiffany gave Dawson one last smile before moving into the porch and exiting the house.

Janine heard the sound of Dawson turning the key in the lock before he stepped back into the room and moved to the window to watch Tiffany. She watched him lift a hand in farewell. She didn't hear the sound of the electric car leaving, but assumed it had when Dawson turned and addressed her.

"So, tell me," he asked in a disgusted tone. "Do we *look* stupid?"

Chapter 29

Dawson saw Janine's eyes widen in confused surprise.

"What?" she said, absently tucking her phone into her right back jeans pocket.

"She thinks we're stupid," Dawson restated as he approached her. "Although, that's entirely to our advantage. But still. It's irksome."

Janine set her beer onto the tower of books beside her chair. "What are you talking about?" she demanded, confronting him.

Dawson made a noise of disgust. "That woman is as fake as my niece's stuffed unicorn," he said. He lifted a hand to tuck a stray strand of her hair behind her ear, but she jerked away from his touch. He dropped his hand and grinned at her. "You were irked, too," he stated, doing nothing to hide his amusement. "You're shockingly gullible, Janine. I think it's on account of not having siblings. You were never teased as a child, were you?"

"What are you *talking* about?" Janine snapped. She lifted the strap of her purse over her head and impatiently tossed it into her chair, then did the same with the long scarf.

Oh, yeah, Dawson applauded silently. Aloud he said, "She thinks we're stupid."

"I heard you the first time. Are you telling me you *knew* she was manipulating you?" Janine demanded, turning to face him as she rested her hands on her hips.

He snorted. "What do you take me for?"

Janine stared at him in open-mouthed astonishment. "*All along?*"

"Yes, all along. She was manipulating both of us." His grin was mischievous. "You were awesome, *pretending* to be jealous. She totally fell for it." In response to the doubt in her eyes, he said, "Oh, come on, Janine. I know we haven't known each other long—as adults, at least—but you can't believe I'm one of those brain-in-the-dick guys who falls under the spell of a cold-blooded viper like that, do you?" He registered Janine's shifting emotions, from annoyance and doubt to chagrin and then mortification.

She dropped her face into her hands. "Oh god. I'm such an idiot," she said, her words muffled.

Dawson gently took her wrists in his hands, remaining silent until she looked up and met his gaze. "No, you're not. Okay, so maybe you weren't *pretending* to be annoyed, and I'm sorry about that. But I had to let her think I was susceptible to her charms, and your reaction helped cement that." He wrapped her in the cocoon of his arms, enjoying the feel of her in his arms, her head under his chin, her palms resting lightly on his chest. She was the perfect fit. "Don't you know, I only fall for women with intelligence, warmth, wit, and beauty all rolled into one?" Dawson realized he'd just inadvertently confessed to falling for her. He hadn't *meant* to use that word, although it was entirely accurate, but she gave no indication she'd even registered his word choice.

Her face had been hidden, but when she lifted her head and looked at him, he saw she was focused on her own whirling kaleidoscope of emotions. He gazed into her solemn eyes, the brown depths a thousand times more appealing than the green ice in Tiffany's. He ran his palms down her straight hair, continuing down her back, letting his hands rest on the inward curve of her waist. "Look, no one would deny she's beautiful." Dawson lifted a hand and gently traced the tip of his finger along Janine's jawline. "But she doesn't hold a candle to you. Any man with half a brain can see she's got more frost in her veins than an iceberg. She tries to camouflage it, but I saw through her the second she stepped out of her car."

Janine rolled her eyes. "I was convinced you were completely enamoured. *She's* convinced, too."

"And that's a *good* thing. You see that, don't you? It's leverage. And anyway, didn't you get my signal?"

"What signal?"

Dawson gave her an intent look, blinked slowly once, then a second time. He'd performed the same action just before they'd followed Tiffany into the house.

"That?" Janine flattened her palms against his chest and tried to push away, but he tightened his hold on her waist. "That was your *signal?"*

"Yeah. I thought you saw it, understood what I meant."

"Yes, I saw it. I assumed it meant your brain was addled." She shook her head at him. "It was a little on the subtle side, don't you think?"

He chuckled, taking her hands and lifting them to his neck, inviting her to keep them there. He dropped his own hands to her waist again and pulled her close, wiggling his eyebrows in mock seduction. "Once you get to know me better, you'll be able to read *all* my signals." He bent his head and trailed his lips along her collarbone, loving the sound of her soft sigh as she tilted her head to improve his access. The heat between them was like a radar signal sending out a continuous pulse at two-second intervals. "Are you reading this signal?" he asked, his tone teasingly low.

When Janine pushed out of his embrace, he let her go. She was still too rattled, he realized, to be distracted by his lame attempts at either humour or seduction.

"We need to figure out what to do, Dawson," she stated in a no-nonsense tone. "Kevin isn't here; so, where is he? And you do realize that Tiffany and Dick Irish are, if not related, then in cahoots, right?" Janine looked contemplative as another thought came to her. "Will Dick Irish still phone in…" She looked at her Fitbit, "forty-seven minutes? And why do they want us to meet Kevin at the left lion at 10:00 pm? Why not now? What's going to happen at 10:00?"

Dawson moved across the room and retrieved his beer. He watched Janine as he sipped the lukewarm beverage, waiting for her to run out of questions. When she looked at him expectantly, he replied, "Dick Irish-Asshole will still call. And he'll tell you to meet him, only the time he offers will be *after* 10:00 pm."

Janine frowned, shaking her head. "I don't follow."

"Because they suspected I might be with you, and because my presence is a game-changer, they need time to refine Plan B. Tiffany didn't leave because she has a job in a pub." He snorted and shook his head. "I mean, who wears a wristwatch worth ten grand and works as a waitress? She really does think we're stupid. No, she left to debrief with Dick Irish-Asshole. Scheduling a meet for 10:00 pm gives them time to plan their next move."

"So you agree they're collaborating?"

"Oh yeah," Dawson said, trying not to get distracted by the way Janine was chewing on her bottom lip. "They expected me to be with you, despite Dick Irish-Asshole's threats to you. They also assumed I'm heterosexual and therefore susceptible to a woman's charms. That's why they sent drop-dead gorgeous Tiffany—to spin her web and catch a sycophant. She thinks she's succeeded. So, yes, Dick Irish-Asshole will phone at the scheduled time. When he does, he won't mention me. He'll give a location for a bogus meet, but it will be *after* our scheduled meet at the left lion, which, by the way, won't be with Kev but with Tiffany and Dick Irish-Asshole."

Janine had been nodding as she followed along with Dawson's logic. She absently picked up her beer and took a swig, then pulled a face. "God, this is disgusting! I need a coffee," she said, turning and heading into the kitchen.

Chapter 30

Dawson followed Janine into the kitchen. Leaning a shoulder against the wall beside the miniature table with its two plastic chairs tucked under it, he appreciatively eyed her curves as she opened a cupboard. Failing to find what she was looking for, she opened another.

He wished he could take her by the hand and lead her up that narrow staircase to the nearest bed, peel off her clothes, and make love to her. More than 24 hours had passed since he'd last had his hands on her, and he'd been walking around with a semi-boner ever since. Not that he wasn't worried about Kevin. He was. Absolutely. And he remained wholly dedicated to helping resolve whatever trouble Kevin had gotten himself into. But needing to find Kevin didn't stop him from wanting Janine. How could she not know that she was a hundred—a thousand—times sexier than Tiffany?

He watched with interest as Janine found a stainless-steel canister with a hinged locking clamp, then smiled when he heard her mutter, "There better be coffee in here, Kevin."

She gave an audible exclamation of relief as she opened the container. When she stuck her nose in the wide mouth of the jar and closed her eyes, taking a long sniff, she reminded him of a sommelier assessing wine, only she was doing it with coffee. She half-turned towards him, still focused on assessing the quality and freshness of the tin's contents. Her eyes, he saw, had a far-away, almost glazed expression.

Dawson couldn't help but picture her with the same unfocused expression at the same counter, only in his mind she was naked, and he was inside her. He was listening as she told him about coffee, but he was distracted by the images in his mind, seeing himself cup the weight of her breasts in his palms as he dipped his head, first to one hard nipple, then the other, all the while revelling in the sounds she made at the back of her throat as she moaned her pleasure. *Jesus!* He was getting hard just thinking about it.

Dawson surreptitiously adjusted his jeans and shook his head to clear the distracting image from his mind, scolding away his lascivious thoughts.

"It's important to store coffee properly even if you don't buy the best quality." Janine was saying. She moved aside the clutter of dirty dishes on Kevin's kitchen counter so she could reach the old-style drip coffee machine. She plugged it in, then filled the pot with water. "Too many people don't store the grinds correctly," she continued. "Never keep coffee in a clear jar—the light will compromise the taste—or in a cupboard near the stove. It's too warm." After pouring water into the coffee machine's reservoir, she opened all three drawers in the small kitchen before locating the filters. "And don't leave the canister on the counter, even one as high quality as this one. Strong sunlight will warm it. Coffee needs to be stored in a cool place—but not the fridge," she amended, "That's too cold."

She glanced over her shoulder at him, then stopped when she noticed how intently he was regarding her. "What?" she asked, clearly self-conscious.

Dawson liked hearing her talk about coffee. Her voice and

tone conveyed her passion for the subject. It was sexy as hell. "And? Was it stored correctly?"

Janine smiled as she measured the coffee grinds. "It was. This canister is designed with a one-way, air-tight valve to vent trapped CO_2 gas, which would otherwise destroy the flavour. The silicone seal—BPA-free—and the locking clamp stops air and light entering. That's key. Moisture is anathema to good coffee."

Dawson drained his can of beer, depositing the empty on the table. "I would've thought Kev would care more about storing his beer in the fridge than storing coffee in an expensive canister."

"Oh, I bought this canister. And I made him promise to purchase only good quality coffee. There," Janine said, pressing the button to start the drip. She turned and faced Dawson, glancing at her Fitbit before crossing her arms and leaning her butt against the counter.

"ETC?" he asked.

She cocked her head to the side as she smiled at him. "Estimated time of call?" At his nod, she added, "Thirty-six minutes. So, now what?"

"Now?" In two strides he was across the room, finally losing himself in the taste of her mouth. She'd only had a few sips of the warm beer, but on her tongue it was sweet nectar. He was an addict and she was his drug of choice.

She was kissing him back, her ardour matching his, her fingers on his scalp practically making his eyes roll back in his head in bliss. His hands filled with her breasts, his thumbs teasing her nipples through the fabric of her T-shirt and bra. The sound of her soft, purring moan against his mouth ignited a pulsing need in his crotch. She arched her own need against his. Jesus, but he loved her lack of inhibition. He wanted her naked, wanted to lick, tease, and suckle every inch of her.

He tore his lips from hers and lifted his head, his gaze

falling to her swollen lips before lifting his eyes to meet hers. The haze of desire had turned their soft brown depths into a mesmerizing velvet abyss he'd happily get lost in. "God, woman," he whispered. "You kill me."

He dropped his head, trailing kisses down the column of her long neck, shifting lower until his mouth joined his hands at her breasts, his lips mouthing a hardened nipple. She arched her back, her fingers in his hair sending sizzling currents of electricity from his head to his toes. The taste of her through two layers of fabric was freaking fantastic, but it wasn't enough. He was about to lift her T-shirt, but she pushed him away, sidling out of his embrace.

"Kevin," she gasped.

Startled, Dawson looked behind them, expecting to see her cousin, but the room was empty.

"No, I mean…" Janine's right hand clutched the edge of the kitchen counter as if it was the only thing holding her up. When he reached for her, she side-stepped and held up her left hand like a traffic cop halting a line of vehicles. "We can't." she repeated, glancing at her Fitbit. "He'll be calling in… thirty-two minutes. We need a plan. I mean, do I…?"

When she paused, taking in a deep breath, his eyes fell to the delectable patch of wet on her breast. She seemed unaware of the mark his mouth and tongue had made, but he found it mesmerizing.

"Do I mention you?" She turned and opened a cupboard door, reaching with both hands to retrieve two mugs.

Dawson couldn't help himself, the curves of her silhouette too tempting to resist. He stepped behind her, lifting his hands to cup her breasts, loving the feel of her perfect, jean-clad ass against his crotch.

He felt her shiver as he feathered his lips against the skin at the base of her neck, letting his hands explore the contours of her breasts. He wanted her naked, wanted to tweak her hard nipples with his hands and his wet tongue.

She dropped her arms, placing the mugs on the counter. He assumed she'd push him away again—she would be right to do so. They needed to talk about what Dick Irish-Asshole would likely say when he called. But she didn't; instead, she rested the back of her head against his shoulder and placed her hands on top of his. He hissed out a breath as she urged him to caress her curves far more roughly than he would've on his own. *Jesus, she was so goddamn sexy.*

"Your hands," she moaned.

"What about my hands?" he growled, his voice hoarse with desire as he nibbled her neck.

"They're magic." She raised an arm to tangle her fingers in his hair, which lifted her breasts in silent invitation for further exploration.

He lifted the hem of her shirt high, exposing the barely contained swell of her breasts in a white, lace bra. His cock surged in response to the glorious sight. He dipped his hand into one of the cups, groaning at the feel of her bare nipple between his exploring fingers. "You scramble my goddamn brain. I haven't been this horny since…" He pictured fifteen-year-old Janine in her cut-off shorts and girls-gone-wild tank top. No way was he admitting to *that.* He'd sound like a lecherous pervert.

The coffee pot gurgled loudly, signalling the end of its drip cycle. This time he was the one who tore himself away, stepping back until he was leaning his butt against the back of a kitchen chair, his hands gripping the chairback behind him.

"Jesus," he said again, eyeing Janine as she adjusted her shirt and turned to face him. He saw her eyes drop to the bulge in his pants. Having her heated gaze practically salivating over his obvious arousal was not helping. Not helping at all. They needed to cool things down, not heat them up. He needed to focus on…Jesus, his brain was a fucking fog. What did he need to focus on?

Kevin! Right. Nothing sexy about Kevin's mess. What other

non-sexy images could he inject into his brain? He pictured Tiffany. *Perfect*! Definitely nothing sexy about brittle-as-ice Tiffany. His pounding pulse begin to slow.

"Coffee?" Janine squeaked.

"Yes, please," Dawson said, his tone über polite. He turned, pulled out a chair and took a seat.

"Black, right?"

"Yup," he answered, realizing she remembered this from their refreshments on the plane.

He noticed the faint tremble in her hands as she placed a mug of coffee on the table in front of him, knew she was likely as wet now as she'd been that morning in the cave. He wanted to pull her onto his lap and bury his fingers in her slick depths, then replace his fingers with his cock. *Not helping!* he scolded himself.

The fact that he kept his hands to himself instead of grabbing her was a minor freaking miracle. He reached for the coffee, took a too-large gulp, then slammed it back onto the table, sloshing coffee over the rim. *"Fuck.* Hot. Jesus!"

Janine gave him an amused look from where she stood by the half-sized fridge splashing milk from a glass pint into her coffee.

He scowled at her in mock anger. "Just so you know, I bought *two* boxes of condoms at Ivy's Pies. And I intend to run out of those real quick."

Janine raised an eyebrow. "And where are they now?"

Dawson's expression darkened. *They were in the goddamn car.*

Janine grinned, clearly enjoying herself. "Seems that's a bad habit of yours, not having condoms when you need them."

"Ha, ha," he said, unamused.

"Well…not that we're going to have sex right now, because we're not, but…just so you know…" Janine patted the left back pocket of her jeans before taking the seat on Dawson's left.

Dawson dropped his forehead to the table and groaned. "Jesus," he said, his voice muffled. She'd had the foresight to put one of those god-awful neon condoms she'd purchased at the airport into the pocket of her jeans. He sat up as an idea came to him. "How much time until the call?"

Janine glanced at her Fitbit. "Twenty-nine minutes."

"That's plenty. Nine minutes to fuck. Twenty to plan." He was kidding, but it seemed Janine was actually considering his proposal, so he quickly added, "We'll both be better able to focus if we…"

His words were cut off by the loud pinging of her phone.

Chapter 31

The message was sent from Kevin's fake cell, and its arrival sobered them, forcing them to focus on the task at hand.

Janine read the text aloud. *Hi Janine! Tiff let me know you arrived. Sorry I wasn't there. Am looking fwd to seeing you tonight. Did you bring the coin? We'll catch up over a pint later, k?*

"This is *not* from Kevin," Janine stated, shaking her head emphatically.

She eyed Dawson as he got up and started scrounging through the cupboards, returning to the table with two bags of chips, what Kevin now called crisps. He opened both, set them on the table within her reach, shoved a handful into his mouth, and held out his free hand for her phone. He silently re-read the text as he munched on the chips, at the same time reaching into the bag and tossing another handful into his mouth. After wiping his greasy fingers on his jeans, he used both thumbs to type a response. He didn't send it but handed the phone back to Janine.

She read his response out loud. "*Of course I have it. But Kevin, where are you?!! I'm worried!!!!* She looked up at Dawson. "Hit send?"

At his nod, she sent it, then looked at her watch and announced, "Twenty-two minutes."

Dawson got up again, saying, "The text messages on Tiffany's phone, they weren't from Kev either." He topped up their mugs with coffee from the pot, then retrieved the milk and dabbled another few drops into Janine's mug. "You know that, right?"

"Tiff, *darling*? My cousin, *Janine*? Signing off with an I-*heart*-Tiff?" Janine blew a raspberry.

Dawson chuckled as he put away the pint of milk, then grabbed both open bags of crisps in one hand and his coffee mug in the other, jerking his head towards the front room. "Come on. Let's Google Tiffany."

Janine settled on the sofa beside Dawson, Kevin's landline phone on her right. "Kevin's not the type to *darling* anyone," she added as she typed Tiffany's name into the browser.

Dawson crunched a mouthful of chips, then added, "He's more the *hey-babe* type."

Janine nodded. "And even if he did buy a cellphone—which he didn't or he would've told me—he'd *never* use emoticons. *I-heart-Tiff*, my ass!"

Janine found a Facebook and a Linked-In site, shifting closer to Dawson so he could more easily read her screen. The Linked-In profile gave Tiffany's job title—vice-president of acquisitions at O'Sullivan Auctioneers—and described the business as an antiquities auctioneer in London specializing in rare finds. Strangely, the most recent post on Tiffany's Facebook page was eighteen months old. Prior to that, her posts showed a mixture of personal and business activities, glamorous holidays, evenings out, auctions, antiquities fairs, and museum shows.

"What happened eighteen months ago that made her stop posting to Facebook?"

"I was wondering the same thing," Janine said, tossing her

phone onto the cushions between them and snagging a handful of chips.

"Do you mind if I contact someone?" Dawson asked, picking up the phone.

"Not at all. Your sister?"

Dawson shook his head. "No. A buddy of mind who's a whiz at overturning rocks."

"An investigator with the Secret Service?"

"A military lawyer with the JAG corps."

Balancing her mug carefully on her knee as she reached for another handful of chips, Janine asked, "You think he can dig up some dirt on Tiffany?"

"For sure. I'll also ask him to research *Rex Alfred* coins."

"So, it's total bogus she lost her phone, right?" Janine bit into a chip.

"Uh-huh." After sending the email, he set the phone down and grabbed another handful of crisps.

Janine crunched the remainder of her chip, then asked, "But what about the phone call? How did she fake that?"

"Did anything about our Tiffany suggest she was a klutz?"

Janine pictured her. "No," she answered. "So…you think Dick Irish and Tiffany had a pre-arranged time for the phone call?"

"I think she sent a text to Dick Irish-Asshole when she got the beer. Something like, *call in ten.*"

"Ah," Janine said, nodding. "And when it rang, Tiffany deliberately fumbled the phone. But does that mean Kevin is with Dick Irish and was being forced to leave that message?"

Dawson had been nodding, but now he shook his head, taking a sip of his coffee before saying, "That was a recording. Had to be."

Janine stared down at her coffee as her brain sorted out the jumbled puzzle pieces. The biggest question still remained: Where was her cousin? Somewhere in Nottingham? And wherever he was, was he badly hurt? An alarming thought suddenly occurred to her. She turned to Dawson. "Do you think it's a recording because Kevin is…" She couldn't say it, but her vision blurred as her eyes filled with moisture.

Dawson rested his hand on her leg and spoke with firm reassurance. "Don't go there, honey. It won't help us find him."

She nodded, taking a moment to regain her composure. With her voice once again steady, she said, "Okay, so they suspected you would accompany me. Which meant they never intended for Kevin or Dick Irish to be here when I arrived, right?"

Dawson nodded, setting his empty mug on a book whose cover depicted colourful Medieval scrollwork.

Janine emptied her coffee, set her mug on the end table, then checked the time. "Five minutes," she announced, turning the timer on her Fitbit off. "So, do I negotiate?"

Dawson shook his head. "No point. Agree to whatever he says. Keep the call short." He picked up one of the bags of crisps, looked inside, then fished out the last few crumbs, then picked up the other bag. "Do you mind if I finish these off?" At her inviting gesture, he made short work of the remaining contents.

"And after that? Then what?"

"We need to recon the location of the left lion before it gets dark. You know it's a statue at the city hall building, right?" He looked longingly into the empty bag, adding, "And we need to eat something more substantial than *crisps*. Kevin *never* has any decent food in his kitchen."

Kevin's phone rang then, two short rings in quick succession.

Tossing aside the empty bag, Dawson sat up and levelled his intense gaze at Janine. "Ready?" he asked.

She nodded, then turned and picked up the receiver, holding it tilted at her ear so Dawson could listen in.

"Hello?"

Janine recognized the man's voice. It no longer held an amused lilt, which was confirmation that Tiffany had brought him up to speed about Dawson's presence.

"Do you have the package?" the man demanded.

"I do, yes."

"Bring it to the Jerusalem at half-ten. You know it?"

Janine knew the pub. Its full name was *Ye Olde Trip To Jerusalem.* It was built on the foundation rocks of Nottingham Castle, which towered on a cliff above the pub. The famous landmark made the claim of being England's oldest inn, a resting place for the pilgrims and crusaders on their journeys to Jerusalem. His request to meet at half-ten, thirty minutes *after* the meet with Kevin, meant Dawson's prediction was correct.

"I know it. I'll be there."

"You better be," the man said, then hung up.

Janine replaced the receiver.

Dawson pumped his fist into the air. "Yes! Did you hear him? He is *pissed.* He's so fucking pissed, he can barely get the words out."

"And that's *good* news? What if he takes it out on Kevin?"

Dawson's glee immediately evaporated. He leaned forward, resting his elbows on his knees as he ran his fingers through his hair. "Yeah. *Fuck.*" He stared moodily into the distance, then turned to Janine. "Assuming there are more coins at the dig site, wherever it is, they must be worth a small fortune."

Janine nodded, chewed on her lip for a moment, then said, "So, his plan A was for me to come alone. Then he'd basically drag me off to wherever he's holding Kevin and threaten to do me harm unless Kevin tells him where he found the coin, right?"

"That's my guess," Dawson said. "Because you didn't conveniently walk into that trap, he's launched plan B."

"And plan B is to kidnap me at the left lion? Then accomplish the same goal as Plan A, using me as leverage to make Kevin tell them where he found the coin?"

"Yes." Dawson's expression was somber as he frowned. "It makes no sense, though. From what I remember of the town square, it's too open, too public, even at 10:00 pm."

Janine was still confused. "So, they think we believe everything Tiffany told us about her being Kevin's girlfriend, and about Kevin not being able to get away from work until late this evening."

"They think we're stupid," Dawson said, shaking his head in disgust. "They don't know that *we* know that Tiffany is working with Dick Irish-Asshole."

"So, they think we believe we're going to meet Kevin at the left lion tonight?"

"Uh-huh."

Janine frowned at him. "But, Dawson, why did Dick Irish even bother to phone? Why even tell me to meet him?"

"Two reasons. First, he told you he would ring at the 24-hour mark, so he needed to follow through with that. Second, he wants you to feel safe, let your guard down. He thinks—because of Tiffany's visit—that *you* think you're meeting Kev at 10:00 pm tonight at the left lion. He's assuming you and I are devising a plan where Kev joins us at the *Jerusalem* to sort out once and for all the ownership of the package Kev sent you."

Janine was beyond grateful Dawson had used whatever connections were open to him to ensure he got on that plane with her. She couldn't imagine having to navigate this mess on her own. She regarded him in silence for a moment, then asked in a resigned tone, "It's wishful thinking on my part to hope Kevin will be at the left lion, right?"

Dawson nodded his head. "Yeah. Sorry." He rubbed his palms over his face, then said, "I'm missing something, though. But for the life of me I can't think what it is."

Janine stared glumly into space, then said, "If Tiffany and

Bart are creating all these hoops for us to jump through, that must mean Kevin still isn't talking, right?"

"He must not be. And without you, they don't have leverage."

"Not true," Janine said, frowning at Dawson. "They have Kevin. I call that leverage." Janine rubbed her fingers on her temples, hating the thought of *persuasive fists* trying to get Kevin to talk. She checked the time. "It's just after 4:00 now, which gives us six hours—" She shrieked when Dawson pounced on her.

"To get naked?" he stated, his tone hopeful. "That's how you were going to end that sentence, right?"

Janine found herself considering having sex with Dawson, simply for the distraction. Well, that and it would probably be beyond amazing. He surprised her when he gave her a perfunctory kiss and got to his feet.

"As much as I hate to say it, we have to go. We need to recon the location in daylight."

Janine's priority was—absolutely, positively—finding her cousin. *Unequivocally*. But had Dawson kissed her for one second longer, she knew without a doubt she would've made a grab for that neon pink condom tucked into her back pocket.

Chapter 32

Nottingham's iconic Council House with its sprawling square was humming with late afternoon activity. Janine always enjoyed a visit to the square, but she found it most charming at night when the ground-level arches of Council House were bathed with warm yellow lights and the impressive central dome—two hundred feet above—glowed with a pale amethyst hue that became a deep magenta in full dark. Her favourite vantage point was from the opposite end of the square where the shallow water feature reflected the dome's light. The previous year when Janine visited Kevin at Christmas, she'd been delighted to see the square transformed into an ice rink flanked by rows of delightful market stalls.

Although Janine was familiar with the huge market square and its wide selection of bars, restaurants, and shops, this time she was viewing it through Dawson's eyes. His inspection assessed every detail, including pointing out to her where a person could be concealed in the dark shadows come nightfall.

He gave particular attention to the two stone lions lounging on their rectangular bases at either side of the steps leading up to the Council House. They weren't massive, their backs only as high as the top of his head. Mirror images of each other, the statues were positioned on their stomachs with their forepaws crossed, looking out into the square with what Janine had always thought were mournful expressions, as if resigned under duress to their busy, urban location. For some unfathomable reason, the left lion had become a popular meeting place.

When Little John—the deep-sounding clock bell in the Council House dome—chimed six bells, Dawson called it quits and suggested they find a pub and have a meal. Janine knew she wouldn't be able to get a decent cup of coffee in a pub, and instead suggested they dine at 200 Degrees Coffee Shop & Barista, telling Dawson that their homemade soups, sandwiches, and baking were bar none, as was their coffee. The restaurant was located in Nottingham's Flying Horse Walk, kitty-corner from the square.

On her previous visits, Janine never failed to frequent 200 Degrees, which also housed a barista school. She'd once taken a course in latte art, subsequently wowing her Whistler customers with micro-foam swans and elaborate leaf designs. In fact, her ideas for expanding Café Art were inspired by Nottingham's successful barista school.

Janine led the way to the 300-year-old Tudor-style building. Once inside she paused, breathing in the fecund fragrance of quality coffee. The décor was as welcoming as she remembered, its rich wood paneling and saloon-style bar original features, she knew, from when the venue had been the Flying Horse Hotel. As expected, the food was artfully and thoughtfully displayed. Janine ordered the ham, cheddar, and apple baguette, while Dawson chose the sausage and stilton with a slice of salted caramel cake. After paying for their order, they took seats at a table by the window looking out at the retail shops on the street level of the Council House.

After they finished their sandwiches, and while Dawson made short work of his dessert, Janine went back to the counter and ordered a flat white for herself and an americano for Dawson, chatting with the barista while the drinks were being prepared. Rejoining Dawson, she showed off the multi-leaf foam art decorating her beverage, then couldn't help but close her eyes in pleasure as she savoured her first sip of the expertly brewed beverage.

"IF FOR ANY REASON WE GET SEPARATED, HEAD TO THE nearest group of people, okay?" Dawson told her. "Ask them to wait with you until you're in a cab, then go to the Premier Inn. If I can't meet you there within a day, go to the Canadian Embassy in London and tell them everything."

He frowned at Janine. She was nodding her agreement, but it felt like she was humouring him, which irked him. He liked that she was self-sufficient, smart, and knew her own mind, but in this case, she needed to abide by his rules.

His annoyance evaporated as he saw her eyes briefly close. He got a kick out of watching her love affair with coffee; actually, he got a kick out of watching her, full stop. He liked her expressive face, liked the way her eyes sparkled or darkened depending on what she was thinking. The longer they spent together, the more his admiration for her grew. She could've complained during their wet, nighttime trek through the woods, but she hadn't. Since bundling her into his van, she'd exhibited strength, courage, determination, sharp wit, and resourcefulness. He especially liked her unapologetically healthy appetite for sex. *God, he liked everything about her.* He couldn't think of anything he *didn't* like.

"What are you smiling at?" she asked, interrupting his thoughts.

Was he smiling? He hadn't realized. "You," he answered, without hesitation.

She coloured slightly at his forthright response. He knew she thought he'd been thinking about sex. His smile turned into a teasing grin as he watched her. "I wasn't smiling about *that*...although I am now." That wasn't entirely true. He had been thinking about sex, but he'd been thinking of it as one thing in a long list of things he liked about her. But now, because of her response, he was *only* thinking about sex.

He watched as she buried her face in the steam rising from her coffee, and knew she was averting her gaze because of the warning he'd given her on the mountainside. *The next time you look at me like that, with that come-fuck-me look in your eyes, make damn sure you've got a condom.*

He chuckled as he captured her free hand. He waited for her to meet his gaze before he started speaking. "I was thinking about how amazing you've been. A lot of people would've fallen apart, you know. As my grandmother would say, you've been a real trooper." It was so easy to lose himself in the warm depths of her gorgeous brown eyes. "I want you to know that being here with you, crazy Kev scenario aside, beats the hell out of camping in the Cascades." Dawson brushed his lips across her knuckles, imaging where his lips would like to stray. "That's why I *was* smiling. But now I'm smiling because I'm picturing you naked."

She shook her head at him, giving him an indulgent smile. "Shouldn't we be focusing on Kevin, and on what we can anticipate will happen at 10:00 pm?

Releasing her hand, he leaned back in his chair. Picking up his coffee and eyeing her over the rim, he said, "Righty then. Hocus, pocus, focus." She looked intrigued, which is exactly what he'd intended.

"Hocus, pocus, focus?" she asked.

He took a sip, then said, "It's what I say to my nieces when I'm babysitting and I need them to chill. You know, dinner time, bath time, bed time, clean-up-the-toys time." He gestured with his hand as if waving a wand. "Hocus, pocus, focus."

"You *babysit?*"

"I'll have you know I'm a devoted uncle."

"Somehow that doesn't surprise me." She paused, and when she resumed speaking, her tone was tentative. "You're also a devoted friend. Tell me if it's not okay to ask this, but I seem to recall that you and Kevin had a falling out right before you finished university. Kevin wouldn't give me any details, but I know it had something to do with a woman. What happened?"

Dawson grimaced. "You know how guys have this rule that your buddies aren't allowed to date your sisters?"

"Yeah, but why is that?" Janine asked, looking genuinely perplexed.

He flashed a humourless grin. "Because the person who knows best what kind of bastard a guy can be is his best friend. I made the mistake of thinking it was okay for Kev to date Joanie."

Janine's eyebrows raised. "Your sister? I didn't know that. And he broke her heart and you hated him for it?"

"No." Dawson gave her a sheepish smile, watching with amusement as she finished her coffee, then gazed into the cup as if hoping another drop or two would magically materialize. "Just the opposite. Joanie broke *his* heart. Dumped him flat just before we graduated from UW when she met Patrick—who's now her husband, by the way, and my business partner." He shook his head in a show of disgust. "She cheated on Kev, and I was furious with her. Kev was devastated. I know she still feels bad about that. Back then, being around me only made him feel worse. When he first moved to England for grad school, we lost touch. Early in 2010, I was here planning security for the Olympics. I had a few spare days and looked him up. We had a great time together. I've seen him fairly often since then."

Memories of how much he'd relied on Kev's friendship in the darkest months following Cassie's death momentarily distracted him. *Hocus, pocus, focus,* he chanted to himself, then added, "Neither of us will win any awards for keeping in touch," he added. "We're guys. But when we do see each other, we pick up right where we left off."

Dawson glanced at his watch. They had three hours yet before their scheduled meet. "Let's go back to Kev's place," he suggested, draining his drink.

He had to hide his smile when he saw Janine's eyes flare with heat, saw her scramble to her feet. *Now,* who had sex on the brain?

Chapter 33

Dawson stood close behind Janine as she inserted the key into the lock of Kevin's front door, his left hand at her waist. The appealing scent of her was quite literally overwhelming him. He was imagining brushing her shoulder-length hair aside and feathering his lips along the nape of her neck, when he felt a presence behind them.

He whirled, his right hand instinctively going to his holster—which was stupid; he hadn't carried a weapon since leaving the Service three years before. With his other arm, he thrust Janine behind him, the two overnight bags slung over his shoulder jostling against her.

There was nothing obviously threatening about the stranger who stood an arm's length away from them, although Dawson remained on guard. He pegged the man's age at mid-fifties. He was of average height, and well dressed in dark grey trousers, a tweed sports jacket over a white dress shirt, and black oxfords. His hair was white, but his bushy eyebrows and generous moustache were brown with only a hint of grey, the striking contrast giving the man a rather distinguished look.

If he hadn't been so consumed by thoughts of divesting Janine of her clothes within seconds of stepping into Kev's house, Dawson would've heard the stranger's approach. The thought that his lack of focus could've gotten Janine killed made him weak at the knees. It also pissed him off. He took his anger out on the stranger.

"Who the fuck are you?" he growled as his senses kicked into high gear. He scanned the street, half expecting a threat to materialize.

The sun was low in the sky, but it was not yet dusk. There were only two trees blocking what would otherwise be a clear view of the street; one to his left, two doors up from Kev's house, and the other at the bottom of the street. A woman pushing a stroller was moving away from them on the opposite side of the road, animatedly chatting on her phone; a young couple was retrieving bags of what looked like groceries from the back of a blue Kia three doors down; an older woman who looked to be in her seventies was walking towards them, a small, heavy-breather-type dog on a long leash. No obvious danger lurked; yet, Dawson's Spidey senses were on high alert. *Something* wasn't right.

"I apologize if I startled you," the man stated in a cultured British accent.

Dawson tensed when the stranger reached into his sports jacket. Was he going for a weapon?

The stranger paused. "My business card. May I?" The man waited for Dawson's nod, then withdrew a large, flat wallet from his inside breast pocket. He rested his gaze on Janine, who remained slightly behind Dawson's shoulder. "It wasn't my intention to startle you," he said again as he extracted a business card. "But when I realized who you might be—you resemble your cousin—I was eager to catch your attention." He handed the card to Dawson, tucking his wallet into his jacket as he asked, "Are you former military?"

Dawson ignored his question as he tilted the card so Janine, who peered around his shoulder, could read it.

"*Alfred H. Buckley. President, Folkestone Auctioneers,*" she recited.

Dawson flipped the card over. He read the line out loud. *"Specializing in rare and antique coins."*

Dawson met Janine's gaze briefly before they returned their attention to the new arrival. "Why are you here, Mr. Buckley?" Janine asked.

"You're Dr. Kirby's Canadian cousin?"

Dawson cut in before Janine could respond. *"We'll* ask the questions. Why are you *here?* And why sneak up on us?" he added with a snarl.

The man was clearly affronted at the accusation. "I did not *sneak.* You would've heard my approach had you not been so focused on this young lady." He gestured towards Janine.

The stranger was right, which didn't improve Dawson's mood. He levelled a gaze at the man and spoke through gritted teeth, enunciating each word. "What. Are you doing. Here?"

"I would be happy to answer that question. Will you at least invite me in?"

"We will not," Dawson stated in a tone that allowed no room for negotiation. His eyes continued to sweep the neighbourhood, alert to any changes in the activity on the street. "If you don't answer the question in the next five seconds, my boot print will be on your ass."

"Dawson!" Janine sputtered. "Maybe—"

Dawson interrupted her. "We're not presently in the mood to issue invitations to strangers who *sneak* up unannounced." No way was he going to have an argument with Janine on the street about whether to invite this man inside. He'd add Alfred's name to the research his JAG buddy was conducting. Once he got the results, they'd decide whether the man was trustworthy. Until then, they would proceed with caution. "You still haven't answered the question."

Alfred sighed. Mr....?"

"Delaney."

"Mr. Delaney, your aggression makes me all the more

anxious for Dr. Kirby's well-being." He turned his attention to Janine. "Since it's been made abundantly clear that an invitation isn't forthcoming, I have no option but to divulge my concerns while standing in the street."

The man hesitated, as if expecting Janine to override Dawson. When she remained silent, he continued. "I am an associate of Dr. Kirby's. The reason I'm here is because he hasn't returned my calls. That in itself is not strange given his frequent absences and his aversion for mobile technology. What is alarming is that his colleagues at the University of Nottingham also do not know where he is. My contacts there confirmed he has no dig scheduled and he isn't on holiday."

Dawson's instinct told him Alfred was speaking the truth. All the same, he would ask his JAG friend to do some digging. Until then, he wasn't about to take the man into his confidence.

Alfred's face creased with concern as he regarded them. "May I ask, do *you* know where he is? He lifted a hand, adding, "I'm not suggesting you *tell* me. I'm simply trying to verify if there is cause for concern when it comes to Dr. Kirby's whereabouts."

Dawson looked at Janine briefly, silently asking permission to take the lead in responding. She understood his look, and nodded almost imperceptibly. *God, she was savvy. He loved that about her!*

He turned back to face the stranger. "Suppose, and I do mean *suppose*, we were to say we *don't* know where he is. What would you say? Keep in mind I'm asking hypothetically, of course."

Alfred grimaced, then said, "Of course. Well, I would say you have cause to be concerned."

"Why?" Janine demanded. "What do you know?"

"I *know* nothing, Ms. Kirby, but if I were to speculate…"

Dawson made a sweeping gesture with his open palm. "Speculate away, Alfred."

"Then I would say Dr. Kirby's grad student, Mr. Jackson Jones, a young, foolish man who has the rather grandiose ambition of following in the footsteps of his namesake—"

"*Indiana* Jones?" Janine interrupted.

"That's right, Ms. Kirby. Mr. Jones sees himself as the real life Indiana Jones. Or, at least, sees himself on a career track to becoming the equivalent of the iconic character. As you may have ascertained from my business card, Folkestone Auctioneers specializes in authenticating, selling, and purchasing rare coins. I'm a professional numismatist."

"What the fuck is a numismatist?" Dawson demanded.

Janine's question was significantly more polite. "You're an expert in coins, Mr. Buckley?"

Dawson hoped Janine wouldn't be tempted to show this man Kevin's coin. That would *not* be a good idea. He gave her hand a warning squeeze, felt her answering squeeze of understanding in response.

"Yes. I authenticate and grade coins for commercial purposes. Like your cousin, my academic discipline is archeology, but in graduate school I diverged and became a scholar numismatic specializing in post-Roman era British coins. Are you an amateur collector?"

"No, but Kevin and I spent a lot of time with our grandfather, who collects Victorian currency," Janine said. "Our grandfather's interest was sparked by *his* grandfather's occupation—my great-great—who was a metal worker at the London mint."

Alfred Buckley's pale grey eyes sparked with interest. "Ah. So some of the coins in your grandfather's collection might very well have been handled by his ancestor. Fascinating."

"*Not* fascinating," snapped Dawson. "Could we get out of the weeds here, Alfred?"

The stranger sobered, nodding. "Mr. Jones approached me a number of days ago claiming Dr. Kirby discovered a coin that, if it exists, is potentially priceless. I've since learned he also approached others in the business who are less reputable than Folkestone's."

Dawson felt Janine's gaze on him and knew her expression was likely betraying everything she was thinking. She might be smart, but her face was an open book. This stranger, his eyes trained on Janine, drew the obvious conclusion.

"You've seen it?"

"No. I haven't seen it." Janine shook her head, but her response didn't ring with truth.

She can't lie worth shit, Dawson thought with a mixture of frustration and admiration.

Alfred eventually shifted his gaze to Dawson, saying, "The coin Young Jones described shouldn't *exist.* Not if it's gold. And *certainly* not if it's embossed with the words Rex Alfred. History gives no hint of King Alfred minting coins other than copper and silver. This coin, *if* it exists, would be the most astonishing and potentially priceless archeological discovery since the Sutton Hoo, or The Staffordshire Hoard, or even King Tut's tomb! If Dr. Kirby had come to me—"

"If Kev didn't go to you," Dawson interrupted, "maybe it's because he doesn't trust you."

Alfred's thick eyebrows jerked down over flinty eyes. "That is preposterous!" His next words fell like flakes of chipped granite. "Folkestone's is above reproach. Ours is a stellar reputation, one instilled by my great-grandfather and continued by each subsequent generation." As he regarded first Dawson then Janine, his astonishment grew. "You don't seem to understand. The coin, if it exists, if it were sold at auction, would fetch upwards of *hundreds of thousands of pounds.*"

Dawson heard Janine's gasp, but he didn't look at her or betray any emotion. When he spoke, his tone was deliberately light, his intention to keep the stranger off balance. "You're telling us that Kevin *allegedly* found a coin, showed this *alleged* coin to Jackson *Indiana* Jones, who in turn has been visiting establishments like yours, without Kevin or the *alleged* coin, and that this *alleged* coin is *allegedly* worth a small fortune?" He gave Alfred a humourless grin. "If you're that gullible, then I've got some ocean-front property in Arizona for sale."

Into the silence that followed, Janine said, "Mr. Buckley, you still haven't explained why you're here."

"I'm here because I am deeply concerned about Dr. Kirby. I'm here because you should know that Mr. Jackson Jones, *Dr.* Jones if he matriculates, lacks integrity and cannot be trusted. I am also here because, although Folkestone Auctioneers' sterling reputation is unblemished, there are others in the business who have tarnished the industry's reputation by consorting with the criminal underbelly of the antiquities world."

"And unlike them, or Jones, we should trust *you?*" Dawson taunted.

It seemed to be taking great effort for Alfred to mask his irritation. "Yes," was his simple response.

A part of Dawson's mind noted that the old woman and her dog were now walking on the opposite side of the street, and a middle-aged couple had exited their house and were getting into the slate-blue Audi sedan parked behind his rental car.

"And who are these others in the business who are consorting with criminals…?" Dawson waited for Alfred to respond, fully expecting to hear Tiffany's last name.

"An auction house called O'Sullivan's," Alfred said.

Dawson felt Janine squeeze his hand.

"It's based in Dublin, with offices in London, Sydney, San Francisco, and Vancouver." Alfred turned to Janine. "O'Sullivan's has been in existence for five generations. The present CEO is Bartholomew O'Sullivan."

Dawson didn't need to wonder if Janine remembered the name he'd overheard when they'd been chased up the mountain. *Bart.* She was squeezing the shit out of his hand. He squeezed hers in response.

"He has three sons," Alfred was saying. "The two oldest

are forces to be reckoned with, just like their father. They run the international offices. The youngest is based in London. He's inept, and grossly overshadowed by his brilliant cousin, a young woman named Tiffany. I, and others, believe the family has strong ties to the criminal community, but they have yet to be held formally accountable for their more nefarious activities."

Dawson kept an ear tuned to all that the man was divulging, but his mind was whirling as it connected some of the previously unknown dots. Bart and Tiffany O'Sullivan were uncle and niece. The O'Sullivan's had learned about the coin from Kev's blabbermouth grad student, Jackson Jones. They'd also somehow learned Kev had couriered the object to Janine. The thugs sent to Janine's house in Whistler must be attached to the O'Sullivan's Vancouver office. The question still remained, who was the other man, the one who'd been knifed on Janine's lawn? And, far more pressing, *where was Kevin?*

"Eighteen months ago," Alfred told them, "Bartholomew was accused of selling looted antiquities from Syria using forged provenance documents. He was exonerated due to lack of evidence. At the time, Tiffany O'Sullivan seemed to view her uncle's involvement in this scandal as an opportunity to not only publicly criticize his leadership, but to make a bid to take over the business. She succeeded with the former and failed at the latter. If rumours are to be believed, the legacy of her failed coup escalated already existing tensions within that family, both financial and personal. Auctioning a rare and unquestionably priceless coin—perhaps more than one—would, at the very least, alleviate the financial side of those tensions and, equally as important, re-establish their reputation in the industry.

"As for Folkestone's," Alfred continued, "we've been in business only half as long as O'Sullivan's, but my father made it a public entity more than thirty years ago. It is entirely transparent. If you were to investigate," he nodded at Dawson, "you'll discover our financial portfolio is stable and sound, and our reputation unblemished by even a hint of scandal."

"You claim to be worried about Kevin," Dawson countered. "Yet you're waxing eloquent about your reputation and financial stability."

Alfred made an impatient gesture. "Of course it would be very prestigious and lucrative if Dr. Kirby allowed Folkestone's to authenticate and auction whatever coins he unearths, especially one that shouldn't exist. But that is not the reason I drove here from London. I'm deeply concerned for his safety." The man grew impatient. "What you don't seem to understand, Mr. Delaney, is that there are players in this game who would stoop to any level of criminal pursuits to get what they want. I came here to assure myself of Dr. Kirby's whereabouts. And, yes, if I found him, offer my professional services for the safekeeping, authenticating, and auctioning of whatever he's unearthed, all while remaining within the full authority of the law. Others in my industry lack such scruples."

Alfred turned to Janine. "Please confirm for me," he said, nodding at Kevin's house. "Your cousin is not in?"

"No, Mr. Buckley, he's not," Janine said, her tone gentle.

"Ms. Kirby…Jaynie…" He saw her look of surprise at his use of her nickname. "Dr. Kirby has talked about you often. I know he values your relationship, all the more so because you are like siblings. You're surprised I know this? Well," he said, giving Dawson a brief, telling look before resting his gaze on Janine. "Perhaps I have proved to you that I am a friend who is here out of genuine concern." He lifted his shoulder in a resigned shrug. "But I doubt your Mr. Delaney believes me when I say I can be trusted, so I think it is time I take my leave."

Alfred addressed Dawson. "You have my card. Please call

my mobile when Dr. Kirby returns. I would appreciate having my concerns alleviated. And if I can be of service in the meantime, don't hesitate to ring me."

The man gave Janine a formal nod as he said, "I'll bid you good evening, Ms. Kirby, and wish you a pleasant visit."

Chapter 34

Janine eyed Dawson. He'd dropped their bags on the floor before closing and locking the door behind them. "Why were you so hostile?" she asked. "Maybe he can help us find Kevin."

He was gazing down at the business card in his hands, absently flicking the corner with his thumbnail. When he lifted his head and met her gaze, she could see his focus remained inward. He shook his head and said, "I'm not saying he *can't* be trusted. But first we need to verify his story." Dawson held out a hand. "Can I use your phone? Does it have enough juice?"

Janine withdrew her phone from her purse and glanced at the screen. "22%," she stated, handing it to Dawson. "Is the cord and converter in your bag?"

"Yeah, let me get them." Dawson tucked Alfred's business card into the back pocket of his jeans, then rummaged through his bag and retrieved the cords. He plugged in the phone beside the sofa, then took a seat and began tapping out a message.

While he was doing that, Janine removed the bubble-wrapped coin from her purse, absently staring down at it as she lifted the crossbody strap over her head and tossed the bag onto the Victorian armchair, then unwound and tossed the scarf beside her purse. After joining Dawson on the sofa, she slid the object out of the plastic sleeve. Examining it, she found it impossible to believe it was as valuable as Alfred suggested. Although, if it was, she didn't want to be responsible for it.

Unlike Dawson, she'd immediately liked Alfred Buckley. If she'd been alone, she wouldn't have hesitated to invite him in. She might even have shown him the coin.

"It can't possibly be worth what he claims, can it?" she asked, studying the disc in her palm. Could such an insignificant looking object, even if it was more than a thousand years old, really be worth hundreds of thousands of pounds? "Why would Kevin send it to *me*, knowing its value? And to courier it? That was utterly foolish. What if the plane crashed?"

Dawson chuckled. *"Cast Away?"* He set aside the phone, then turned towards her.

Eyeing the coin in her palm, he nudged it with his fingertips, his brief touch generating a sizzle against her skin. Janine sighed inwardly, annoyed with herself for being so susceptible to his touch, even one this brief.

"What about Kev strikes you as 'utterly foolish'?" he asked.

She swivelled her head and looked at him. He was slouched against the back of the sofa, his hands folded across his flat stomach. His long legs were stretched out, booted feet crossed at the ankles under the coffee table. He was deliciously distracting. She had to force herself to look away. What was the phrase he used with his nieces? *Hocus, pocus, focus.* She needed to focus on the question he'd posed.

"There is *nothing* foolish about Kevin," she said, putting the coin back into the bubble envelope and tucking it into the front pocket of her jeans, adding, "We need a safer place than my pocket for this."

"It's safe enough for now," Dawson said, less bothered, obviously, than she was by the fact that the coin might be worth more than her house. "But first, to your point, explain why he was *foolish* enough to send you something that valuable."

Janine frowned, leaning back against the sofa beside Dawson. She thought about what made her cousin tick. Above all else, he was passionate about his career. When he was conducting an archeological dig, his focus was unwavering. He unearthed all kinds of objects he defined as treasures—animal bones, shards of pottery, metalwork and glasswork, even bits of broken weapons, tools, and jewelry. But when he was with her, away from all that, whether exploring a nearby city or national park or simply chatting on the phone, he was curious and interested in whatever they were discussing, from the merits of a pint of bitter versus coffee, to the legacy of Stephen Hawking. Easy going, and with a goofy sense of humour much like Dawson's, he also had a competitive streak that surfaced when they played board or card games. Janine won more often than not, a state of affairs that both baffled Kevin and kept him coming back for more. He was the kind of person who understood the world's concern over climate change but didn't understand a single person's obsession with professional sports. He was a lot of things, her cousin, but what he wasn't, was foolish. In fact, he was risk-averse—which was why, she was only now realizing, he never won at Hearts.

Janine finally answered Dawson's question. "He sent it to me because he was backed into a corner." She looked at him. "He was out of options, wasn't he? He didn't have a choice."

Dawson nodded in agreement. "That's what I think."

Janine frowned her concern. "But *why* was he out of options?"

"If we knew the answer to that, we'd probably also know where he is."

Janine's gaze dropped to her phone. Reaching across

Dawson, she disconnected it, then read the emails he'd sent to someone named Lieutenant Commander Ross Sheridan. Dawson's first message to LC Sheridan explained that he was in the UK on a personal matter. In it, he asked his friend to research Tiffany O'Sullivan, O'Sullivan Auctioneers, as well as King Alfred coins. The second email, the one he'd just sent, tagged Bartholomew O'Sullivan, Jackson Jones, Alfred Buckley, and Folkestone Auctioneers to his original request.

The recipient's response to Dawson's first email was, *Sure thing, bro. What's up? You okay?*

When the phone dinged in Janine's hand with the JAG lawyer's second response, she read it out loud. "*Helping out another damsel, I take it?*" She snorted with amusement as she regarded Dawson. "Another damsel? *That* sounds like an interesting story."

Dawson, his head resting on the back of the sofa, gave her an amused look. "Not that interesting. And it was a long, *long* time ago."

She chuckled. "That won't make the tale any less fascinating. I'm going to do a quick search for Folkestone's." She opened a browser and typed, then said, "Listen to what it says here on their website. *Folkestone Auctioneers is the result of three generations of growth and development, beginning in 1954 thanks to the vision of Bernard Buckley. Bernard was born in Paddlesworth, Kent...* yada, yada, yada." Janine scrolled down before continuing. *"The Folkestone Auction firm has developed a global client base of collectors and coin dealers, with a long-standing history of notable sales. Folkestone catalogues provide meticulous descriptions and colourful illustrations that showcase our extensive numismatic holdings. We have gained a solid regional and international reputation thanks to our numismatic experts, and remain an excellent choice for bidder and consignors alike. Contact us today to obtain consignment or appraisal information, or to discuss your personal want lists and collecting goals."*

Janine continued to skim the info on the website. "Alfred Buckley was born in Lambeth...he studied in London and

Rome…and he's been at the helm of Folkestone's for twelve years."

"Ross will send me a dossier. Knowing him, it will be comprehensive. He'll let me know if Alfred can be trusted."

Janine sighed, handing the phone to Dawson, who reattached it to the power cord. She slouched against the sofa, her thoughts on her cousin. *Where are you?*

"We'll find him," Dawson said.

Janine rolled her head to regard him. He had a knack for reading her mind. She liked that about him. "When? And…" She didn't finish her sentence, unwilling to speak her worrisome thoughts aloud. *And will he be alive when we do?*

"We *will* find him. And he *will* be okay."

Janine read the promise in Dawson's eyes. She wanted to believe him, knew he wanted to make good on his promise, but she also knew he didn't have the power to make such assurances. There were simply too many variables outside of their control.

"Janine," Dawson said, shifting his arm and inviting her to lay against him. He momentarily rested his lips against her temple, then said, "I'm going to do everything in my power to help you find him. We will find him. And when we do, I feel certain he'll be okay."

She lifted her head and looked into Dawson's eyes, their inky blue depths reminding her of the young man he'd been fifteen years ago when she'd tried so hard to make him see her as a woman. As their gazes held, his eyes darkened, desire glittering in them like dark sapphires.

"You're so beautiful," he said in a breathless whisper.

Suddenly desperate with need, she lifted her lips to his, at the same time shifting and crawling onto his lap. Her hands, trembling with urgency and need, wrestled with the buttons of his shirt.

She tore her lips from his. "Off," she ordered. "Take it

off," at the same time leaning back and pulling her borrowed T-shirt up and over her head.

When she heard Dawson's strangled breath, she laughed, knowing he was responding with approval to Nicolette's ultra-sexy, too-skimpy bra. *Well, with that kind of reaction, no way was Nicolette ever getting it back.*

Chapter 35

Whatever Dawson had been thinking about—Kevin and Alfred Buckley and the O'Sullivan's and the coin —evaporated when Janine straddled him. Jesus! Did anything feel better than Janine's legs, open and inviting, above his pulsing cock?

He scrambled to obey when she ordered him to take off his shirt, and had three buttons undone in the space of half a heartbeat, but then she was shirtless and he was trying to say something like, *holy hotness, you are so goddamn hot,* but what came out of his mouth was, "Fuhhaaah." If only he could redirect some of the blood from his cock to his brain, he'd be able to speak in coherent sentences. *Sentences?* He'd settle for the ability to utter a single, coherent word.

His brain may not have been able to function, but his hands knew what to do. He was in a state of sensation overload, his eyes feasting, his hands exploring, his skin sizzling, his blood pulsing. Speech was over-rated, he decided, as he felt the delicious caress of Janine's hands inside his shirt.

His brain cells finally unfroze. "Wherever you buy your lingerie…*A-fucking-plus.*"

"It's not mine," Janine said, unbuttoning the rest of his

shirt and pulling the tail out of his jeans. The touch of her fingers against his skin sent delicious rivulets of heat sizzling at high speed through his body. Dawson pushed aside the lace cups of her bra, mesmerized by her lush curves as his thumbs brushed each dark areola, watching in fascination as her nipples hardened in response to his touch. As if from a distance he heard her say, "I had to borrow it. Remember?"

Her voice hitched on the last word. He'd leaned forward and closed his mouth over her nipple. *God, she tasted good.* He let his hands roam at will, from her magnificent breasts to the long, velvet length of her spine, then slipping into the back waistband of her jeans. When his hand encountered the minuscule panties, he felt his cock surge with need, and tore his lips from devouring her breasts to once again feasting on her mouth.

Her hands were as impatient as his, moving down his chest to fumble with his belt, her tongue in his mouth sending a message of hunger that matched his own.

He shifted a hand to the front of her jeans, unclasping the button and pushing down the zip, not willing, just yet, to have her move off his lap. Ever since their mind-blowing encounter in the cave, he'd been longing to return his hands to where they'd been. And now, finally, he'd achieved it. He pulled his head back, breaking off their kiss so he could luxuriate in the sight of her as he sank two fingers into her slick folds.

The liquid pleasure on her face was more erotic than the whole of his previous sexual experiences combined. Her cheeks were flushed, her hair mussed, and her breasts—*god, her beautiful breasts*—were spilling out of flimsy lace some idiot might call a bra but he would forever after designate as a slice of Janine heaven.

He moved his hand inside her, saw the answering flutter of her eye-lids dropping to half-mast. Janine's lack of poker face might have been a handicap when talking to Alfred Buckley, but it was a goddamn aphrodisiac during sex. He dropped his gaze to her breasts, his thumb grazing her nipple. He felt himself getting drunk on her sumptuous beauty.

"Your breasts…this bra…god, Janine. You are so freaking gorgeous."

Her hands on his chest were sparking flames of heat in his veins, his cock surging with the pulsing demand to replace his hand. He heard her moan, felt her press her hips into his hand, felt her hands still momentarily on the zip of his jeans as she focused inward on the sensations his touch was evoking.

He watched her face, revelling in the pleasure he was giving her as he moved his thumb against her most sensitive spot. He deliberately stilled his hand for a heartbeat, then two, waiting for her to look at him so he could drown in the dark nectar of her glorious eyes. "Are your own as sexy?" he asked, his voice gravelly with desire.

Her eyes were feasting on him as her hands mapped out his chest, thumbing his nipples, then twining her fingers in his chest hair. She leaned forward, her lips and tongue tasting the length of his collarbone, sending currents of heat into every pulse point of his body. He deliberately stilled his hands, waited for her to lean back and meet his gaze. "Wh-at?" she asked.

"I said," he repeated with a smile, "Is your own lingerie as sexy?"

Dawson sucked in a breath when her knuckles brushed against the tip of his cock. He answered her gambit, moving his fingers inside her, felt her breath on his face as she gasped her pleasure. She lifted her hands and buried her fingers in his hair as she bent her head and gave him another scorching kiss.

"Your own bra and panties?" he asked again when they finally came up for air. "Are they equally as sexy?"

She smiled against his lips, then leaned back and looked at him, languidly moving her hips, her melted chocolate eyes filled with a teasing heat that would've buckled his knees had he been standing. "Not even close," she said, her voice low and husky, trailing her hands lightly down his chest. "You'll be deeply disappointed," she teased.

He chuckled low in his throat, and said, "Not likely." She could wear a burlap sack and he'd still hunger for her. He stopped breathing entirely when her cool fingers shifted down, staking a claim on his swollen shaft. *Mother of god!* He wanted his cock inside her slick heat.

She seemed to have drawn the same conclusion for she was suddenly pushing off of him. His eyes followed her as his hands blindly fumbled to remove his clothes. Needing more room to manoeuvre, he placed a booted foot on the coffee table and pushed, not caring that half the books and journals, as well as the empty coffee mug he'd left there, crashed to the floor. He got to his feet and shrugged out of his shirt, his gaze feasting on the sight of Janine, smiling in delight as he watched her hop on one leg, tugging at the jeans twisted at her ankle, her ample breasts bouncing above the wire cups of her bra. Unable to tear his gaze from her perfection, he tugged blindly at his own jeans, which were now stuck around his ankles. He was fumbling with equal fervour to remove his boots—*stupid cowboy boots that needed a stupider boot jack*—mildly disappointed when she succeeded in removing her pants. When she turned her back and raced to the window to pull the curtains closed, he got an eyeful of her sculpted ass in the barely there scrap of thong underwear, making his cock leap to even more rigid attention. And then his boots were finally off and he was kicking them aside, his hands reaching for the waistband of his boxers.

He laughed his delight when he saw Janine's eyes hungrily eying his hands as if he was about to unwrap a much anticipated present, her own hand extending the neon pink foil packet she'd obviously retrieved from her jeans. He'd seen that come-fuck-me look on her face before. This time he could do something about it.

He snatched the condom from her with one hand,

shucking off his boxers with the other, then got distracted when she unhooked her bra and dropped the scrap of lace.

"Woman, you are killing me," he muttered, tearing open the packet. He froze, staring at the rolled latex. "What the fuck? It's *Pepto-Bismol* pink!" His cock had never worn a pink jacket before.

He lifted his eyes and met her amused gaze, shifting to head over to his overnight bag and retrieve the normal-coloured condoms he'd bought at Ivy's Pies.

"Uh-uh. No you don't," she warned, holding out a palm to stop him. "I went to a lot of trouble to buy that for you," she teased, nodding at his hand. "If you don't want to wear that, then I'm not sure I want to take this off." Her hands moved to rest on the barely there bit of fabric hugging her hips.

His eyes sparked. She wanted to play, did she? Well, he was up for that. "Oh, I'll put this on. *After* you take *that* off," he bargained, nodding at her panties.

He couldn't tear his eyes away as she slowly, teasingly, rocked her hips, slipping the scrap of fabric down the curve of her hips, down her strong, gorgeous thighs, finally stepping out and kicking them aside. He stared at her. Had he ever seen anything as beautiful as Janine?

"Your turn," she said.

He looked down, making quick work of the condom, but he couldn't help frowning at how ridiculous he looked sheathed in *neon fucking pink*.

"Oh, believe me," Janine assured, her voice husky, clearly reading his mind. "You don't look ridiculous to me."

And then she was in his arms, her bare skin scorching his as she nudged him backwards. When his calves hit the sofa, unwilling to break the kiss, he pulled her down onto his lap and—*holy fuck*—she didn't wait even a second but simply adjusted herself over him and sank onto his cock. *God, was she trying to undo him before they even got started?* Every slick muscle inside her was locked around him like a vice, her tight, wet heat enveloping his length. He had his hands on her ass, her back, her breasts, then back on her ass. Every inch of her was silk.

She broke the kiss, tilting her head back and moving in perfect rhythm above him. His lips and tongue trailed kisses over every inch of skin he could reach, gorging on her satin smoothness as he inhaled her intoxicating mix of summer sunshine and coffee. *Janine heaven.*

He filled his hands with the weight of her breasts as she lifted her hips, his eyes glued to her beautiful face as he worked her nipple with his mouth and tongue, mesmerized by the unfocused pleasure warming her eyes. As he dusted wet kisses around her dark areola, he asked, "How many colours did you get?"

She made a murmuring sound of approval before answering, her voice husky and low, "Three."

Her focus, he could see, was inward as she slowly, exquisitely, lifted her hips, releasing almost the full length of him before sinking back down. They gasped in perfect unison, the intensity of his pleasure excruciating in its bliss.

He worked her breasts so he could lick both nipples with one sweep of his tongue, heard her moan, felt himself grow harder, if that was even possible. *He could do this all day.* "You are so beautiful," he gasped. He couldn't believe he'd complained about wearing pink. He'd wear every colour under the sun if he could have Janine in his arms like this, soft, pliable, wet, *so goddamn hot.*

"I hope you like..." She took him deeper, then paused and exclaimed, *oh god,* echoing the sentiment in his head. "Radioactive lavender," she added, finishing her sentence as she lifted her hips.

He smiled against her skin. "I love radioactive lavender." He looked down, took in the sight of her hips lifting, lifting, almost releasing him, pausing with just the tip of his pink-sheathed cock at the apex of her triangle of hair. “Hell, I fucking adore neon pink.”

She laughed as she sank down, paused there for a moment, clearly enjoying the sensation. “You feel so good, Dawson. *Sooooohhh! Gooooood.*”

He shifted his hand to touch her, there, the press of his thumb making her gasp and increase the pace of her movements.

He was about to lose his shit. “Are you close?” he asked, shifting his hand, loving the sigh that escaped her lips as he looked into her expressive face.

When she opened her eyes, something in her gaze made him catch his breath.

She stilled, reaching up to cup his face with both her hands. With a breathless smile, her eyes shimmering with light, she breathed out his name, slowly, drawing it out. “Dawson. *Freaking.* Delaney.”

The way she said his name, triumphant, almost reverent, made him feel weightless with joy.

And then his ability to have anything resembling a coherent thought evaporated as she once again began to move.

Chapter 36

They were due to arrive at the left lion in less than an hour.

While Dawson showered, Janine dressed in Nicolette's slim-fitting jeans and a taupe T-shirt embellished with an embroidered dreamcatcher. Her own clothes were unpleasantly musty, but since Dawson advised that they'd take everything with them when they left Kevin's house, she repacked her overnight bag and brought it downstairs, tucking the aqua scarf in a side pocket and setting her things, including Nicolette's riding boots, by the front door. Her Nike's, at least, were dry enough to wear.

She headed to Kevin's small kitchen, intending to prepare an iced coffee with what was left in the pot. As she set about making the drink, she was preoccupied with thoughts of Dawson and whether he would disappear from her life once this business with Kevin was resolved. Was it too much to hope that he would want to see where their mutual attraction would lead? Now wasn't the time to have that conversation, she knew, but it didn't stop her from trying to guess what his answer might be.

Her thoughts turned to her cousin. She couldn't help

anticipating, despite Dawson's prediction, that Kevin would be at the left lion. Janine knew Dawson was as anxious about the meet as she was, but where she was concerned about Kevin—not only whether he'd be at the square, but how hurt he might be—Dawson was preoccupied with the lack of information. He was still convinced the O'Sullivan's intended to kidnap Janine, but it bugged him that he couldn't figure out why they'd chosen such a busy, public venue when the roads around the large square were too distant from the left lion to perform what he called a successful grab-and-toss.

Not that any of that mattered, he'd repeatedly assured her, adding that he had no intention of letting her out of his sight. Which suited her just fine.

Janine retrieved the ice-cube tray from the miniature freezer section of Kevin's fridge. She heard the shower shut off as she popped a handful of the frozen cubes into the re-usable travel cup with straw she'd purchased on a previous visit, dumping the remaining ice into the sink. She had her hand outstretched for the coffee pot when she paused, frowning at the cubes in the sink, some of which appeared strangely soiled. Had the tray not been clean when Kevin filled it?

She reclaimed a cube, slippery and cold in her hand. As she inspected it, the hairs on her arms rose.

Quickly scooping the rest of the ice cubes out of the sink before they could melt, she dropped them into the travel cup, then held it under the hot water tap. Twenty seconds later, with the cup half full of water, she gaped at the three golden discs as they settled onto the bottom. Unable to tear her gaze away, and aware that her wet, trembling hands were making the cup slippery to hold, she set the beverage container on the cluttered countertop.

"Dawson," she called, but her voice was croaky. She had to clear her throat. "Dawson!" This time she had sufficient volume and urgency to get his attention.

She heard him pounding down the stairs, knew by his footfalls he was taking them three at a time, knew as well he was expecting to see someone attempting to kidnap her from Kevin's kitchen. She heard him enter the room, heard him mumble an expletive when he saw she wasn't in danger. Yet still, she couldn't tear her eyes away from the contents of the cup.

Dawson was beside her then, barefoot, wearing jeans but with his plaid shirt hanging open. His gaze followed hers. "Jesus! Is that…?" Unlike Janine, he didn't hesitate to pour the rest of the water out of the cup, allowing the coins to fall into his palm.

She stared at the objects in his hand, feeling mildly light-headed. If Alfred Buckley could be believed, the four coins now in their possession could be worth upwards of a million pounds. *Two million Canadian dollars.*

She felt rather than saw Dawson shift his attention to her. She must've looked ready to faint, as he immediately led her to one of the kitchen chairs. He slapped the coins on the table as he squatted in front of her, peering into her face. "You okay?" he asked.

"I'm fine," Janine said, staring at the coins where they sat in an innocuous puddle of water. "It's just…" she waved a hand. "They're worth…"

Dawson pulled out the other chair and sat facing her, his knees bumping hers. He dried his wet hands on his jeans, then took her hands in his. "Honey, it's what we were expecting. This shitstorm was never on account of a single coin." He nodded towards the coins. "This proves our theory."

Janine finally tore her gaze from the coins and looked at him. "*Your* theory," she said. He'd been interrupted half-way through shaving, she saw. He would've looked comical had the situation been less outlandish.

She suddenly sucked in a breath as the full significance of her discovery dawned. "This explains…" She paused, tried again. "This means…" But she couldn't form words around her thoughts. *If they killed a man in hopes of gaining possession of the single coin they knew she had—assuming that's why the man on her lawn had been killed—what would they do to gain possession of four?*

"What this *means,*" Dawson said with an amused grin, "is that Dick Irish-Asshole was within reach of those three coins while he was ordering you to bring him *one* all the way from Canada."

Janine couldn't match his nonchalance. "But we're about to leave. What are we supposed to do with them?"

Dawson nodded at her hip. "I can't think of a safer place than that snug pocket. It's certainly more secure than any of mine."

"I meant…they belong in a safety deposit box." Janine hated the thought of having millions of dollars' worth of historic treasure in the pocket of her jeans.

"Yeah, they do, but that will have to wait until tomorrow, or the day after. We'll see how things go." He patted her knees in reassurance. "Think of them as loonies," he suggested, referring to the Canadian dollar coin etched with a loon. With a glance at his watch, he said, "I better finish getting dressed." He kissed her, then left.

She heard him jog up the stairs. How could he be so cavalier? Having a fortune on his person might not disconcert Dawson, but it made Janine more than a little uncomfortable. "Pretend they're loonies? Fat bloody chance," she muttered as she got to her feet.

She retrieved the bubble envelope from her pocket, added the three additional coins, then tucked the packet as deep as the pocket allowed. Dawson was right. The jeans were snug. There was no way the coins would fall out. But still. First thing tomorrow, she would insist they get a safety deposit box. Alternatively, she suddenly thought, they could bring the coins to Alfred Buckley. She felt certain he was trustworthy. And he would have adequate facilities on hand—and insurance—to store them.

As there was now no ice, Janine dumped the leftover coffee down the sink and rinsed the pot. Hearing Dawson enter the front room, she went to join him, positioning the long strap of her purse across her body as she absently eyed him with undisguised appreciation. Freshly shaved and with his hair still damp, he looked good enough to eat.

Dawson stopped in his tracks, heat flaring in his eyes when their gazes met. "What did I say about looking at me like that?" he grumbled in feigned annoyance as he hefted both their bags over his shoulder.

She *had* been mentally licking her lips at the sight of him. *Oops*. "Sorry," she said with a smile as she retrieved her cell from where it was plugged in beside the sofa. She stashed the cord, adaptor, and phone into her purse, which also had her Canadian and pounds sterling cash, her passport, and the three remaining neon-coloured condoms. Then she slipped her arms into Nicolette's white jacket and joined Dawson at the door, gathering up the tall boots.

When she made to step out of the house in front of him, he stopped her, a hand on her arm.

"What's the plan?"

His question sent a geyser of anxiety whooshing through her body. *Kevin, please be there! Please be safe!* She breathed deep, then recited his instructions. "Don't let go of your hand. Stay with you in well-lit areas. Be aware of others in the square. If need be, claim refuge from a group of strangers. If separated from you, get to the Premier Inn here or the Canadian Embassy in London, whichever makes the most sense."

Dawson nodded once, then bent his head and kissed her. Holding her gaze, he said, "For the record? None of that really matters. Because I don't intend to let you out of my sight."

Chapter 37

And Dawson meant it. The heart-stopping fear he'd felt at Ivy's Pies when he thought the bastards chasing them had grabbed her was not worth repeating.

He led them out into the night, scanning the neighbourhood while Janine locked the door. The streetlights weren't as bright or as numerous as he preferred, but he could easily spot the activity on the street. Two young men, one carrying a large pizza box, the other a sack of beer, were heading into a house at the bottom of the street. A handful of young women had just vacated one of the terraced houses opposite Dawson's rental car, all laughing and chatting, clearly excited about their Thursday evening out on the town.

Dawson took Janine's hand in his as they stepped onto the cracked flagstones in front of Kevin's house. He stopped abruptly when he saw movement on his left behind the neighbour's tree, but it was only the same elderly lady he'd spotted earlier in the day when they'd been talking to Alfred Buckley, walking the same bow-legged, heavy-breathing dog. They waited, nodding to her as she moved past them.

"The square will have better lighting," Dawson said in a low tone, meeting Janine's concerned gaze.

"It's okay," she said. "I'm jittery, too."

He felt something shift inside him as he looked into her eyes, as if his world had been slightly canted and was only now righting itself. It was an odd sensation, one he didn't understand. But whatever it was, now was not the time to evaluate it.

He leaned in and lightly touched his lips to hers. He couldn't imagine anywhere he'd rather be than here with Janine, although he could do without Kev's shit-show.

They began walking towards the rental car, Janine's hand in his as his gaze swept the street. After taking half-a-dozen steps, he heard a noise behind them and swung around, on full alert, then relaxed when he saw three skinny teenage boys on skateboards heading towards them from the top of the street.

Jesus, but he was jumpy. He knew his feelings of responsibility for Janine's safety—exacerbated by his growing affection for her—contributed to his tension, but he also felt vulnerable without a goddamn weapon. What with airport security, he no longer even had his Swiss Army knife.

He shared a brief apologetic glance with Janine as they turned and continued walking.

The old lady ahead of them suddenly tripped, emitting a bone-chilling cry of pain as she did a face-plant on the unforgiving slate. Instinctively, Dawson let go of Janine's hand and rushed forward to help.

It wasn't until he was beside her and felt her clamp his wrist in her bony hand that he realized his first mistake. *The old lady was O'Sullivan's eyes!*

After that, everything happened at high speed; yet, he seemed able to dissect the events frame-by-frame. He yelled Janine's name at the same time he heard the sound of a vehicle's engine revving behind him, heard the seemingly thunderous click-click-clacking of the approaching skateboarders. He shook off the woman's hold and pivoted on his heels, his heart slamming in horror when he saw Janine step between two parked cars to wait for the skateboarders to pass. Heard himself yelling *noooohhh* as he leapt towards her. But there was no time to explain the danger, no time to tell her that she'd positioned herself exactly where it would be most convenient for the approaching attackers to seize her.

The black van descended upon her like a swooping bird of prey. He saw two figures wearing balaclavas spring out the open side door of the moving vehicle, heard Janine shriek, saw the boots she'd been carrying fly from her grasp as she began to struggle. There was only a handful of strides between them, but even that short space was too distant for him to prevent the horror from unfolding.

Her assailants thrust her inside the van, then jumped in behind her. Dawson heard one of them shout, *go, go go!* And then the vehicle was accelerating towards him.

He could still save her! He could launch himself off the hood of the nearest parked car and dive into the van's side door; that was, as long as they didn't slam it closed in his face.

At the same moment that he pivoted to fling himself towards the street instead of continuing his momentum towards where Janine had been standing, the nearest skate-boarder slammed into him, the speed of the slightly built teenager sufficient to knock Dawson off balance.

That he hadn't given a thought to the skateboarders was his second mistake, he realized. Despite their deceptively scrawny, youthful appearance, *they were O'Sullivan's brawn!*

Dawson staggered, snarling his frustration, the sound of Janine's screams of protest igniting a boiling rage. He had two seconds, max, to make it inside the moving vehicle.

But in that last second, the remaining two teenagers threw themselves off their skateboards and body-slammed him, causing all three of them to fall hard against a parked vehicle, setting off its alarm.

His third mistake—his worst mistake—had been failing to

answer the question that had been nagging at him all afternoon and evening. *Why would Dick Irish-Asshole and Tiffany choose the popular, well-lit city square for their meet?* He had his answer. *They hadn't! Their grab-and-toss had always been scheduled to occur on Kevin's quiet street.* Dawson had been so goddamn hot for Janine, so single-minded about getting her naked, he hadn't properly tuned his inner ear to what his own intuition was trying to tell him; he hadn't taken the time to unpick the threads of that niggling discomfort to unravel the knowledge that the location for the meet was bogus.

Had one of the skateboarders still been within easy reach as he staggered to his feet on the cobblestoned street behind the speeding van, he would've pummelled him senseless. Except that would've taken too much time.

Cursing himself for his reckless stupidity, he began sprinting down the middle of the street in pursuit, memorizing the van's license plate numbers as he dug the car keys from his pocket and pressed the unlock button on the fob. He saw the brake lights flash on at the bottom of the street, and then the van—with Janine in it—was rocketing around the corner, disappearing from view.

His car was facing the same direction the van was travelling—*thank Christ!* He jerked open the door, tossed in the bags he'd instinctively held, and slid behind the wheel. He had the car in reverse a split second after it started. He slammed his back bumper into the car behind him, disregarding the sudden, shrill alarm, then shifted into drive.

As he swung onto the street, he called to Janine in his mind. *I'm coming for you! Don't stop fighting, I'm coming for you!*

He ignored the other voice, the one that taunted him, the one that said, *And here's yet more proof, Delaney, that you can't keep anyone safe.*

Chapter 38

Janine felt a sense of déjà vu as she was tossed into the moving van. This time she knew she wouldn't soon learn her kidnapper was a friend.

She screamed in protest as the man behind her pinned her arms. Janine could tell he was a large man, significantly bigger than the man at her feet who was no taller than Janine but solid and thick with muscle. He held one of her ankles and was trying to grab the other. She kicked and flailed with her free leg, connecting with his shoulder and knocking him off balance at the same time as the van careened around a corner. The van's tires squealed as it fish-tailed momentarily on the tarmac before straightening.

With a snarl, the man at her feet finally overpowered her, pinning her to the rough floor of the otherwise empty cargo van.

"Let me go!" she screamed.

Her words were abruptly cut off when her assailant back-handed her, his fist connecting with her cheekbone.

Pain exploded in her face, causing Janine to collapse against the man behind her. In high school, she'd been hit in the face by a softball while on the pitcher's mound. That had been excruciating. This pain was far worse. For a moment, all she could see were points of bright light exploding like fire-crackers against the black void of her vision.

"Bloody hell!" exclaimed the man behind Janine. "He's behind us."

He? Dawson?

"Lose him, Richie," barked the man at her feet who'd shifted to straddle her thighs.

"Right-oh," the driver said as he gunned the accelerator.

The man at her feet removed his balaclava and tossed it aside, then said, "Hand me a cable tie, Jones."

Janine's struggles had been feeble, temporarily overcome by the pain in her cheek, but at the sound of the man's name, she froze. *Jones?* Jackson Jones? Kevin's grad student?

"What ties?" Jones asked.

Janine squeezed her eyes shut, partly against the pain still radiating from her cheekbone and partly in a desperate, silent plea. *Please don't have any cable ties.* She wouldn't have a chance of escaping if her ankles and wrists were bound.

As her vision began to clear, and aware of the uncomfortable lump of her purse underneath her right hip, she blinked up at the back windows of the van finally able to think. She couldn't see the road, but if Dawson was in pursuit, then all she had to do was remain alert for an opportunity to escape. Her gaze, the black spots finally fading, fell on the van's back door handles. They were within easy reach. If she could free herself from her assailants, she could flee out the back doors, if the vehicle slowed. For now, she would feign terror—which wouldn't actually require any acting—ready to run or fight or do whatever was needed when Dawson executed the escape plan he must surely be hatching.

She opened her eyes and saw the man at her feet gaping at Jones. In the light reflecting into the van from the street and headlights of whatever well-lit thoroughfare they were on, she saw he was about thirty, clean-shaven, with pale hair, a flat face, and deep-set, mean-looking eyes. A spider-web tattoo crept up the left side of his neck.

"What do you mean, *what ties?* The fecking ties I told you to grab when we left the fecking warehouse."

Another Irish accent. Was this the London-based O'Sullivan son, the one Alfred Buckley had described as inept? If so, he sure as hell wasn't inept at kidnapping!

"You *didn't* tell me," Jones stated in an undefinable—at least to Janine—British accent.

"You bloomin' knobhead! Are you telling me you didn't bring anything to tie her up with?"

"It wasn't my idea to grab her. I keep telling you, this is crazy!"

His words sparked hope in Janine. She didn't have to inject fear into her tone as she bargained, "You don't need to tie me up. I'll cooperate. Please, just don't hit me again." If she could pretend to cower, she might have a better chance of escaping.

When the man at her feet glared at her with eyes that glinted like cold steel, she shivered with fear.

The driver suddenly slammed on the brakes.

"No fecking stopping!" shouted the man at her feet, swinging his head to glare at the driver.

"I'm not stopping," The driver called back as he swerved, then went too fast over a series of speed bumps.

Janine saw the headlights of the car behind them bouncing on the van's ceiling. *Dawson?*

"You wearing a belt?" the Irishman asked Jones.

"No." Jones tightened his grip on her. "I'll hold her."

"All the way to fecking London?"

They were going to London? That was a two-hour drive, at the very least. She wished she knew how much gas was in the rental car's tank. Dawson couldn't follow them if he ran out of gas.

"Shite! There's a motor accident up ahead," the driver called out.

"Then take a bloody detour," the man at her feet growled, then had to brace his hand on the wall of the van as the driver took a sharp right turn. Janine could hear the van's tires squealing. She kept her eyes on the van's ceiling. *Stay close, Dawson! Please, stay close!*

When the van straightened, the man at her feet settled onto her thighs. "Bloody plonker," he muttered. "Thinks he's so fecking clever. Fecking idiot."

Janine wasn't sure if he was muttering about the driver or Jones. Not that it mattered.

"Stop wasting time, Gerald!" Jones urged. "Find the coin!"

Gerald? She'd heard *that* name before. Dick Irish had credited someone named Gerald with having *persuasive fists.* Gerald must be the London-based son who'd beaten Kevin!

"You don't have to search for it," Janine volunteered, surprised her voice was steady. "Let go of me, and I'll give it to you." It was silly to bargain, she knew. If he searched her, Gerald would find the coins. But if she convinced Jones to release her arms, she could…*what?* What *could* she do? They were travelling too fast for her to jump out the back doors. And while inside the vehicle, she was up against three kidnappers. What were her options?

Gerald had been tugging at the strap of her purse, clearly intent on searching its contents for the coin. A knife suddenly appeared in his hands. *Holy Christ!* Was he intending to slit her throat like the dead man on her lawn?

Janine squeezed her eyes shut, expecting any moment to feel the cold edge of the blade at her throat. Even Jones was freaking out, demanding to know what the hell Gerald was intending. But then she felt Gerald pawing at her abdomen and realized he was slicing through the strap of her purse. She didn't know why he hadn't forced her to sit up and remove it —although the strap was under her jacket. Maybe he simply liked an excuse to flash his switchblade.

After cutting the strap, Gerald set the knife on the floor beside his knee, then yanked hard, tugging her purse free.

Janine drew breath to continue bargaining, but then remained silent when her eyes fell on the discarded weapon. It lay beside her left hip, the blade glinting invitingly. She stared at it for a heartbeat, then forced herself to look away so as not to telegraph her intention. If she could grab it, she would… what would she do? In all her life, she'd never willingly harmed another human being. Yet, if an opportunity for escape presented itself and it involved using that knife on these men, she would do it. She had to.

She did her best to look meek and cowering—it wasn't difficult—as she watched Gerald dig through the contents of her purse. He tucked the wad of cash into his jacket pocket, then tossed the ruined purse aside. Looking down at her, he said, "You've got it in your pocket, yeah? Well, I don't mind looking." Without warning, he palmed Janine's crotch. "Nice snatch," he added in a casual tone.

Janine erupted, bucking beneath him. "Get off me!" she screamed. But she didn't have sufficient strength or leverage to dislodge his significant weight, although she did feel a momentary lessening in Jones's grip as if he was as shocked as she by the Irishman's outrageous pawing. *Was this her chance to grab the knife?* But then Jones renewed his hold, gripping her even tighter than before. Her small window of opportunity to confiscate the weapon evaporated.

Gerald was clearly enjoying how her struggles made him rock and sway on his perch atop her thighs. He leaned forward, grinning with lecherous pleasure as his hands moved to grope her jutting breasts, making her wish she'd zipped her jacket before leaving Kevin's house. "Nice fecking tits, too."

"Get your hands off me!" Janine screamed, at the same time realizing she had to stop struggling. Her thrashing was only increasing his enjoyment.

"Fucking hell, Gerald!" Jones was roaring. "I'm not going to hold her down while you bloody well *rape* her."

Jones's words told Janine he, at least, had a moral compass. *Would he help her escape when an opportunity presented itself?*

Janine forced herself to lay still while Gerald continued to molest her. Glaring up at him, she spat, "*You disgusting, sick pig!*"

His gaze lit with fury and he lifted his arm to backhand her again, but Jones's next words stayed his hand.

"What will Bart say when he hears you lost your shit before we even searched for the coin?" Jones accused.

Mention of Bart seemed to check Gerald's behaviour. Janine filed that for future reference.

"Bloody hell," Jones continued as Gerald dropped his arm. "Just check her pockets and be done with it!"

"Sod off," Gerald snarled, sitting back and glaring at Jones. "Who the feck do you think you are, telling me what to do?"

The driver braked, snaring Gerald's attention. "Richie!" he shouted over his shoulder as he began searching the left front pocket of Janine's jeans. "Why the feck are you slowing down?"

She heard Richie describing roadworks up ahead, felt the van slowing even further.

"Do *not* stop this vehicle!" Gerald warned, lifting his head to snarl an obscenity at the driver before returning his attention to her other pocket.

Janine dared a glance at the floor of the van beside her left hip. The knife was still there.

Gerald's face registered triumph when he realized there was a small object in Janine's pocket. He pushed his hand into the pocket, deliberately brushing his other against her crotch. Janine willed herself to lay still, her head turned away, her gaze towards the driver, the knife in her peripheral vision.

Tugging out the plastic bubble envelope, Gerald crowed as

he held it up in his left hand, at the same time lifting his right, searching blindly for the ceiling light.

Janine felt the van slowing even further, felt too a slackening of Jones's hold on her arms.

"Let me see!" Jones begged.

Gerald looked up, found the light switch, then flicked it on. Keeping the knife in her peripheral vision, Janine watched as he opened the plastic envelope and tilted the contents onto his palm.

The coins—or perhaps the surprising number of them—seemed to enthral the two men. As Jones leaned forward, gaping at the unexpected sight, his grip slackened. Neither man seemed aware that the van was now almost crawling, their attention fixated on the luminous gold in Gerald's palm.

Now! Janine told herself.

Wrenching her arms out of Jackson's slack hold, she grabbed the handle of the knife with her nearest hand, her left, the weapon clumsy in her non-dominant hold. Leveraging her upper body towards the back doors, she arced her left arm up, towards Gerald, noticing the blade glinting in the light a split second before it found its mark. She saw blood gush from his throat, heard Gerald screech, felt his weight lift from her thighs as he flung himself backwards, away from the source of pain.

She had the vague sense of the discs flying out of Gerald's grasp and of Jones lunging for the falling coins as if trying to save them from a bottomless abyss. Her right hand found the door handle and jerked it down. In the next instant, she was diving head first out the open door of the van.

The vehicle had been travelling slow, but not so slow that it didn't hurt when she slammed into the pavement. The impact knocked the knife out of her grasp. She heard it skittering away across the tarmac, heard as well the screech of tires directly in front of her. She braced herself for the inevitable, unable to stop her momentum as she rolled, once, twice, three times, towards the approaching vehicle. In the next instant, she was scrambling to her feet, intent on taking refuge in Dawson's black Golf.

But the car behind her was red, not black, and the driver a wild-haired blond woman gaping at Janine over the steering wheel in round-eyed disbelief.

Aware that Dawson wasn't there, that she'd lost her weapon, and that Gerald was squealing his rage like a stuck pig—*she hadn't killed the bastard, more's the pity*—she took the only action available to her. She ran.

Chapter 39

Dawson managed to talk himself down from the ledge he was teetering on as he shadowed the black van. *You can get her back, Delaney. Traffic is light. You have half a tank of gas. No matter what, stay focused; stay in control. Do NOT panic.*

The van was travelling fast through Nottingham's city limits, heading west, likely to the M-1, Dawson guessed. His heart pounding, he stayed glued to its bumper as he bounced over a series of speedbumps, his mind scrambling for a way to get Janine the hell out of there. He considered ramming the van, but dismissed the idea, envisioning the resulting crash, envisioning Cassie.

No! Janine is *not* going to die!

He swerved to hug the left rear bumper of the van, then the right, scanning the road ahead of them. No traffic lights. Nothing that would force the van to stop. He could pass the vehicle, then force it to stop. But there were too many intersecting roads onto which the van could divert. Even if there wasn't, that would give him maybe three seconds max to get from his car to the van on foot. If the van's occupants had weapons and were willing to use them, he was as good as dead in the first second.

He needed a workable plan. *What he needed was a goddamn weapon!*

The van suddenly took a sharp right turn. Avoiding an accident and congested traffic, Dawson saw as he followed, thankful the Golf was responsive to the sudden change of direction. He stayed on the van's tail as it merged and accelerated onto a busy, four-lane thoroughfare. *How to rescue Janine?*

Within a quarter mile, traffic began to slow. Another accident? Construction? *Please god, give me a break. Let me get her the hell out of there!*

Dawson swerved to the right so he could see what was on the road in front of the van. He saw a fire hydrant shooting out a geyser of water, the dark tarmac reflecting the emergency vehicles' flashing red lights. Work crews on the scene had placed neon orange traffic cones, funnelling the two-way traffic into single lanes, one each way. This was his chance to get it front of the van! If those motherfuckers had weapons, they wouldn't shoot, not with a hundred witnesses and no available escape route.

Don't fuck up this time, Delaney!

Dawson swerved into the left lane, closest to the sidewalk, intending to shoot ahead of the van before the two lanes funnelled into a single, but his lane suddenly slowed to a crawl as traffic began to bottleneck. A car length separated him from the van, then two. *Jesus Christ!* Dawson banged his fist on the wheel and shouted obscenities as the space between him and the van continued to increase.

He was about to slam the car into park and start chasing the vehicle on foot when the back door of the van swung open and Janine's limp body tumbled out, head first, white jacket open and flaring at her sides like angels' wings. The unexpected sight nearly stopped his heart. They'd killed her and were tossing her body! But then she was scrambling onto her feet.

He slammed his hand on the all-window release button.

"Janine!" he yelled, but she was in flight mode and didn't hear him. He slammed the car into park and leapt out, leaving his door gaping open. Oblivious to the honking horns around him, he sprinted towards her, shouting her name.

She saw him—*thank fuck!*—and changed direction. Then she was in his arms, and he could breathe. *He was never, ever letting her go!*

But then he did release her, and they were both sprinting back towards the Golf. As he slid behind the wheel, Dawson caught a brief glimpse of a man inside the van, his features lit by the glow of the interior light as he reached out to pull the door closed. He was crouching, but Dawson would peg him to be over six-feet tall, Caucasian, Robert Redford handsome, wearing a black leather jacket and a white, button-front shirt. He glimpsed wide, startled eyes before the van door swung closed.

Dawson shifted into drive, yanking the steering wheel hard to the left and maneuvering onto the raised sidewalk so that he was parallel with the road. He took a moment to chuck their overnight bags, which were in Janine's way, into the back seat. As he shifted into reverse, he saw that Janine was in a state of shock. "You okay?" he demanded as he braced a hand on the back of the passenger seat. Keeping his eyes trained out the rear window, he sent the car speeding backwards towards the nearest intersection behind them, one set of wheels in the gutter and the other on the sidewalk. A cacophony of honking horns erupted. He tuned them out.

"Janine?" he prompted, without looking at her. He was hyper aware of her presence in the car with him, and of the relief coursing through his veins. His heart still felt oversize in his chest, hammering out a tempo of fear. *Never. Again. Never fucking again would he let her out of his sight.*

Just before the intersection, he swerved back onto the road, barely avoiding the sign post and a street light pole, and forcing an oncoming car to swerve out of the way. He heard the sound of crunching metal as that car collided with another. He ignored it, knowing neither vehicle had been travelling fast enough to cause any major injury.

The next instant, the Golf was careening, still in reverse, onto a cobbled side street. Dawson swerved around a black mini Cooper, it's chrome accents glittering angrily as it veered out of the way, its horn beep-beep-beeping a discordantly cheerful reprimand.

Dawson faced front, shifted into drive, and accelerated, remembering at the last moment to keep to the left. *Damn Brits driving on the* wrong *goddamn side of the road.*

Chapter 40

"Are you okay?" Dawson repeated when Janine remained silent.

His eyes darted from the road to her profile, then back to the road, barely slowing as he turned right onto a wide street with sparse but steady traffic. He pressed the button on his door console to close his windows, flicking his gaze to the road sign as they sped through an intersection. *Robin Hood Way.* He had no idea where that was, but according to the compass indicator, they were heading northeast, the opposite direction the van had been travelling. His eyes darted from the road ahead of them to the mirrors, searching for the black van. He knew it couldn't have followed them, but he would remain watchful just the same.

He was very aware of his pounding heart and chalk-dry mouth. He gripped the wheel with both hands so Janine wouldn't see them shaking. He wondered how many years of nightmares he'd be having of Janine's limp body getting tossed out the back of the van.

They'd been in the car for barely half a minute, but she still hadn't spoken. "Talk to me, Janine," he said in a gentle but insistent tone as he slowed to navigate a round-about, taking it three-quarters the way around and exiting north onto Sheriff's Way.

"I could've killed him," she finally stated, her trembling voice almost unrecognizable.

As he sped under a streetlight, he glanced at her, saw she was staring down at her shaking hands, saw as well the blood. Not hers, he knew. The blood spatter told him that. But still he demanded, "Did they hurt you?"

"No," she said, wiping her hands on her jeans. Her words tumbled out in a rush. "I knew you were behind us. And then we were going so slow, and his knife was right there, and I just grabbed it and…and swung." She gestured with her left hand.

They had *a knife* on her? *Jesus!* He glanced at her again. She was staring straight ahead, but he knew she wasn't seeing the road.

"I could've sliced right through his neck! Just like the man on my lawn. I could've…" Her head snapped to face him. "My purse! It has…*shit!* It has my phone, my cash, *my passport!*"

"Don't worry about your goddamn purse," Dawson snapped, keeping his eyes on the road as he navigated a succession of dog-leg turns. At the next intersection, Queens Road, he turned east. When he saw a mileage sign for Radcliffe-on-Trent, he knew he was on a road that would eventually intersect with the A-1. In the back of his mind, he'd already decided to head for London. There, he'd enlist the help of Steve Jacobson, a buddy of his who worked for the National Crime Agency. He'd give him the van's plate number and report the kidnapping. He'd also acquire a weapon because, *holy weaponless, Batman,* it was a fucking miracle she'd escaped. And no goddamn thanks to him! He had to do a better job of protecting her. And to do that, he needed a goddamn weapon.

"But I can't get home without my passport," Janine argued.

"The Canadian embassy will replace it, don't worry," Dawson said, forcing himself to speak in a calm, easy tone that belied his horror over her narrow escape.

The road straightened as they began travelling parallel with a narrow canal.

"Pull over!" she suddenly demanded, her hands scrambling for the door handle.

"We need to keep go—"

"I'm going to be sick! Pull over!"

An embankment on the passenger side of the road prevented him from doing as Janine asked, but as there was no oncoming traffic, Dawson swerved to the left, glimpsing a road sign—*Rutland?*—before they bumped over a single-arched bridge and came to a screeching halt in front of a bus stop.

Janine practically fell out of the car,.

Dawson slammed into park, then ran around the nose of the car, gently guiding her to the empty bus stop bench, urging her to drop her head between her knees. He ran back to the car, grabbed his jacket and a bottle of water from the 12-pack they'd purchased on the drive to Nottingham. In seconds, he was beside her again, draping his jacket over her trembling shoulders.

As he stroked her back and murmured soft reassurances, his gaze swept their surroundings. The bus stop was well lit and the street quiet, with only an occasional car passing. He gripped the water bottle between his knees, twisting off the cap. "You're safe now, honey," he reassured her. "You're safe."

His own adrenaline rush was in retreat, but thinking about what might have happened had she not had the ability and wherewithal to escape made his stomach roil. How had she gotten hold of the bastard's knife? Her courage was off the freaking charts!

Janine sat up, slowly, her trembling hands pressed between her knees.

"Here, sip this," he said, holding out the water. "Are you still feeling like you're going to be sick?"

"No. I think I'm okay," she said, her voice unsteady. Her shaking hand froze as she reached for the bottle, noting the splatters of blood. "I need to wash my hands."

He helped her, splashing water until she was satisfied they were clean, then getting her to dry them on his jeans.

"You did good," he said in a low, encouraging tone as she sipped what was left of the water. He took her free hand in his, rubbing it gently to get the blood flowing back to her extremities.

When she lifted her gaze to meet his, he saw lingering fear and terror. His throat closed as he pictured the man he'd glimpsed holding a knife at her throat. *He'd kill the bastard!* "I don't know how you did it, but you got away. You did good, honey. Better than good. You were awesome." *Unlike you, Delaney. You did nothing. You're a fucking joke!*

Janine gave him a brave smile as she raised an eyebrow. "I was? Does that put me in league with Princess Leia?"

It took a moment for him to process her meaning, but then he barked out a laugh, although his grin held no humour as he challenged, "Princess Leia who?"

Despite her ability to joke, her eyes, he saw, were still clouded with fear. "Tell me what happened in there," he asked.

By the time she got to the end of her short tale, Dawson felt like he'd ground his teeth into stubs. He was leaning forward with his elbows on his knees, his head down, his shaking hands buried in his hair. *This was all his fault. He hadn't kept her safe.*

He finally sat up and looked at her. "I'm so fucking sorry, Janine. I should've figured out what they would do."

She pulled a face. "I know you think that, but I wish you wouldn't. You couldn't have known. And anyway, our main concern is still Kevin. Now that they have all four coins, they will conclude there's a bigger cache, right?"

"There has to be. And you know what that means, right?"

"What?" Janine asked.

"It means Kevin's *life* is valuable to them. He's the *only* one who knows the location."

Hope dimmed the worry in Janine's eyes. "Then they won't kill him," she said, her voice finally sounding normal. She drained the rest of the water, absently twisting the cap onto the empty bottle.

Dawson scanned their surroundings. All was quiet, but they were too exposed in the bright glare of the streetlights. "If you're up for it," he said, "we should get going."

As they stood, Janine shrugged out of his jacket, handing it to him. She frowned down at the blood spatters on her clothes. "I owe Nicolette some new clothes," she observed, then added, her tone thoughtful. "Dawson, if they were taking me to London, then Kevin must be there, right?"

"I think so, yes." Holding his coat in one hand, Dawson lifted his other to her face, tenderly tracing the yellowing bruise on her cheek with his knuckle. "Things have gotten way serious now. I have a contact at the National Crime Agency. We'll enlist his help. We should also contact your favourite numismatist." He cupped her face. "Are you okay?"

"I am now."

"Gerald O'Sullivan is going to pay for what he did to you," he growled.

Janine shuddered. "God! Just promise me I never have to see him again."

Dawson nodded. "Now that's a promise I can keep," he said.

Chapter 41

"I didn't assign you the role of my protector," Janine insisted. "Why did you? Why are you being so hard on yourself?"

His whole life, Dawson had been surrounded by strong, smart, independent women—his mother, his sisters, Cassie. His protective instincts had been deeply imprinted when he'd rescued his sister from drowning. Years later, it had been honed by his line of work. At this point in his life, he couldn't simply turn it off.

Dawson was still upset with himself for not realizing the meet at the left lion had been a ruse; that, all along, the O'Sullivan's had been planning to nab Janine on Kevin's doorstep using the old lady and the teenagers as unexpected eyes and brawn. Since resuming their drive to London, he'd been berating himself for his lack of foresight and the mistakes he'd made that allowed the kidnappers to abduct Janine right under his nose. Had that water main not burst and forced traffic to slow, had Janine not been so exceptionally courageous and resourceful, he might still be chasing the van. Thinking about his mistakes, about everything that could've gone wrong, made him feel sick. His heart-rate was still accelerated; he could feel it beating a wild tempo in his chest. His hands wouldn't stop shaking, and drawing a full breath into his lungs was proving impossible, as was dislodging the constriction that gripped his throat. If he didn't know better, he would say he was on the verge of a panic attack. But he didn't get panic attacks. What he was experiencing must simply be an adrenaline crash, more intense than usual because it was combined with the overwhelming relief that Janine was safe and the sick knowledge that he'd failed.

"Do you have a superhero complex?" Janine accused when he didn't answer.

"Of course not," he denied. "But that doesn't change the fact that I didn't keep you safe. *Jesus,*" he added in a frustrated undertone. "I'm fucking useless at keeping *anyone* safe." Feeling the intensity of Janine's gaze in the dark interior of the car, he wished he'd kept that last thought to himself. "Look, forget about it, okay?"

"No, I won't forget about it. What do you mean, *you can't keep anyone safe?* Explain that."

Every time he'd verbally chastised himself, she would counter with a reassuring statement that he'd done everything right, that he couldn't have predicted how events would unfold. But she was wrong. He should've figured it out. He hated that word, *should*, but in this instance, it was appropriate. He *should* have realized the left lion was a decoy location. He should've realized the old lady and the skateboarders were part of the take-down. He should've paid attention to his gut and figured out what his intuition was trying to tell him. Because he hadn't taken that time, Janine had been abducted, physically harmed, molested, and terrorized.

What he really wanted to do was pull over, then just sit and hold her, letting himself be soothed by her presence, even letting her stroke away his own tears. He wanted to hear her telling him that he was a good man, that he'd done his best, and his best was enough, even if he didn't believe her. Holy god, he wanted it to be true. But it wasn't, and he couldn't let himself off the hook.

Dawson geared down to navigate yet another roundabout. Half-way through, he accelerated, then clamped his shaking hand back onto the wheel.

When he remained silent, Janine continued. "Dawson, if your self-imposed protector role is on account of your sister Joanie's accident, that was eons ago. And besides, you *saved* her. You can't still castigate yourself for that."

He made a scoffing noise. No way was he ever, in his lifetime, forgiving himself for almost drowning his sister. The fact that he'd saved her didn't negate his reckless wrongdoing. And anyway, years later, he hadn't saved Cassie. That was a sticking point. And he hadn't saved Janine, either. She'd saved herself.

"Dawson," Janine insisted when he still didn't respond. In his peripheral vision, he could see the white of her jacket almost glowing in the ambient light of approaching headlights. "I think what happened to me is making you relive the panic of what happened to Joanie when you were kids." Then she added, her tone puzzled, clearly speaking to herself, "Although, that doesn't make sense. It was so long ago."

He heard Janine suddenly suck in a breath. When she spoke, her tone was cautious and exploratory. "Dawson, did something happen to make you leave the Secret Service, something you're still blaming yourself for?" When he remained silent, she added, "Every time I've mentioned your former job, you clam up. Look, you don't have to tell me. Honestly, you don't. But you might feel better if you did."

He wasn't surprised at her perception. She was too smart, her heart was too big. *No, never too big.* But right now she was being overly forgiving because she didn't have all the facts. If she knew the truth, she would change her tune. And besides, talking about it would only make him relive the godawful self-loathing and powerlessness he'd felt after Cassie's accident. How would that help anything? He'd been officially exonerated from any wrong-doing, but that was just stupid-ass politics. Cassie's death *was* his fault. There was no getting around that.

"Dawson, I'm not pressuring you." Janine's voice was soft as she placed a hand on his thigh, left it there. "I only want to help."

His hand automatically lifted to clasp hers, but he wouldn't let himself. Instead, he lifted his hand and ran his fingers through his hair, then gripped the steering wheel once more, tapping his thumb in agitation as he stared out at the snaking line of lights.

"Dawson? Say *something,* at least," echoing his earlier request of her.

He realized not telling Janine would make him more of a coward, on top of everything else. *Tell her, Delaney! Let her see you for the worthless, reckless bastard you truly are.* But telling her meant she would disappear from his life. Whatever might be going on between them, it would be over before it even begun. *All part of the shit cards life deals out.*

"Fine," he said, his tone brittle.

Shit! Was he really going to do this? Was he really going to talk about her after more than three years of radio silence? He heaved a half-sob, half-sigh. When he finally spoke, his tone was harsh.

"I didn't join the Service because I wanted to be on the detail to protect the highest ranking US politician. That didn't interest me." He paused. *God, was he really doing this?* He tried to take in a deep breath, but his lungs wouldn't expand. His breathing shallow, he said, "I've always been interested in the operation behind the scenes."

In fits and starts, he went on to tell her that, after completing his training, he'd been assigned to an investigative team that specialized in assessing threats. His next seven years were spent under the mentorship of Patrick Brooks, a man

Dawson considered the smartest and best investigator in the business.

When Patrick retired, Dawson took on the role of mentor to an eager new recruit, a young woman named Cassandra Straker. In their two years as partners, Dawson grew to admire and respect Cassie for her fearlessness, her courage, her acutely intuitive thought processes, her integrity, her high energy, as well as her vivacious, upbeat personality. Dawson also liked Cassie's fiancé, Matthew Bishop, a financial analyst whose unflappable strength was a perfect foil to Cassie's effervescence. The men met weekly for a round of golf or a game of squash, followed by beers at the nearest sports bar.

A few weeks before Matthew and Cassie's wedding, Dawson and Cassie were investigating the boyfriend of the President's niece, an alleged member of a violent extremist group. They'd tracked the man to a residential neighbourhood in Portland, but he'd eluded them by climbing through a basement window and speeding away in his souped-up car.

They gave chase, with Dawson behind the wheel. He'd been hyper alert to his surroundings, as always, mindful of the danger of speeding on residential streets. He was aware of an elderly gentleman in his flower patch rising from his knees; aware of a woman of undetermined age wearing a floppy straw hat and wielding a watering can; aware, too, of a young mother on the sidewalk ahead of them, walking in the same direction as the cars and pushing a stroller, a kid of about four walking at her side and leading a small dog on a leash.

He'd seen the quarrelling squirrels the instant they darted onto the road directly in front of his vehicle. Thanks to his training and years of experience, he knew it was safer to allow the inevitable than to try and dodge the silly creatures. But when the kid's dog chased after the squirrels, jerking its leash out of the youngster's hand, and the child went running into the street in pursuit, Dawson had to react. He avoided the kid, thank Christ.

He couldn't avoid the dog. And he should've avoided clipping the driver's front wheel against the curb. At the speed they'd been travelling, that impact launched the car into the air briefly. It flipped sideways and slammed into a fire hydrant, the metal protrusion a giant steel fist punching through the passenger door.

By the time the car stopped its momentum, landing on all four wheels with the air bags deployed, Dawson didn't have a scratch on him. Cassie, though, lay broken and bloodied in the seat beside him, barely conscious, barely even recognizable.

At the hospital, the medical staff wouldn't tell Dawson anything. Matthew and Cassie's families were behind closed doors. When Matthew finally emerged with an older woman Dawson assumed was his mother, the look on Matthew's face told him everything he didn't want to know. Cassie was dead.

"*You killed her!*" Matthew snarled when he saw Dawson.

The accusation, resonating with truth, fell like a whip on the open wound of Dawson's heart.

Dawson choked out an apology, but the heartbroken man interrupted him, shouting in a voice hoarse with tears, *"Get away from me; get out of my sight!"* before collapsing onto a chair.

Dawson gazed at Matthew, trying and failing to find words to express his grief and shame and mortification for the role he'd played in Cassie's death, but the hovering woman at the sobbing man's side was gesturing at him, urging him to leave.

Dawson slowly turned away, lifting one heavy foot in front of the next, his head low, his heart achingly heavy, knowing he would never in all his years forgive himself for what he'd done.

He'd seen Cassie's grieving fiancé once more, at her funeral, but he hadn't had the courage to approach him, then or since.

The months following Cassie's death were hell. Dawson was forced to undergo multiple psych evaluations while on paid leave. Eventually, he ended up at Kevin's house in Nottingham, drowning his grief and self-loathing in copious amounts of alcohol. His loyal childhood friend frequently got drunk with him, drawing the proverbial sword and standing at his friend's side as Dawson battled his demons of self-loathing and recriminations. After six weeks in England, Dawson returned to the US where he resigned from his job, convinced that, if he couldn't keep his own partner safe, then he had no business in the Service. A few months later, Dawson and his brother-in-law opened a security company in Seattle.

Janine's hand was still resting on his left thigh. It felt so damn good there, *so right.* But he kept both his shaking hands on the wheel, dropping his left only to change gears.

"God, Dawson," she said, her voice gentle and soothing. "It's so awful, heart-breakingly so. I'm so, so sorry Cassie died. But you can't burden yourself with this misplaced blame."

"A residential neighbourhood, Janine," Dawson ground out through clenched teeth. "Even a mall cop knows the idiocy of engaging in a high-speed chase through a residential neighbourhood. But I was cocky and arrogant, certain I was in control, convinced I was striking the right balance. With my training, my so-called expert ability to control a speeding vehicle, it was worth the risk of preventing this asshole from escaping our net. And this guy *was* dangerous. Later that day, my unit found a hoard of stolen weapons in his basement. But that still doesn't change the fact that Cassie's death was entirely my fault."

"You can't live the rest of your life with this self-imposed affliction," Janine argued.

"I can and I will."

"Haven't you punished yourself long enough?"

"But I *deserve* to be punished. I saw the look on Matthew's face. And he was right. I killed Cassie. I was reckless. I overcompensated when I ran over that damn dog. If I hadn't clipped the curb—"

"If! Dawson, don't do this. If the man you were chasing hadn't fled in his car, if the child had kept hold of his dog, if the fire hydrant hadn't been in that exact spot, *if, if if.* Don't you realize, *none of what happened is your fault.* There's simply too many variables."

"It *is* my fault. It's *all* my fault. I didn't do what I'd been trained to do. I didn't maintain control of that car. Cassie died because of it. Because of me."

"Dawson, if you truly embrace that belief, then you're letting that belief define who you are."

"How can it *not* define me?" he practically shouted. *"I* was the reckless one. *I* should've died in that accident. *Not* Cassie!"

Dawson was aware of Janine shaking her head, but all she said was, *"Jesus, Dawson."*

He could hear the anguish in her tone, felt his vision blur knowing her heart was breaking for him. Her hand was warm on his thigh, a physical link between them. He wanted to grab hold of it and never let go, but he forced himself to keep his hands on the wheel, his eyes on the motorway. If he touched her, he felt certain he would weep, although he wasn't sure if he'd be weeping for Janine's unfounded, persistent belief in him, Cassie's needless death, Matthew's heartbreak, or his own bruised and battered soul.

Talking about it had *not* helped!

After a few minutes of silence, Janine asked, "How is Matthew now?"

Dawson blinked away his unshed tears. He hadn't expected her question, and it took him a minute to respond. "What? But…I told you. I haven't seen him."

"You haven't contacted him at all?"

"Of course not. Didn't you hear me? I killed the love of his life. Thanks to me, his wedding guests attended a funeral. Why would he want to see me?"

"But Dawson, *you* lost something precious to you, too. And I don't just mean Cassie. You lost Matthew's friendship. Your heart took a major hit that day, and so did your self-worth. It's time for you to have all of that back again."

He wanted to shout, *I don't deserve to have it back!* But

he couldn't speak around the fisting lump of sorrow closing his throat. Janine's words hit a raw and open wound he'd never allowed himself to treat. No one, including himself, had ever acknowledged exactly what he'd lost that day.

"Oh, Dawson," Janine said when he didn't speak. Her simple words were weighted with tenderness and compassion. He sensed that she wanted to say more. Perhaps because he remained stubbornly silent, she held her tongue. He felt her gaze return to the road, to the glow of light pollution on the horizon and the winding string of lights snaking ahead of them. Her hand remained on his thigh, a steady, tenacious warmth.

Strangely, as the minutes passed in silence, Dawson felt the tension slowly uncoiling from his shoulders. His hands loosened on the wheel. The painful conscription that had prevented him from filling his lungs with anything more than shallow breaths lifted. Maybe he *had* needed to talk about Cassie, share the misery of the tale, not to free himself from his burden of blame—never that—but to lessen the pain of remembering.

Dawson stole a glance at Janine, her steadfast touch and her patient, profound silence conveying her genuine concern and acceptance. His heart filled with longing, for what exactly, he couldn't say.

His hands no longer trembling, he finally reached down and claimed hers, raising it to his lips and planting a tender kiss on the tip of each finger, then dropping both their hands to his thigh, their fingers linked. *I love her.* The words in his mind appeared as silent testimony to what was in his heart; they didn't startle him, although perhaps they should have. He felt a glow in his chest that was due to Janine's presence at his side, a flame that had nothing to do with sexual desire and everything to do with the unknown force that powered her beautiful heart.

Janine finally broke the silence. "Do you know where Matthew is now?"

"I think he moved to California," he said. His voice was gruff, as if he'd been crying, yet he hadn't shed a tear.

"You lost Cassie, Dawson, and you've never properly grieved for her. Don't you see that's why it still hurts so much? It's not because you *deserve* to be hurting. It's because the only person who could truly understand how you felt about Cassie, about losing her, the only person who can give you the helping hand you need to step out of that shadow of pain, he shut you out."

Dawson felt enveloped by the warmth emanating from Janine's beautiful, forgiving, loving heart. He was getting choked up again, but in a happy way this time, as if the turmoil of his dark emotions had gained an opacity that was finally letting in a hint of warmth and light.

"I get it now," she continued, her tone thoughtful. "I think what happened with Joanie made such an impression on you —and at such a young age—it became a kind of calling, which is why you chose a career in the protective services. Given that scenario, it was natural for you to feel that Cassie was your responsibility, especially given your role of mentor. And I understand now why you have a hyperactive goal to keep me safe."

Dawson didn't have the desire or the energy to argue, but Janine was wrong. Or, half wrong, at least. He was motivated to keep her safe, but it was because he freaking loved her. Now didn't feel like the right moment to express his feelings, but he would tell her when the time was right. "Janine, I don't think there's any getting around that I was behind the wheel. That alone made her life my responsibility."

Janine was shaking her head again. "When I lost my parents, I found myself doing a lot of self-reflection about all the things I wished were different. My mom, even though she wasn't warm and fuzzy, still taught me some valuable life lessons, particularly about how to face a problem head on, and how to sort out what I was and wasn't responsible for. After they died, I went through a period of resentment because I no longer had the chance to have a *loving* mother. Whatever opportunities I might've had in our future to understand why she'd been so aloof and emotionally detached, they were gone. Wiped out in a single instant. But I eventually found a kind of equilibrium between the mother she'd been and the mother I realized she'd wanted to be. I take comfort in that." Janine gestured impatiently with her free hand. "Oh, I'm not making any sense, am I? What I'm trying to say is that, at some point in our adult journey, we have to take responsibility for our own selves. But Cassie was not *your* responsibility. Cassie *chose* to be a Secret Service agent. She was fully aware of the danger she might face in the course of her work. And you, Dawson, don't have the right to claim responsibility for *her* choices."

When he didn't respond, Janine asked, "Dawson, would she have seen it your way? That she was *your* responsibility to keep safe?"

An immediate image of Cassie making an abject, vociferous objection to this statement crowded into Dawson's mind. He surprised himself by chuckling. "God, no. Absolutely not. She would've been incensed at the notion. She was…I don't know, fiery. She had strong opinions and didn't mind sharing them." He felt as if he'd finally been granted permission to talk about Cassie and now couldn't stop. "She reminded me of Joanie, actually. I used to tease her, just like I did Joanie, because it was entertaining to watch her blow a fuse and get all bent out of shape before she finally realized I was pushing her buttons on purpose. And then she'd give me a well-deserved punch on the shoulder. If Matthew was around to witness this, he'd start a countdown when that look came into her eye, all sparky and fired up like a lit stick of dynamite." Dawson chuckled again, shaking his head as memories danced through his mind. "It pissed her off something fierce when he did that. God, she was something else. I wish you could have known her. You'd have loved her, too."

His last few words shook with emotion as, for the first time in a very long time, with Janine's hand enfolded in his, Dawson felt the fist of blame loosen its grip on his beleaguered heart.

Part III

Chapter 42

An hour later, just after midnight, Dawson checked them into a Travel Lodge.

Five minutes after entering their hotel room, and after draping her running clothes, still musty, over the radiator, Janine crawled into the king-sized bed in the nightshirt she'd borrowed from Nicolette. Dawson could tell she was as physically and emotionally exhausted as he was. It had been a harrowing evening. He climbed in beside her, clicked off the bedside light, then spooned her against his chest.

Janine sighed into the dark. "I have a million industrious bees buzzing in my head, filling the honeycomb of my brain. I keep thinking of Gerald's *persuasive* fists, and wondering how badly Kevin is hurt..." Her voice wobbled as her words tapered off.

"Shh," Dawson whispered soothingly, lifting his head and pressing his lips against her temple, careful to avoid the small cut in her hairline. Dropping his head back onto his pillow, he said, "Don't let those images in, honey. You need sleep. We won't be able to find him if you're too exhausted to think."

"I know. It's just..."

"Think about what your mom taught you about how to

deal with life's problems," he suggested, his tone soothing and light. "All those things we need to solve? Every question we have that still needs an answer? That will all still be there in the morning, waiting for us to think about them again. And we'll both be better equipped to fix the problems and find the answers after we get some sleep. And we *will* find him, honey. I promise you. We don't know how yet, or…"

Dawson abruptly stopped speaking when he heard a light snore. *Well shit! Not so industrious, after all.*

He waited ten minutes, making sure she was fully asleep before slipping out of bed and moving silently to the desk where he flicked on the small lamp, setting the light to the dimmest setting. Keeping an eye on Janine, he dialed the number for his sister in Seattle. When Joanie answered, he asked her to look up Steve's contact info—all of it, email, home, work, cell—writing it down as she recited it. She wanted to know why he needed it, but he promised to call her later to explain. She would've argued, he knew, but her girls started making a ruckus in the background.

After ending that call, and despite the hour, he dialed again.

Janine stepped into the shower, the water causing the small cut at her temple to sting and her bruised cheek to ache. She closed her eyes and let the hot spray of water drum lightly against her scalp. She didn't have to look in the mirror to know a smile still lingered on her face. Waking up in Dawson's arms, followed by mind-blowing sex, was the perfect anecdote for stress. She wanted to find her cousin, and soon. Today. But she also didn't want her time with Dawson to end. Not just yet.

She loved being held in his arms and in his midnight gaze, loved how the timbre of his voice seemed to strike a chord that resonated deep within her, whether his voice was lifted in laughter or lowered in passion. She especially loved being touched by his big, beautiful, magic hands. And she loved his goofy sense of humour, loved talking with him. It didn't matter if they were sorting through his hang-ups, or addressing her worries, or chatting about his big and boisterous family, or just chit-chatting; it didn't matter, she simply liked being with him.

Was she falling in love with Dawson Delaney?

As she massaged shampoo into her hair, she recalled how the tension had emanated from him as he'd relayed the tragic tale of Cassie's death, recalled too how it had felt when, after he'd told her his heart-wrenching tale, his taunt shoulders had finally relaxed and he'd taken comfort in holding her hand. He came across as confident, straightforward, and competent —and he *was* all of those things—but under the façade of his pragmatic approach to life and goofy sense of humour, he had a bruised, hurting heart. She wanted to be a bridge for him that helped him navigate away from the pain of Cassie's death and towards the blameless life he deserved.

Janine leaned her head back and rinsed the shampoo from her hair, considering her feelings for this intriguing man. Half a lifetime ago, she'd had a pretty terminal crush on him. Were those feelings a sufficient foundation for what she was now experiencing? And even if they were, how could she reconcile a future with him, short- or long-term, where she ran her business in Whistler and he ran his in Seattle?

You're being premature, she scolded herself as she finger-combed conditioner into her wet hair. She knew full well it wasn't practical wasting time contemplating anything long-term when their immediate future was rife with so many unknowns. Right here, right now, their first priority was finding Kevin. She would stick to that, and so would Dawson, she knew. But, while they pursued that goal, she would make the most of her time with him. Which included having sex at every opportunity, *including jumping his bones again as soon as she stepped out of the shower.*

She shrieked in surprise when the shower curtain was yanked aside and Dawson joined her, but that changed to a strangled sort of half-sigh, half-moan when his lips found hers and his hands began stroking the length of her body.

She lifted her arms, her fingers doing what they always wanted to do—tangle in his thick hair. Her body hummed in anticipation as she felt the evidence of his arousal against her abdomen. When his lips left hers to sketch hot, moist kisses across her jaw and along the base of her neck, his touch and the light abrasiveness of his stubble sent shivers of delight to every nerve ending in her body. Wanting more, always wanting more, she stood on tiptoe, curling a leg around him in invitation as she began stroking his cock, her movements sure and demanding, her lips lifting into a smile at the intoxicating *gah-ah-ah* sound he made in response to her touch. She could get addicted to that. She could get addicted to him.

He took her hands, bringing them up and holding them against his chest as he looked down at her. She lost herself in his dark sapphire eyes framed in their wet, sooty lashes. There was desire there, and heat, but also a knee-buckling tenderness that made her catch her breath.

"Janine," he breathed, pressing his lips against the tip of her index finger.

The inflection in his voice when he uttered her name made her heart swell with wanting, need, and love.

He lifted his hand and gently traced the outline of the bruise on her cheekbone with his knuckle.

She saw his eyes darken with storm clouds. Wanting to chase them away, she pressed her lips to his, her kiss full of all the feelings that were too soon to express in words.

He turned them, pressing her against the wall, the spray of water cascading down his back as his hands and lips and tongue explored her. She wanted him. Now, without delay. "I need you inside me," she moaned in an urgent whisper. "Now."

He shifted out of her grasp, but instead of opening the curtain to grab the foil packet he must surely have laid ready, he trailed kisses down her neck, along the swell of her breasts, stopping to suck and lick first one, then the other of her taut nipples. She let her head drop back, let her eyes drift closed, loving the sensation of his wet tongue and lips on her skin, loving the feel of his muscled shoulders under her fingers, her hands lifting once again to his hair as if being called home.

He dropped to one knee in front of her, and all thought of the urgency of getting him sheathed in a condom got vacuumed out of her brain as his mouth began exploring her folds, his tongue and lips pressing, just so, on her most sensitive spot.

"Oh, god!" she gasped. She wanted to say more, but the heart-stopping pleasure she was feeling robbed her of speech.

When he lifted her leg and draped it over his shoulder, improving access for his mouth and hands to explore, she resorted to moans of pleasure, gripping his shoulders with her hands, incapable of all thought beyond the momentum of bliss building inside her, swelling, blossoming, intensifying until, in the next instant, she shattered.

If he hadn't been bracing her, she would've collapsed.

Eons later, she heard him murmuring her name, the sound coming to her as if through a fog. She looked down, cupping his face in her hands as the shower thrummed against his back. *"Janine,"* he whispered again, holding her gaze as he pressed his lips to the curve of her waist. She was mesmerized by the vision of him, his face against her abdomen, his midnight eyes, framed by dark, wet eyelashes, holding her captive.

"Janine," he whispered again as he rose to his feet, cupping her face, his thumbs stroking her swollen lips. *"My beautiful Janine."*

She tasted herself on his tongue as he kissed her, his touch making her dizzy with need again. She reached blindly behind him, searching the edge of the tub surround until her fingers found the foil packet.

Sheathed, he filled her with his length, igniting bliss at her core as he thrust into her until, for the third time that morning, Janine felt herself bursting into a rapturous kaleidoscope of ecstasy.

Chapter 43

Janine was impressed that Dawson was able to maneuver the rented Golf into the compact parking space on a crowded street near Holland Park in Kensington, two blocks from Folkestone Auctioneers. They were taking a stab in the dark, visiting Alfred unannounced, but earlier they'd agreed it was the obvious place to start. Dawson was still waiting for the investigative reports from his JAG friend, but at least they had a meeting scheduled with his contact at the National Crime Agency for later that afternoon.

They agreed it made sense to tell Alfred Buckley everything. Dawson wasn't certain they could trust him but, at the very least, Alfred could shed some light on the O'Sullivan's and perhaps give them a sense of what they were up against—as if they didn't already know.

Janine had finally donned her own clothes that morning, including her long-sleeved running shirt, despite the warm, dry spell that wasn't showing any signs of abating. She climbed out of the car and waited for Dawson on the busy sidewalk, stepping aside to avoid a fashionably dressed woman wearing earbuds and talking on a cellphone while pushing a wide two-seater stroller with identical fashion-forward toddlers.

Noticing a dent in the Golf's back bumper, she turned to ask Dawson about it, but instead remained silent, admiring his lean form as he edged gracefully between the two parked cars. He had an unhurried way of moving, a kind of natural elegance that made her catch her breath.

As he got closer to her, Janine gestured at the dent in the Golf's back bumper. "How did that happen?"

He pulled a face, absently scratching his jaw. "Yeah, that. There's a red Ford Fiesta on Kev's street with a matching dent on its front bumper. I'll figure out who it belongs to later and make the necessary reparations."

"I'm happy to pay for the damages," Janine said.

"We've got bigger problems to solve than who's paying for what," he stated as he drew her into his arms. "The biggest one being, it's been far too long since you last kissed me."

Janine laughed. It had been less than an hour. When he dipped his head and touched his lips to hers, she couldn't help but respond, her kiss full of erotic promise. *Would she ever be immune to this man's touch?* She didn't think so.

When the kiss ended, they remained in their embrace, their gazes locked, their eyes conveying an unspoken acknowledgement of their growing feelings.

"As soon as we extract Kev from his shitstorm," Dawson finally said in a low voice. "I intend to do a whole lot more of that."

Janine felt a shiver pass through her. She wasn't sure if it was in response to his mention of Kevin's predicament or Dawson's promise of continued intimacy beyond their sojourn in the UK. They hadn't discussed what would happen between them after this mess was sorted out. It was as if they were both avoiding the topic, knowing Kevin was the priority. But Dawson's statement told Janine he was contemplating their future, just as she was.

She leaned her forehead against his chest for a moment, basking in the knowledge that he seemed to reciprocate what she was feeling. After a moment, she lifted her head and said, "Well, we'd better get on with it then, hadn't we?"

They shared a humourless smile, then turned and headed down the congested sidewalk hand-in-hand. Her thoughts immediately drifted to her cousin. Would Alfred Buckley be able to help them locate Kevin? And, if so, when they found him—as surely they must—how badly hurt would he be? She gave voice to some of her worries. "What if Alfred refuses to help? Or can't? What if—?"

"Honey," Dawson interrupted in a soothing tone, shaking his head. "Remember? We agreed not to get suckered in by what-ifs. Anticipate, yes. What-ifs? No."

Janine forced herself to take a deep breath, deliberately pivoting her attention away from everything that could go wrong and onto appreciating the pretty, tree-lined street. She assumed the elegant buildings that lined both sides of the wide street, with their large, white-trimmed windows and sweeping sidewalks, had once been terraced mansions. Most were built from an oyster-coloured stone with accents of orange or red brick and with multiple chimney pots lining the gabled roofs. The street-level frontages boasted a mixture of shops, galleries, restaurants, and cafés, while the entrances to the upper stories made it obvious the mansions had been transformed into multi-unit apartments.

A few minutes later, they stood in front of Folkestone's Auctioneers, the name stencilled in old-fashioned gold lettering on the plate-glass windows. A taupe and garnet striped canopy perched invitingly above the entrance, while the ground-level windows were framed in slabs of dark marble, capped by an elaborate gold crest mounted in the centre of the elegant transom. The upper stories of this building, Janine guessed as she looked up at the three levels, had not been converted into apartments. Rather, the small arches of black marble above each window, each boasting the Folkestone crest, suggested the entire former mansion belonged to the auction house.

The pleasant sound of a bell chiming greeted them as they entered the shop. The interior was smaller than Janine expected, although high-ceilinged, with a feature wall at the rear in beautiful pale stone. An arched doorway in the centre was draped with cranberry-coloured curtains, held to each side with thick braided cords of gold. Their footfalls were silent on the thick red and gold carpet as they made their way into the room. Showcases were configured in a horseshoe, split in the centre by a small opening that was blocked from entry by another gold cord. The interior looked little different from a jewelry store, but when Janine glanced at the nearest cabinet, she saw the shelves were lined with trays of coins in varying sizes and metals.

An elegantly dressed woman, her long, black braids wound in a sophisticated up-do, stood behind the counter. She set aside the coins she'd been sorting as she greeted them. "Welcome to Folkestone's. My name is Areta. How may I help you?"

Janine couldn't place her accent, but didn't think it was British. "Is Alfred Buckley here?" she asked.

"Yes, he is in the back. May I tell him who is asking?" She lifted an inquiring eyebrow as she picked up her cellphone.

"Dawson Delaney."

He'd spoken before she could, and Janine gave him a puzzled look. When he gave her a minute shake of his head, she realized he hadn't wanted her to mention her last name, which made sense given it matched Kevin's.

She returned her gaze to Areta, watching as the woman tapped out a short message with long, elegant fingers. Was she in league with the O'Sullivan's, Janine wondered. But the woman gave no overt indication of curiosity about either Janine or Dawson.

Janine expected Alfred to be pleased to see them given the concern he'd displayed for Kevin the previous day, but when he stepped through the draped opening and saw her, his face blanched. She must've imagined his reaction, for in the next instant, he was smiling and greeting them warmly. With a glance at his employee, he asked Janine if she had any news of her cousin, seeming as disinclined as Dawson to speak Kevin's name aloud.

As a wave of disappointment swept through her, Janine realized she'd been harbouring a hope that Kevin was with Alfred.

"Not yet," Janine answered in a too-cheery tone.

"Would you care to join me for a refreshment?" Alfred asked, unclipping the velvet cord between the showcases.

After they walked through, Alfred led them through the draped archway and along a carpeted corridor. After climbing a wide staircase, the nearest wall lined with framed auction posters advertising estate sales and archeological finds, Alfred led them down another carpeted hallway. Janine glimpsed a figure in a nearby room standing over a table working on what appeared to be a large painting. Noting her interest, Alfred told her this was one of their restoration rooms. He gave no further explanation, instead leading them up a second, narrower staircase to a landing on the third floor.

Once on the smaller landing, he extracted a key from his pocket, unlocked a door, and stepped into a small foyer floored in black and white, hexagon-shaped tiles. Closing the door, he inserted his key into the interior keyhole and locked it.

"This is my private flat," Alfred said. They followed him down a short corridor, the walls papered in striped wallpaper much like the Folkestone awning and decorated with small, elaborately framed paintings hung from a picture rail. "I don't live here, but I often stay the night. London traffic can cut a swath into one's day."

The tall casement windows in the compact, elegantly

furnished reception room made it seem larger than it was. Alfred gestured for them to sit on an off-white Victorian sofa, the tufted upholstery an elegant contrast to the carved swirls of dark wood along its back and arms.

"Can I offer you a refreshment? Tea? Coffee?" he asked.

"Just water for me, please," Janine said, eying Dawson with a frown. He'd moved across the room and was poking his head into an archway.

The older gentleman tilted his head as he, too, eyed Dawson. "You are a careful man, Mr. Delaney." He seemed unbothered by Dawson's snooping. "As you can see, that is the kitchenette." When Dawson turned to regard him, Alfred gestured back the way they'd come, addressing his guest in a pleasant tone. "At the other end of the corridor is a lavatory, utility room, linen closet, and bedroom. Go ahead. Investigate."

"I'll do that," Dawson said, disappearing down the corridor.

Alfred gave Janine a tight smile before leaving the room. She could no longer see him, but heard the sound of the faucet, then of glasses being filled.

Dawson reappeared a minute later, finally taking a seat beside her. "Empty," he stated.

Alfred re-entered the room with a tray bearing three tall glasses of water, none of which had ice. "Now that you've established no one is listening at the keyhole, perhaps you can indulge my curiosity and tell me why you're here."

He placed coasters on the oval coffee table, set their glasses in front of them, then settled into an armchair on Janine's left, which was positioned in such a way that the occupant could both see down the corridor and out the window.

Janine gave him a summary of recent events, ending with her fortuitous escape from the van. It took her a full ten minutes to recite, with Dawson adding a few details along the way. Alfred remained silent, interrupting only twice, once with deep suspicion as to what she'd found in Kevin's ice-cube tray, and a second time with profound concern—*and trepidation?*—about the previous evening's kidnapping.

Janine eyed Alfred as she sipped her water. His expression was doleful, and she wondered if he was despondent that she'd lost possession of the coins or if he was worried about Kevin. Perhaps both. She glanced at Dawson, but he simply shrugged and returned his gaze to Alfred.

"The authenticity of the coins can't be established without examining them in what you academics call 'in situ', correct?" Dawson asked.

Alfred seemed to make an effort to focus on and respond to Dawson's question. "Yes," he finally said. "The site would need to be subjected to carbon testing, which would confirm the date range of the coins—or, at least of the surrounding earth in which the coins were found. But that would only be the first step. If these coins were proven to be minted by Alfred the Great…" He shook his head as if in disbelief.

"Why is it so hard to believe that Alfred the Great might have minted them?" Janine asked.

Their host rested his elbows on the arms of his chair and formed a steeple with his fingers. "As a Canadian, you may not realize that my namesake is a very significant figure in British history. He was the first ruler to officially make peace with the warring Danes." Alfred's admiration for the historic figure was evident as he continued describing him. "Because of that peace, he was able to nurture cultural growth. As an adult, he learned to read and write Latin, and promoted education, at least for those whose station in life allowed such a pursuit." He regarded Janine, then Dawson, before adding, "Throughout his reign, Alfred the Great minted many coins. But what he *didn't* do was mint *gold* coins. You're certain it was gold?"

Janine and Dawson both nodded.

"You didn't happen to take a photo of it, did you?"

"Even if I did, which I didn't," Janine said, "I no longer have my phone."

"Yes, of course," Alfred stated in a bleak tone.

"Wouldn't Kevin know if something he dug up was authentic?" Dawson asked.

Alfred nodded reluctantly. "Indeed. Dr. Kirby is an expert. I would stake my reputation on his ability to determine the authenticity of any Anglo-Saxon artifact."

"Let's just say the coins are authentic. Then…" Dawson paused, lifting an eyebrow in invitation for Alfred to complete the sentence.

"Then?" Alfred's gaze went to Janine. She thought she read concern, even apology, in his watery grey eyes. "Then, I'm afraid, you, I mean to say, Dr. Kirby, is in grave trouble. Last night's appalling events are evidence that the O'Sullivan's will stop at nothing to get their hands on this treasure, including…" he hesitated for a fraction of a second, touching his temple with his index finger as he added, "kidnapping, to achieve their goal."

"They *won't* get another opportunity to snatch Janine," Dawson snapped. "I'll make certain of that.

Alfred eyed Dawson, looking utterly weary. His tone was strangely accusatory when he asked, "Why did you come here?"

Dawson leaned forward, resting his elbows on his knees. "We don't have any leads, Alfred. Not a one. You're more familiar with the O'Sullivan's than we are. Can you guess where Kevin might be?"

"Oh," Alfred gave a dismissive wave of his hand. "I don't have to *guess*."

Chapter 44

Hope flared in Janine's chest as Alfred informed them that the O'Sullivan's had a warehouse somewhere in east Barking, but it died when he admitted the precise location was a closely guarded secret known only to those in the O'Sullivan's inner circle.

When a knock sounded on the door of Alfred's flat, Janine startled at the unexpected sound. Dawson leapt to his feet.

Alfred didn't look at them as he rose and murmured his apologies.

Janine felt certain she'd seen alarm on Alfred's face before he left the room. Dawson must've seen it as well. His body was poised like a predator eyeing its prey.

"What's wrong?" Janine asked, getting to her feet.

She heard Alfred unlock and open the door, then saw Dawson's shoulders relax as the conversation between Alfred and his visitor, easy to hear from the front room, drifted their way. A youthful male voice was informing Alfred that his mail had arrived. She heard Alfred thank him, heard the sound of the door closing.

Something wasn't right, though. Some faint bell was ringing in her mind as she listened to the sound of Alfred's returning footsteps. *But what?* When Alfred reappeared in the front room, his gaze remained on the manila envelope in his hands.

Janine realized she hadn't heard the sound of Alfred re-locking the door.

She spoke Dawson's name, her tone filled with alarm, but Dawson had already grabbed her hand.

"We're leaving," he said.

They'd taken only a single step when Janine heard the flat door swing open. A burly man of medium height with thinning, grey-streaked hair hurried into the room, a pistol in his hand. He stopped, blocking their access to the short corridor.

"Hands where I can see them, Delaney."

Janine recognized the lilting Irish accent. *Dick Irish!* Or, rather, Bartholomew O'Sullivan.

"Stay behind me," Dawson instructed Janine as he lifted his hands.

Janine realized Alfred must've texted Bartholomew O'Sullivan when he'd filled their water glasses in the kitchenette. It hadn't dawned on her that the benign numismatist would double-cross them.

She whirled on him. He'd remained standing beside his chair, his hand clutching what Janine felt certain was an empty envelope. "*How could you?*" she accused.

Alfred's expression was mournful. "You don't understand," he said, shaking his head. "They know—"

"I don't *care!*" Janine snapped. She didn't want to know what dirt the O'Sullivan's had on him. Evidence of embezzlement, or forgery, or perhaps a sex tape. It didn't matter. He'd sold them out.

Janine turned back to face Bartholomew, trusting that Dawson was devising a plan. With his skills, she assured herself, he'd disarm the man. She'd wait for his signal, and then act accordingly.

She felt the blood drain from her face as a shorter man

stepped out from behind Bartholomew, a wide swath of white bandage taped to the underside of his jaw. Gerald! He remained slightly behind his father, keeping his distance from Dawson, but his eyes, filled with a malicious kind of glee, devoured her. She felt a shudder of dread convulse her body. *I should've stabbed the bastard in the heart when I had the chance.*

"You!" Dawson spat, his eyes on Gerald.

She could see Dawson struggling to balance his desire to pounce on Gerald and wring his neck for what he did to Janine, with the need to stay calm in order to extricate themselves from this tricky situation.

Gerald was gesturing emphatically at Dawson. "Shoot him, Dad."

Janine saw Bartholomew half close his eyes, as if in the habit of calling forth patience from within when it came to dealing with his son.

"I told you to keep your fecking mouth shut, Gerald," Bartholomew growled without looking at him.

"Look," said Dawson. "I'll take you to the dig site where Kev found the coins, but not until Janine is safely away."

Bartholomew spoke in an amused tone, unwittingly echoing what Dawson had said after meeting the Irishman's niece. "Do I look fecking stupid?"

Janine heard a soft, snapping sound, was confused when she saw Dawson jerk and stiffen, heard him emit a guttural exhalation of air. Dawson's body, as rigid as granite, was pitching backwards. She tried to catch him, but he crashed to the floor like a felled tree, splintering the coffee table and sending their water glasses flying.

She dropped to her knees beside him, staring in confusion at the twin reels of what looked like fishing wire that led from Dawson's chest to the muzzle of Bartholomew's gun. An unpleasant guttural sound was coming from the back of Dawson's throat as he spasmed on the floor.

Bartholomew's weapon wasn't a gun with bullets, Janine realized. It was a taser pistol.

"Stop it!" she shouted. "Turn it off. *Please! Stop!*"

She was about to seize the ends of the two wires to pull them out of Dawson's chest, uncertain if doing so would also electrocute her, but before she could touch them, her arms were gripped from behind and Gerald was yanking her to her feet.

"Got you now, fine thing," he snarled into her ear as he man-handled her past Bartholomew and into the corridor. "And this time you're *not* escaping!"

"Alfred, help him!" Janine shouted, hoping to appeal to Alfred's better side, feeling certain he had one. Somewhere.

She couldn't see what was going on behind them, didn't know if Dawson was still spasming. *How long had the tasering lasted so far? Eight seconds? Ten? How long could a human body sustain an electrical charge from a taser gun?* She had no idea, but she was certain she'd heard reports of people dying from the experience.

She was aware of pain in her arms and shoulders from Gerald's grip, but her fear for Dawson overshadowed her discomfort as she battled to free herself. "Let me go, you bastard! Let me go!" She kicked at anything and everything in her path. Her flailing feet slammed into a narrow side-table. Something shattered as it hit the tiled floor behind them.

"Jesus fecking Christ!" Gerald grunted, tightening his hold. "Hold still, you bitch."

Behind them, she was grateful to hear Alfred shouting at Bartholomew to stop.

Gerald, barely taller than her, was broader and far stronger. Unable to shake his punishing grip, she yelled for help, despite knowing none would arrive. At the closed door, sobbing with effort, Janine lifted her feet and slammed the soles of her Nike's as hard as she could against the door jamb.

Gerald staggered back, losing his grip on her.

"Dawson!" she shouted, launching herself forward.

Her momentum was rudely checked when the door swung open from the landing, clocking her in the face. She staggered back against Gerald, her blurred vision vaguely aware of a tall man, his blue eyes wide beneath a thick shock of straw-blond hair. Then something heavy hit her in the back of the head and the world went black.

ALFRED DIDN'T KNOW WHAT HE WAS GOING TO SAY TO HIS employees if they came to investigate the noise. Gerald and Jones were already gone. They'd scurried out of the flat with Janine unconscious between them.

But he had a more pressing issue to address. He trailed after Bartholomew, who'd finally turned off his terrible gun and was rushing to exit the flat.

"Wait! Where is she?" Alfred insisted, grabbing the taller man's arm. "I did what you asked."

Bartholomew shook him off and snarled, "Get your bloody hands off me."

"Where is she?" Alfred demanded, standing his ground.

"The Seven Oaks Mews in Barking," Bartholomew answered, then added with a humourless smile. "Probably OD'd by now."

When Bartholomew's eyes widened, Alfred whirled and saw Dawson staggering towards them. The big man, looking dazed, was listing to one side. He tripped on the overturned side table and stumbled into the wall, slid to his knees, then struggled to get back up as he gasped Janine's name.

Alfred hated the role he'd played in her abduction. With a muttered sob, and with a glance over his shoulder to confirm Bartholomew had flown, he slammed the door closed and moved to help Dawson, all the while praying, *please be alive, darling girl, please be alive.*

Chapter 45

Janine thought she heard her gentle-souled father calling her name. Only, it wasn't her father, she realized. *It was Kevin!*

Her eyes flew open. She was lying on her left side in the semi-dark on a cold cement floor. Her immediate field of vision was filled with a wall of chain-link fencing. A bare bulb hung from the ceiling high above her.

"Jaynie!"

At the sound of her cousin's voice, she swivelled around, but when pain exploded at the base of her skull, she cried out and curled into a fetal position. Squeezing her eyes shut, she fought to suppress the waves of nausea. As the spots of blinding white began to fade from her vision, she opened her eyes again, pushing herself up onto an elbow, slowly this time, cautiously turning her head towards the sound of her cousin's voice. It took a moment for the tall form behind the chain link fencing to come into focus.

"Kevin?" Tears of relief blurred her vision. "Is it really you?"

Her cousin was alive, and only an arm's length away from her. Janine scrambled to her feet, then almost fell over as another wave of nausea sought to flatten her. She grabbed hold of the nearest fencing, linking her fingers through the metal wire to stop herself from falling. Leaning forward, she waited for the dizziness to pass, all the while aware of her cousin calling to her.

"Jaynie! Jaynie, are you okay?"

"I'm fine," she finally answered, her voice barely above a whisper. Keeping her eyes closed, she repeated the words silently, trying to convince herself. As the nausea once again began to recede, she lifted her head, slowly, turning her gaze towards Kevin.

Her cousin was standing behind a wall of chain-link perpendicular to the one she was clutching, the fingers of both his hands gripping the wire as he stared at her in wide-eyed concern. "Christ, Jay-Jay," he said, his voice close to a sob. "When they dumped you in there, they wouldn't tell me if you were dead or alive!"

Janine slowly advanced towards him, clutching the fence for support as she took in their surroundings. She saw they were in side-by-side enclosures, the high walls entirely constructed of chain-link fencing. More than a dozen others just like theirs were in her field of vision, but with palettes of merchandise wrapped in plastic.

She stopped in front of Kevin, touching her fingers to his through the diamond-shaped holes. Her vision blurred again as she took in his bruised, swollen face, his fat lip, his filthy T-shirt and jeans. Equivalent concern for her was radiating from his honey brown eyes.

"You're hurt," she observed in a tremulous voice, unable to withhold her tears.

He leaned his forehead against the cold metal. "Don't cry, Jaynie, please don't cry." He left her briefly, returning immediately and pushing a half-used roll of toilet paper through one of the holes. "Bog paper," he said. "God, Jaynie, what did they do to you?"

She heard a slight lisp in his words, the remnants of the fat lip he'd had the day Bart answered his phone. Janine unrolled a length of tissue, her tears abating. "I forgot that's what they call it here."

"When in Rome," her cousin said, his tone devoid of humour.

She lifted her hand to her forehead, felt the small lump swelling above her right eyebrow where Alfred Buckley's door had hit her, then explored the back of her head. She winced, hissing, as she felt the tender lump. She looked at her fingers. No blood.

"Are you okay?"

"How long have I been here?"

"About ten minutes. God, Jaynie, I'm so goddamn sorry I got you into this mess!"

"I know." Behind him in his enclosure, she saw a rumpled sleeping bag atop two empty wooden pallets, a flat of water bottles beside the makeshift bed. In the far corner, she spied a tall bucket with a closed toilet seat. She frowned, looked over her shoulder, but her enclosure was empty. Her gaze roamed the dim, seemingly cavernous room, trying to make sense of their surroundings. Facing her cousin again, she asked, "What is this place? Are we in…*cages?*"

"Sort of. They're added security for storing valuables in warehouses."

"I never did like your idea of roughing it."

She saw one side of his mouth lift in a lop-sided smile, but the humour didn't reach his eyes. "You're white as a ghost, Jay-Jay. Look, plant your ass on the floor, okay? I know it's cold, but I don't want you toppling over."

Once seated, facing the locked door of the enclosure, Janine pulled her knees to her chest and leaned the right side of her body against the chain-link. On his side of the fencing, Kevin joined her on the floor, passing her a bottle of water. Keeping her gaze on him, she opened the bottle and drank, then replaced the cap and set it on the floor beside her, taking comfort from the feel of his shoulder against hers.

"You look awful," she said.

Kevin wagged his head, ignoring her observation. "I'm a total fucking loser for involving you. I thought I was being smart, sending you the coin and getting it out of their reach, but then they saw me coming out of the FedEx store. I phoned Dawz and asked for his help. You remember Dawson Delaney?"

As if she could ever forget. "Of course, he's—"

"Christ, Jay-Jay," Kevin interrupted before she could tell him Dawson was in London with her. "I was so certain he'd be able to help you. I thought, of all people, Dawz could keep you safe. But then you phoned, and that shithead Bart answered, and he made all those threats, and…Shite!" Kevin dropped his head, tangling his hands in his disheveled brown hair. He lifted his head and met her gaze. "I'm so fucking sorry, Jaynie."

"Stop apologizing. I really am okay. I'm just so thankful you're alive." Janine pictured Dawson spasming on the floor of Alfred Buckley's elegant front room. "But Dawson was shot with a taser gun, and—"

"What?" Kevin's head swivelled, sweeping his gaze around the warehouse. "Dawson's *here?*"

"Well, not *here*, obviously."

He returned his gaze to Janine. "But he's in London? He came with you?"

She nodded, "Yes, but—"

Kevin sagged against the fence. *"Thank bloody Christ!* Hell, that's…wow!" He sat up straighter. "Wait a minute. He was shot with a taser gun? Who shot him?" He made a disgusted sound. "That nasty bitch Tiffany?"

"No. Bartholomew."

"Is he okay?"

Janine shook her head as tears welled in her eyes. She

poked the fingers of her left hand through the holes, seeking physical contact with her cousin for what little reassurance it could provide. Kevin gripped her fingers in his. "I don't know," she said, her voice thick. "We were in Alfred Buckley's apartment—"

"Alfred Buckley! How…" Kevin shook his head. "Sorry, I need to stop interrupting. Tell me what's been going on, Jaynie. Tell me everything."

An hour later Janine finally finished her tale. She'd shifted and now sat with her back leaning against the chain-link and her legs stretched out in front of her, the warmth of her cousin's back behind her. She fiddled absently with the empty water bottle as she asked, "Do you think Dawson will be okay? I mean, god, you should've seen him. It was awful."

She felt Kevin's fingertips on her shoulder as he said, "Believe me, he's got the skills that will keep him alive for a very long time." He shifted, sitting sideways to her, his left shoulder against her back. He gently poked her. "So, you and Dawz, huh?"

Startled, Janine swung around to meet her cousin's gaze, thankful doing so no longer made her dizzy. "I didn't say anything about that!"

Kevin shrugged, giving her his characteristic lop-sided grin. "You didn't have to. Finally acting on your teenage crush, huh?"

"Oh god, you *knew* about that?"

Kevin gave her a look of sympathy. "It was pretty obvious. Well, to me, at least. I honestly don't think Dawson knew. I certainly didn't tell him." He paused, then added in a soft tone. "He's an amazing guy, Jay-Jay, but…"

When he hesitated, Janine couldn't help but smile. "But? You're thinking about his nickname? George?"

Kevin looked surprised. "You know about that?"

"He told me on the plane."

"He *told* you?" Kevin looked astonished, but then gave her

a genuinely pleased smile. "Well, shit…I'll be goddamned. I'm happy for you, Jay-Jay."

Janine shifted to lean her shoulder against his. "Your turn. I know wanna-be Indiana is at the root of this, but Kevin, how the hell did all this start?"

Chapter 46

Kevin Kirby stood at the bar of his local pub, sipping his pint of bitter. Oblivious to the growing darkness outside and the increasing volume inside the pub, he was trying to predict the sequence of events that were sure to unfold if that arrogant prick Jones started flapping his mouth about what he'd glimpsed.

On academic probation, and mere months away from finishing the requirements for his PhD, Jones had been foisted on Kevin by his Department Head. The kid was smart, yes, and as passionate as Kevin when it came to Anglo-Saxon artifacts, but he was a conniving, puffed up, self-aggrandizing ass. Jackson's most recent academic infraction had been to list himself instead of his former supervisor as first author on a submission to the *Journal of Anglo-Saxon England.* Kevin later found out that, in two term papers over the past two years, Jones had failed to acknowledge original phraseology, both times claiming this plagiarism had been an unintended oversight. Kevin understood giving students second chances, but he wasn't sure the university had made the right decision when it came to Jackson. In fact, he suspected the kid had been getting away with borderline academic misconduct for years.

What Kevin needed to do was convene a team of experts he could trust. Every inch of the site where he found the coins needed to be meticulously documented to extract every glimmer of knowledge about the people who'd once lived there. If word got out about what he'd unearthed, the field and woods would be overrun by treasure seekers, with Jackass Jones and his grandiose ambitions at the head of the pack.

Standing at the bar, Kevin suddenly became aware of a hulking presence hovering behind his left shoulder.

A mobile was shoved in front of his face. "You *fookin* recognize this?"

Well, there's a Notts accent if I ever heard one, Kevin thought, looking up at the man who'd spoken. This goon was far taller and broader than Kevin's lean six-foot frame, with a face only a mother could love, made even less appealing on account of a badly set broken nose. Kevin nodded at him—no point being unfriendly—then glanced to his right where a second goon stood, only slightly less big and broad as Goon One. Kevin nodded a greeting to him before checking over his shoulder—*nope, no third goon*—then finally allowed his gaze to fall on the screen of the mobile.

"*Aw, bloody hell,*" he muttered.

The man's thick, sausage-like fingers could've crushed the phone as easily as a beer can, Kevin suspected, but the size of his intimidator's paw wasn't why he'd cursed. Rather, it was the rough drawing of the Rex Alfred coin. So much for hoping Jackson hadn't snagged a good look. *Damn!*

The day before, Kevin had taken Jackson—and, more precisely, the kid's high-tech drone outfitted with a camera—to a farmer's field in Lincolnshire. From an archeologist's perspective, the summer of 2018—the driest in decades—was exciting. The drought revealed parch marks—bare patterns in open fields—reflecting the location of buried stone or brick structures a foot or more below the surface. The buried stone inhibited crops or grass from growing on the overlying topsoil. In this particular farmer's field, the pattern was suggestive of a large Anglo-Saxon community. If the landowner gave the University permission to dig the following spring, Kevin would be able to focus on that site for years, an endeavour that thoroughly appealed to him. The video footage from the drone, combined with old-fashioned measurements, would help Kevin plot what structures might once have stood there.

As the day progressed, Kevin began to suspect the extensive parch marks were revealing the ruins of a previously unknown market town rather than a small settlement. After retiring the drone, he assigned Jackson the task of taking further measurements while he began exploring on foot, pencil and notebook in hand. Evening had fallen by then, and Kevin was in a patch of scrub trees at the top end of the field, sketching out where he thought a structure might have stood based on intermittent markings. Calculating steps in his head as to where a cornerstone might lay buried, he stopped about twenty feet away from a dead tree that had been hit by lightning years before, its roots exposed from years of erosion.

Retrieving a gardening trowel from his belt, and although he didn't yet have permission from the landowner for an actual dig, he sank to his haunches and carved a narrow trench a foot deep to assess the soil's composition. He wasn't expecting to find anything so was suitably astonished when he unearthed a small object that, in the last rays of the setting sun, had the unmistakable glint of dirt-encrusted gold. Kevin brushed the soil from the object, revealing a coin the size of his thumbnail, but the lengthening shadows made it difficult to distinguish the markings. Because the object was gold, the most non-reactive of all metals, Kevin knew it was unlikely to be Anglo-Saxon.

Coins had rarely been used in the early Anglo-Saxon period, but if they were, they were generally gold pieces that came from the continent, namely the rare and rather large 'solidus' coin that weighed four grams. In the UK, archeologists were more likely to unearth the smaller 'tremissis', one third the value of a solidus. But even the wealthiest of Anglo-Saxons wouldn't have used these coins as currency; they were too high in value, rendering them useless for everyday transactions. Instead, seventh-century Anglo-Saxons minted smaller gold coins called 'thrymsas' that, according to some historians, were the ancestor of the British shilling. The coins, created by artisans with no knowledge of Latin, were often decorated with nonsensical Roman numerals and lettering. After the seventh century, gold currency disappeared entirely from the British archeological record.

It was rare to discover a tremissis coin on British soil, but if there were more of these coins to be found at this site, the area had to be handled with the care of experts—*trusted* experts. Kevin rose to his feet and craned his neck, searching for Jones and finally spotting him packing up the bins that held his drone equipment. Squatting back down beside the hole, Kevin reached into the narrow trench, carefully brushing away more of the dirt to see if another loose coin appeared. Within a few minutes, he'd unearthed three more.

Knowing he had the leeway of a fortnight to file a report to the proper authorities if the coins turned out to be more than 300 years old, he tucked them into one of the pockets on his cargo shorts. Finders of gold and silver objects were legally required to report their discoveries under the UK's Treasure Act, a law that also mandated the formation of a valuation committee to determine the value of the find and how the profits were to be divided amongst the finders and owners of the land. Over the years, Kevin had reported a wide range of valuable metal work, including a few coins.

He dug for another minute—it was getting too dim in the trees to continue for much longer—but froze when his fingertip brushed against the unmistakable edge of a small piece of metal. He felt his heart-rate accelerate with excitement. Had he not found the coins first, he would have surmised that this as yet unidentified object could be any number of artifacts, from jewelry to weapons to something as functional as a buckle. But given he'd already found four gold coins, the realm of possibilities was narrow. The metal—likely almost rusted through depending on its chemistry—might very well be the remains of forged metalwork that had once bound a wooden chest, one potentially filled with gold coins.

Kevin sat back on his haunches. With hands that trembled, he carefully refilled the trench, the surest means of safekeeping what lay buried. He didn't know the extent of what was there, but as soon as the object was exposed to air, especially if it had wooden components, it would quickly deteriorate. After refilling the hole, Kevin stood up, looking around for something to mark the location. He was about to start collecting rocks to make a cairn, when he spied a watermelon-sized boulder at the base of the dead tree. It was too large to lift, but he might be able to roll it end-over-end. Five minutes later, the boulder sat atop the freshly dug hole looking as if it had been there for hundreds of years, while the eroded roots of the tree showed no evidence of tampering.

With twilight approaching, Kevin headed back to rejoin Jackson, his hand in his pocket fingering the coins. But at the edge of the sparse woods, he stopped. His grad student was busy packing the last items into the van. Once in Jackson's company, Kevin wouldn't be able to examine the objects—no way was he trusting Jackson with knowledge of this unusual find—and Nottingham was more than an hour's drive away. Impatient to examine what he'd found, he stepped behind a tree and withdrew one of the coins.

After cleaning it on his T-shirt, he held up the object to catch the last light of dusk. What he read on the gold coin literally stopped his breath. The light was dim, and he initially thought he must be mistaken, but the lettering was clear and very uniform. R E X A L F R E D. *King Alfred.*

Kevin struggled to process the staggering significance of his discovery.

"Bloody hell!"

Kevin, mesmerized by the coin and lost in thought, nearly jumped out of his skin at the sound of Jackson's voice. He stuffed the coin into his pocket with feigned nonchalance, then turned and started striding across the field, ignoring the young man who trotted beside him, making demands.

"Let me see!"

Jackson grabbed his arm, but Kevin shook him off and kept walking, saying, "When I authenticate it, I'll tell you about it. Not before."

"Not cool, Dr. Kirby. *Not. Cool.* Goddamn it!" Jackson stopped and looked over his shoulder towards the woods as if doing so would indicate where his doctorate supervisor had found the coin. But darkness was falling and he didn't stand a chance of figuring it out.

Ninety minutes later, after a hellishly long drive back from the field with the annoyingly persistent Jones, Kevin had a quick shower, then set three of the cleaned coins in an ice-cube tray, filled it with water, and slipped it into the miniature freezer box of his refrigerator. Upstairs in his office, he moved armfuls of academic journals and books from his desk to the futon sofa, then flicked on the desk light to examine the coin under a magnifying glass, all the while making notes and sketches. After examining every detail of both sides of the coin, he got out his laptop and began an internet search, then scrounged through his stacks of books and journals, reading everything he could find about King Alfred's mint.

He awoke late the next morning, still at his desk, his head pillowed on his arms. For a dreadful moment, he thought it had all been a dream, but the coin was in his hand, his fingers curled around it even while he slept. In the daylight, it was even more astonishing; the gold as shiny and bright as if it had been forged that very day. The artifact—artifacts, Kevin corrected, thinking of what he'd placed in his freezer—was the greatest find of the century. Archaeologically speaking, he amended, it was the greatest find of *the millennium!*

KEVIN FELT THE FINGERS OF GOON ONE'S FREE HAND DIG into his shoulder.

"I said, do ya *fookin* recognize this?" Goon One, who must've thought Kevin was near-sighted, brought the mobile closer to the archeologist's face.

He didn't know who these assholes were, but knew there would be a short line connecting them to Jackass Jones. He wanted nothing to do with them. Maybe he could create a diversion, perhaps start a bar fight like in the movies.

Kevin turned to regard Goon One. "You lose a fight?" he asked in a conversational tone, nodding at the broken nose.

The man clearly took offence to the question. In the next instant, Kevin was being herded out of the pub, his arms gripped by a bruiser on either side of him. As they emerged into the poorly lit, cobblestoned street, they abruptly stopped so as not to crash into half-a-dozen young men and women, the girls wobbling on high heels, the boys wearing baggy T-shirts and jeans. Their high voices and shrill laughter indicated that, although the night was still young, they were already in an advanced state of inebriation.

"*Jul-eh!* Watch out!" one of the women complained as the girl in question stumbled.

Kevin took the opportunity fate offered and called out, "Julie? Julie, is that you?"

When all six heads swivelled to look at him, Kevin stepped forward, forcing the goons to release him. He saw the puzzled frown of the tallest girl—or, rather, the one in the highest heels. Kevin went to her and gave her an exuberant hug, which she enthusiastically returned. "Oh my god, it's been years!" he said.

"Jul-eh!" one of the girls said, clearly envious. "You didn't tell us you knew any *Americans!*"

With a promise to shout the next round, Kevin inserted himself into their midst, herding the group down the street as he invented a story about how he and Julie knew each other. He glanced over his shoulder, saw the goons following. It took almost an hour to ditch his hulking shadows.

Twenty minutes later, half a block from his house, Kevin noticed the unmistakable glow of a cigarette being lit, warning him of the presence of a loiterer. He stopped abruptly, ducking behind a parked car. After a few minutes of observation, it was clear the guy was waiting for Kevin to return. Retracing his steps, Kevin eventually hopped on a tram that took him into downtown Nottingham. He jumped off at Station Street, then checked into the nearest hotel.

He was agitated by then, knowing he was out of his depth. In his hotel room, he startled at every noise. Who the hell were these goons, and what were their intentions, besides the obvious intent of stealing the coin? He wished his old mentor Professor Abernathy was available to consult, but the old man had the shit luck of having recently been diagnosed with cancer. Regardless, Kevin needed someone he could trust who was also politically savvy. Even if the site didn't reveal a chest of gold coins minted by King Alfred, the four he'd found could unleash a media circus. Kevin didn't have the knowledge, finesse, or even the desire to successfully navigate that kind of minefield.

His mind spinning, he lay awake for most of the night, eventually falling asleep shortly before dawn, waking late the next morning when the cleaners knocked on his door.

When he tentatively stepped out into the sunny street, his right hand in the pocket of his trousers fingering the gold coin, he didn't have a destination, but knew his first priority was to find a safe place for the coin, somewhere no one would think to look for it. He'd never had any need for a safety deposit box, so the next best thing was to give it to someone he could trust. Again, his first thought was Professor Abernathy, but as much as the man would be delighted with the discovery, he was simply too sick to involve, at least for now.

He considered Jaynie. He trusted his cousin above anyone else, except maybe his childhood friend Dawson. If only she lived in the UK, he thought. At that moment, his gaze fell on a bus stop advertisement for FedEx. He abruptly stopped walking.

He could courier it to her! No one would dream to look for it in Canada.

Five minutes later, he entered a FedEx store at a busy intersection. The young man working the counter recognized him, telling Kevin he'd taken his first-year undergrad course. He also said he'd enrolled in Kevin's second-year class, which would commence in a few weeks.

Kevin felt better after the kid put the envelope on a conveyor belt, but as it disappeared from view he began second-guessing his decision. Had he done the tight thing? Regardless, he should call Jaynie and explain.

He asked the kid, "I need to make an international call. Can I do that here?"

Apparently not, Kevin learned. But for twenty pounds, the kid was willing to let him use his mobile. After making note of the kid's name—and giving himself a mental reminder to bump up the kid's mark the next time he graded one of his papers—he tapped out Jaynie's number, noting it was early morning on the west coast of Canada. He got her voicemail —she was probably out on her morning run. Mid-way through leaving his message, the FedEx door opened. Kevin swung around, worried the goons had found him. But the new arrival was a young man in a business suit. Kevin ended his call and gave the kid back his mobile, along with a twenty-pound note.

When he stepped out of the FedEx store, folding the receipt for the package into his pocket, he hesitated in the doorway, uncertain what to do next. He needed to consult with someone who had a network of trusted experts to call upon. *Dawson!* His friend was both trustworthy and connected. Why hadn't he thought of calling Dawson last night when he had access to his hotel room phone? Maybe Jaynie was right. Perhaps it was time he bought a mobile. For now, he'd borrow the kid's.

He was about to re-enter the FedEx store when he saw Goon Two hurrying towards him as he loped across the busy crosswalk. Clearly, Kevin had been spotted as soon as he'd stepped onto the sidewalk. *Whatever*, Kevin thought, knowing he could outrun a hulk like that. He turned in the opposite direction, about to break into a jog, but saw Goon One lumbering toward him. *No worries*. Faster and nimbler than the goons, he would simply weave his way across four lanes of traffic.

He froze suddenly, feeling his heart hammering in his chest as he comprehended the significance of having been spotted exiting the FedEx store. They were brawny goons, but likely still smart enough to put two-and-two together and conclude he'd just sent a courier package. *Damn it!* He didn't need Dawson to recommend expert help. He needed Dawson to protect his cousin.

Kevin swung around and re-entered the store. When the kid handed his phone over without question, still busy with business-suit man, Kevin gave another mental bump to his grade.

He had just enough time to leave a message on Dawson's work phone, the only number he could remember, before the goons entered the store. While doing that, he at least had the presence of mind to tear up his copy of the courier chit. It lay in confetti pieces on the counter. Likely whoever these assholes worked for would still be able to discover where he'd sent the package, but they'd have to work for it, and his call to Dawson would give his friend time to ensure Jaynie was safe.

They eyed Kevin with suspicion as he handed the mobile and a fifty-pound note to the young man behind the counter.

"You better *fookin* come with us," Goon One threatened under his breath.

Kevin must've looked uncooperative because Goon Two added, "I'll break that *fookin* kid's arm if you don't."

As soon as the three of them exited the shop, Goon One, his mobile to his ear, made a call. When it was answered, he said, "We got him, boss. Now what?"

Chapter 47

Janine was dumfounded. "Kevin, is keeping silent really worth it?"

"Not now that you're bloody hurt!"

As the cold, cement floor had become too uncomfortable, they'd both risen to their feet.

"Do you have any idea of the significance of what I found?" Kevin's tone and gestures were animated as he walked in small circles inside his enclosure. "It's indescribable, Jaynie! It's akin to finding the Rosetta Stone. It's a discovery that will rock the world."

Despite their circumstances, she couldn't help but smile at him. "Is this your Kevin-who?"

He gave her a lop-sided grin. "Yeah, it is." But his smile quickly faded. "Point being," he continued. "It's *my* find. And I don't mean it's my claim to fame. I don't need any of that shit. But the site needs to be registered, the work properly and meticulously conducted. Jackass Jones and his ambition will ruin it, especially now that he's involved the O'Sullivan's."

"But Kevin, they *killed* that man on my lawn. They shot at us, and they *kidnapped* me."

"Holy hell, Jaynie, don't remind me," he growled. "When

you called and Bart answered?" Kevin dropped his head, stuffing his fists into the pockets of his rumpled jeans. "After that, of course I couldn't reveal the location. Not without a guarantee that you'd be unharmed. That's why I agreed to make that recording—the one you said Tiff played. It was a bargain to ensure they wouldn't hurt you." Kevin scoffed in disgust. *"That* turned out really well! But really, I was counting on Dawz to keep you safe."

"But *none* of us is safe now."

"I know that. And it's my fault. So, of course I tell them where I found the coins. But I won't do that until *after* Dawson and you are safely back in Canada."

They both startled at the distant sound of a heavy door opening and clanging closed. Bright overhead lights flicked on high above them, followed by the sound of two sets of footsteps approaching on the bare cement floor.

Janine felt the pounding of her heart as she gripped the metal fencing. Was it Dawson? Would they toss him into one of the enclosures along with Kevin and Janine? But that made no sense. If that was their intention, they would've taken him at the same time they'd grabbed Janine.

She could feel the tension coming off Kevin, felt her own hackles rise as they waited with apprehension for the newcomers to appear.

A moment later, Tiffany and Gerald stepped into view. He still sported the swath of white bandage on the underside of his jaw. Tiffany was wearing camel-coloured slacks tucked into high-heeled boots and a butter-yellow leather jacket, her red hair rippling in loose waves over her shoulders.

"Where's Dawson?" Janine demanded.

Tiffany's smile was calculating as she sauntered towards them. "Forget about him. He's probably already forgotten about you."

Janine wanted to kick the smug woman in the shins.

"I don't intend to tell you a bloody thing, Tiffany," Kevin

pre-empted in a growl. "Not until Jaynie's back home in Canada and Dawson confirms they're safe. *Then* I'll bring you to the site, but not a minute before."

Gerald poked the muzzle of a pistol through one of the diamond openings of Janine's enclosure. She sucked in a breath and stepped back. She hadn't gotten a good look at Bartholomew's taser gun, but this weapon looked like the kind that held real bullets.

"I can *make* you tell." Gerald taunted Kevin, keeping his ominous gaze on Janine.

Irritation passed over Tiffany's face. "For Christ's sake, Gerald, put that away before you put a bullet through your own foot."

Tiffany waited, an eyebrow raised, until Gerald tucked the pistol into the back of his jeans, the weapon concealed under his lightweight jacket. Then she nodded at the door to Janine's cage. "Open it."

Janine shared a nervous glance with Kevin. Were they letting her go? "Let Kevin go, too!" she demanded. Her trepidation escalated when Gerald swung open the wide door and stepped into her cage, slowly advancing on her.

"What are you doing?" Kevin demanded, his tone filled with the same fear that was pulsing through Janine's veins, making her heart pound and sucking all the moisture from her mouth. "Don't you hurt her!" he warned.

Janine backed up. Over Gerald's shoulder, she saw Tiffany move to stand in the open door, regarding them with a calculating eye. Kevin moved parallel with his cousin as Janine continued backing away. She kept her eyes on Gerald, but heard Kevin slamming his palms against the chain link, making it rattle ominously as he vented his impotent rage.

"Don't you fucking hurt her!" he warned again.

"You should never have knifed me," Gerald sneered as he cornered Janine.

She defiantly met his malevolent gaze, trying not to reveal

her fear. Could she dart past him? If she succeeded, could she push past Tiffany? She knew vaguely in what direction the door to the warehouse lay, at least the one Tiffany and Gerald had used, but even if she got through it without being caught, what then? And what about Kevin? Could she abandon him? No, she decided. Not without some guarantee he wouldn't be harmed. Escape wasn't an option, not right this moment, at least, and not alone.

"I wished I'd stabbed you in the heart!" she spat.

She heard Kevin yelling at Tiffany. "Bloody hell, Tiffany, you're honestly not setting your sick bastard of a cousin loose on her, are you?"

When Gerald lunged toward her, Janine dodged, but he anticipated her response and used his momentum to smash his fist into her cheekbone in the exact spot he'd hit her the day before.

Pain exploded in her face, the waves of agony almost overwhelming her. She stumbled backwards, barely able to breath, only just managing to grab hold of the wire fencing to stop herself from falling. But she could do nothing to prevent Gerald from grabbing both her arms and twisting them high and hard behind her back. The pain in her face was blinding, blurring her vision, shortening her breaths, and now her rotator cuffs felt ready to pop out of their sockets.

Gerald slammed her face-front against the back wall of her cage, his body trapping her between him and the unforgiving metal. She was aware of her cousin yelling, and of the rattling sound as he futilely launched himself against the chain link. Recalling how Gerald had pawed at her in the van, she told herself not to let terror overtake her. She had to use her brain. She would *not* let this disgusting pig of a man beat her or, worse, rape her.

Then she remembered the pistol he'd tucked behind his back. If she could grab it, just as she had the knife, they'd be able to escape. She'd never held a gun before, but she knew which was the business end.

Gerald forced her to turn, releasing her left arm, at the same time trapping her left side against the chain link. "Get off me, you freak!" she bawled. But he held her right arm in his left, twisted behind her back, forcing her to bend forward. Wedging her between him and the fencing, he grabbed at her breasts with his free hand, laughing in her ear. She felt his spittle land on her cheek. It sickened her. He sickened her. "Get off me!" she screamed.

Janine could hear Kevin shouting. "Leave her alone! You bastard! Don't fucking touch her! I'll *kill* you!" And then his tone changed as he pleaded with Tiffany. "For Christ's sake, Tiffany! Do something! *Stop him!"*

Janine tried to kick at Gerald. If she could make him stumble, perhaps she could free one of her arms and make a grab for the gun. "Fucking bastard!" she cried, kicking out. But he kept her securely pinned, laughing his pleasure. She abruptly ceased struggling when she felt him grinding his erection against her hip, felt his hand fumbling at the front waistband of her leggings. *Oh god! She was going to be raped, in front of her cousin, and with Tiffany doing nothing to prevent it!*

Janine could hear Kevin punching at the metal fence, shaking and rattling it. "Tiffany!" Kevin was roaring. "For Christ's sake, make him stop."

"There's only one way to make him stop," she heard Tiffany say in a lilting, conversational tone. Janine knew she'd never be able to hear the Irish accent again without shuddering.

"Then do it!" shouted Kevin.

Gerald kicked out, swiping Janine's feet out from under her. She landed hard on her back, but her legs and arms were free at last. She kicked and hit and screamed like a mad, trapped animal.

When Gerald smashed his fist into her face a second time,

the liquid sensation of intense, white-hot pain consumed her. She tasted blood at the back of her throat and felt certain she would pass out. She willed herself not to let the agony overwhelm her, knew she had to keep fighting, knew also that her struggles had diminished into barely more than feeble gestures of protest. She struggled to breath, her nose, her entire face, on fire.

Somewhere within the abyss of pain from her shattered nose, pain so intense it seemed to take up every molecule of her brain, she remembered his gun.

"It's not *me* who can make him stop," she heard Tiffany say in a casual tone as if she and Kevin were chatting in a coffee shop rather than witnessing an attempted rape. "Only *you* can do that, Kevie."

"I'll *tell* you! Christ! Make him stop!" he shouted. *"I'll tell you! For fuck's sake, Tiff, I'll fucking tell you!"*

"That's more like it," Tiffany said, a satisfied purr in her tone.

Janine heard Tiffany telling Gerald to stop, that he'd frightened Kevin into submission, but Gerald didn't seem aware of his cousin's directive, or possibly he had no intention of obeying. He panted above Janine, one hand grabbing at her breasts, the other pulling at the waistband of her leggings.

She needed that gun. And then she would shoot the bastard in his non-existent heart.

And then she had it, in her right hand this time.

In that instant, Gerald must've become aware that she wasn't as defeated as he'd assumed. He rolled to the side, breaking their contact, his abrupt movement causing Janine to lose her grip on the pistol, sending it clattering across the cement floor. The weapon came to a stop inches from the toe of Tiffany's polished boot.

The Irishwoman bent gracefully and picked it up. Instead of pointing it at Janine, she stepped into the enclosure and aimed it at Gerald, who lay on his back staring up at her.

Free of the weight of her attacker, Janine scuttled across the floor towards Kevin, grateful for the reassuring touch of his hands on her shoulders as she whimpered and pressed her back against their shared wall of chain link.

"Christ, Jaynie! Jesus Christ!" she heard him sobbing behind her.

She didn't turn to look at him, but kept her gaze on Gerald and Tiffany, her mouth open as she gulped much needed air into her lungs, her hands searching blindly for the roll of toilet paper.

Gerald was looking up at his cousin in snarling disbelief as Tiffany held her stiletto heel threateningly above his crotch.

Janine found the tissue, unrolled a length, then almost blinded herself with the pain of dabbing at her bloodied nose. She could already feel the tissue around her left eye swelling. As she kept her wary gaze on the O'Sullivan cousins, she heard Kevin behind her whispering in a broken sob, *Jesus Christ! Jesus Christ!*

"You fecking idiot, Gerald," Tiffany was saying, her mild tone at odds with her threatening stance. "You're worse than a rutting stag."

"Get off me, Tiff," Gerald growled.

Tiffany didn't shift. "Two seconds later, *she* would've been the one aiming this here weapon at your empty head. And, unlike me, I'm guessing that there colonial wouldn't have hesitated to pull the trigger. I'm considering letting her. What do you think of that, *cousin?*"

"If you shoot me, you still won't get control of the company." Gerald's tone was taunting as he added, "You can't outsmart Dad, no matter how hard you try."

"Oh? That's what you think, yeah?" Tiffany made a scoffing sound. "Shows how smart *you* are." Abruptly, Tiffany stepped away from Gerald and sauntered out of Janine's cage.

Gerald leapt to his feet, snarling. "Give me my pistol," he demanded, chasing after her.

Tiffany handed it to him without a backward glance, but she must've known what her angry cousin would attempt in retaliation for, in the next instant, she whirled to face him. With a cry of protest from Gerald, the pistol he'd been lifting to point at her was once again in Tiffany's hand. This time she pressed the muzzle against his chest.

"Don't feck with me, Gerald," Tiffany stated, her tone deadly.

Gerald's look of fury didn't dim, but he lifted his hands, palms up, and took a backward step.

Tiffany lowered her arm. "Unlock his door," she said, with a nod at Kevin. Then she looked towards Janine, showing no compassion for the battering she'd suffered. "Get up. Gerald is taking you two for a drive."

Gerald's hands paused on the padlock of Kevin's cage as he looked over at Tiffany. "You're not coming?"

"I'll meet you there."

Kevin launched himself at the locked door of his cage, causing Gerald to leap back in alarm. "Tiffany," Kevin demanded. *"He's* not taking Jaynie *anywhere!* Let me get her somewhere safe. *Then* I'll bring you to the site."

Tiffany was shaking her head. "Kevie, I'll ask you for the hundredth time—and this time your answer better be different than the first ninety-nine. Are you ready to lead us to the site? The *exact* spot?"

"Not until Jaynie's safely away," Kevin snapped.

Tiffany shook her head. "You're down to two options, Kevie. I leave her here with Gerald. Or, she comes with us to the site."

When Kevin only glared at her, Tiffany arched an eyebrow. "Well? What will it be?"

"She comes with us," Kevin finally said.

Janine had never before heard that tone of strangled dread and hopelessness in her cousin's voice.

Tiffany smiled triumphantly. "I always knew there was a

way to make you see things our way, Kevie. I'm glad you value your cousin as much as I value mine." She handed the pistol back to Gerald. He took it with a scowl, tucking it under his coat.

"Hardly," Kevin spat out.

Tiffany eyed Gerald almost affectionately, then gave an elegant shrug. "He has his uses."

While Gerald unlocked Kevin's door, Janine met her cousin's gaze. She saw his face blanche. In the glaring overhead lights, she realized he was getting his first good look at her injuries. From his expression, she knew she it must be bad.

"Christ, Jay-Jay!" he said, stepping towards her, his fingers curling helplessly through the open weave of the fencing. "I'm so sorry," he practically sobbed.

Janine wanted to tell Kevin he'd done nothing wrong, but it would hurt to speak so she simply lifted a hand and touched his fingers in reassurance.

A moment later, Kevin's door swung open on creaking hinges. He stepped through slowly, threateningly, stopping inches from Tiffany. The tall woman held her ground, one eyebrow arched.

"Kevie," Tiffany stated. There was no disguising the threat in her cold tone. "I shall turn Gerald loose on your cousin, so help me god, if you screw us over. *Do you understand?"*

They glared at each other until Kevin said, *"Keep him. The fuck. Away from her."*

He turned and shoved past Gerald, then stepped into Janine's cage.

She stood watching him approach, half blind, clutching a blood-stained wad of tissue in one hand and the roll of toilet paper in the other. Ever so gently, with an arm around her waist, she let her cousin lead her out of the cage.

Chapter 48

Janine felt Kevin nudge her leg with the toe of his boot.

They were in an unmarked cargo van, their wrists bound, and their arms secured with cable ties to rings above each of their heads. Janine's arms were tingling, and her bottom ached from sitting on the bare metal flooring, but that discomfort was nothing compared to the throbbing agony of her face.

At Kevin's touch, she lifted her head and looked out the back windows on her left. There was no ambient light from passing traffic. She turned to look out the front of the van—Bart was driving, with Jackson in the front passenger seat and Gerald on an overturned plastic crate behind the driver's seat—but she could see nothing to indicate where they might be. She checked the time. Ninety-eight minutes had passed since they'd left the warehouse.

The van turned off the paved road and began bumping along what felt like a farmer's track. A few minutes later, Bart stopped the vehicle. The sudden brightness of the interior lights when the front and side doors opened was almost blinding. Then the back doors were also opened and their three assailants stood regarding them.

Bart gestured. "Get them out," he said.

"But leave the ties on, yeah?" Gerald's tone was both eager and sinister.

Bart rolled his eyes, "Your brilliance never fails to amaze me, Gerald. *Of course,* leave the ties on. I'll get the torches and shovels," he added, disappearing from view.

When Jackson had been enlisted to bind her wrists before bundling her and Kevin into the van, he'd shown alarm at the sight of her battered face. She'd whispered, *help me*, as he secured the cable ties, but he'd pretended not to hear and refused to meet her gaze. Now, at their destination, and even with her impaired vision, she could see only eager avarice in his expression. Gaining possession of the buried coins—and one-upping his supervisor, Janine thought, seeing the look of triumph on his face as he cut the ties that held Kevin's wrists above his head—took precedence.

As soon as he exited the van, his wrists still bound in front of him, Kevin turned to help Janine, reaching for her as Jackson cut her free. She assumed his arms must be tingling as intensely as hers now that the blood was once again allowed to flow.

"Are you okay?" Kevin asked.

Before Janine could respond, Gerald snarled, "I told you, shut the feck up!"

Janine and Kevin had spoken to each other when they'd initially been confined to the back of the van, but when Gerald threatened to haul Janine onto his lap so she could talk to him instead, they'd stopped, remaining silent for the duration of the journey.

"I need to go to the bathroom—" Janine abruptly stopped talking, flinching and reflexively jerking her head back when Gerald raised his fist as if to strike her. She dreaded what it would feel like to be hit in the face again. She didn't actually need to pee—they'd each been allowed to use the bathroom before leaving the warehouse—but she'd wanted to find out how accommodating their captors would be. She had her answer.

With their hands bound in front of them, Kevin and Janine were led around the side of the van where Bart was removing two shovels and two large torches. Janine shrieked suddenly, leaping forward to escape Gerald's groping hand. "Get off me!" she yelled, a stab of pain shooting through her broken nose as she projected her voice.

"You fucking bastard!" Kevin shouted as he shoulder-checked Janine's assailant.

Gerald went slamming into the side of the van, then fell to his knees. As he regained his feet, he whipped out his pistol and jabbed the muzzle into Kevin's chest.

Kevin didn't back away. He loomed over the shorter man and spoke through gritted teeth. "Go ahead. Shoot me. Then you'll never find what you're looking for. Which suits me fine. *But don't. Fucking. Touch her.*"

"Leave off, Gerald," Bart snarled. "For Christ's sake, your timing, as usual, is fecking atrocious. You can have your fun with her later."

Bart's promise caused an icy fist to close around her throat. Janine could only see out of one eye, but in the light streaming from the open side door, she saw Kevin's look of revulsion and horror, and knew it mirrored her own. She forced herself not to panic as Gerald slavered at her side like a dog waiting for a promised treat.

"*When* later?" he demanded

Bart whirled on his son. "Don't turn this into a cock-up, you fecking knobber. Christ, you're as brainless as your bitch of a mother. If you can't fecking control yourself, then you're out. *And this time it will be for good.*"

Janine shared a look with Kevin and knew they were thinking along the same lines. *Get Gerald to cock things up, set Bart loose on him, then escape during whatever O'Sullivan mayhem ensued.*

Jackson was holding a shovel, his wide-eyed gaze going from Bart to Gerald and back to Bart.

"Well?" Bart demanded as father and son glared at each other.

Janine felt certain Gerald was toying with the idea of shooting his father, but after a moment, with an avaricious glance towards her, the younger man stepped back. "I can control myself," he muttered.

"You sure? Cuz I'm not fecking convinced."

At the sound of a vehicle approaching, all five heads swivelled to look behind them, Janine's heart leapt with hope. *Was Dawson coming to their rescue?* But their captors showed no concern over the approaching headlights, and Janine realized the visitor was expected.

Moments later, the vehicle stopped behind them. The headlights flicked off, and Tiffany stepped out of the driver's door. It wasn't the little car she'd driven in Nottingham, Janine saw, but a rugged SUV. The redhead had also exchanged her high-heeled fashion boots for a pair of hunter-green rubber boots. As Tiffany approached, Janine saw she was holding a pistol, pointing it at Kevin. The muzzle was covered by a square of yellow. *A taser gun.*

Tiffany stood silent for a moment, looking from Bart to her cousin, then back to Bart. "Christ, you two," she stated in a scornful tone. "You're at it *again?* Eye on the prize, for feck's sake." She moved to Jackson, keeping her gun trained on Kevin as she kissed the handsome man on the lips. "Hi, you. Are you ready to unearth our treasure?"

Jackson looked as eager as a five-year-old in a candy store who'd just been told to fill a bag with treats. "Oh, I'm ready."

Tiffany smiled, then addressed Kevin. "Lead the way, Kevie darling," she invited, gesturing with her gun.

Janine could see Bart growing annoyed as Tiffany assumed the role of leader, but the older man remained silent, his lips pinched together.

Kevin ignored Tiffany, stared instead at his grad student. "Jackson, you're a goddamn fool. Don't you know, she'll drop you like a hot potato as soon as you're no longer useful?"

Jackson gave Tiffany a worried look.

"Of course I won't, darling," Tiffany assured, stroking a hand up Jackson's arm. "Don't listen to him. He doesn't understand how special it is between us."

Kevin turned to Tiffany and made a last-ditch effort to safeguard his cousin. "Let Jaynie go."

"You should've cooperated from the start," Bart snapped, handing Jackson one of the torches, then flicking on the one he held.

When Kevin didn't budge, Tiffany aimed her weapon at Janine. "I'll taser her if I have to. Then we'll lock her in the van with Gerald. She'll be nice and docile. Although, my cousin prefers feisty women. Don't you, Gerald?"

Janine was sickened by the image Tiffany painted. The entire O'Sullivan clan was absolutely stark, raving mad. She couldn't panic, though. If she and Kevin wanted to escape, she had to keep her wits about her.

Kevin seemed to draw the same conclusion. "Bloody hell," he muttered in defeat. He looked over at Janine. His face, she saw, was haggard with dread and regret. *"I'm so fucking sorry, Jaynie."*

Janine couldn't prevent her silent tears from falling, aware of the salt stinging her battered face. She hated the self-loathing and misery in her cousin's eyes and voice, but hated even more the terror of what was to come if they didn't escape.

The light suddenly flicked off as Bart pulled the side door of the van closed. With their torches on, Jackson led the way into the field. There was no moon, but the clear night sky was filled with stars. Janine could see the distant glow of light on the horizon. She wondered what city it was.

As they walked, Tiffany carried on a dialogue with Kevin.

"You understand, yeah? By claiming this treasure, we can save O'Sullivan's. Without it, we'll fold, and then six generations of work will be for naught."

Kevin made a disgusted sound. "That's horseshit. You've been dabbling in stolen artifacts and forgeries for years."

"We've had to, thanks to some poor business decisions."

Janine assumed Tiffany's barbed remark was aimed at Bart, but the older man remained moodily silent.

"If you let Jaynie go," Kevin bargained, "you can still claim the site. Both you and the landowner stand to make a hell of a lot of dough. I won't lay claim to a penny of it. I'll walk away."

Tiffany gave an inelegant snort. "You don't expect me to *believe* you, do you?"

"Just because *you* don't keep *your* promises, doesn't mean I won't. Seriously, Tiffany. Let Jaynie go. I'll bring you to the site. And then I'll walk away and never breathe a word."

"Enough!" Bart barked. "You have only yourself to blame. *You* brought the girl into this."

Janine stumbled on a clod of dirt, felt Gerald grip her upper arm more securely as he dragged her along beside him. He held her with his left hand, his right still pointing the pistol at Kevin. When he deliberately brushed his knuckles against the side of her breast, she instinctively jerked away, yelling, "Stop it! You goddamn *freak!*"

Kevin whirled to face Gerald, making everyone stop. "Let her go," he snarled. "She won't say a thing. I *know* that. You can trust her. You can trust *me*."

Bart's laughter was devoid of humour. "Trust," he scoffed, spitting out the word as if it were dirt. He gestured at Tiffany. "I can't even trust my own flesh and blood. Why would I trust you?"

Tiffany's tone was affronted. "I thought we agreed to let bygones be bygones, yeah?"

Bart gestured and they all resumed walking. The Irishman

addressed Kevin. "You're a fecking idiot if you think your eleventh-hour bargaining will get you anywhere. You say you'd walk away, but when news of this find explodes across the globe? When your arse of a grad student here takes the credit for the find? And when we get paid millions for the treasure? You know what you would do? You'd get greedy. You'd tell yourself you deserve some of *my* profits. You'd go to the police and spin your yarn. Your cousin there would corroborate your story. No," he added, shaking his head. "You two are a liability. It ends here and now. And that money is *mine*."

"Ours," Tiffany immediately corrected. "That money is *ours."*

"Fine. *Ours*."

As they entered a sparse woodland on a slightly higher elevation than the field, Tiffany scowled at Jackson. "You swore he couldn't have found the coin in these woods."

Jackson, who'd remained silent up until then, retorted, "I've gone over every inch of ground in there. Nothing's been disturbed."

"Indiana Jones would've found it," Kevin mocked.

"He's trying to trick us," Jackson argued.

Kevin remained silent as he led the way through the sparse trees, coming to a stop beside a small boulder. He turned to regard Jackson, tapping the rock with the toe of his boot. "Did you look under this?"

Jackson gave Kevin a startled look. "That hasn't been moved recently."

"You sure about that?" Kevin's tone was scornful.

Tiffany spoke before Jackson could respond, addressing Kevin. "You marked the spot with this boulder? Where did it come from?"

"That root base there, the one that's eroding," Kevin said, nodding his head at a tree behind her. Both Jackson and Bart momentarily shone their torches at the tree.

Tiffany whirled on Jackson, whacking the fist of her free hand into his abdomen, making him double over in surprise more than pain. "You fecking knob! And you call yourself an archeologist? You should've spotted that this boulder had been moved."

"Never mind that," Bart growled, setting down his shovel and torch. "Jackson, give me a hand. Gerald, take the safety off your gun."

"Already done. I'm just waiting for you to tell me I can shoot him. *And then you're all mine,*" he added in a low tone only Janine could hear.

She shuddered, dreading what was to come if she and Kevin didn't succeed in escaping. *But how could they manage to escape?*

She watched as Jackson and Bart shifted the boulder aside. Once that was done, Bart and Tiffany took up positions on either side of Jackson, shining the torch light at the ground as Jackson sunk a spade into the dirt. Gerald stood opposite Tiffany, gripping Janine's upper arm in his left hand and keeping his gun pointed at Kevin, who stood a couple metres to Gerald's right, slightly behind Jackson.

As he started digging, Jackson exclaimed, "This dirt… bloody shite, it's *loose!* It's been recently dug up. This *is* the site!"

The three O'Sullivan's had all leaned forward. The muzzle of the taser pistol Tiffany held was pointed at the ground, and Gerald had half lowered the arm that held his pistol. In the peripheral beam of the bright torches, Janine caught Kevin's gaze, saw the minuscule nod of his head towards Gerald's pistol. *He intended to make a grab for it!* Janine knew it was risky, but also knew it was their only chance. She closed her eyes briefly, readying herself to run. *Don't get shot, Kevin! Please, don't get shot.*

Kevin took a slow, half step forwards, then another.

Bart snapped up his head. "On your knees," he barked at

Kevin. He gestured angrily at Gerald, causing his beam of light to wobble. "For feck's sake, Gerald, do your job."

Gerald raised his pistol and pointed it at Kevin. "I can shoot him?"

"No!" Bart shouted. "Do *not* shoot him. For feck's sake, you half-wit." He gestured at Jackson's efforts. "This might still be a trick, don't you know?"

Clearly disappointed, Gerald gestured at Kevin with the pistol until the archeologist dropped to his knees. Janine closed her eyes, fighting tears. *Now what?*

When she opened her eyes, she saw that Jackson was crouched beside the hole, reaching in with his right hand. The young man suddenly emitted a strangled sort of exclamation, then sat back on his haunches, brushing dirt off an object he held. The glint of gold as both Tiffany and Bart shone their lights on him was unmistakable.

Tiffany leaned over Jackson's shoulder. "You found it!" she breathed.

Gerald leaned forward as well, his pistol arm dropping.

Bart dropped to one knee. "That's it?" he demanded. "That's the Rex Alfred coin?"

Jackson, his eyes glued to the coin, was struck speechless for a moment. When he spoke, his tone was filled with wonder. "It is! It's real. Bloody shite! It's fucking real."

At Jackson's confirmation, Janine saw Gerald lifting his pistol, clearly having drawn the conclusion that a living, breathing Kevin was now superfluous. She shifted her weight, aware in her peripheral vision that Tiffany was also lifting her weapon.

"Nooohhh!" Janine shouted as she shoulder-checked Gerald. But she was too late. She heard the ear-splitting crack of the bullet leaving the chamber of his pistol, heard Kevin's grunt of pain, saw her cousin jerk back and fall to the ground.

She fully expected Gerald to whirl on her, but in the next

instant, he stiffened and fell beside Kevin, two thin wires attached to his left side shining in the torchlight.

Tiffany hadn't shot Kevin or Janine with her taser gun. She'd shot Gerald!

But Janine didn't care about Gerald, or any of the O'Sullivan's. She cared only about Kevin. Screaming his name, she sidestepped Gerald's spasming body and fell to her knees beside her cousin. He lay on his back, his eyes open, looking up at her. In the torchlight, Janine could see a dark patch of wet glistening ominously on his chest. "Kevin!" she screamed, pressing the heels of her bound hands against the wound, his blood warm and sticky.

"Jaynie?" Kevin croaked.

She looked over her shoulder at the others. Even though it was useless, she couldn't stop herself from shouting, "Help me! Please, help me!"

The two torches were abandoned on the ground, she saw, the cones of light shining haphazardly up into the night sky. Bart was wrestling with Tiffany for possession of the laser gun. Gerald was still grunting and spasming in the dirt.

Jackson seemed oblivious to the O'Sullivan's drama. He remained stooped over the hole, digging with both hands.

Desperate to save her cousin from bleeding to death, Janine cried out again, "Help me!"

Her words were drowned out as dozens of voices began shouting for everyone to *get the fuck down.* The woods came alive, suddenly swarming with figures in night camouflage gear, sub-machine guns at their shoulders.

Dawson knew he should be grateful that Steve Jacobson had talked his superiors at the National Crime Agency into allowing Dawson to join the ground team following Tiffany O'Sullivan, but he was fuming that Steve refused to issue him a weapon. Of course he hadn't expected to be allowed to join Steve and the SWAT team in the stealth Black Hawk helicopter, but he felt naked without a weapon. He hadn't been allowed with the ground crew either; instead, he'd been relegated to the tech team van that was now parked a half mile behind Tiffany's Land Rover. He could see her tracker signal flashing on one of the monitors in the back of the van.

Six minutes earlier, the ground crew had departed, night vision goggles in place. At least Dawson had been issued an ear piece and he could listen to the team's radio chatter. Steve had promised to let him know when it was safe for Dawson to approach the take-down site. Until then, Dawson had been ordered to stay with the tech team.

But the ground and air teams were now on radio silence, and Dawson was a hair's breadth away from losing his shit.

When the single gunshot sounded, nothing could have kept him in that van. He catapulted out of it, sprinting blindly across the field in the semi-darkness. In his ear, he heard the Team Lead issuing the command for the take down, then saw the powerful search light of the helicopter suddenly illuminate the distant patch of trees at the far end of the field. Dawson could hear shouts—*get down, get the fuck down*—and indistinct words and screams coming through the team's microphones. A distinctly female voice was shouting for help, but it didn't sound like Janine's. He didn't care who'd been shot, as long as it wasn't Janine.

Dawson tripped, sprawling ass over tea kettle in the middle of the field. *"Can't fucking see,"* he snarled as he scrambled to his feet. It didn't actually matter, though. He could run. Janine needed him, and he would run to the ends of the earth to get to her.

He launched himself into the trees, making no effort to be silent as he strained to pick out and analyze every sound coming through his ear piece and from the opposite end of the wooded area. Was she hurt? Was she—god forbid—dead? *Please, Janine, don't be dead!*

He snarled at the corporal who stopped him at the perimeter of the scene, the MP5 aimed at Dawson's chest. But then Steve was there, issuing the command to let him through and uttering the most beautiful three words Dawson had ever heard: *She's not hurt.* But then Steve followed it with a fourth word—bad. *She's not hurt* bad.

He saw her then beside the corporals who were strapping a man to a stretcher with quick, efficient movements, the scene as bright as day. He felt his knees weaken. *Her face. Jesus!* In that moment, if he'd known who'd done that to her, he would've grabbed Steve's MP5 and emptied the chamber into the bastard's chest. Instead, he launched himself towards her, at the same time realizing that the man on the stretcher was Kev. *Jesus Christ, he'd been shot in the chest!*

Janine was crouched at the crown of her cousin's head, murmuring words of reassurance and shaking off the efforts of a corporal who was trying to entice her away.

And then, thank fuck, he had her in his arms, and was cradling her against his heart, exactly where she belonged.

Chapter 49

"Are you telling me Tiff is getting off scot free?" Kevin's tone was indignant.

Janine smiled indulgently at her cousin. "For now, but put a little faith in karma," she said.

"And Steve Jacobson," Dawson added. "He's tenacious. He'll nail her to the wall. He just needs time."

That morning, for the first time in the five days they'd been coming to the hospital, Janine and Dawson found Kevin sitting up in bed. They drew up a chair each on either side of his bed. Janine pulled the curtain around the bed, shutting out the other three patients in the shared room.

According to the surgeon, Janine knew removing the bullet that fractured Kevin's collarbone had been relatively straightforward. His recovery had proven slower than anticipated on account of an infection, which was finally responding to a new round of antibiotics. He was on the mend, thank god, although his bruised face was still hollow-cheeked from his ordeal and he wouldn't be permitted to leave the hospital for a number of days. They'd been assured that, once he was well enough to start physio, it would be a matter of months for him to regain full use of his shoulder.

The only plus side of Kevin's hospital stay was his parents' arrival in London. Janine always enjoyed spending time with her aunt and uncle. Now that Kevin was on the mend, her and Dawson were scheduled to meet them that evening for a celebratory dinner.

Janine's injuries were also healing. Her nose had been reset and she could finally breathe comfortably, although she would wear the nose brace for another few days. The discolouration from the bruising would take far longer to fade.

Kevin had insisted on being given a full account of all that had transpired since he'd been shot. They'd just finished telling him, their voices pitched low so as not to disturb the other patients, what they'd gleaned over the past few days about the O'Sullivan's, some of it factual, other elements speculation. Tiffany was working with the police as an inside informant, and claiming her innocence, of course. Given her cooperation, she wouldn't be facing charges, which is why Kevin had taken offence.

She agreed it wasn't fair. The woman had done nothing to prevent Gerald from terrorizing Janine—for that alone she deserved to be jailed. But Tiffany had also orchestrated the events that resulted in their rescue. She might be eluding punishment at the moment, but Janine felt certain Tiffany would get her just desserts given time.

"The investigative report from my JAG buddy will help nail them all to the wall," Dawson added. "Unfortunately, it can't be part of the jurisdictional record, but it will open avenues for further investigation."

"And the guys at your house in Whistler?" Kevin asked Janine. "Who were they? Working for Bart or for Tiffany?"

"Both," she said.

"But that murder had little to do with the Rex Alfred coin and more to do with a long history of bad blood," Dawson explained. "The guy killed on Janine's lawn—he was working for Tiffany. Not long ago, he apparently stole a speedboat belonging to the other two guys—they were working for Bart. The boat allegedly had a fortune in cocaine onboard, so his days had already been numbered long before the coin was thrown into the mix."

"Bloody hell," Kevin said, giving Janine a mournful look. "It's my fault you ended up rubbing shoulders with lowlifes like that. I don't want to sound like I'm passing the buck here—I know I played a role in all this—but Jackass Jones... Christ, I could wring his neck. He and Tiffany are a match made in hell, I'll say that much."

"She claimed to have met you at the Winfarthing Pendant exhibit," Janine said, "but that's apparently where she met Jackson."

"Only Tiffany soon lost interest," Dawson added.

"But why didn't he go straight to Tiffany when he saw my coin? Why involve Alfred? That's someone else's neck I'd like to wring."

"From what Steve tells me," Dawson said. "Jackson hoped Alfred would strong-arm you into making an official report about the coin, which would of course also reveal the precise location. When Alfred refused to believe the coin existed, Jackson had no choice but to go to the O'Sullivan's. He knew nothing of the friction between Tiffany and Bart, and apparently blurted out his astonishing news to the both of them."

"Do you think, if he'd found only her, things would've turned out different?" Janine asked. She looked from Dawson to her cousin, then back to Dawson. Both men were shaking their heads.

"It would've been a different mess," Kevin said, "but a mess all the same."

"Agreed. The O'Sullivan's are reprobates, every one of them. On the surface, Bart and Tiffany were working together," Dawson added. "First to intimidate Kevin into revealing the coin's location; then, when Kevin refused to cooperate and they discovered where the coin had been couriered, they hatched a plan to use Janine as leverage. Without her uncle's knowing—and Steve says we can't prove this so it doesn't factor into the case, unfortunately—Tiffany sent her own guy to Janine's, all the while scheming to set up Bart to take the fall that was sure to come. Her intent all along has been to take over her uncle's empire. She snared Jackson in her web of lies, and tried to do the same with us."

"I just can't believe Alfred is in cahoots with the O'Sullivan's."

Janine was smiling as she shook her head. "He's not."

Kevin scoffed in disgust.

"Honestly," she added. "You'll understand when you know why he did it."

She proceeded to tell him that the O'Sullivan's knew a little of Alfred's personal life, including the fact that his niece Christine was living with him. Three years before, at age fifteen, the girl's parents and little brother had been tragically killed in a rockfall accident on the Mediterranean coast during a family holiday. Since then, she'd lived with Alfred, her only surviving relative. But the lively, inquisitive child he'd always indulged was irrevocably changed by the tragedy. He'd done his best by her, but she'd fallen prey to her misery and grief and, within two years of her changed circumstances, had become a hardcore drug addict. Twice he'd searched for and found her on the streets. Both times she'd agreed to enter rehab. Within months after leaving her second round of rehab, she'd once again disappeared. Alfred had been searching the streets of London for weeks, without success.

Somehow, Bartholomew O'Sullivan learned of Christine's location, likely through his criminal contacts. But Bartholomew hadn't passed on that information to Alfred; at least, not until he learned, thanks to the elderly woman in Bart's employ, of the visit of a distinguished looking man who had a long conversation with Dawson and Janine on Kevin's front stoop. That woman passed on the license plate number of the visitor's Jaguar.

After Bartholomew confirmed the identity of the visitor, he contacted Alfred, telling him he knew where his niece was, then coercing the distraught man to bait and trap Janine in exchange for information about where his niece was living. When Dawson and Janine made their fortuitous visit to Folkestone's the very next day, Alfred put the life of his niece ahead of the well-being of these strangers, hesitating only briefly before texting Bartholomew.

"I was ready to drag him to the nearest police station and insist they arrest him as an accessory to kidnapping," Dawson added.

"Christ. Poor sod." Kevin sipped from the bendy straw in the water cup on his overbed table, then asked, "Did he find her?"

"Yes," Janine said. "The good news is she's once again in a rehabilitation program. This time, hopefully, it will have a lasting benefit. He loves her, that much is clear."

Kevin regarded Dawson. "I suppose you have a connection with someone here in law enforcement? That's how you engineered the successful rescue?"

It was Dawson's turn to scoff. "You call getting shot successful?"

Kevin gave his old friend a lop-sided grin. "I call getting medevac'd and surviving getting shot successful."

"Regardless, it wasn't thanks to me. As hard as it is to say, it's all thanks to Tiffany. I want her in jail for what she let Gerald do to Janine, but we wouldn't have found you without her."

Dawson explained that Tiffany had contacted Alfred soon after Janine had been abducted. Within the hour, the Irishwoman was sobbing out a story to Dawson and, more importantly, Steve Jacobsen at the National Crime Agency, as well as to a military liaison from the Canadian Embassy, Jillian Shreeves.

"I was there," Dawson said, "and let me tell you, she gave an Oscar-worthy performance, claiming her horror over the abduction of two Canadians, and that Bart intended using Janine to force Kevin to reveal the location of the coins. She also told them the location of the Barking warehouse. The team sent to raid it found the four coins Gerald took from Janine, and a whole lot of stolen Syrian artifacts, including some fakes that concealed smuggled drugs. She claimed Bart would kill you both once the location of the buried coins was revealed. Thank Christ the National Crime Agency took her seriously, or you'd be dead by now, and Janine…" Dawson's face looked grey as he shook his head.

"Well, they didn't succeed," Janine murmured. She took Kevin's hand in hers, shuddering at the thought of how close she'd come to losing him.

"She knew the location of the field thanks to Jones, right?"

"Yes, but she also agreed to wear a GPS tracker." Dawson shook his head in disgust. "She's doing everything in her power to come across as the cooperative innocent in all this."

Kevin blew a raspberry, although it sounded rather lame given his lack of robust health. "She hasn't got an innocent bone in her scrawny body. But what about Jones? What's he saying?"

"He's singing a tune we assume Tiffany composed," Dawson answered. "About how he'd been forced at gunpoint by Bart to go along with them that night. But Janine's testimony, and yours too, when you're well enough to give it, will ensure he gets what he deserves."

"And the site?"

"Your department head is apparently coming to see you tomorrow, now that you're finally on the mend," Janine said. "He'll give you a full update."

"It needs to be secured," Kevin stated, growing agitated. "If anyone—"

"Bro, it's under control," Dawson quickly reassured. "Responsibility for the archeological discovery has been officially assigned to the University of Nottingham, along with 24/7 security to protect the historical integrity."

"This bit hasn't yet been released to the media," Janine said, "but they found more coins and the remains of a wooden chest. Your suspicion was correct. You found your Kevin-who."

Delighted to see a spark of keen interest lightening Kevin's golden-brown eyes, she shared a pleased smile with Dawson. She'd earlier filled him in on why she teased her cousin about his Kevin-who.

"Well, holy Christ," he said, his tone filled with awe. "And Alfred is authenticating them? He's the best in the business." He frowned as he muttered, "Bloody bastard."

"Give the guy a break. He was gutted when he learned how close you both came to being killed," Dawson said. "We've got plenty enough villains to hold accountable for this shit-show, we don't need to throw Alfred in the mix. Anyway, he'll be visiting you soon. He wants to apologize in person."

Kevin sighed. "I'm still mad as hell at him." Despite his claim, he shook his head in sympathy, his eyes lifting to Janine's when she rose to her feet and began fluffing her cousin's pillows. "God, Jaynie," Kevin said, his eyes shimmering with unshed tears. "Thanks to me, you were almost killed. I'll never forgive myself for putting you in danger. I'm sorry I ever found that damn coin. Sorrier I sent it to you."

Janine hated seeing the self-loathing marring his kind eyes, saw also that he was tired out from their talk. "Stop berating yourself, okay?" she said, her tone gentle. She remained beside him, holding his hand. "We should go. You need your rest."

As Dawson got to his feet, Kevin shifted his troubled gaze to his old friend. "All I can say is thank god you went to

Whistler." His tone hoarse with emotion, he added. "I owe you big time, man."

Dawson scowled darkly and jerked his chin towards Janine. "Jesus, don't *thank* me! Look at her."

When Kevin and Dawson turned their mournful expressions her way, Janine sighed. She couldn't wait for the bruises to fade, not so much because they were ugly, but so people would stop looking at her as if she were a victim.

Kevin squeezed her hand. "You're freaking amazing, Jay-Jay. Will you ever be able to forgive me?" he asked.

As Janine pretended to consider this, an idea occurred to her. "On one condition."

"Sure, Jay-Jay. Anything."

"I'm going to buy you a cellphone. And you have to use it, with me at least. Will you promise to do that?"

Kevin grimaced. "You're letting me off the hook too easy, Jaynie. I deserve the guillotine. But yeah, I promise, and gladly."

"You know they found Dawson's cellphone on my front yard?"

Kevin smiled tiredly at his friend. "Does that mean you're a wanted man in Canada? Don't you know, the Mounties always get their man?"

Dawson chuckled. "Well, the Mountie's now know the full story, so you won't see my ugly mug on any wanted posters."

When Kevin seemed barely able to lift the corners of his mouth in a smile, Janine realized they'd exhausted him. "We should let you rest. Your parents said they'd bring you a decent lunch so you wouldn't have to face another hospital meal."

"Mom said you didn't tell Grandma and Grandpa how badly you were injured."

Janine shrugged. "They don't need to know.

Kevin sighed. "But I'll feel like a fraud the next time I see them, not owning up to the role I played in you getting hurt."

"Can we please change the topic?" Janine nodded at Dawson. "We're heading to the Embassy to pick up my new passport."

"Your other one didn't turn up?" Kevin asked, smothering a yawn.

Janine shook her head. "No. Whatever Gerald did with my stuff, he's not admitting to it. It's nap time for you. We're leaving."

She bent down and kissed his cheek, then watched in amusement as Dawson and Kevin did their man-grip handshake as they said their goodbyes.

Chapter 50

"You're letting me off the hook too easily, too," Dawson stated, his tone glum.

They were strolling hand-in-hand towards their rental car, but at Dawson's words, Janine stopped, then quickly pulled them a half step to the side so they wouldn't block the other pedestrians hurrying into and out of the hospital. "I thought we addressed this already?"

"Addressed what?" Dawson said with a frown. "My inability to keep you safe? That will haunt me my entire life."

Janine enfolded his big hands in both of hers, clasping them against her heart. She was beginning to realize he was the more emotional of the two of them. If they were to carve out a future together—something they'd been discussing and to which they were both wholly committed—then he would have to set aside, or at least somehow govern, his misplaced self-loathing. He needed to see himself the way she saw him, someone whose every action and motivation arose from the tenderness, compassion, and love that formed the wellspring of his beautiful heart. How could she convey to this man—this dear, big-hearted, caring man—that he'd done nothing wrong? It was how one responded that counted. And he'd responded exactly right, in every way.

"Dawson, you blamed yourself for what happened to Joanie as a kid, and later for what happened to Cassie. That didn't get you anywhere. And now you want to add what happened to me to that burden?"

He jerked his chin in emphasis, muted anguish in his eyes. "Yeah, and rightly so!"

She shook her head emphatically. "No! *Not* rightly so."

She despised the storm clouds that lurked in the midnight depths of his eyes and wished she could dispel them once and for all. She knew it would take time, though. Rome wasn't built in a day. Over the upcoming months, even years, they'd likely have variations of this conversation. That was okay with her. She was willing to have it every day for the rest of her life if that's what it took. "Do you not see that choosing to carry the burden of blame for what happened to me gets in the way of us? Don't do that to yourself, Dawson. *Don't do that to us!*"

She lifted her lips to his, her gentle caress transmitting all the words she had yet to find that would express how she felt about this man. Their kiss was gentle by necessity, both mindful of her tender face.

"I love you, Janine," he said a moment later, his voice gruff with emotion.

They'd been exchanging these three words a lot lately. She'd never tire of hearing him uttering the sentiment while holding her captivated in his gaze. She cupped his face in her hands. The storm clouds were still lurking, but they'd receded to the distant horizon. Instead of reciprocating the sentiment, and hoping to instil some levity into their conversation, she smiled and said, *"Dawson. Freaking. Delaney."*

Those three words made him smile, as she knew they would, calling to mind the first time they'd made love. A mix of amusement, adoration, and desire sparked new galaxies in Dawson's dark eyes, finally chasing the storm clouds away.

They would be back, Janine knew, but each time less threatening until eventually, hopefully, they wouldn't return.

As they resumed walking, hand-in-hand, she retrieved her new cellphone from her pocket and turned it back on. "Shoot!" she exclaimed, pausing outside the passenger door of their rental car. "I missed a call from my grandmother."

"Hop in, honey. Let's hear what she has to say."

They settled into their seats, Dawson delaying starting the car while they listened to Janine's voicemail on speaker. The message was short, simply asking Janine to call.

"Do you mind if I call her back now? It's dinner time there, so I know they'll be home."

"Of course not," he said, giving her a warm smile. "But it's been at least five minutes since you last kissed me. Can your grandmother wait ten seconds?"

Janine laughed as she leaned in for his kiss. Ten seconds turned into twenty, then thirty, before they finally broke apart.

Dawson rested his forehead on hers. "Your cousin's right, you know," he said softly. "You're freaking amazing."

"You're just saying that so I don't repeat the mistake of threatening to take you shopping."

When she'd borrowed his credit card to buy some clothes—sending him an e-transfer that he had yet to accept—she'd made the mistake of suggesting he come with her to get some clothes of his own. He'd been affronted when she pointed out that two pairs of jeans, two plaid shirts, three boxers, and three pairs of socks were insufficient wardrobe for a prolonged stay in London.

"It'll take a half hour at least to get to the Embassy," Dawson said with a laugh as he started the car. "Go ahead and call her."

Janine didn't put the phone on speaker because she knew from past experience this compromised how well her grandparents could hear her. When her grandfather answered the call on the second ring, he told her they'd just finished dinner, then asked about Kevin. After reassuring him that Kevin was getting stronger every day, her grandfather passed the phone to his wife. In the background, Janine heard him say that he'd finish loading the dishwasher, and then her grandmother's sweet voice was greeting her.

"Did I hear correctly, sweetheart? Is Kevin doing better today?"

"Yes, Grandma. He's definitely on the mend," said Janine. "The doctor says he'll be released in a couple of days."

"Oh my," her grandmother said with genuine relief. "I can't believe what a kerfuffle that boy caused with his discovery. It's on the news here, you know. They didn't give his name, but they reported that the coins were discovered by an archeologist from the University of Nottingham."

"Kevin's colleagues have been ordered not to talk to the press. Hopefully the media doesn't get wind of his name. He'd hate that."

"When are you coming home, sweetheart?"

"I'll wait until after Kevin is settled at his place, then I'll book my flight. I actually don't yet have permission to leave the country. I have to provide more statements to the authorities here. But at least my new passport is ready. We're on our way to the Embassy now."

"We? Is Dawson still with you?"

Although it had been years, Margaret and Anthony Kirby had met Dawson a time or two when they'd visited their son's family in Seattle. Janine knew her grandmother could hear the smile in her voice as she responded. "Yes, Dawson is still with me."

"Well I sure hope we get to see him again soon. We want to thank him in person for all he's done to keep our granddaughter and grandson safe."

Janine glanced at Dawson, who was being a good driver and paying attention to the road. She would like nothing better than to have him join her at her grandparents' small farm on the Saanich Peninsula, but she had no intention of visiting them until her face was free of discolouration.

"You left a message on my voicemail, Grandma. Was there something you wanted to tell me?"

"Yes, sweetheart, although I don't know if it's important. It's just something I remembered about your mom."

"My mom?" Janine was surprised. This time when she glanced at Dawson, he gave her a questioning glance. Since receiving Kevin's package, Janine had barely given the mystery of her mother's early pregnancy and the child she'd given birth to a second thought. In fact, she hadn't yet told her grandparents about the private investigator's report. And she didn't want to do that on the phone. She would bring it with her the next time she visited.

When her grandmother began telling Janine about a dreadful wind storm they'd had the night before, Janine wondered if this change of topic was the first sign of senility. But then her grandmother was explaining that the reason this storm made her think of Janine's mother was because a tree had fallen onto the woodshed, the very same shed whose roof had been crushed by a fallen tree when Paul and Brenda had been visiting years before. This recent storm made Margaret remember a conversation she'd had with her reserved, aloof daughter-in-law when the men had been wielding their chain-saws and the ladies had been stacking the debris. While letting Janine—who'd been a toddler at the time—make a messy pile of the smallest sticks, Margaret recalled Brenda expressing her longing for a large family. Given that Paul and Brenda were still young and their daughter barely two years old, Margaret had reassured her daughter-in-law that she might yet be blessed with many more children.

"Sweetheart, now that I remembered what she said that day, I wanted to let you know I understand her so much better."

"What do you mean? What did she say?"

"She said, and it breaks my heart now just like it did then, *I don't deserve to have more children.*"

Janine frowned. She'd always assumed her mother didn't want more children, and had blamed herself for that despite knowing she'd never been a handful to raise. "Why would she say that?"

"I didn't know *then*. In fact, I remember being utterly astonished and challenging her, but she seemed to regret her words. There was never any point in badgering that woman. You know how she could clam up."

"I still don't understand, Grandma."

"Sweetheart," Margaret said in an excited tone. "You discovered the birth of Esme!"

"Yes. Three months ago."

"I know, I know. But I think your mother gave Esme up for adoption. And I think all her adult life she felt guilty about that. I think giving that child away—if that's indeed what happened—made her feel undeserving of finding happiness and love in a second child, or third or fourth. Her words that day prove that, don't you think? All her adult life, I believe she was carrying a great burden of guilt, telling herself she didn't deserve to be happy, didn't deserve to have a family, all because she'd once given up a child. Don't you think her attitude makes sense now that you know about Esme?"

"Yes," Janine answered, her mind whirling. "Wow, you're so wise, Grandma. That makes *perfect* sense."

Her grandmother made a sympathetic tisking sound. "You know, it just about breaks my heart thinking of Brenda now. She seemed to deliberately keep herself at an emotional distance, didn't she? I know underneath her standoffishness, she loved Paul, and you, and us. But it was from a galaxy away, wasn't it?"

"That's so true." And it was. Her mother had done everything a mother should do, all the while keeping all of them at an arm's length distance.

"I think she was like that because of this other baby. Saying she didn't deserve more children, well!" Margaret made a disgusted sound. "That's absurd, isn't it? Everyone deserves a happy family, even if many aren't blessed with one, more's the pity. But I feel Brenda wouldn't *allow* herself to be happy. She didn't give herself *permission* to experience the true joy and fulfillment from being Paul's wife and your mother. Now I know why. I feel I understand her so much better than I did then. And I have so much compassion for her, which I'm ashamed to say I didn't always have back then."

"Me too, Grandma," Janine said, suddenly choking back the tears. "Me too."

Chapter 51

Janine lay against Dawson, her head pillowed on his shoulder, the fingers of her left hand absently tangling in his chest hair. They'd made love, slowly and languidly, and now seemed reluctant to drift into sleep even though it was nearing midnight and they had a 5:00 am wake-up call.

It was their last night together in London. After two weeks in England, they would fly to Vancouver the next day. Dawson would go south to Seattle and she'd head north to Whistler. Due to work commitments that he couldn't get out of, three full weeks would pass before Dawson would be able to come to Whistler to see her. On the plus side, her face would finally look normal by then. Regardless, she felt certain it would be the longest three weeks of her life.

Even though they'd been together 24/7 in the fourteen days they'd spent in the UK, her desire to keep Dawson in her life hadn't diminished. Fifteen years ago, during that long-ago lakeside holiday, she'd fantasized about being loved by Dawson. Now it was a reality to which she was still adjusting, with joy and wonder, and a great deal of satisfaction.

"Do you remember that summer you came waterskiing with us?"

Janine smiled. *Yet more evidence this man could read her mind.* "I was just thinking about that," she said, doing nothing to hide the smile in her voice. She entertained the idea of confessing what she'd dreamed of doing with him that weekend, but decided it would be too embarrassing. She'd tell him down the road sometime, once their relationship was more cemented.

"You were so goddamn sexy," he confessed. "I kept having to remind myself to keep my hands off of you." As if in defiance of the restrictions he'd imposed on himself back then, he stroked his hand along her skin, stopping to cup her breast.

Janine pushed up on her elbow so she could look him in the eye. *"What?"* she demanded.

The curtains of their hotel room were closed, but the lamp on his side of the bed was on low and she could see the sudden look of consternation on his face. By his rapid, backpedalling response, he clearly misunderstood her vehement, one-word response.

"I know, I know, you were only fifteen, and that's technically statutory rape, *but Jesus!* You can't blame a guy for where his mind goes when…I mean, your *legs* in those cut-offs and your *boobs* in that tank top, and your face with that gorgeous smile, and your liquid chocolate eyes all trusting. And me, feeling like a pedophile pervert, and… Hey!" he said in wounded indignation when he realized Janine was laughing at him. "What's so funny? I'm being serious here."

Janine shifted, resting her forearms on his chest, her chin on her knuckles. She grinned in amusement, her tone filled with delight as she asked, "You were attracted to me back then? Really?"

He gave her a dumbfounded look. "Hell, yeah! Do you not know how gorgeous you were?" He raised a hand and tucked a strand of hair behind her ear, then cupped her cheek, his thumb lightly caressing the fading bruises. He softened his voice, and said, "Do you not know how gorgeous you *are?*"

Janine smiled, unable to contain her pleasure at his words. "Do *you* not know what I wanted to do that weekend?"

His hand stilled. "What do you mean?"

"Dawson. I wanted to gift you my virginity. I tried all weekend, but I was an abysmal failure at flirting. I went home royally disappointed."

"You're kidding me," he said, after a shocked moment of silence.

She bit her lip in amusement as she shook her head at him. "Nope, not kidding."

He sucked in a deep breath as he raised his arm and draped it across his face, hiding his eyes in the crook of his elbow. *"Jesus,"* he murmured. "I can't tell you how glad I am I didn't know that then." He lifted his arm, dropping his hand to stroke her bare shoulder. "I hope I wouldn't have…but Jesus Christ, if I had known…" He swore again. *"Thank fuck* I didn't know."

Janine moved her hips invitingly. "So…" she said, her tone low and teasing. "If I hadn't been underage, what would you have done?"

He growled, then proceeded to show her.

Chapter 52

Janine stood back and perused the three new paintings leaning against the bare wall, sipping her macchiato as she assessed how best to display them. The encaustic landscapes were painted by an artist who'd recently relocated from Quebec to Squamish, and featured Blackcomb Mountain from different angles, the glimpse of ski runs recognizable to Janine despite their semi-abstract perspective. She was drawn to the paintings because they suggested, at least to her, the pleasing union of nature—mountains, sky, trees, and snow—and man—the graceful swath of cleared trees crisscrossing the mountain—together conveying an overall sensation of peace, exhilaration, adventure, and joy. She predicted the painting, *Addicted to White Powder,* with its depiction of velvety, pristine snow, would be the first to sell, although the remaining two would not be far behind.

She glanced impatiently towards the entrance. Dawson was due to arrive soon. He'd hinted at having a surprise for her, and she found herself picturing an engagement ring. Was it too soon? In the three months since their return from the UK, they'd only seen each other four times. Was that sufficient foundation to build a life together?

She too had a surprise for Dawson. Kevin had fulfilled his promise to her, communicating regularly with Janine by text and email on his new mobile. Earlier that afternoon, he'd sent a link to an internet article defaming O'Sullivan's recently appointed CEO, Tiffany O'Sullivan, who was under suspicion for forgery, fraud, and blackmail. An "inside source" claimed to have proof of Tiffany forging the provenance papers her uncle had been accused of faking almost two years before.

Janine hadn't read the rest of the article. She'd gotten the gist, and took satisfaction in knowing that karma was indeed doing what karma did best.

DAWSON STOOD IN FRONT OF THE CAFÉ ART PEERING through the window. He could see Janine leaning some paintings along the wall, then standing back to assess them, head tilted to the side as she sipped her coffee, then stepping forward and rearranging them.

It was barely mid-afternoon, but it was already dusk. Snow was falling lightly in big, giant flakes, melting on the sidewalk thanks to the underground heating that kept the snow off the walkways and roads in the pedestrian section of the resort town. He couldn't see Janine's face, but knew she would be chewing her lower lip, a habit that never failed to make him want to kiss the shit out of her.

This was the third time he'd driven to Whistler to see her, but it was the first time he felt unsure; the first time he was second guessing himself; the first time he hesitated before entering Café Art. *How would she respond to his surprise?* He'd been so certain leading up to this moment—all the planning, all the hours he'd spent imagining her delight—but now, with the gently falling snow settling on his shoulders, he felt unsure.

He hoped she would be pleased. He wanted to spend a lifetime pleasing her. She was the most amazing person he knew. A week ago, he'd been in San Francisco on business and, thanks to her encouragement and support, he'd found the courage to make a phone call, one that had his stomach in knots and his hands clammy with sweat. But what he'd expected to happen—a blast of unabridged cursing and a resounding click—hadn't occurred. Instead, he'd been warmly invited for a long overdue visit.

The next evening, Dawson went to the home of Matthew Bishop—the man who should've been married to Cassie—and his pregnant partner Birgitta. The unreserved pleasure Matthew displayed at seeing his old friend had Dawson hugging him a heartbeat longer than was strictly appropriate.

When the two men took their beers to Matthew's man-cave in the garage, their conversation was stilted at first, but before long they were talking freely and, after an hour, were conversing frankly and openly about the woman who'd so profoundly—and all too briefly—touched their lives.

Matthew offered a heartfelt apology to Dawson, telling him how sorry he was for uttering such harsh, unforgiving words at the time of Cassie's death. He'd needed someone to blame, he said, and Dawson had been the easiest target. Matthew added that he'd been haunted with regret for years now, but hadn't had the courage to reach out to Dawson, then thanked him for doing exactly that.

Back at his hotel, Dawson poured himself a bourbon. He positioned a chair by the windows, the curtains open, the lights off, staring out at the nighttime view of the bay. He nursed his drink, then poured another. For the first time in more than three years, he was remembering Cassie—deliberately bringing to mind the remembered warmth of her loyalty and friendship, deliberately recalling images of her smiling face, effervescent personality, sharp wit, and overloud laughter. Some of his memories made him chuckle—she'd been so comical in her outrage when he teased her—some made him laugh outright—she truly had an awful honking loud laugh—

but not a single one shredded his heart. For the first time since her death, thinking about Cassie wasn't agonizingly painful. He found himself wiping moisture from his eyes, knowing the tears weren't grief per se, but more an evaporation of grief.

After polishing off his second whisky, he was feeling almost weightless, and knew this feeling had little to do with the alcohol. Thanks to Janine's steadfast love and encouragement and her belief in his goodness, he'd found the courage to face his demons. Janine was the key, to his heart, to his life, to his future. He had her to thank for believing in him. He smiled to himself then, wondering if his sisters would stop calling him George after he proposed to Janine.

Dawson was brought back to the present by the sound of a woman speaking his name, her tone laced with uncertainty. He started, then turned to face the tall, blond woman who, he hoped, would be a significant part of his life. "Hey, you," he said, hoping his smile concealed his apprehension. "Are you ready?"

Her smile trembled, but her nod was confident.

Was he doing the right thing? Would the events he was about to unfurl alienate Janine? Or would she understand he was doing this for her, for the woman he loved and would love for all eternity?

It was too late for self-doubt, he realized. He'd set too many events in motion to do anything now but let the momentum of what was about to unfold carry them forward.

With a nod at his companion, he opened the door to Café Art and gestured her inside.

JANINE HAD THE NEW PAINTINGS ARRANGED IN A PLEASING display when she heard soft footfalls behind her. She immediately recognized Dawson's cowboy-boot tread. She felt her heart glow as she turned to greet him.

His shaggy hair needed another trim and he hadn't shaved, but somehow that made him all the more gorgeous. He was wearing a parka, the zip open to reveal a dark blue shirt that perfectly matched the colour of his eyes.

She was taken aback when he gave her only a perfunctory kiss, so unlike his usual ardent enthusiasm. She frowned, about to scold him that a peck on the lips was insufficient greeting after having been apart for almost two weeks. She stayed her words when she noticed the woman hovering behind Dawson's shoulder.

She was about forty, Janine guessed, dressed elegantly in a double-breasted wool coat, the oxblood colour complementing her clear, pale skin and blond, shoulder-length bob, hair as thick and stubbornly straight as Janine's. The woman was staring at Janine with an intensity that seemed inappropriate, her blue eyes drinking in every detail of the younger woman's face. Janine knew this woman wasn't one of Dawson's sisters. Who was she?

Bewildered, Janine looked up at Dawson, but the apprehensive look on his face only served to elevate her confusion. Why was *he* nervous? "What's going on, Dawson?" she asked.

Her gaze drifted back to the woman, whose blond head was canted slightly to the side as she stared at Janine with hungry absorption. Something about the way the woman held her head, just so, reminded Janine of someone. Who?

"Honey, I..." Dawson hesitated, then pushed the air out of his lungs with a nervous laugh as he ran a hand through his dishevelled hair. "Well...I guess you could say, I brought you a present." He gestured at the woman. "Janine, I'd like you to meet Riley Knoweldon."

The woman smiled at Janine as if the name should mean something to her. It didn't.

"You know her as Esme," Dawson added, his tone low, gentle, uncertain.

All thoughts in Janine's mind ground to a halt as she stared at the woman.

You know her as Esme.

The woman's eyes, bright with longing and hope, held her captive. Janine finally found her voice. *"Esme?"* She wanted to look at Dawson, but she couldn't tear her gaze away from this woman. *Her sister!* "You're Esme?"

The woman nodded and began to cry silently, although she didn't appear to notice and did nothing to brush away the tears. She held out her hands to Janine, who automatically lifted her own. As their hands touched, Janine felt a shift, as if a painting had been hung slightly skewed and had now been put right.

"Hello, Janine," Riley said, the low register of her voice a warm, pleasing tone. "I'm so very happy to meet you."

The surprise Dawson had planned for her, she realized, wasn't an engagement ring; it was introducing Janine to her long-lost sister. In Janine's mind, in her heart, there was no greater treasure.

Lifting her tear-filled gaze to Dawson, she managed to whisper, "Thank you," as she began weeping in earnest. She leaned against him for support, all the while clinging to her sister's hands, utterly captivated by the blurry form of her mother's beloved first child.

Note from the Author

Thank you for joining Janine and Dawson on their crazy adventure. I hope you enjoyed *A King's Ransom*.

Your positive reviews are a huge help to indie authors like me. Please take a moment to submit a review on any platform of your choice. Thank you!

I love to hear from my readers. If you want to contact me or are interested in my other books, please email me through my website at CorinneAarsenBooks.com.

From my heart to yours, thanks for reading!

Acknowledgments

Publishing a book is only possible thanks to a team of supporters, readers, and experts. Thank you to graphic designer Christine Astle at Rook Book Designs for creating just the right cover design for this book, as well as Anne Correia at West Coast Editing Services for helping me craft the jacket description.

I want to especially thank my test readers for their enthusiastic feedback and support, specifically my dear friends Angie Neal (say "hi, Angie!"), Sashie Steenstra, Karen Payne, my talented writer and friend, A.K. White, and my sister Grace Berkenbosch.

A special heartfelt nod goes to my sister Gwen Bosch for her meticulous and detailed edits to multiple early drafts, and her boundless support and encouragement. Thank you!